LESLEY AND TRÉVILLE'S LOVE STORY

By

Lesley Tréville

ISBN-13: 978-1979531887
ISBN-10: 1979531889

CONTENTS

CHAPTER 1 *England to Paris* 1
CHAPTER 2 *The Ball* 9
CHAPTER 3 *Childhood* 17
CHAPTER 4 *Katherine* 25
CHAPTER 5 *The Bakery* 34
CHAPTER 6 *The Castle Wedding* 39
CHAPTER 7 *The Wolves* 47
CHAPTER 8 *Renovations* 54
CHAPTER 9 *The Dagger* 62
CHAPTER 10 *Healing and Upset* 70
CHAPTER 11 *Reunion and Philip* 79
CHAPTER 12 *What Happened Next?* 87
CHAPTER 13 *The Return* 93
CHAPTER 14 *End of an Era* 102
CHAPTER 15 *Tréville's Story* 119
CHAPTER 16 *Rochefort* 129
CHAPTER 17 *After the Incident* 141
CHAPTER 18 *Recovery* 155
CHAPTER 19 *Betrayal* 168
CHAPTER 20 *Leaving Chartres* 185
CHAPTER 21 *Meeting George* 201
CHAPTER 22 *Sadness, Love and Laughter* 211
CHAPTER 23 *Happiness* 224
CHAPTER 24 *Death* 235
CHAPTER 25 *War* 244
CHAPTER 26 *Reminiscing* 256
CHAPTER 27 *Surprise* 268
CHAPTER 28 *The Village and Return* 280
CHAPTER 29 *What Happened to Rochefort?* 296
CHAPTER 30 *The Summer Ball* 315
CHAPTER 31 *The Twins* 327
CHAPTER 32 *The Cave* 337
CHAPTER 33 *Paradise* 350

CHAPTER 34 *Last Breath* 359
CHAPTER 35 *Edouard and An Apology* 370
CHAPTER 36 *New Beginnings* 381
CHAPTER 37 *Resignation* 392
CHAPTER 38 *Memories* 400
CHAPTER 39 *Ritual and Return* 413
CHAPTER 40 *My Purrfect Friend* 425
CHAPTER 41 *Back Together* 434
CHAPTER 42 *The Epilogue – Part 1* 439
CHAPTER 43 *The Epilogue – Part 2* 454

ACKNOWLEDGMENTS

First of all, I must say a huge thank you to Amanda Harris. Amanda and I met on Twitter and she decided to write a story called *For the Love of Porthos* which hopefully is also going to be published. Amanda wanted to include me in her story, so I sat down with a cuppa, and started writing my very first chapter. After that, we decided to mirror each other's chapters, and hence you have my story.

I would like to say a thank you to everyone who has followed my story, especially all my friends on Twitter, mainly Lindy, Helen, Karen and Remy, and on Facebook, mainly The Musketeers BBC UK site, Musketeer Maids and Perfectly Porthos. All your comments have been greatly appreciated.

A special thank you goes to Hugo Speer, who portrayed Captain, Minister and Regent Tréville. Without his portrayal in the series of The Musketeers, this story would never have been written. Lots of love Hugo xx.

CHAPTER 1

England to Paris

I'm on my way to France to track down my best friend Amanda. With help, I got on a passenger ship from Dover in England and luckily a cabin with no one else sharing. The Captain advised the few passengers he had that hopefully, sea-wise, it would remain calm. Small meals would be brought to us three times a day. In the morning a jug of water, along with a bowl, would be brought for us to wash. As I entered my cabin I saw it had two small bunk beds with straw pallets. There was a small window, which could be opened to let the sea air in. I sat on the straw pallet, and started reminiscing.

I was born twenty-four years ago on an Indian Reservation, somewhere in the state of South Dakota in the Americas. My mother was English and my father Indian. My mother had apparently been on a long line of wagons when the Indians attacked and she was taken, but to cut a long story short, she fell in love with her captor and along I came. My Indian name is Spirit of the Wolf, as the wolves would always come and stay with me, wherever I was. My spirit wolf is called Tala. The wolf that stayed with me the most I named Motomo (he who comes first). My mother gave me the English name of Lacey but this ended up as Lesley. Soldiers killed my father when I was five, and my mother decided she wanted to go back to England. I have very little recollection of the trip to England. I just remember being on a very big ship and I was very hungry, sick and homesick, and a lot of people in the one room. I'm still homesick some days. What I would give to go back to my tribe, but that will never be; but at least Tala is content, at the moment. Wherever I go I will need to find somewhere quiet, like a forest, where she can run free now and then. I vaguely remember some of my Indian language, but sadly it's fading now as English has taken over.

We arrived at a place called Dover, early morning. My mother found something called a carriage and we went to a place called London. I was used to riding bareback horses, this was bumpy and very uncomfortable.

We had nowhere to stay but my mother had a sister in London called Katherine and her husband was called James. We made our way, with what little baggage we had, to their house. I clung to my mother's gown, as I was very frightened. What was this place? It was dirty, very noisy, people staggering and shouting. When we arrived at this thing called a house my mother banged on the door. A lady opened the door and took my mother in her arms, then she hugged me – this was Katherine. She was very surprised to see us. My mother explained what had happened and it was decided that we would stay with them until things were sorted out. I'd never been in a house before and was confused by it.

James died two years later, but unbeknown to me, he had left Katherine very well off, as funds go. I had to go to a place called petty school (infant) until I was seven, then to a middle-class school. I hated it. We had to wear long dresses and make sure our ankles were not on show, and bonnets!! As my skin was darker I was called horrible names and obviously knew little English. However, I soon learned how to read, write and other subjects, and later went on to stand my ground and get my own back on those bullies. The school hours were very long, starting at six in the morning until eleven. Then we had a break for a meal and drink. Lessons carried on from one until five, and then time for home. The only day we didn't go was a Sunday. We had two weeks off at Easter and Christmas. When I wasn't at school my mother taught me manners, household chores and needlework. Everything was all right until I reached the age of eight when my mother died of fever. My life was shattered. What would I do, where would I be sent to? I need not have worried, as Katherine said I would stay with her.

After I left school (about ten years old) Katherine said I had to try and get some sort of position, but what? I trudged round for days until I spotted a notice in a baker's shop. They wanted a kitchen helper, so I went in, after I'd made sure I looked presentable, and enquired. I was given the position, but it was hard, backbreaking work. The cook took a liking to me and said if I did things right I might have a good fortune as a baker.

I was there for about five years and I learnt everything I could and became a good baker, but wanted to learn more. Katherine had friends in high places and a position came up for a kitchen maid in a mansion. I was coming up sixteen and got the position. It was a very, very industrious kitchen but I loved it. There was a pastry cook and after a few months I was put with her, and what I learnt about cake baking was beyond my imagination. While I was there, if any spare time happened, one of the older butlers taught me how to dance. I worked my way up the ladder until I became the pastry cook. Things were going well until the master passed. No more resplendent balls, no need for half the staff, so we had to go. I had by then reached the age of twenty-four. Oh, if only I could open my own baker's shop. I had been very frugal and saved a little bit of money but not enough to buy a shop, and being a woman was a problem as well. Men had to buy properties.

It was during my time at school that I met Amanda. I first encountered her crying under the oak tree in the schoolyard. Some of the girls were taunting her, pulling her pigtails or poking her. Why? Because her mother had died giving birth to her. Girls can be so cruel. I sauntered up to a girl who seemed to be the leader, and very graciously tapped her on the shoulder, and as she turned round I gave her the Indian fist in the face! Let's just say it was such a shame she walked into the oak tree! I put my arm around Amanda and asked if she would like to come to Katherine's house and have some lemon water. Amanda and I became great friends from then on. Her father was a physician and eventually re-married. I didn't like her new stepmother and not only that, she came with a son as well! They were nasty people and both picked on Amanda, but only when her father wasn't around.

Alas, the unthinkable happened and Amanda's father died and she was left at the mercy of her stepmother and her son. Amanda still misses her father very much, even to this day. In the end it got too much for her, and one day there was a handwritten note from her, saying:

To my dearest friend Lesley,

It is with great sadness that I write this note to you. You know how hard it has been for me since my father died and I know you are aware, and you often saw, the abuse I received from my stepmother and her son Philip.

My father left his fortune solely to me. The London house and a country home, all money is held in trust for me, with a yearly allowance. He left nothing to Henrietta or Philip, and on his deathbed my stepmother told him she has always despised him and only married him for his fortune. Whether my father knew of this I do not know, but I feel he must have otherwise he would not have left everything to me. The Will also stated they had to vacate the premises. She hatched a plan to marry me off to Philip. Something awful happened last night that I cannot put in this letter to you. One day I may be able to tell you. I cannot marry Philip, ever. I will never marry a man who could do such a thing.

These are the reasons I can no longer remain here in England. I am not running away from you my dearest and only friend. You have been there for me since we were children.

Please take the greatest care my friend, I will think of you always, and one day we will meet again.

Amanda xx

Needless to say, her stepmother came to our dwelling demanding to see me to find out where Amanda was. I said I didn't know she'd gone, I hadn't seen her for a couple of days and just thought she'd come down with something, and hopefully I looked very worried. Her stepmother went off in a huff.

About six months had passed and with another friend I frequented a tavern. Not likely to do that again, they thought I was a prostitute! However, I noticed a familiar face – it was Philip, very drunk. Good job as he might have recognised me. He took a liking to me, so I played along to see what he would say about his mother and Amanda. They had found out Amanda was somewhere just outside Paris, and he was getting passage to go and find her, as he missed her so much and wanted to be reunited. Reunited, I don't think so. He ordered more ale for himself and I said what a lovely thoughtful man he was to go to France to find his woman. It was then he said something that shocked me.

He was going to find Amanda to kill her so his mother would inherit. I nearly fell off the stool. I had to do something, but first I had to get out of the tavern. My friend was, let's say occupied! I spotted a back entrance but as I went to get up he grabbed my arm and yanked me back down again, and said he wanted his money's worth for the drink he'd bought me – what drink? I suggested I slip out the back way, and he follow. Luckily I knew the back of the tavern and a quick, safe way home. It was not a good idea for a woman, on her own, to be out late at night on the London streets. He duly followed but could hardly stand up, so as a refined lady, he got the Indian fist in the face, with an Indian chop on his neck. I knew where to hit on the neck to knock someone out, not kill him, although I do wonder if I should have done, but I don't particularly want to be hanged for murder.

When I got back, I told Katherine everything, and showed her Amanda's letter. She was shocked. She said it was time for me to go to France and try and find Amanda. Katherine paid all my passage and gave me funds to make sure I would be all right. All I knew was that Amanda was somewhere outside Paris, but in what direction?

So here I am on the passenger ship. I hear lots of shouting all of a sudden and peek out of the cabin to see what is happening. We've arrived at the French port of Calais, two long days after we had left. I travelled with a small case, just a couple of dresses to change and underclothes, and other personal things. I ask the Captain if he can advise me how to get to Paris. He advises me it's a very long way, about two hundred miles. The only way is for me to get different carriages along the route. He is concerned about me travelling on my own and asks me to wait. He came back with a very well-dressed gentleman and his wife, Monsieur and Madame DelaCroix, who are going to Chartres via Paris, for their daughter's wedding. Monsieur DelaCroix asks me quietly and after apologising for his forwardness, if I have enough funds to pay for the various carriage rides to Paris. I reply I have enough funds and not to apologise, I would be wary as well. We left the docks of Calais and Monsieur DelaCroix suggested it would be a good idea for him to pay for the carriages and then I reimburse him. We had four stops along the way. I reimbursed Monsieur DelaCroix each time, and naturally paid for my own room and food.

After what I term a horrendous journey, we finally arrive in Paris. I say my goodbyes to Monsieur and Madame DelaCroix. Before they went he gave me the name of a reputable tavern where I could stay. As I made my way to the tavern I passed lots of guards; I later found out they were called Red Guards and you didn't go near them. I was weary and spotted a cafe and went in and ordered a lemon drink and it was delicious, I was so thirsty. Eventually I reached the tavern and as I went up the stairs I noticed a group of five guards, but they weren't in Red Guards uniform. When I later came down from my room, I sat at a table, in the corner, out of the way to eat my meal, which was passable. I felt very vulnerable, and as the night went on the tavern got rowdier. The ladies of the night were in full flow, and everyone was merry. All of a sudden the Red Guards came in and all sorts of chaos broke out. A fight broke out over a game of cards and suddenly I was pinned against the wall.

The owner of the tavern spotted me, and came over and gently eased me away from the fight and up the steps to my room. He advised me to put the chair up against my door, just in case.

Later on that night there was a loud banging on my door, and it frightened me. "Open the door now or we will break it down," said a very fierce voice.

"Please, you're frightening me. What do you want?"

"We are Red Guards and are looking for a convict," he said.

"I swear I'm on my own, sire, please ask the owner. If he comes I promise I will open the door." I heard footsteps retreat and then come back.

"Please, miss, open the door as I can't afford a new one," asked the owner.

I removed the chair and opened the door. Two guards pushed past me and confirmed I had been telling the truth. They did apologise but said it was necessary. I replied it was fine, but could I now get some sleep? The door was slammed shut and I put the chair back immediately and returned to my now cold bed.

For a couple of days I walked round Paris, admiring the buildings, the river, it was a lovely city, but time came when I somehow had to try and find Amanda.

I was walking through a part of Paris and had accidentally taken a wrong turning and found myself in a rather dingy square. I stayed close to the walls and kept my head down as I retraced my steps. All of a sudden a hand touched my shoulder and with fist ready I turned to see four Red Guard soldiers. They asked me who I was and I explained I had come to find a friend. They just laughed, but one mentioned "another English wench". I had ever so slowly moved backward along the wall and was almost back to the street when a fight broke out in the square. Thank heavens the Red Guards went to see what was going on and I fled back to the tavern.

It wasn't until the following day that I remembered what the guard had said: "another English wench". Had they by any chance seen Amanda? I didn't want to go back but I had to find them and ask. This might be a lead. I got to the turning for the square, when two other guards on horses approached me. They were not Red Guards. They enquired as to why a lady should be in such an area. I felt rather flattered to be called a lady. I asked who they were and they introduced themselves as the Kings Guards – the Musketeers. Guards to the King, now that made me feel better. They introduced themselves as Captain Tréville and Porthos. I looked at them more closely and realised they were the ones in the tavern with three others. I introduced myself as Lesley and mentioned I'd seen them in the tavern the previous evening. They dismounted their horses and escorted me back to the tavern. We partook of a drink and I told them my story. Captain Tréville asked me if I had this letter as proof of who I was. I said I did and showed them the letter I received from Amanda. They both looked at each other and grinned.

They told me they had rescued Amanda from the Red Guards after she tried to save a child, just like her father would have done, and they knew where she was. They told me Amanda worked at the palace and a ball was being held that night, and they came to Paris as they were picking up a ball gown for Amanda as a surprise. I couldn't believe my luck. Much to their surprise I flung my arms round both of them and kissed each of them on the cheek. I then blushed, as I'd never done that before. Captain Tréville suggested that I attend the ball and then I could surprise Amanda, and just to call him Tréville. I explained I had never attended a ball before, and therefore had no ball gown to wear. Tréville replied that would not be a problem, as I would be able to purchase one from where they were picking up Amanda's ball gown. I needed to see Amanda's gown to know what to purchase. I paid the landlord for my stay and thanked him for his hospitality.

The gowns, in the shop, were the most beautiful gowns I had ever seen. I couldn't see Amanda's gown as it had already been boxed up, but the lady showed me a similar one. I had no idea what to get but the lady helped me and one gown was purchased. I was a bit concerned about the neckline being low, for me, but the lady assured me it was correct.

Tréville and Porthos were outside waiting with another horse. Porthos took the boxed gowns and placed them on the spare horse, along with my small bag. I looked at both of them, then at the spare horse and made my way to it. "No, no," said Porthos, "you're going to ride with Captain Tréville." I would rather have ridden on the spare horse bareback. Porthos helped me onto Tréville's horse and I have to be honest, blushing, I felt rather comfortable riding in Tréville's arms. After a short journey we arrived back at the garrison where Tréville took me up to his office, much to Porthos's amusement. Porthos rode off to deliver Amanda's gown. I was so excited to think I would be seeing her later on. Tréville suggested I stay in his office after the ball, where he had a bed, and he would sleep in the spare room next to his office. I decided I rather liked Captain Tréville.

CHAPTER 2

The Ball

After the sun was high in the sky, Tréville brought some food and drink up to his office for me. "Don't want you fainting at the ball, do we?" he said. I smiled and thanked him. He told me that his Musketeers and himself had to be at the palace before everyone started arriving, and he had arranged for a carriage to take me there. They would ride at the side of the carriage. Heavens, I felt like royalty. I did wonder if I was dreaming, but a quick pinch assured me I was not.

Tréville and I talked and then he said it was time to get ready for the ball. He kindly brought me a jug of fresh water so I could refresh myself. I undressed and washed, and then unplaited my long hair, brushed and replaited it and arranged it so it looked presentable. A lot of pins were used! My gown was in midnight blue with a black V-shaped bodice, which was pinched at the waist, and then went down into a small portion of the front of the dress. The sleeves were long and fluted out at the ends. The fluted ends were edged in black lace with a small bow. The lady in the shop had also given me a midnight blue ribbon, which I tied into a bow around my neck. I had also purchased a pair of dark sapphire earrings. I was still a little embarrassed about how low the neckline was. At last I was ready. There was a gentle tap on the door, I replied to enter and Tréville walked in. Heavens, did he look handsome. He had his "special" Captain's uniform on with a long flowing blue robe attached from his shoulder. His sword hung down at his side. He smiled and said, "You look beautiful, Lesley." I blushed and thanked him.

He escorted me down to the waiting carriage. Porthos was waiting, also looking handsome. Once I was seated in the carriage they mounted their horses and off we went. When we arrived at the palace, it was a hive of activity. Tréville helped me from the carriage and escorted me into the palace and then the ballroom. My eyes went wide and I looked everywhere. I had never seen anything so wonderful. It was decorated to perfection. Tréville made his apologies, as he had to check on several matters.

Porthos said, "Are you all right, Lesley? You look rather bewildered."

I replied, "I suppose I am in a small way. I have attended balls before, but as a servant, not a guest. I hope the King and Queen will not be annoyed at me for attending?"

Porthos laughed and replied, "Of course they will not be annoyed, as you are Captain Tréville's guest." People had started to arrive and I found a seat to sit on, so I could just observe. I noticed Musketeers walking around along with Red Guards. Why were they here? I later found out they served the Cardinal. I glanced at the ladies' ball gowns and was relieved to see some of the gowns were lower than mine, so my confidence grew slightly.

Tréville appeared from nowhere and took my hand. "Time to meet Amanda," he said. "Stand behind Porthos and myself." Which I did.

Amanda finally appears with three other Musketeers at her side. She looks absolutely beautiful in a gown of ivory, with an overskirt decorated with beautiful flowers. The waist is pinched and the sleeves long and fluted in two places. The neckline and flutes are edged in white lace. Porthos and Tréville kiss her hand, and say how beautiful she looks.

Porthos then said, "We have a surprise for you." Tréville and Porthos move aside so I'm facing her. We are like the two children we used to be, hugging each other, both full of questions, but this must be left until later, when both of us are alone so I can relate the reason I'm there. Amanda introduces me to the rest of Tréville's elite Musketeers – Aramis, D'Artagnan and Athos. I curtsy to each of them, but for some reason the hairs on the back of my neck have risen with regards to Athos. Why, I have no idea. I have never met him before.

Suddenly an announcement is made. "The King and Queen."

Everyone bowed or curtsied. Once they were seated upon their thrones the music began. Amanda wanted to talk to me but I told her Porthos had been waiting all day to dance with her. We would talk later or the following day. Tréville takes my hand and we start to dance. He is a very good dancer. The ball goes well and I meet lots of people, either talking or dancing.

I danced with each of the Musketeers; Porthos is too large for me to hold onto properly, Aramis is very smooth with a twinkle in his eyes for every lady, D'Artagnan is more reserved but I do understand he has a love. Tréville, well, we fitted together rather nicely. My curiosity about this man is intriguing; I must get to know him better. Athos, however, seems to be rather strange to me, and would not dance. I managed to talk to Amanda for a short time and she told me he had a history, but of what I didn't know. Naturally, quite a lot of the evening Tréville and his men were at the side of the King and Queen. They were on duty, but I was surprised at how many gentlemen came and asked me to dance. I partook of some of the wonderful fare and then decided to look for Amanda, but I could not see her, which was strange, unless it had brought back memories of her twenty-first birthday when she danced with her father. I decided to walk to the window that led out to the gardens to get a breath of fresh air. All of a sudden I saw a movement and see Amanda with Porthos, sitting on the top of the step talking. Amanda looks to be crying, and I start to go to her when I stop abruptly. She's telling Porthos about Phillip; my hands go to my face when I hear that Phillip had raped her. I'm stunned into absolute silence. I know I've gone white with rage. If I ever get my hands on him! I also feel I have betrayed a confidence by showing Porthos and Tréville the letter, but I had to prove to them who I was.

My mind wanders to Phillip. The night I met him he said something about getting a ship from England to France in a couple of days. It took Katherine over a week to help me get passage. Oh no, what if he's already here? He is very crafty and has ways with the ladies of getting information.

I return to the ballroom and nervously glance around, but there are too many people. A touch on my shoulder has me jumping out of my skin. I turn and look into Tréville's gentle face. "Are you all right, Lesley? You look pale and worried." I tell him I'm fine, maybe just tired from my long journey. He raises one eyebrow and a look that says, 'Something else is going on here.' I don't know why, but I knew I could trust him and put my arm in his, and as we walked around the ballroom, I asked if we could leave the ball before the end. "Alas, my dear, I cannot. I must ensure that the King and Queen are safely escorted to their chambers and the guests leave the palace."

I reply that I understand.

"Ah, Captain Tréville, might I enquire as to who this captivating creature is?"

I turned to see it was the King and immediately curtsied, and Tréville bowed. "Sire, may I introduce you to Lesley, who has just arrived from England to surprise Amanda."

"Oh, how wonderful for Amanda," said the King. He looked at me and said, "Forgive me for asking, but you don't seem like the usual English Rose."

I smiled and replied, "I was born in the Americas, Your Majesty."

"Interesting, we must get together one day and have a talk. I would love to hear about the Americas. Now I really must 'mingle', as they say. Look after our guest, Tréville, or I will be upset."

Tréville replied, "Yes, sire," and with that the King left us. I couldn't believe I had just spoken to the King of France.

I mingle with the rest of the Musketeers and the guests, still not knowing why Athos has me so curious. Time goes by and the next thing I know the guests are leaving. The Musketeers volunteer to take me back to the garrison, but Tréville says it would be his pleasure to escort me back. I curtsy to the King and Queen as they pass to go to their chambers. When Tréville is content that everything is secure, he guides me out of the palace to where I arrived in the carriage. All that's left is his horse. I ride back with him to the garrison wondering if this is where Amanda is with Porthos. Tréville and I enter his office, but as I go to bid him goodnight he asks me what is wrong. I advise him that I must first speak with Amanda, and that showing him her letter, I felt I had betrayed her confidence. He replied that Amanda would understand and if we needed their help they were there for us. I thanked him and very timidly gave him a kiss on his cheek and bade him goodnight.

The following morning, after I had washed and dressed, I looked out of the window and saw Porthos carrying a tray towards his rooms, so I assumed Amanda was with him. There was a gentle knock on the door, which I opened to see Tréville stood there. "Good morning, Tréville," I said.

"Good morning, Lesley. I hope you slept well?" I replied that I did. The next minute there was another knock and two Musketeers entered with food and drink and placed it upon the table. I had gone back to looking out of the window, watching the garrison come to life. Tréville came up behind me and said to help myself to the food and drink. I thanked him. While we were talking Tréville said, "I need to talk with Amanda about the letter you showed us. Something is not right and I'm worried with regards to her and Porthos. Please may I ask if I could kindly borrow the letter from you, my dear?"

I looked at Tréville and my heart felt like I was betraying Amanda all over again. "I will give you the letter but I'm not happy about it," I said, and with that, got the letter and gave it to him.

He went out and called over the balcony, "Athos, tell Porthos I want to see him and Amanda now."

I went to stand back by the window again, a dread coming over me. What was going to happen? I saw Amanda come out of Porthos's room looking worried. Porthos was striding ahead of her, and she was shouting at him, and then to my surprise, Porthos picked Amanda up and put her over his shoulder and carried her up the stairs to the office, then put her down. Men, really!

They were both grinning at each other. Amanda and I hugged and sat down. Tréville asked Amanda what happened in England, and he wanted the truth.

"Tréville, it doesn't matter what happened, it is all over," said Amanda.

Tréville shook his head. "Amanda, have we not told you that you are safe with us and you would be protected by us? You need to be honest with us."

Amanda looked at Porthos with tears in her eyes. She then stood and turned to face Porthos and myself, so her back was to Tréville. She lowered her dress to her hips and crossed her arm over her chest. "This is what he did to me," she said, "before he raped me." I saw the colour drain away from Tréville's face. My reaction is one of horror – Philip had whipped her and the result was three huge whip marks on her back and one across her stomach. Oh, how I would love a whip now, I would show that swine what a whipping is and hoped he would hurt so much he would beg for mercy, and get none.

The pain Amanda must have endured leaves me feeling sick. I go to her and pull her gown back up. Porthos tries to go to her but Amanda flees down the steps and runs for the gate. Porthos goes to go but I stop him. "No, this is my mess, it's me that needs to apologise to her. I betrayed her and for that I will never forgive myself."

I caught up with Amanda at the garrison gates, where a Musketeer is trying to stop her. "It's all right. Thank you, young man, I will look after Amanda. Come, Amanda, let's walk down to the river," I said, and then take her arm. "Oh Amanda, I'm so sorry. I knew Philip had raped you, I overheard you talking to Porthos at the ball, but the whip marks, I could kill him. I feel I have betrayed you in such a bad way, can you ever forgive me?"

Tears start to fall and Amanda hugs me and says, "Oh, Lesley, you have nothing to apologise for. You did it because you care, you didn't know what Philip had done to me. Since we were children you have always been there. Please do not cry for me, Lesley, as I have cried every night since it happened. I look in the mirror every day and I am reminded of what he did. Porthos is right, I cannot run away from it anymore. Anyway, he cannot hurt me anymore, he will never find me here, and one day I may return to England only to visit. I have made my home here now, and as for my inheritance, I will decide what to do with the property one day, but not now. We have a lot to catch up on," she said, smiling. "Do you remember the first day we met?"

"Oh yes," I replied. "I found you crying under that big old oak tree in the school yard, those girls picking on you, pulling your pigtails and jabbing you in the ribs and laughing, and why? All because your mother had died giving birth to you. I didn't like bullies, so I wandered up to the leader and gave her a fist in the face."

Amanda smiled and said, "Yes, and you put your arm around me that day too. I'm sorry I did not say goodbye to you personally when I left, Lesley, I really didn't feel safe after my father died, and with what happened that night I really had to get away. I have never forgotten you, my Indian sister."

I notice Amanda keeps looking at the river and say, "You need to swim, don't you? Go, I will stay and ensure you are not disturbed." I remember the way she keeps her fears down by being in water. We walk towards a clump of tall trees, where she undresses and slips naked into the river. Luckily no one else is around.

A short while later, I hear a couple of voices behind me, and turn to see Porthos and Tréville. Porthos sees Amanda swimming in the river and a glint comes into his eyes. "What a good idea, going for a swim, I feel so sweaty," says Porthos. Tréville and I look at each other and grin.

"Would you like to take Amanda's clothes with you?" I ask. Porthos grins and winks and moves off towards the trees by the river's edge. Tréville and I walk off arm in arm. I turn and see Porthos in the water swimming towards Amanda. Amanda waves at me and I wave back.

A couple of weeks pass; it's a beautiful day and Amanda and I are, again, walking by the river. The scenery reminds me of home in the Americas. Eventually Athos's name crops up and she tells me of his past. As soon as she says he was the Comte de la Fere I see red. I turn and storm back to the garrison, Amanda absolutely stunned with my change of temper. I see Athos talking to his men, and not wanting to embarrass him, I wait patiently until he is on his own. While waiting I look around to see if I can see the handsome Tréville, but alas, no.

"Monsieur Athos, may I have a word with you please?" I ask, curtsying as I speak. He turns and walks over to me. When he is within inches of me, I give him the Indian fist in the face and he falls to the floor.

"What the hell was that for?" he asks.

"Does the name DelaCroix mean anything to you, sire?" I ask.

His face goes a deathly white at the name. Amanda has come to my side to enquire what I'm doing. These are her friends, and there are laws for striking a Musketeer. I tell her I can't repeat what was said to me by Monsieur and Madame DelaCroix, and I doubt Athos will ever tell the story. I turn to look at Athos, my fury now gone. He raises his eyebrow and I notice a bruise is appearing on his cheek. "I have an ointment that will rid you of the bruising, if you would like it?"

"I think you've done enough damage to me for one day, madam. I will get something from Amanda," and with that stomps off.

Amanda has to go to work at the palace, so I decide to return to the river and read the book I had with me. As I go to leave my attention is drawn up to the balcony, where Tréville is leaning on the rail, smiling a smile that leaves me breathless.

CHAPTER 3

Childhood

With Amanda working at the palace, and Tréville kindly letting me use his bed, the time has come for me to find work and lodgings. Tréville heard of a position going at a bakery shop and so I went to see what they required. Luckily for me they wanted someone who could make pastries and cakes, which is what I had done in my last position in England. I offered them a free day's work so they could access my capabilities. I was hired, thank heavens – Katherine's funds were getting low. After a couple of weeks I found a nice clean lodging house and, rather sadly, moved out from Tréville's office. After just over a month, I expect Tréville was probably very pleased to get it returned, clean and tidy!!

I saw Amanda as much as I could and we always tried to meet up once a week to catch up on news, if possible. Porthos and Amanda were getting quite close now and it was lovely to see her so happy. I also stayed in touch with Tréville and the other Musketeers, although Athos would still glare at me.

Life was going along quite rosy and news came in of a huge wedding at one of the chateaus about a mile from the garrison. Cakes, pastries and a wedding cake all had to be done within two weeks, oh mon dieu. Yes, I was learning French! Two weeks of working virtually all day and night was extremely hard; I was so tired I met myself coming backwards. I was determined to make sure everything went well. Who knows? Maybe then the bakery would really thrive, and I really wanted to please Monsieur Rennard, the owner.

At last the day of the wedding arrived and disaster struck. The horses that Monsieur Rennard had were ill. How on earth were we going to get the food to the chateau? I hitched up my skirts and ran through the small lanes as though my life depended on it to the garrison. Oh, thank heavens Tréville was in his office.

"My dear Lesley, what on earth is wrong? Please sit and try and sip some water to calm yourself?" I explained what had happened. "Is that all?" he said, to which I gave him a shocked look.

"Is that all?" I said. "My position in the bakery and all the hard work that has been done must get to the chateau or we are all ruined, ruined!" I snapped.

Tréville looked at me and smiled. "My dear Lesley I have two wagons, with horses, you can borrow. Not only that, I will also let you have four of my recruits to help you load and unload your goods at the chateau. I will also feel better knowing that you will be well guarded, the road is not good."

The journey to the chateau was long and slow, mainly to the fact I was trying to make sure the three differently decorated wedding cakes didn't crush. At last we arrived at the chateau. What a beautiful place it was, too. A moat went all the way round, beautiful gardens, and a huge lake towards the rear of the chateau. An English word came to my mind – idyllic.

The recruits helped with all the food, and at last everything was set up ready for the wedding party. Guests were arriving and we took our leave via the back entrance, as they went in the front. A voice called out to us and Monsieur Rennard stopped the wagon and went to see what was wrong. When he returned the smile on his face was beaming. The bride's father had expressed his thanks for a beautiful variety of food and was extremely impressed with the wedding cakes, and he would be advising his friends to use him in future. I was so relieved.

As we pulled away from the chateau, I was looking at the guests arriving on horseback. No, it can't be, it was. On a large grey horse there was Phillip. The shock on my face must have alerted one of the recruits as he asked if I was quite well, as I looked frightened. I replied I thought I saw someone I knew but it must be the light playing tricks on me.

When we eventually got back to the bakery I said my goodbye to Monsieur Rennard, and then carried on to the garrison. I saw Athos, Aramis, Porthos and D'Artagnan were sword fencing, and when the opportunity arose I called Porthos over. "Is Amanda here?" I asked.

"No, she's at the palace, dear Lesley. Are you all right? You look worried about something."

I looked at Porthos and asked if I could kindly whisper in his ear. He grinned and said yes. Being such a well-built Musketeer, I had to stand on my tiptoes and I whispered three words. "Phillip is here."

***

At last, a well-earned weekend off work for both Amanda and myself. We had decided to go to Paris as a treat. Porthos had recommended a nice lodging house for us to stay. The weather was sunny and so one afternoon we decided we would have a picnic and go sit by the River Seine. Amanda started asking me about my childhood in the Americas. My mind started to wander and my eyes hazed over. Looking back now there was so much I'd forgotten but I always remember the story my mother told me, just before she died. I was eight and we were in England.

We had had a really hard winter and snow so deep, like I'd never seen it before. Katherine had lit a huge fire and the room felt cosy and the smell of pinewood filled the air. Katherine decided to go and visit her friend Liz to make sure she was well. My mother and I snuggled together and I asked her to tell me about her life in the Americas. Her eyes misted at the thought of my father; she still loved him deeply even though he passed three years ago. She was born in England, just outside of London, and was called Elizabeth. Times were very hard and her parents decided to go to the Americas, as it was the New World. She said the passage was dreadful – rough seas, people dying, and after six months on board they were lucky to survive. Her father had made arrangements with a scout to have a wagon for his family and then they were bound for a place called Virginia. They never got to Virginia. The scout was always drunk and took them in the wrong direction.

There was a line of about 30 wagons. After a couple of months travelling an Indian War Party attacked them. They escaped but quite a few were killed, horrible to see dead bodies and two dead horses lying in the dirt. This happened three times as they journeyed on, and in the end the settlers stopped by a forest and went no further. There was a river and a variety of game. They started building some sort of shelter, grew crops and life was as good as it could be, but alas, it didn't stay like that. They had been there about six months when a huge Indian War Party came upon them. Some of the settlers started shooting and the war cries went up and a fight began. After the Indians had left, the settlers realised all the young women were gone, including her. My mother paused with a tear in her eye – it was the last time she saw her parents alive.

She continued that all the young women had fled to the forest thinking they would be safe, but unbeknown to them, the leader of the Indian party had spotted them and followed with others on their horses. There were about twelve of them and each one was captured and put on the horses with their captors. The leader had captured her, but was not rough, he was gentle and made sure she was comfortable before they rode off to heavens know where. Even though she was frightened she remembers she also felt a calm around her. After what seemed a long time they arrived at the Indian camp. It was huge, and seemed to be spread out over a vast area. There was lots of shouting and chanting and the captured women became very frightened. Children touched them then ran off, men looked at them with savageness in their eyes. The Indian women just looked. All twelve of them were taken to a very large tipi (tent) and the leader who had captured her sort of did sign language for them to stay there. About an hour passed and an Indian lady walked in, and she spoke English and she said her name was Woman with a Temper. She explained not to be frightened. They were in no danger, unless they went against them. Many moons ago the same had happened to her, she learnt to live with them and their ways. She ended up marrying the Chief, and had given him four children.

All the women said they wanted to go back to their families. They didn't want to stay. She explained they were already breaking camp as news of bad soldiers with bad Indian scouts were headed their way, a very ruthless army who killed everyone and everything. A wagon was brought to the tipi and those who refused to get in were forcibly put into it. They travelled for a week, stopping only now and then to eat, wash and feed their horses, and the Chief to talk to his people. Slowly all the women started to behave and were treated well, a couple of them even had admirers, including her.

The leader who had captured her was called White Wolf. When he was a child he had been followed by a white wolf and was hence given the name, and the wolf was always with him. He was very handsome in a rugged way, strong, but spoke no English. Slowly, over time White Wolf became very attached to her, and she to him, and eventually he asked the Chief if he would allow him to marry her. This was against tradition as wives were normally picked out from the tribe, or another tribe, but the Chief had seen the way White Wolf cared for this woman and, after asking his elders, he agreed. The wedding lasted two days, but the most embarrassing thing she had to endure was the night of the honeymoon. Once they had lain with each other, White Wolf had to show evidence that she had not lain with another man. As the proof was shown there was much cheering and dancing, and they were then left alone to enjoy the rest of the honeymoon. She was then given the name Chipara (rainbow). My mother fell pregnant with me straight away. Each season and month had its own name. The seasons were:

Spring was Moon of the Birth of Buffalo Calves (April, May, June)

Summer was Moon when Strawberries are Ripe (when the Sun Dance was performed – July, August, September)

Fall was The Harvest Moon (hunting season for Buffalo for winter – October, November, December)

Winter was The Winter Moon (January, February, March)

The months were:

January – wolves run together

February – dark red calves

March – sore eye moon

April – red grass appearing

May – moon when ponies shed

June – strawberry moon

July – red blooming lilies

August – cherries turn black

September – calves grow hair

October – changing season

November – falling leaves

December – when deer shed their horns

I was born in the summer season in July. My mother told me as an infant I was very good, hardly cried and my father doted on me and said I had a special blessing within me. I used to play with all the other children, rode horses bareback and always did as I was told. She said I'd seen the results of naughty children. She asked me if I remembered how I got my name, Spirit of the Wolf. I replied that I did.

When I was about four I had wandered far from camp to the edge of a huge forest. Unbeknown to me, within the forest was a huge wolf pack. I didn't know what danger was and because I had run/walked a long way I lay down to rest. When I woke about twelve wolves surrounded me; for some reason I knew not to scream. I heard a horse galloping towards me and turned, it was my father with his wolf running at his side. My father slowly got off his horse and motioned me to stay still. The pack leader of the wolves slowly walked towards me. He was snarling and showing his fangs, and then stopped. I felt something brush my legs and looked down. I had two white wolves stood either side of me, and they were both spirit wolves.

I looked back to the pack leader who had both his front legs out in front of him and he looked like he was bowing. He then stood and howled like I'd never heard a wolf howl before. He then turned and with the rest of his pack headed back into the forest. (The pack wolf was always around the Reservation and I named him Motomo – he who comes first.) My father came slowly over to me and told me to sit down with him. Both the wolves stayed at my side. My father chanted to both of the wolves, they walked over to him and were gone. My father tried to explain to me I had been born with a wolf spirit inside of me, hence the name Spirit of the Wolf, and placed his hand on my chest and tummy. Now and then she had to be set free. It was about a year later when I understood what he meant.

My mother carried on with the story. All of the women slowly learnt the Indian language but at the same time they taught them English. Two of the women did run away, they never knew what happened to them. White Wolf told her that children were called

Wakanisha and were extremely important and the centre of attraction. Their Great Spirit was Wakan Tanka. The tribe was deeply spiritual, intertwined with the spirit world by music and dance. One of the tribal dances was an endurance of pain self-inflicted with terrible wounds but it reasserted their identity. Boys of twelve would be taken to a place where they would not be able to eat or drink until they had had their vision – this could take days or weeks, but they all survived. He also told her that all the animals had a spirit for luck and strength. Life was a Sacred Circle, all connected, nature, animals and humans. It was also called a Sacred Hoop. The moon told time. If different tribes arrived they communicated by sign language. In the season of the fall, many buffalo were killed, but only what they needed, no more. The women made the hides into robes for the winter and moccasin soles. Most of the clothing was made from deerskin. The women also raised the children; boys were taught the Four Great Virtues of Life: Bravery, Fortitude, Generosity and Wisdom. The girls were also taught Bravery, how to make tipis and clothing, and care for the sick.

She had adapted to Indian life nicely, and hardly thought of England, this was now her home. She loved her husband and myself with all her heart. I had just celebrated my fifth birth year when tragedy struck. Soldiers were trying to round up the tribes and much fighting was taking place. The tribe had been lucky and we hadn't moved camp at all. The Chief called his elders and leaders to his tipi, and much talk and smoking of the peace pipe was held. I told my mother I remembered the events vividly.

My father and his warriors had donned their war paint, the horses the same. The only people left were some of his elders, women and children, and those not well enough to fight. They were gone for days and then the scout arrived back with grim news. Many of the warriors had either been killed or captured. My father, White Wolf, had been killed. My mother broke down. I just stood looking out of the tipi. The rest of the warriors arrived back, some with makeshift sleds with the dead on them, some covered with blankets. I recognised the sled my father was on, with covered blanket, because of the feathers and the white wolf at his side. I ran to him but the warriors held me back, I learned later on he had been decapitated and so had the wolf. The whole tribe went into mourning, the women wailing loudly, lots of chanting.

The funeral pyre was made and my father and his wolf gently placed on the top. It was custom for the wife to go on the pyre too but my mother was saved because of me. The fire was lit and I saw my father's spirit rise along with the wolf. The other pyres were lit, some with the wives, some not. After it was all over I told my mother I was going for a walk. I was going to the river but something led me towards the forest. About halfway there I saw the two white spirit wolves. They both came to me and I sat down and cried so much I hurt. The wolves were nuzzling me, so I looked at them. They were running back and forth. I didn't understand, then I realised they wanted me to run with them. I took off my dress and moccasins and ran, I was getting faster and faster and that was the first time I let Tala, my spirit wolf, out. I felt so free; even though I was only five, we ran for what seemed like miles. When we stopped and had rested for a while, I put my clothes on, turned and then saw my father and his white wolf stood in front of me, he came to me and told me things were going to change but he would always be with me and wherever I was, my wolf had to run but I had to be very careful.

Weeks passed but my spirit wolf didn't want to run. I had to learn to listen to her, she would tell me when. My mother was heartbroken and made the decision that she wanted to leave the tribe and go back to England. I didn't want to go. I loved my people, I loved Motomo, and I ran away. I went to the forest but as night drew in I got scared and started crying. A bright light shined on me, and it was my father and his wolf. The two white wolves also appeared. My father came towards me and held me in his arms. He told me my mother was frantic, she had lost him and now she thought she had lost me as well. He was sorry he had passed, but life had to go on even if it meant me leaving his tribe. It was then I heard the horses, my father kissed me and told me to be good, and then he and the wolves were gone. I returned with the warriors to camp and flew into my mother's opened arms. We left two months later.

CHAPTER 4

Katherine

I have been in France now for just over six months. In that time I have received one letter from Katherine, which is strange, as I have written to her every month with all the news, especially about seeing Phillip. My employment at the bakery with Monsieur Rennard has been hard work but very rewarding. He now looks upon me as the daughter he never had. His wife died giving birth and sadly the baby, a girl, was stillborn. The bakery was flourishing, and the small shop window was always full of bread and cakes, but I felt so sad seeing the small children begging for crumbs. I had a word with Monsieur Rennard, saying that perhaps we could give the very stale bread and pastries to them. He agreed, but some days everything went and I had nothing to give them. There was about six of them that came regularly, and I made them promise they must keep quiet, because if everyone knew they would get nothing.

I was walking back to my lodgings early one evening, when all of a sudden I froze on the spot. I looked round to make sure nobody else could see what I was seeing. Sitting in the middle of the lane were the two white wolves. All of a sudden I was overwhelmed with grief. The two wolves sort of melted into one and there stood Katherine. As quick as she was there she was gone. Oh no, Katherine must have passed. Why hadn't I heard? What had happened? My heart was pounding in my chest and slowly I made my way to my lodgings. At the end of the lane where my lodgings were, was a tavern. I thought I heard someone shout my name but took no notice. A hand touched my shoulder and I jumped. It was Captain Tréville. "My dear, whatever is wrong? You look like you've seen a ghost?" he said. Little did he know that was exactly what I had just seen! Only Amanda knew about my "gift", but she didn't know the full extent.

Tréville and I had become very close, but alas not in a romantic way. We were more like brother and sister, and I was extremely content with that. I also trusted him implicitly. I tried to speak but fainted instead. When I came to, I had been placed upon my bed, with my landlady Madame DuPresse, and Tréville, watching over me. When I went to move, my landlady rushed to my side and gave me some water to drink. "Oh, my dear Lesley, are you ill?" she asked.

I had to think quickly and replied, "My apologies Madame and Tréville for worrying you, I have not eaten today, I have been too busy."

Tréville looked at me and raised his eyebrow. "Do you think you can walk to the garrison, my dear, where I will make sure you have a good meal inside you?" I nodded yes, and slowly we walked back to the garrison and went to Tréville's office.

Within five minutes a variety of foods was laid on his table. I nibbled at bits of this and that. "Now you want to tell me what really happened out there," he asked, "and no story about not eating?" He knew me too well.

I couldn't tell him the whole truth, so replied, "You know I've been writing to Katherine in England, well I have only had one reply, which I find odd. This is going to sound rather strange but I saw her this evening as a ghost, and my heart filled with grief. Oh, Tréville, I think she has passed. I somehow must go to England and find out."

Tréville rubbed his chin and told me that four of his Musketeers were bound for England in two days' time. They were going to Calais for a ship to England, which would take about six days. (Paris to Calais would take four days and then Calais to Dover two days. Dover to London was about four hours on horseback). They were going to deliver high-security papers from the King. I went quiet for a minute to gather my thoughts, but Tréville, as usual, read my thoughts. "Would you by any chance like to go with them?" he asked. "I can arrange it for you and I would be happier knowing you had four of my best Musketeers with you, just in case of any trouble."

I looked at this kind hearted, understanding man, so I put my arms around him and gave him a kiss on each cheek. How could I turn down such an offer? I was concerned that his four best Musketeers were going to be going to England. Who was going to guard the King and Queen? Tréville smiled and said it was four other Musketeers that were going, and I had met them before. I smiled and said I must go as I had a lot to sort out before I went. The following day I explained to Madame DuPresse and Monsieur Rennard that I would be away for over just two weeks. They both wished me god speed and to return safely. A couple of days later I packed a small bag and went to the garrison. I noticed six horses were saddled, ready to go. Six, I wondered who else was joining us. Tréville came down from his office and gave me a worried look. I asked what was wrong. He was a bit hesitant and then said riding in a gown might be a bit uncomfortable for me and as we had to go through some rough areas and it might be better if I wore men's clothes.

I was rather taken aback by this, but then realised he was probably right, but I didn't have any men's clothes. The last time I had worn breeches was on the Reservation. Tréville advised me to go to his office and what I required was there. I was amazed at the clothes he had found and as soon as I was dressed I felt so comfy. I'm sure I felt a sigh from my wolf. I descended the steps to the waiting Musketeers and horses. Athos, Porthos, D'Artagnan and Aramis were there along with Tréville. I felt rather conscious of how I looked but they all approved. "Not training then today, gentlemen?" I asked.

They just grinned and then Porthos stepped forward and placed a hat on my head. "Not dressed without a hat," he said.

I gave him a hug and a kiss on his cheek, and then whispered, "Please take care of Amanda, especially now we know Philip is here," and he nodded.

Aramis and D'Artagnan both gave me a hug and a kiss on the cheek and wished me a safe journey and to hurry back. Athos stepped forward, I'm sure he's still wary of me, and he took my hand and kissed it, saying, "Safe journey, Lesley. You will be missed, especially by Amanda, but we will look after her."

I smiled at him and then whispered to him, "I will never tell anyone what I know, your secret will go with me to my grave."

At that he surprised me and gave me a hug and whispered in my ear, "Thank you," and he was smiling. At last, I hope Athos and myself have come to an understanding.

"Lesley, Lesley! Oh, I thought I had missed you." It was Amanda, running into the garrison like she was on fire.

We gave each other a hug and a kiss on the cheek. "Stay safe," I said, and she then went to Porthos.

"Come, my dear, it is time to go," said Tréville.

The four Musketeers were already on their horses waiting to go. I noticed none of them were in uniform. Tréville helped me onto my horse and then mounted the spare one. I looked at him quizzically. "I'm riding with you until you get past the forest, it's a bad road for Red Guards," he said. I smiled, waved goodbye to my friends and trotted out of the garrison. When we pulled into a tavern for the night, I mentioned to Tréville it was no good, I just could not ride with a saddle. He said not to worry, they would leave the saddle with the innkeeper and collect it later. The next morning after a good breakfast we set off to clear the forest; luckily nothing befell us and then it was time for me to say goodbye to Tréville. He held me tight, told me to stay with the Musketeers at all times, especially on the ship. He had given his Musketeers instructions that one of them had to stay with me. He kissed me on both cheeks, wished me well and looked forward to my return and hopefully not with bad news.

My Musketeers were called Andre, Tomas, Loup and Rogier. After we left Tréville we carried on to Calais, where the ship was waiting for us. It wasn't a large ship, rather small in fact. The conditions were cramped, no cabins as such, so we slept and ate on the decks. The sea was rough in places, no one had the seasickness, and the food was adequate. We arrived in Dover two days later. We then had a four-hour journey on horseback into London. On the outskirts of London, Tomas suggested I changed back into one of my gowns or people would stare and alert soldiers. I found a secluded place to change and then we rode into London. Katherine's house was north of London, so Loup volunteered to accompany me whilst the others attended to the King's orders. We arranged to meet back at the secluded spot where I would change again, four days later.

Loup and I carried onto Katherine's house. After my mother died

Katherine decided to move away from the city and bought a dwelling near a small village, surrounded by fields and a forest. It was a brick house, with a chimney, and had three rooms. The first thing I noticed was the garden, as it was a mess. My bones felt a chill as I dismounted, and much to my concern, I saw my two white wolves. I looked at Loup – no reaction. Obviously he couldn't see them, thank heavens. I walked up to the door and saw that it and the windows were all nailed shut. Loup called to me and said someone was coming. I saw it was Katherine's neighbour, Liz, and we both ran into each other's arms. It was so good to see her. She explained Katherine had died over a month ago, and they thought it was her heart. She was buried at the cemetery up the road. Tears came and they wouldn't stop, I never said goodbye to her, and that broke my heart, as she had been like my second mother. Liz asked me where I was staying and I said we were going to find a tavern in the city, to which she replied we must stay with her. I looked at Loup who motioned me over and asked if I would be all right on my own, I had a good friend to stay with, and he could join the other Musketeers. I knew I would be welcomed at Liz's and not only that, I might be able to run in the forest. I assured him I would be all right, but I would prefer it if he came back for me in three days, as I didn't want to ride to the secluded spot on my own. He agreed and went on his way.

Liz and I talked about lots of things, but not Katherine, for a couple of hours, and then it was time to retire. "Tomorrow will be Katherine's day," she said. I smiled and said that would be good. I slept on and off and eventually got up and tiptoed to the window. My two white wolves were playing, so very quietly I opened the door and crept out. They both came to me and led me to the edge of the small forest. I glanced around to make sure no one was around, slipped out of my clothes and started running. Oh, it felt so good to run free again, Tala loved every minute. We all played, rolled over and then laid down together. Later on I felt the wolves nudging me; daybreak was coming so I hurried back to where my clothes were, dressed and again, very quietly, crept back to my bed. Tala was satisfied and I felt more at ease. Later on I heard Liz moving around so I went into the kitchen where she was making breakfast.

We decided to go for a walk and soon Katherine came into our conversation and Liz suggested we go to the cemetery and then into the city to see Katherine's lawyer. I looked at her. "Lawyer? I said.

"What do we have to go there for?" Liz told me Katherine had left a thing called a will, and her lawyers were trying to find me. "What have I done wrong? I know nothing about a will," I said rather anxiously. Liz put her arm around me and said there was nothing to worry about. A will was what a person had written down by a lawyer, leaving whatever to whoever it had to go to, and Katherine was a lady with means. I'd never heard of it, but Liz's explanation did make me feel better.

We got to the gates of the cemetery, and Liz showed me where Katherine had been buried. It was just a mound of dirt with some flowers on and a wooden cross. I just stood and stared and silently said a prayer, with tears rolling down my cheeks. I felt such a loss, and as we turned to walk away I left a bit of my heart with her. I looked around to see if the wolves were there, but nothing. Later on, Liz hitched her horse to a very small cart and we travelled into the city.

The city hadn't changed much, still the smog, the filthy sewage-filled lanes, mongrels and beggars scrounging for food. There was death in the streets. The houses were made of wood and pitch, the upper storeys overhanging the lower ones, so the sun was blocked out. We passed a thing that looked horrendous. I'd never seen it before. It was a wooden structure with ropes hanging around people's necks, and there were four adults and a child. Quite a crowd was surrounding them and as I looked there was a loud noise and then all five were jolted down and a huge cheer went up from the crowd. Their bodies were twitching. Oh God, I felt the nausea rising within and put my hand to my mouth.

I heard a horse galloping and someone calling my name and turned to see Loup. "What on earth are you doing in this part of the city? I couldn't believe my eyes when I saw you drive past, it's dangerous for two women on their own, and not a sight you should be seeing," he said angrily. "If anything happens to you Tréville will kick me out of the Musketeers." I explained we were going to a lawyer, and Loup asked Liz the address. Alas, we had taken a wrong turn so Loup escorted us away from that scene to the road where the lawyer was situated. He explained to Liz the correct way to return to the road, which would lead us out of the city. I thanked him and he rode off, to wherever he was going.

The lawyer we were going to see was a Mr Burrows. His office was above a tavern, and was dimly lit. We entered the office and a clerk, I believe that was what he was called, came to us and Liz explained why we were there. Alas, Mr Burrows had gone out for about half an hour so we decided to go and have a drink at a teashop across the way, informing the clerk where we would be. We were given a table for two by the window, and the tea and cakes were delicious. A short while later I saw a rather rotund gentleman enter the lawyer's and then the clerk came over and advised us Mr Burrows was back.

We returned and met Mr Burrows. He was quiet a well-spoken gentleman, with red rosy cheeks and spectacles on the end of his nose. He produced Katherine's will and proceeded to read it. He ended up telling us that Katherine had invested very wisely. I understood that after all Katherine's funeral expenses, and all debts paid and promises had been adhered to, whatever was left would be inherited to me. I asked about the house and he replied that if I decided to sell it, it would be better to do it sooner rather than later. He also advised that a gentleman had already enquired about the house and would pay a reasonable amount to include all the furniture and the small barn. I needed time to think, Tala was very restless, and I suggested I went back tomorrow with an answer. My dilemma – did I stay in England or France? I didn't have much time to make that decision.

After Liz had gone to bed, I crept out and headed towards the forest. I undressed and let my wolf run. After an hour of running I returned and dressed. As I turned my father and his wolf, and my two white wolves, appeared before me. "Sit, my child," my father said, and I did. He said my spirit wolf had called to him. He asked me what was wrong and I slowly told him of the day I'd had. When I'd finished he hugged me and said, "My little one, it was written that life would not be easy and hard decisions would have to be made, you have come to that crossroad in your life. I will always be with you, wherever you are. You have to think of life here and in France. I cannot guide you to the right path, only you can do that, but I think maybe in your heart you know which path you will take. Like all of humanity you will have a crisis in your life many times, and many times I will appear to you. I have met Katherine in the spirit world and she is with James and happy again." I smiled at this and a single tear fell. "Little one, it is time for me to go. Tala will guide you along with others, listen to her." I gave him a hug, but just before he left, he said something that brought tears to my eyes and flowed for some time. "Your mother sends her love." And he was gone.

The following day Liz and I returned to see Mr Burrows. I told him to sell the house as I had decided to go back to France, where my friends now were. He suggested that we go back to him in a couple of hours and he would try and sort things out, and he would return with us, so that I may gain entrance to the house, in case there was anything I needed. Liz and I had a lovely time going in and out of the shops, and by the time we had returned to Mr Burrows' office and then onto Katherine's house I was exhausted. Mr Burrows somehow removed the nailed boards to the door and we went in, and he told me to take whatever I needed, within reason of course. The house felt musty and a bit damp and everything was covered in dust. Memories came flooding back. I had had such a good life here. I knew where Katherine had hidden her jewellery box in her bedchamber. I asked Mr Burrows if it would be all right for me to take it. He said it was mine anyway. I went into my bedchamber and got the rest of my gowns (three) and undergarments, and other things I needed. Nothing else caught my attention until I entered the parlour, where I spotted Katherine's cookbooks. I took all four of them with me. I shook Mr Burrows by the hand, curtseyed and thanked him for everything. In return he dropped two heavy bags of coins into my hands. "I managed to contact the gentleman interested in buying Katherine's dwelling and we agreed a good price, and because of the urgency he left and then returned with the funds. There are three thousand livres in each bag, which is your inheritance after deductions. A goldsmith did the exchange for me." I was stunned. I was rich, but nobody must know, I didn't want to lose my new friends in France.

That night Liz and I were talking and she asked me why I went to France. I explained why – to find my friend Amanda, and about her stepmother and brother. Liz was stunned at first and then said, "Was she the one who married the physician? His daughter was called Amanda. I never met them." I replied it was. She then told me Amanda's stepmother had passed, as her son had strangled her, and then went missing. He was wanted for murder. She started looking for something and then gave me a rolled-up poster. It was Phillip. I was stunned and said I didn't leave until two weeks after I'd seen him in the tavern and I'd heard nothing. Liz said that apparently he had come home drunk, strangled her and laid her in her bed with a blanket over her, locked the house and went. She was found a month later when a friend visited her and all she could see was blowflies. I couldn't wait to tell Amanda and Porthos. I was also missing Captain Tréville.

The following day I packed everything up into four bags, which I borrowed from Liz. Must return them to her when I can. Two of them had a hiding place in the bottom and I hid most of the coins in there. One book went on top, and then I divided the rest of my things into each bag. Loup arrived as arranged. I hugged and thanked and said goodbye to Liz. Loup took my bags with a groan. "You robbed the book shop?" he asked. I apologised and said I did have a heavy cookbook in each bag, a memento from Katherine. I grinned (if only he knew) and mounted my horse, which had had a lovely rest in the field. Two bags were put on each horse. We rode to the secluded area, I got changed and the rest of the Musketeers arrived a short time later.

"We need to talk," I said. "If Captain Tréville finds out you left me with my friend he will go into a rage, not a pretty sight, and your lives will be hell on earth. You all know what he's like, so we mustn't say anything. Loup, you stayed in the small barn, escorted both of us into the city and back on both days. I don't want to get any of you into trouble because of me, do we all agree?" They agreed and we rode back to Dover; the ship was waiting for us and six days later we arrived back on the outskirts of Paris. They stopped at my lodgings first, and Loup kindly carried my bags up to my chamber. I asked him to inform Captain Tréville I would call upon him tomorrow, and thanked him for looking out for Liz and myself. He bowed and left. I was absolutely exhausted. I had to decide where to put my money, but for now a quick wash and slumber.

CHAPTER 5

The Bakery

The day after I returned from England, I made sure I saw my landlady to inform her I was back, as I had arrived late and she had retired for the evening, and then went to the bakery and then on to the garrison. I looked up to Tréville's office and saw him leaning on the rail. I waved, and he waved back. I went up the steps to his office, where he gave me a huge hug. It felt so good to be with him again. "Lovely to have you back, Lesley, how did it all go?" I told him it was a long story and he replied he had time to listen. I told him the whole story, apart from the money and Philip, I had to see Amanda first to tell her about Henrietta (Philip's mother), and my decision. I just hoped while I'd been away Philip had not found her. Tréville looked at me, raised an eyebrow and just said, "And your decision is?" I just smiled and said I'd let him know later.

The following day I fell back into my routine, up and at the bakery very early. Mr Rennard welcomed me back with a hug. "I have missed you, Lesley. I'm glad you are safely returned to us," he said. I went into the kitchen and was surprised to see one of the young street girls I'd been giving stale bread to there. "I needed more help whilst you were away," Monsieur Rennard said.

I smiled and asked what she was called. She replied, "Catherine, milady."

My eyes went to hers and I stuttered, "Did you say Catherine?"

She looked a bit frightened and replied, "Yes."

My heart missed a beat. I looked at her, smiled and said, "I'm sorry, I didn't mean to frighten you, I have just lost a very good friend called Katherine, and you surprised me, and my name is Lesley, not milady." She smiled back and over time we became good friends, and I called her my little sister.

Several weeks passed, and I'd been far too busy to catch up with Amanda and Tréville. I had noticed that Monsieur Rennard had been looking tired of late and was concerned. Eventually I convinced him to go to his physician. The result was not good, as his heart wasn't working too well. The physician suggested he gave up the bakery. My heart dropped at the thought of having to look for another position. A couple of evenings later he came and sat with me in the kitchen. "Lesley, I want to speak to you," he said gently. "I don't want to give up the bakery, so I have had an idea. I would like you to take over the running of the bakery instead of me." He took my hands in his and said he knew it would be in good hands, but I had to think about it.

As it was still light I decided to go to the garrison to see Tréville, I needed to speak to him. Alas, he was at the palace, so I went to my lodgings. The following day as I entered the garrison I saw Amanda speaking to Porthos. I went over to them and hugged each of them and said I had some important news to tell them, and could we go somewhere quieter. Amanda looked at Porthos and suggested a walk by the river. "A walk by the river, that seems a good idea." I turned to see Tréville behind me, grinning. Tréville left word as to his whereabouts in case he was needed, as the Red Guards had been causing trouble again! The four of us walked down to the river, and then I asked them if they minded if Amanda and I had some time on our own. There was a small tavern, so they headed there.

I told Amanda what had happened in England and that I had decided to stay in France. She was so pleased, so hopefully we would now always be there for each other. "That's not the only news, Amanda," I said. I put my hand in my bag and brought out the rolled piece of paper. Amanda unrolled it and went white. I suggested we sat down.

"Oh my god, what has he done?" she asked.

I explained that before he got to France he had strangled

Henrietta, left her in a bed with a blanket on her, to be found about a month later by a friend. I put my arm around her. "Philip is more dangerous than we thought," I said, "and he's here. I saw him the day of the wedding and before I left I told Porthos." Amanda started crying and I tried to console her. Amanda composed herself and we returned to the tavern. "Tréville, will you walk with me please?" I asked. He looked and nodded as though he knew something was up.

As we walked I explained about me seeing Philip at the wedding. He was outraged. "Why wasn't I told this before? You have both been in danger and if anything had happened, how do you think my Musketeers and myself would have felt? You are both family to us all now."

I apologised. We walked back to Amanda and Porthos. The two men nodded at each other.

The following day I popped in to see Tréville to pick up a bag I had left with him for safe keeping. Whilst I was in the spare room retrieving it, I heard Tréville raise his voice and went to see what the commotion was. Amanda stood there with her lovely dress ripped and a guilty-looking Athos. What had he done now? Athos was explaining it had been an accident. At that moment the door burst opened and in walked Porthos, Aramis and D'Artagnan, who had been sent to Montmartre on business. They all looked at Amanda and then Athos. I pulled a shawl from my bag and put it around Amanda's shoulders. Amanda looked at Tréville. "We need to tell them," she said. Tréville then told Aramis and D'Artagnan the situation and the looks on their faces were shock. Porthos put his arms around Amanda.

Athos then addressed Porthos and said, "You need to tell them what he did to her, the scars on her back."

I looked at Porthos and his eyes narrowed. "How do you know that?" he said.

Athos replied, "We were in my room."

I looked at both of them, surprised. I have never seen Porthos move so fast, he was on Athos before I could blink. Amanda was desperately trying to explain but Porthos ignored her. What Athos said next stunned me. He thought we were spies because when we met we whispered a lot – don't men realise that some things are private and not to be spoken aloud!

Tréville asked Amanda for a description of Philip and when she had relayed it, I turned and said, "Would this help?" and gave him the poster. Tréville looked at Porthos and Athos, and begrudgingly they shook hands, then Porthos said something to Tréville and then walked out. Tréville escorted Amanda to her carriage and then came back with a grin on his face. "Why are you smiling like that?" I asked.

"Let's just say Porthos has something planned," he replied. I knew exactly what he meant and also smiled.

Now everyone had gone I told Tréville that I personally had something to discuss with him. First of all, I told him my decision and he was delighted, not just for himself but for Amanda as well. I then told him about my inheritance and the bakery. He said the bakery was easy, and I should take the position. The money was a different matter. "Where is the money now?" he asked. I replied it was still in my bags with the hidden bottoms and I had left the cookery books in them. He leant against the table and rubbed his hand over his chin, as he usually did when he had a problem to sort. "You could think about buying the bakery if Monsieur Rennard is agreeable, but you would have to have a private agreement, as you know a woman cannot buy property," he said. I had thought about that but then, as I explained to Tréville, people would know I had money and I was worried in case I lost my friends over it. He understood my dilemma.

I then had a bad thought. "I'm not going to lose your friendship, am I, Tréville, now I've told you the truth." Tears welled in my eyes and he took me in his arms.

"My dear, I am so pleased for you. Katherine wanted you to have the inheritance and the last thing I would do is break our friendship over such a matter. We just need to find somewhere where the funds can be left securely." I was so relieved, as he was the only person I really trusted, apart from Amanda of course. The evening was drawing in and Tréville walked me back to my lodgings, kissed me goodnight, on my cheek, and we agreed to see each other tomorrow.

I had a restless night and wondered if Tala needed to run. But she was quiet. The following day I went back to the garrison to see Tréville but he wasn't there. The Red Guards had caused a fight with some of the Musketeers and Tréville had gone to the palace to defend his men. I decided I would walk round some of the lanes by the garrison and there I bumped into Monsieur Rennard taking his morning constitutional. "Ah, my dear Lesley, how are you? Isn't it a lovely day?" he said. I agreed it was indeed a lovely day and wondered if we might go back to the bakery and talk about my position. "Of course, my dear. Here, please take my arm."

Once there I made us some tea, and advised him I would love to run the bakery for him; he was delighted and then made another suggestion, which took me by surprise. He had a dwelling on the outskirts of Paris, in the country, and instead of staying at the bakery, he wanted to move there, and so the rooms above the bakery would be available for me. I wasn't sure about this, what would people think? Would they think I'd moved in with him, or worse? He replied for me not to worry, he had already conversed with most of his friends, and they agreed the bakery would be in good hands and he really did need to rest. He would still come to the bakery some days, and make sure everything was in order, sort the orders and pay the wages.

We went up to the rooms above the bakery. There were three rooms – one was small and was Monsieur Rennard's office, which he wanted to keep, and the other two would be mine. Two rooms for me! One had a small bed in it, but he told me he would replace it with a new bed. The other room had a couple of pieces of furniture, which would stay. He then showed me something that was a wondrous sight. In his office he removed some bricks and there was a safe, where he kept his funds. He then showed me another one in the bedchamber. I had somewhere to hide my inheritance. There were separate keys for each. What could I do? I agreed to his terms. My own rooms and somewhere to put my funds, I was a very happy person.

CHAPTER 6

The Castle Wedding

A few weeks after I'd moved into the bakery, on the Sunday, I went to see Tréville to see if he would like a picnic by the river, but alas, he was away on King's business. I decided to go to the river on my own, as Amanda was also busy. I found a quiet spot, sat down and started reading a book I'd taken with me. "Lesley, is that you?" I heard a familiar voice say. I looked up.

"Monsieur DelaCroix, how lovely to see you again," I said.

"My wife is at the tavern and said she saw you walking, and we wondered if you would care to partake of a meal with us?" he said. I accepted his kind invitation, as with Tréville not being with me I didn't bring anything. We walked back to the tavern where I greeted Madame DelaCroix and sat down next to her.

"Oh Lesley, how lovely to see you again. How have you been? Did you find your friend?"

"My dear, please let Lesley get her breath, so many questions." I looked at both of them and smiled and told them of my life in France so far, but not mentioning Philip.

"That's wonderful, Lesley," said Monsieur DelaCroix. "I'm so pleased things have turned out well for you and your friend, but so sorry for the loss of Katherine. I think we were meant to meet today, as you could be the answer to our prayers." I looked at him, wondering what he meant. "Let me explain. As you probably remember we came home to see our youngest daughter get married. Due to the passing of her sister it was postponed. The wedding is now in two weeks' time and we came to Paris to look for a baker to come to our castle and do the preparations. (Did he just say "castle"!) Lesley, can I persuade you to come and do the preparations? I would send a carriage for you, and naturally you can have one of the bedchambers."

"Oh, please Lesley, say you will come," said Madame DelaCroix. I explained I would have to ask Monsieur Rennard first, and if I did go I would prefer to stay in the servants' quarters, it wouldn't be right otherwise. They both looked at each other and smiled and then I suggested, if they had the time now, we could go and see Monsieur Rennard, as I knew he was doing various jobs at the bakery whilst it was quiet. They agreed but before we left I knew I had to tell them about Athos.

"Before we depart there is something I must tell you both and I'm worried it might upset you," I said.

"Please tell us, Lesley, surely it can't be that upsetting?" said Monsieur DelaCroix. I started shaking a little bit and Madame DelaCroix held my hand.

"I have met and know the Comte de la Fere," I said. They both looked at each other and paled slightly. "He does not hold that title any longer, and is now, along with his Captain and three others, one of the top men in the King's Musketeers. When I found out from my friend who he was I'm sorry to say I was rather hasty and hit him in the face. I told him I would take his secret with me to my grave. As I live near the garrison there may be a possibility you would see him, or he could come into the bakery."

Monsieur DelaCroix took my hands in his and said, "Thank you for telling us, Lesley. Yes, it would have been a shock to see him after all this time, but time heals wounds and since being at the castle I have been informed more of the circumstances that led to what took place. Did you come by carriage or horse, Lesley?"

I replied, "By carriage."

We all left in his carriage and went back to the bakery after I had given his driver instructions on how to get there. I looked around as I alighted from the carriage and luckily saw no Musketeers. We entered the bakery and I called for Monsieur Rennard, who came out from the kitchen. I introduced Monsieur and Madame DelaCroix to him and then related what had happened.

"Please, please come into the kitchen, I will make a new pot of tea for us all," said Monsieur Rennard.

As we walked in I stopped dead in my tracks. Oh dear, sitting at the table were Tréville, Athos, Aramis and D'Artagnan. I assumed Porthos was with Amanda. Athos looked up and went white, and glared at me. I looked at Monsieur DelaCroix who walked over to them and shook their hands. Had he not recognised Athos? Tréville looked at me and said, "Apologies, my dear, I understood you were looking for me. Perhaps we can talk later? Gentlemen, I think it's time for us to take our leave. Nice to meet you, Monsieur and Madame DelaCroix."

As they walked past me Monsieur DelaCroix looked at Athos and then his face showed he recognised him. "Athos, may I have a quiet word with you please?"

I looked at both men and said, "Oh, do you two know each other?" I was worried in case things turned nasty. Athos nodded and asked me if they could use my parlour. Naturally, I agreed. Tréville told Athos they'd see him back at the garrison.

"Please don't do anything that could lead to something bad," I heard Madame DelaCroix say to her husband. He kissed her on the cheek and followed Athos upstairs. I asked Madame DelaCroix to explain about her daughter's wedding to Monsieur Rennard and I slipped out to make sure nothing untoward happened upstairs. All I could hear was raised voices, and then it went quiet, then normal voices. All of a sudden the door opened and both came down the stairs. I crept back into the kitchen but looked through the crack in the door. I saw both men shake hands and Athos depart. Looks like they had reached an understanding.

Monsieur Rennard agreed he would be more than happy for me to go and do the wedding preparation. It was arranged that two days later Monsieur DelaCroix's carriage would come for me and I would stay for seven to ten days. After they had left I went to the garrison to see Tréville and tell him what had transpired. He was pleased for me but said he would miss my company. "Where do they live, my dear?" he asked.

"I'm going to the outskirts of Chartres, which I believe is about fifty miles away, and apparently it's a castle," I said.

"Um, a castle you say? Interesting," Tréville said as he raised his eyebrow.

"Have you ever been to Chartres, Tréville?"

He replied he had but some time ago. We said our farewells and as usual I left him looking out over his balcony. As I went to leave I saw Athos. "Everything all right, Athos?" I asked.

He just replied, "Fine," nodded and carried on walking. I looked up to Tréville's office and he was still there watching everything going on. I waved and he waved back. I was going to miss him too.

Two days later, rather early, the carriage arrived. We stopped a couple of times and arrived very late evening so I couldn't see much of the castle. Monsieur DelaCroix had been called away on business, so his wife greeted me. She showed me around the rooms, very impressive, and then took me down to meet the lady in charge of the household servants. She was called Madame Guillochon, but said I could call her Theresa. As it was late she showed me to my room and said she would introduce me to the rest of the servants in the morning. My room was clean, had a small cabinet with a jug and bowl on top, and a bed, which was very comfy and I slept well. I was up early, as normal, and could hear the hustle and bustle of a very busy kitchen. There was a knock at my door and a young girl stood there with a jug of water for me to wash. I thanked her, hurriedly washed and dressed and made my way down to the kitchen.

"Morning Lesley, please come and join us," said Theresa. She introduced me to everyone who worked in the kitchen and advised me that Madame DelaCroix was going to speak to us about the wedding menu. The kitchen was huge and divided into two. Fish and meat was one end and the other was for bread, cakes and pastries. Apparently the DelaCroix's did a lot of entertaining. Theresa said I would have three girls to help me with whatever was needed. I was getting acquainted with the girls when Theresa came over and said we'd been asked to go to the drawing room.

I followed Theresa, this castle was huge, and we entered the drawing room where Madame DelaCroix was seated. "Ah, ladies, please come sit, we have a lot to discuss," she said. She then told us there would be two hundred guests, and the menu for the food was roasted hog, fish, lamb, chicken, geese and ducks. This was to be Theresa's domain. Mine was to make the wedding cakes, individual cakes for each guest, various breads and pastries and small cakes to make a Croquembouche.

"I apologise, Madame DelaCroix," I said, "what is a croque?"

"Oh, do not worry, Lesley, it's small round cakes that are placed on top of each other by the wedding guests. It's believed to be good luck if a newly married couple kiss over the mound of cakes without knocking it over," she replied. I just smiled and said it wouldn't be a problem! I had six days to do all this, heavens above. As we went to leave I noticed Theresa curtsy so I did the same. Afterwards Theresa advised me I didn't need to curtsy – they were servants, and I was a friend. Theresa suggested I go outside and have a look around, see the castle in the daylight. She showed we where the servants' entrance was and I stepped out into brilliant sunshine and gasped. The castle was beautiful.

It was surround by a moat that went all the way round, with lovely trees and flowers on all sides. Tala whimpered. "Yes, I know, Tala," I whispered. "I see the forest which is huge and I'll have to check it out first, it's new territory for us." There were four bridges to cross the moat, each going in various directions. At the side of the servants' entrance was a large garden that had vegetables, spices and herbs growing. I walked towards the forest and at the same time viewing the castle from different angles. It was the biggest dwelling I had ever seen. As I walked closer to the forest I could see it was very dense with shrubs, trees and other plants. Good place for Tala to run, if I got the chance. I retraced my steps back to the servants' door and bumped into one of the girls that were going to help me. "Hello Lesley, are you taking some air?" she asked.

"I'm sorry, I've forgotten your name?" I replied.

"It's Francine but all call me Fran," she replied.

"I have never seen a castle before and the beautiful garden and forest take my breath away."

She smiled and filled me in about everyone. We returned to the kitchen.

Theresa had a small room off the kitchen where she did all of the ordering, and then gave it Monsieur DelaCroix for his approval. From what I could gather they were a very wealthy family. "Lesley, please come and join me for tea," she said. I accepted and Theresa started telling me about the castle and the DelaCroix's. They had two daughters and a son. Sadly, the son had been shot whilst out hunting. It was the younger daughter getting married, the other daughter "had a past" but had now also passed away, leaving a child. This got me interested, as I knew this was to do with Athos. Theresa asked me about my life and I told her only what I wanted her to know.

Slowly we got back to the daughter with a past. I said that Monsieur and Madame DelaCroix must have been bereft at having lost a second child. Theresa replied, "Chantelle caused them heartache long before she passed. She had a childhood sweetheart, we all knew him as the Comte de la Fere. They made such a lovely couple and we all knew they would eventually marry. When they thought they were old enough, they asked her father if he would consent to their marriage. He refused them. "Too young," he said, and so they ran away. Searches were mounted but nobody found them. The master and mistress were in despair. Two years later the daughter returned, and she was dreadfully ill and with child. The master asked where the Comte was. She told him the Comte had refused to marry her, he was always drunk, beat her and had abandoned her when he found out she was carrying his child, and had walked for nearly a month to get home, begging where possible. The master, as you can imagine, was full of rage. He got his physician out to look to his daughter and then set out to try and find the Comte. He swore if he ever found him he would either be hanged, shot, or rot in the Bastille. As time went on his daughter regained her health and gave birth to a baby girl, but the master's rage festered. One day he came back from a long journey and said that some justice had been done. We never knew what he meant.

A couple of years later Chantelle was taken seriously ill. It was something to do with her lungs. The master and mistress had just returned from a trip to England. The day before she passed she asked to speak to the master privately. She told him she had a confession to make. When she ran away with the Comte it was a ploy. She had met somebody else and fallen deeply in love with him, but he was not of noble birth. She had told the Comte and he said he would accompany her to her lover, but only after he had seen for himself that she would be happy, would he leave her. All three met up and stayed together for three months, in which time she married her lover and the Comte then said it was time to leave them. She asked the Comte if he would return to his lands and house, but he said he would not, her father would not forgive him for what he had done, and therefore he had to make himself another life. Chantelle and her husband were happy and enjoyed life together, or so she thought. He turned out to be a gambler and everything they had he gambled away. When she told him she was with child, he beat and kicked her and threw her out.

The master was stunned and then told her the consequences of what she had made him do. When they couldn't be found his anger towards the Comte festered badly. He learnt that the Comte had never returned to his house and lands, so one day he burnt his house to the ground and tore all his lands up. After his daughter passed the master went into a decline for months and was only brought out of it by his other daughter and his wife.

"Good heavens, what a story. Did they ever find the Comte?" I asked. Theresa replied he was never found and was either dead or living in another country. Little did she know he was only fifty miles away and a King's Musketeer!

The next three days were hectic to say the least. Fran, Suzanne and Michelle, my helpers, were brilliant. Under my guidance I showed them how to roll the dough for the small and large cakes, they watched and then helped put the white coating on all the cakes and everything else I asked them to do. I had no time to myself and I knew Tala could smell the forest and was restless.

At last the day of the wedding arrived. The tables in the great hall were placed into position, of which there were ten with twenty people around them. At the far end all the meats were placed and the other end the cakes and pastries. In the middle of the hall a table was laid and on it went the wedding cake and a large round empty plate for the Croquembouche. When everything was laid out and ready, Monsieur and Madame DelaCroix came to see the results, and I'm glad to say, they were delighted.

They advised us that some of the food was too be left downstairs and we were all to have our own celebrations, he'd even arranged for wine and ale to be sent down. Madame DelaCroix took my arm and said, "Lesley, we would be honoured if you joined us for the celebrations. As of yet you have not met our daughter and she wishes to thank you personally." I smiled and said I would be happy to join them, but alas I had not brought an appropriate gown with me, and perhaps I could meet their daughter before she went off on honeymoon. They were happy with that and so was I. I would rather be down with the servants than try and mix with people I didn't know. I really wished Amanda, Tréville and the Musketeers were here.

The wedding was a huge success. All the guests commented on what excellent food they had, and the bride, called Bridgette, looked absolutely gorgeous and was a lovely lady, and what a handsome groom. The guests built the Croquembouche and the bride and groom kissed over it and didn't knock it down. Downstairs all the servants had a great time and nobody noticed when I slipped out.

CHAPTER 7

The Wolves

The forest was calling and Tala was desperate to run. I made doubly sure that I wasn't followed and that nobody was around. The forest was very dark but the moon lit a passageway through the trees. When I was far enough away I slipped off my dress and the next thing I knew I was running free. Oh, how Tala loved it; the forest seemed to go on for miles, it was so good. All of a sudden I heard a crackling of twigs and lay down behind a huge shrub. I peered through a gap to see a lovely sight – it was a doe and two young ones. I stayed still as I didn't want to startle them and after a couple of minutes I could see her sniffing the air, and then slowly they ran off. I still stayed still for another couple of minutes, realised all was clear and off I went running again, enjoying every minute. After about two hours I went and found my dress and then slowly and quietly rejoined the party with the servants. They thought I'd gone upstairs!

The following day was clean-up day, we all helped each other and after about four or five hours the grand hall was put back, the floors cleaned and polished, the kitchen scrubbed, the plates and utensils washed and put away until the next time. Theresa called to me and said the master and mistress wanted to see me. I hurried up to the drawing room, smoothing out my skirts and attending to my hair before I knocked at the door. "Enter," came a voice. Monsieur and Madame DelaCroix were sitting having tea. "Lesley, please come and sit and take tea with us." I sat down in a chair next to Madame DelaCroix and opposite her husband. "We wanted to thank you for a wonderful spread that you did, and the wedding cake was beyond words. Our daughter had such a splendid day and most of it was thanks to you. If there is in any way we can repay you taking time away from Monsieur Rennard, we would be honoured to recompense you."

I looked and smiled at both of them and replied, "If a friend cannot help another friend out when needed, then they are not friends."

Monsieur DelaCroix stood and came over to me and took my hands in his and kissed them. "Lesley, you are our angel. Please feel free to visit us whenever you can, you will always be welcome here, and you will not stay in the servants' quarters. I would also like to let you know that I have forgiven the Comte, I mean Athos, for what I thought had happened. I'm sure, if he wants to, he will tell you the story himself." I replied I was pleased they had sorted their differences and I doubted very much if Athos would advise me – it was his memories, not mine. I did not let on that I already knew the story from Theresa.

"Lesley, I believe you leave us the day after tomorrow, is there anywhere you would like to go whilst you're here? Oh, and I believe word has been sent that somebody will be travelling with you back to Paris." I looked quizzical at his last remark and assumed it was one the guests, time will tell.

"If I may, tomorrow I would just love to go walking in your forest, it looks so lovely," I replied.

"Of course, my dear, it's rather a walk but if you stay to the path it leads down to rather a large lake with a variety of birds. If you're very lucky there is a herd of deer and you may seem some of them," said Monsieur DelaCroix.

I nearly said, "I know," but stopped myself. I thanked them for the tea and made my way back down to the kitchen. I took a meal with Theresa and everyone else and then retired for the night. I was quite exhausted.

The following morning after breakfast I left to go to the forest. It took me a good half hour to walk down to the lake, but it was worth it. The lake was huge with lots of swans and ducks and fish, trees bending branches over it full of leaves and flowers, and it was magical. There was even a path either side, but I decided it might be too far for me to walk around. I sat down on the grass with my back against a tree trunk, and just enjoyed the peace and quiet and sunshine. I closed my eyes and started to drift off. My mind wandered back to a time just after my father had passed and my mother was preparing to leave for England. When I could I used to go to the forest to see if I could see Motomo, but never had any success, he would always appear at the Reservation now and then, but if I followed him back to the forest it was like he disappeared. This particular day, for some reason, Motomo let me follow him to where his pack was. I knew better than to follow him into the pack, so found a stone and sat quietly watching them. A hand touched my shoulder and there was my father and his wolves. "What are you up to, child?" he asked.

"Hello Father, I am curious about Motomo and his pack and only today did he let me follow him," I replied.

"That is because he knows you and your mother are about to leave and he will never see you again." I then felt so sad, tears started to flow. I hadn't thought about that. "Hush, child, don't cry, you have Tala now and I will tell you about the wolves.

"A pack is ruled by an Alpha, and the pack could have as many as twenty wolves. Motomo's pack only has twelve. If the Alpha is killed then the female takes over. He will fight others to keep his place at the top of the pack and also earn respect. He will also fight any of his pack if any of them try to mate his female. The Alpha and his mate decide where to stay and where to hunt, they are the first ones to eat after a kill. Should both be killed the next in line takes over and he is called a Beta. The rest of the pack are called Subordinates. Every pack also has an Omega. An Omega is regarded as the lowest wolf in the pack. He is the last to eat after a kill, if the Alpha allows him. Even though he is the lowest he plays an important role in the pack; others will fight him to release their frustrations, but they will never hurt him. Some Omegas have been known to work their way back to the top of the pack. When an Omega dies the whole pack goes into mourning – they won't hunt, they just lay around looking miserable.

"Motomo and his mate breed once a year, usually between Jan and March. Sixty-three days later the pups are born who are blind and deaf, and she can have as many as six pups. She stays with them for the first three weeks keeping them warm, and other pack wolves and

Motomo bring food. After eight weeks they are moved to another site and are now used to eating food that the mother has eaten and then brought back up. They are also learning from the pack the ways of a wolf. Six to eight months, they travel with the pack and join in hunts. Two to three years old, they leave the pack to find their own place and a mate. Usually only half survive.

"The pack mostly eats deer, elk, and bison. Sometimes they will eat rabbits and other small creatures and feed off other dead animals, as they are natural scavengers. Wolves help balance nature in stopping elk and deer trampling new plants so that they can grow, especially trees as this gives nests to birds. They try not to eat beavers as they keep a river clean. They will eat large amounts of meat a day, but sometimes it can be twelve days between meals. We call this feast or famine. Pack territory depends on prey, and if there is no prey around they can travel many miles to find it in a day. Most wolves live around six to eight years, but I have known some older.

"Wolves speak to each other in different ways, which can be high-pitched barks, yips, whines, whimpers, and howls. Whines and whimpers may be a sign of either physical or emotional discomfort, or when the pups are hungry. A yip might be heard when a wolf is suddenly frightened or hurt during play or a fight. Barks or woofs are generally short and warn against the approach of intruders or to attract the attention of another wolf within range. Of all the sounds, none are as beautiful as a wolf's howl.

"Wolves howl alone or together for a number of reasons. To notify other wolves of where they are, such as when they wish to attract a mate, getting the pack together for a hunt, when in trouble, during or after playing, and often just because they want to. Howling sessions among multiple wolves generally begin as a series of short yaps then howls that last for a short or longer time. If you listen the howl can be high, down to low and then back up to high. Two or three howling wolves can sound like a dozen or more. Wolves can howl while standing, sitting, or lying down, it's something they love to do. You look as though you have a question, my child."

"Father, is a coyote a wolf as well?" I asked.

"No, a coyote is different to a wolf. A wolf is longer with rounded ears, but a coyote is tall and has pointed ears. A wolf is broader, has a shorter nose, a coyote has a narrow, pointed nose. A wolf howl is long and drawn out, whereas a coyote has a shorter yapping sound. A wolf and coyote's fur can be the same colour so sometimes it's hard to pick them out in a wolf pack."

"Oh, Father, thank you so much, I feel like I know Motomo and his pack so much better now. Will Tala ever be lonely because she's with me and not in a pack?" I asked.

"No, child. Tala is a spirit wolf and is different to Motomo. You and her are one and always will be until your passing. You will learn to listen to her and she will guide you when she can. I do not know this England to which you go with your mother, but you must be very careful, people outside of our tribe will not understand. Ah, I hear your mother calling, so you must return now, my child. Remember I will always love you, and Spirit of the Wolf do not tell where Motomo is, he has honoured you by letting you follow him today, do not break his trust."

I replied, "Father, I would not do that. I love Motomo, and I love you too. Bye Motomo and thank you for your trust, and I promise I will tell no one." My father vanished and Motomo walked with me to the edge of the forest. I walked slowly towards him and he let me put my arms around his neck and I hugged him. As I moved away he licked my face. I walked out of the forest towards the Reservation and turned and looked. Motomo was still there so I waved and he let out a howl and then ran off.

"Well it's not often I come across a sleeping beauty," I heard a voice say.

I slowly opened my eyes and turned. "Tréville, what on earth are you doing here?" I said. I stood up and we hugged each other.

"What a lovely spot this is," he said. We then both sat down and he said, "Did Monsieur DelaCroix not tell you I was coming? I sent him a note to say I was going to Chartres on the King's business and would call to escort you back to the bakery."

"Yes, he did mention it, but he did not tell me who. Are we returning this afternoon?" I said.

"Oh no, my dear, I'm on my way to Chartres now and will be staying overnight for a reply for the King. Not only that, I know how long a carriage trip is, so I brought one of the horses with me so that we may ride back together," said Tréville with a smile. "I must confess I have missed you not popping into the garrison, there were times when your presence would have been most welcome."

I sat gazing at the lake when an idea came into my head. "Tréville, please do not think me forward, but where are you staying in Chartres?"

"I'm staying with an old friend of mine, why do you ask?"

"I was just thinking I would like to see Chartres and if you were staying at a tavern maybe they would have an extra room and I could stay and after your business we could look at the sights, but as you're staying with a friend..."

"What a splendid idea, Lesley. I would love to show you Chartres. My friend has a large dwelling and I'm more than sure you would be welcome. Come, let's go and you can say your goodbyes," he replied.

We both set off towards the castle, and I felt Tala whimper a bit and just patted my stomach and silently said to her, "I know, I know."

Monsieur and Madame DelaCroix were sorry to see me leave, as were Theresa and the servants. Tréville helped me up onto my horse and we rode off to Chartres. It was only about a half-hour ride, and firstly we went to Tréville's friend, Monsieur L'Enfant. He welcomed me and said it was no problem for me to stay, as he would get another room ready for me. Tréville made his apologies and went off to do what he had to do. A stable boy appeared from nowhere and took leave of my horse. Monsieur L'Enfant, who asked me to call him Henri, was indeed a lovely man. He had a servant called Maria who made us tea, which we had in the parlour with a lovely log-burning fire. I asked how he and Tréville had met. He told me he used to be a Musketeer until he was badly wounded and had to retire; they had fought together for over five years, and he had then married and moved to Chartres. He asked why I was with Tréville and I explained. It turned out he knew the DelaCroix's very well, and told me he made his wealth from money and was, as I'd been told, a very, very wealthy man. Tréville returned about an hour later and sat and talked with Henri for a while and then made our apologies, as he wanted to show me Chartres before it got too dark.

Tréville and I walked arm in arm around the beautiful place of Chartres. We went into one of the taverns and had a lovely meal. It was nice just to be able to sit, talk, laugh and not care about anything else. I had to admit Tréville and I did get on extremely well. He asked me about the wedding and I told him it was extremely hard work, but worth it. As much as I liked being down with the servants I was glad I wasn't in service again and was delighted I was going back to the bakery. By the time we left the tavern it was getting dark and we returned to Henri's dwelling. We all sat round the fire and talked for a couple of hours and then I made my excuses to retire for the night, so Tréville and Henri could catch up with their news.

The following morning, after a good night's sleep, I had a small meal and waited for Tréville to return with the answer for the King and then we both said our goodbyes. Tréville and I travelled back to the bakery and garrison riding through some of the beautiful countryside I had not seen whilst riding in the carriage. I said goodbye to Tréville at the bakery, and said I would see him as soon as I could, as I knew Monsieur Rennard, if he was there, would want to hear all about it. Tréville gave me a hug and kissed my forehead, took my horse and rode off to the garrison. Monsieur Rennard was there and after making a pot of tea we sat round the kitchen table and I told him about most of my adventure.

CHAPTER 8

Renovations

A couple of days after I had returned from Chartres, Monsieur Rennard asked me if we could have some time to discuss something important that had arisen whilst I'd been away. Oh, how I hoped he hadn't changed his mind about me taking the rooms over the bakery. After the workforce had left we went up to the parlour and Monsieur Rennard told me about his news. "I have had some bad news about my brother in Montmartre, he passed over two weeks ago and has left me his rather large dwelling and business," he said.

Oh no, I thought, *he's going to close the bakery and move.*

Monsieur Rennard saw my anxiety and said, "Do not worry, Lesley, I have no intention of going to Montmartre. I already have a couple of gentlemen who want to buy the dwelling and business, and my solicitor is attending to this matter. The other news is that the dwelling next door is to be sold as the owner has passed. I am thinking about buying it and extending the bakery. I have been given a key to the dwelling. What do you think, Lesley?" he asked. I was so relieved it was not the topic of conversation I thought it would be.

"I have to be honest, Monsieur Rennard, I've never taken much notice of the dwelling next door, why don't we go and have a look?" I replied. We both went outside and looked. It was the same height as the bakery, two storeys. Monsieur Rennard unlocked the door and we went in, but it was rather dark. I went back to the bakery and returned with a lit candle in a lantern. The downstairs was the parlour and a small cooking area, and upstairs had two bedchambers. The rooms were quite big and long. "The rooms are a good size, Monsieur Rennard, and I think it would be a good proposition, depending on what you want to do with it," I said. He replied he had a rough idea, but as I would be moving into the rooms above the bakery he wondered if I might have any ideas. I felt honoured that he asked me.

The following morning Monsieur Rennard found me stood outside looking at both dwellings. "You look like you have an idea, Lesley," he said.

I thought he would think I was going beyond my position but plucked up courage and said, "How would you feel about a tearoom, like the ones going up in Paris? Half of the parlour could be the tearoom, and then we could get tables and chairs from the market, the other half somehow part of the bakery. Upstairs, I'm not sure."

"What would you do with a tea room?" he asked.

I explained that whilst I had been at Monsieur and Madame DelaCroix's, Theresa had shown me how to make a drink called "hot chocolate", and it was very popular in Paris. "Customers could sit and have a drink and hopefully partake of some pastries."

"Ummm, now that's something I haven't heard of, but..." And he walked away rubbing his chin. I went back to my duties in the bakery. A couple of hours later I saw Monsieur Rennard talking to Monsieur Belvoir, who I knew was a builder, and then both men went into the dwelling, then came into the bakery, looked outside the back door and then went upstairs to the rooms above. Monsieur Belvoir left about an hour later, after lots of banging had taken place. Naturally, the workforce was curious, as was I.

Monsieur Rennard had to go to Montmartre for a couple of days, and when he arrived back he called me up to the parlour. "Ah, my dear Lesley, I have good news. I'm glad to say that everything in Montmartre has been concluded and sold, also I am now the owner of the dwelling next door." I was so pleased for him. "As you know Monsieur Belvoir has had a look at the dwelling and has advised me of what can be done. I think you will be pleased. The parlour can easily be divided into two areas, and the back area would become part of the bakery with a door leading into it. I thought we could make this the dry storeroom, which would give more space in the kitchen.

The tearoom gave us a problem. If people came in by the front door of the dwelling you would not hear them, so Mr Belvoir suggested another door in the wall from the shop into the tearoom, which would mean the steps in the dwelling up to the next floor would have to be taken away. Above the bakery, as you know, the rooms are only separated by partitions, so Mr Belvoir suggested we take these down. Where my bedchamber and parlour are, I would only now require a small parlour, so it would still be made into two rooms, but my bedchamber entrance would be blocked up. The small office could be made bigger. The other room in the dwelling would also be split into a bedchamber and parlour for you. This would mean when you got to the top of the steps there would be door in front of you, which would lead into my parlour. At the side would be… like a corridor. The door on the right would lead into the office. The door at the end, between the two buildings, would lead into your parlour. Again, another partition would be put up to separate your bedchamber, with another entrance going in to what was my bedchamber. Maybe later on, you could have a tub put in there. Fireplaces will be in both your rooms and one in my parlour. Your rooms would also be private. What do you think?"

"Heavens, I can't take it all in," I replied. "It's going to be an awful lot of work, Monsieur Rennard, and is it going to affect the bakery?" He replied it wouldn't, as the work knocking down the walls to make the door sections and removing the dwelling steps would be done over a weekend, and the bakery would be closed for that time. The partitions could be easily put up. Mr Belvoir said, hopefully, it would all be done in seven to ten days.

When I went back to my lodgings that night I tried to see how it would all look – I couldn't wait for it to be done. I was so excited. That weekend the bakery was closed and Mr Belvoir and his men moved in. On the Monday morning I arrived the same time as the rest of the workforce and when we entered the kitchen we stopped and gasped. The whole place was covered in thick dirt and dust – what a mess! Sleeves rolled up, fire lit, hot water put in buckets and scrubbing started. It took all of us over an hour to get the kitchen clean, before we could start baking. I dreaded to see what the shop looked like. It was immaculate! That shook me and as I turned to return to the kitchen Monsieur Rennard came in, and then explained he had cleaned the shop after Mr Belvoir had left last night. Mr

Belvoir had managed to get more men to help and everything was done and finished. Amazing.

"Let's see upstairs, Lesley," said Monsieur Rennard.

We went up the steps and saw the door to Monsieur Rennard's parlour. I turned down the very small alley, and saw the new office. I walked down to the door and opened it. I entered into a lovely spacious parlour. Ahead a partition with a doorway that led into my bedchamber, with the spare room at the side. Hmm, a tub would go in there nicely. There were also windows front and back. It was wonderful. "Oh, Monsieur Rennard, I don't know what to say, it's beautiful and I will pay you rent every week," I said.

"You most certainly will not," replied Monsieur Rennard. "You are taking over the bakery from me and you need to live on the premises and this is part of your wages, and I will hear no more about it," he said quite sternly. We returned to the shop and, instead of a door was an arch that led into the tearoom. I reckoned we could get about six to eight small tables in. The back bit was partitioned off totally. We then went into the kitchen and again at the end by the back door there was another door that led into the storeroom. Monsieur Rennard asked the men to move all the sacks of flour, sugar, and salt into the new storeroom. Monsieur Rennard told us that shelves were going to be put up and whatever was needed could go on them. He also told us that Mr Belvoir would be back at the weekend to re-do the stables and the back walls, to make it more secure. That weekend the horse and cart were moved out and Mr Belvoir made a bigger stable, the walls were knocked down and rebuilt with a new backyard gate. Now all we had to do was hope the tearoom would work.

One evening as I was walking back to my lodgings, Tréville, Athos, Aramis and D'Artagnan passed me. "Lesley, can you come to the garrison now? It's important," said Tréville. I nodded and Tréville helped me onto his horse.

As we entered the garrison Porthos arrived with Amanda. "What's going on?" said Amanda. I looked at the Musketeers and knew straight away – Philip.

We went up the steps and walked down to Tréville's office, and they all looked unhappy. Tréville said, "Ladies, we have bad news.

Philip is here, we saw him outside the palace today."

Amanda went white and looked faint. I made her sit down and Porthos put his hand on her shoulder. "Oh God, what am I going to do? I don't feel safe anymore. Please, I'm frightened," said Amanda.

Aramis came over to Amanda and took her hands in his, and said, "Amanda, please don't give up, we will protect you. You are our dearest friend and I hope I speak for all of us, but we would die for you before this Philip does anything to you." Amanda burst into tears.

I went out onto the balcony to get some air, and wipe my tears away. A hand touched my shoulder and I turned to see Athos. "Are you all right, Lesley?" he asked. "You know we will all protect you as well. Do you think Philip would recognise you again?" I said he was so drunk that night I wouldn't have thought so. He smiled and said, "Good," and went back in. That left me a bit puzzled, did they have a plan? Amanda came out with Porthos; we hugged each other. I asked if she wanted to stay at my lodgings, but she kindly thanked me and said she would be safer at the palace. Porthos put her on his horse, and they rode out of the garrison. The rest decided to go to the tavern by my lodgings, so we all walked back together. I said goodnight and went to my room. With everything going on I had totally forgotten to tell Tréville my news about the bakery, tearoom and moving in.

Due to extra duties, now I was learning to take over the running of the bakery, another two weeks went by before I saw Tréville again. I said goodbye to Mrs DuPresse and moved my belongings to my new rooms. I borrowed the horse and cart, so did it in one go. Carrying my heavy bags up the stairs nearly crippled me. Straight away my funds went in the safe and I hid the key. Thank heavens for that, now I can relax. Times were very hard and if people knew I had funds I would probably be robbed or murdered for it.

Monsieur Rennard and I took time away from the bakery to go to Paris to find another bed and more furniture for my rooms, and at the same time he showed me his country dwelling on the outskirts of Paris. He advised me that more work was going to be done on the dwelling. It was in a small village, about ten minutes north of Paris by carriage, and had about twenty dwellings, with fields and a small forest surrounding the village, and there was also a small stream flowing through the village with a stone bridge. There was a beautiful small church, and of course, the village tavern. The birds were chirping and to me it looked lovely and peaceful. He will certainly rest well here. I could feel quite content here myself. Aahh, dreams!! We then returned to Paris where I picked out another bed, and got some parlour furniture for myself. I didn't want Monsieur Rennard to pay for it, so I suggested I put some funds towards it. He wouldn't hear of it. Everything was put in the back of the cart and covered. We then went to a market on the outskirts of Paris and got some tables and chairs quite cheaply. When we returned, two of the men removed my old bed and kindly took the new one upstairs to my new bedchamber, and then took the parlour furniture up. When the bakery was empty, Monsieur Rennard suggested to me that because he had such a good workforce he wondered if I would agree to them no longer working on a Sunday. The shop part would open for a couple of hours, with the extra bread and cakes we made on the Saturday. I agreed but told him I was worried because they would all lose a day's pay, and some of them were on the poverty line. He was a fair man and to that extent he made sure the workers weren't out of pocket.

A couple of days later I went off to the garrison and up to Tréville's office. As I approached I could hear Amanda was already in the office talking with Tréville, Porthos, Aramis, D'Artagnan and Athos. Amanda turned and saw me and said, "Talk of the devil," and threw her arms around me. I was slightly confused.

"And where the **hell** have you been, Lesley? We have all been so worried, as we were told you'd gone to Paris. Did you stupidly forget that we have a mad man trying his best to kill Amanda, and yet you decide to disappear and not tell anyone?" said Tréville banging his fist down on his desk.

I lowered my eyes as tears came to them. I was shocked and frightened. Tréville had never raised his voice to me like that before. I said, "I apologise, I had news to tell you the last time we met, but with everything going on I forgot. I did go to Paris with Monsieur Rennard to get another bed and parlour furniture, as I have moved into the bakery." They all stared at me. "Oh no, no, nothing like that," I explained after I realised what I said, and I blushed from head to foot. "Let me explain please. Monsieur Rennard is not well and has decided to move to his dwelling in the country, north of Paris. His brother passed and so he sold his brother's dwelling and business in Montmartre and then bought the dwelling next door to the bakery. He then decided to have the rooms re-done and linked. We now have a tearoom and I have my own private parlour and bedchamber."

Athos coughed and said, "In that case I need to explain, I went to your lodgings and Mrs DuPresse said you'd gone to Paris, I then went to the bakery and it was closed. I think there has been a huge misunderstanding and for that I humbly apologise, Lesley."

Again, tears welled in my eyes. "Again, I'm so sorry to have caused such anxiety. I have been so busy at the bakery and moving that I didn't have time to tell anyone and that was a mistake of mine," I said.

Tréville snapped, "Tell her," and turned his back on me.

Athos said they had seen Philip hanging around the palace quite a few times, but Philip hadn't seen Amanda. The plan was for Amanda and myself to walk round the gardens, hoping Philip would see us and try to seize Amanda. As I had brought the poster back from England, enquiries had been made about arresting him in France. It was within the law to do so. At the moment they were putting a plan together to try and capture Philip, and if all went to plan he would soon be in the Bastille. I looked at Amanda and she said this had to end; she was settled, had a great job (she was also deeply in love with Porthos) and wanted to stop looking over her shoulder. She just wanted her life back. I agreed. The problem was getting Amanda and I together when Philip was there. The palace was about fifteen minutes away on horseback.

Tréville said, "Would everyone please leave? Not you, Lesley, I need to talk with you. Amanda, I still need to speak to you later on, about a certain matter," and looked at Aramis and Amanda.

Oh no, I hope she's not in trouble again passing notes. Amanda has been acting as a go-between for the Queen and Aramis. As Amanda passed me she gave my arm a gentle squeeze and whispered, "He won't be mad with you for long," smiled and left with the others.

Tréville came over to me and put his arms around me, and said, "Come, my dear, dry your tears, we are just all relieved you are well, and still with us. Lesley, I apologise, I should not have spoken to you in that way. We were all concerned that you had fallen into the hands of Philip and he was hurting you in some way to get to Amanda."

"Oh, Tréville, it should be me apologising, not you. I have put you all through so much." My tears started to flow yet again.

"Please, my dear Lesley, don't get upset again," and he put his hands to my face and wiped away my tears, and then kissed me on my forehead. "I have an idea, would you like to partake of a meal with me, not at the normal tavern, but somewhere else?" I looked at him and into his beautiful blue eyes; how could I say no? We went to another tavern a short walk from the garrison and had a lovely meal, good conversation and laughter. Tréville then walked me to back to the bakery, but when he went to kiss me goodnight I moved and our lips accidentally met. We both jumped at the same time and then both burst out laughing. He looked at me and said, "I hope one day I will be invited to see your new quarters." Did I notice his eyes twinkling? I think so.

"Of course, Tréville, when I have finished you are more than welcome," I said. He kissed me on both cheeks and went on his way. I watched him walk away, a Captain with a lot of problems, who spent most of his time on his own and who needed to be loved.

CHAPTER 9

The Dagger

After I had moved into my new rooms at the bakery, I sorted out my parlour furniture. There was a table and four chairs, a couple of better chairs to go by the fire, and a couple of small cabinets. I still needed a bigger cabinet for my bedchamber. Once every two weeks there was a market down the lane, I would have to go and have a look.

I went back down to the kitchen and Catherine said, "Lesley, may I ask you a question please?"

"Yes of course, Catherine, what is it?"

"We were wondering – what is a tearoom?"

I sat down at the kitchen table with Catherine and said, "When I was in England and it was time for us to eat, Katherine would always say it was time to sit round the tea table, so I thought a room with tables, tearoom. It's sounds stupid now, the only tea we have is made from leaves of flowers, which people might not like, and so we're going to serve something new called 'hot chocolate', which is popular in Paris."

"Why call it anything? Everyone knows it's Rennard's Bakery," said Catherine. She was quite right, of course. "How do we make this chocolate drink then?" Catherine asked.

I explained to Catherine that we would have to find a supplier who sold cacao beans first, before we could do anything. The beans were also considered to have medicinal benefits. "We make the drink like this," I said. "Toast the beans slowly, then grind them up, put them in a mug and add hot water. As the taste is rather bitter, we will need to add either sugar or honey. Then with a wooden whisk-like tool it's twirled between the palms of the hands to make a foam on the top."

"Where are you going to get these beans from?" asked Catherine.

"I will have to go to a market in Paris and see what price they are first and then talk to Monsieur Rennard."

"Talk to me about what?" said Monsieur Rennard. I jumped; I hadn't heard him arrive in the kitchen. "I was just telling Catherine how to make this hot chocolate and I need to go to a Paris market to check prices of the beans." Monsieur Rennard looked at both of us and then asked if both of us were free on Sunday, and we could all go together. We both said yes and I think Catherine was really pleased, as it would be her first time in Paris.

On the Sunday the horse and cart were made ready and we all went to Paris. Catherine's face was full of amazement and joy. I was so glad she came. Monsieur Rennard took us to a market, where they seemed to sell everything. Alas, no cacao beans, but one of the stall people told him where a warehouse was that sold them, so off we went. Monsieur Rennard talked business with the owner and we came away with two bags of the beans. I thought one would have been enough, after all we didn't know if this drink was going to be popular where we were. On the way back we stopped at a tavern for a meal. All went well until six Red Guards came in. Monsieur Rennard and I looked at each other, and I hoped there wasn't going to be any trouble. They sat at a table next to us, ordered ale and grabbed a few wenches, then one of the Red Guards said, "Well that was a triumph, men, with a bit of luck that Captain won't be found and when they realise he's missing he'll be dead."

Another guard said, "You sure he won't be found? He is near the forest road by the village north of here."

"Not a chance, we covered him well," said the original guard.

I wondered who they were talking about, and was it the village where Monsieur Rennard had his dwelling? The guards slowly got drunker and drunker and Monsieur Rennard said it would be a good idea for us to leave, he could see trouble happening. As I passed them I overheard one of the Red Guards say to another guard, "Here's to the death of the Musketeers Captain."

The colour from my face drained and my heart pounded, like it had never pounded before. Tala started whimpering at my distress. Once outside Catherine said, "Lesley, what on earth is wrong? You look so ill."

Monsieur Rennard caught me as I started to fall. "Lesley, Lesley, what's wrong?" he asked.

I couldn't speak, my head was spinning, all I could think of was Tréville dead somewhere. Catherine ran back into the tavern and got some water, which I sipped slowly. "Tréville is dead, he's dead," I said, tears flowing down my face. Catherine and Monsieur Rennard looked at me as if I had gone mad.

"Lesley, what on earth do you mean, Tréville is dead?" I told then what I'd overheard. All three of us got back on the cart and Monsieur Rennard said he had heard there had been trouble by the village a couple of weeks before. We wasted no time and went to the village, where Monsieur Rennard "borrowed" another horse, just in case we needed it. We drove to the edge of the forest and could see nothing disturbed. "We need to split up," said Monsieur Rennard, "and look for anything that shows fighting. The grass will be flattened down by footmarks and horses."

After half hour of searching I thought all was lost until Catherine screamed, "He's here, come quick." I rushed to where she was and saw Tréville covered by twigs and then my heart sank – he had a dagger in his back and blood everywhere.

Monsieur Rennard placed his hand on Tréville's neck and said there was a faint pulse, but he needed immediate medical attention. "Lesley, you know your way to the garrison better than Catherine, take the spare horse and get the Musketeers now." I just stood there looking at Tréville's back, I couldn't move, I had lost my best friend in the entire world. "Lesley!" shouted Monsieur Rennard and then came and shook me. I looked at him and he repeated what he said.

"I can't leave him," I said.

"You must, Lesley. He needs you to get to the Musketeers **NOW**."

I was on the spare horse and galloped as fast as it would carry me back to the garrison. How stupid of me to just stand there, every minute counted. I literally charged into the garrison, the poor horse skidded to a halt and I screamed, "Help, someone please help me."

Athos came out of Tréville's office and ran down to me. "Lesley, what's happened? Are you all right?"

"It's Tréville, he's dying with a dagger in his back by Monsieur Rennard's village, it was the Red Guards."

By this time half the garrison, including Aramis, Porthos and D'Artagnan were at my side. Athos told D'Artagnan to go and get the King's physician and we'd meet him on the fork out to the country. I have never seen a Musketeer move so fast. The others were soon mounted and off we galloped.

We must have had about twenty extra Musketeers riding with us, showed how much their Captain meant to them. We eventually got back to Monsieur Rennard and Catherine. Aramis and the King's physician jumped off their horses and rushed to Tréville. Athos stayed with me with his arms around me. Aramis said, "He's alive but we need to get him back to the garrison, we can't remove the dagger here or he will bleed to death." I felt the tears flowing down my cheeks again and Athos just held me.

"My dwelling is nearby if you that would help?" said Monsieur Rennard.

"Alas, thank you sire, but no, we need to get him back to the garrison as the physician needs other implements he does not have. Do you have blankets at your dwelling we could use? We need to make him as comfortable as possible in the back of the cart," said Aramis.

"I will be back in a moment," said Monsieur Rennard and drove off in the cart. About ten minutes later he came back with a straw mattress and blankets in the cart.

"Thank you, monsieur, that will be good," said Aramis.

Aramis looked at Athos and nodded. "Lesley, they need to get Tréville in the cart and it's not going to be pretty sight, it might be better if you look away," said Athos. I looked at Athos and told him I would get in the cart and they could put Tréville's head on my lap.

Aramis shook his head and said he had to be laid straight, and he was going to go in the cart with him in case anything happened. Very, very slowly all the Musketeers somehow picked Tréville up and got him into the cart. He was then wrapped in the blankets either side of the dagger to keep him warm.

After Tréville was in the cart, I saw the amount of blood on the ground. How on earth could he still be alive with all the blood he'd lost? It was a long, slow journey back to the garrison but at last we arrived. D'Artagnan and the King's physician had ridden ahead, and were waiting for us. Again, all the Musketeers carefully got him into his bed in his office. I think I said thank you to all of them.

"Lesley, you need to leave now. He is in good hands, I promise you," said Aramis. I wanted to stay but Monsieur Rennard said it made sense for me to go back to the bakery, with Catherine – we were all in shock. Reluctantly I agreed but made Aramis promise to come and get me immediately if needed. He promised.

As soon as we got back to the bakery, the cacao beans were put in the storeroom, for another day. Catherine made us all a tea from peppermint leaves and we sat quietly round the kitchen table. I was restless, as was Tala, but now was not the time to go for a run! Catherine decided to go back home and Monsieur Rennard accompanied her, mainly to make sure that she was all right. A couple of hours later somebody knocked on the shop door. I looked and saw it was D'Artagnan. "Is he all right, is he dead?"

"Lesley," replied D'Artagnan, "calm yourself please, they have removed the dagger. He is weak but still with us and is asking to see you." D'Artagnan helped me onto his horse and as we rode back to the garrison we saw Monsieur Rennard, so D'Artagnan stopped and told him the news. I could see he was so relieved and he said he would see me later. D'Artagnan also told me that Amanda was upset that she could not be with me, but the Queen had many duties for her and Porthos and the King's physician were on their way back to the palace to report to the King and Queen about Tréville's condition. Porthos would bring Amanda up to date.

I was off D'Artagnan's horse before it had stopped and flew up the garrison steps, not very ladylike! I opened the office door and slowly made my way to where Tréville's bed was. They had moved it away from the wall so they could work on him from all sides. Aramis and Athos were with him and Tréville was lying on his side. I saw the dagger on the table and tears welled in my eyes again, and I turned so Tréville would not see my distress. Athos came over to me and said, "Lesley, Tréville is weak but he will mend. In a couple of weeks he will be out there duelling with the trainees again."

"What are you going to do with the dagger?" I asked.

"Ah," said Aramis. "That is evidence against the Red Guard who stabbed him. We all want justice."

"Lesley, is that you?" I heard Tréville say and immediately went to his bed and sat on the chair that Aramis had vacated.

"Captain, I'm sure you will be in very good hands now, so we'll take our leave and return when Lesley is ready to return to the bakery," said Athos. Tréville just nodded.

Tréville held out his hand to me and I took it. "I'll be fine, my dear, please don't look so distressed. I understand you were with Monsieur Rennard and Catherine and thank heavens you were in the same tavern as the Red Guards," he said.

At that remark, for about the tenth time that day, the tears started to flow and I sniffed and said, "Oh Tréville, what if they hadn't come into that tavern? You would have died and I would have lost the best friend I've ever had." He tried to put his hand to my face, but I stopped him when I saw the pain in his face and wiped away my own tears.

"Please, my dear, I didn't die. I am here and always will be. I will never leave you." We then changed the subject and I told him why we had been to Paris, and we talked until I saw Tréville had quietly slipped into a deep slumber. I kissed his forehead, made sure his blanket covered him and then took my leave.

Athos was sitting at the bottom of the steps and escorted me back to the bakery.

"Thank you, Athos," I said.

"You're more than welcome, Lesley. Sleep well and don't worry about the Captain. He will have his justice and he's a fighter, as you know. We will look after him, and we have arranged to stay with him this night and will take turns between the four of us. I promise if there is any change in him, we will come for you." I gave Athos a kiss on his cheek and then went into the bakery. Monsieur Rennard had left me a note saying he had gone back to his friends and if I needed him to go to him straight away. I was so tired I went up to my bedchamber, not expecting to sleep, but I did.

The following morning I made sure that Catherine was all right, and I promised her we would go to Paris again. She smiled and gave me a hug. When most of the work was done, I went off to the garrison. "At last, someone who might talk some sense into him," said Porthos. "He's refusing to do what he's told and is up and doing his duties."

"What?" I said, and went up to his office. Tréville was sitting at his desk looking like death warmed up.

"And what do you think you're doing? Does the word 'rest' not come to your mind?" I said to him.

"Lesley, I'm sitting at my desk doing paperwork which has to be done, I'm not out there with the trainees as I should be," he replied. "I've somehow now got four babysitters who are driving me to distraction. Don't do this, let me do that, I'm not an invalid."

I took Tréville's hands in mine and said gently, "Tréville, this time yesterday we found you with a dagger in your back and we all thought you were going to die. You might have four babysitters, but they think the world of you. You are their Captain and the thought of losing you was hard for them to bear. So they want to help, let them. How many times have you helped them? Now I want you back in that bed and I will go and get you something to eat and drink." Tréville went to say something but I put my finger on his lips and said, "For once, Tréville, please do as I ask." He knew he'd lost the battle. I helped him up and slowly he walked to his bed.

I went out onto the balcony and saw Aramis coming up the steps. "How's the Captain behaving?" he asked. I replied I'd made him go back to his bed and was going to get him some food and drink. Aramis smiled and told me he would do that and off he went to the kitchen. I waited for Aramis to return and we went to Tréville together. Aramis had got him some chicken broth and bread, plus fruit for after. Tréville was in his bed and Aramis told him he wanted to look at his wound, and he would need to remove his shirt. So I didn't embarrass him, I walked out to the balcony to give them privacy. A couple of minute later Aramis came out and told me his wound looked to be healing well, but only time would tell. "Tell him to rest more, Lesley, I worry he will overdo things."

I replied, "I'll try, Aramis, but you know what a stubborn goat he is," and we both smiled.

I went back to Tréville and most of the broth was gone and he looked as though he was asleep. I quietly went to go when he said, "Please stay with me, Lesley, as I love your company so much. How's your new rooms looking now? What else do you need?"

We talked for some time and then I saw his eyes drifting so I said, "You need your rest, Tréville, so I will take my leave now. Please let the Musketeers look after you, and then you will get better sooner and we can go back to the river for a picnic." He smiled and put his hands out to me, so I leant forward and we gave each other a hug and a kiss on the cheek.

Two days later Tréville couldn't breathe.

CHAPTER 10

Healing and Upset

It was just after midnight when I was awoken by banging on the door. I left my bedchamber and looked out of the parlour window above the shop. It was Athos. My first thought was Tréville. I dressed hurriedly and went down. "What's wrong, Athos?" I said.

"It's Tréville, he can't breathe, we have sent word to the palace and the physician is on his way," he said. We mounted his horse and went to the garrison and just as we arrived so did D'Artagnan and the King's physician. We all rushed up to his office and went to his bed. He looked dreadful, and was gasping for air. Aramis was with him and I asked him where Amanda was, she needed to be here. D'Artagnan told me that the King had specifically asked that his physician only be sent. With Philip being around, the King did not want Amanda away from the palace, at the moment. I understood that she was to move to the garrison into Porthos's rooms. Amanda wasn't going to like that, as she would feel like a caged animal. I knew she would look for every opportunity to run.

The physician examined Tréville and said the wound had become badly infected, inside, not outside of his body, and the infection was spreading.

"Please, you can help him can't you, Monsieur...?" I said.

"My name is Monsieur Verde, and just so you know I have a great appreciation for your friend Amanda, but this is something she would have had a problem with. I have to drain the infection from his back which is complicated and Aramis needs to hold Tréville down whilst I perform this, and I would also prefer it if you left," he said abruptly.

I looked at him and replied, "You will not speak to me in that tone, Monsieur Verde, and I will not be dismissed, I will stay."

Monsieur Verde looked at Aramis, who then came over to me and put his arm around my shoulder. "Lesley, this is going to be hard to watch, believe me. I have seen this done before and Tréville will be screaming with pain, which I know will upset you." I told Aramis I would be on the balcony.

Aramis was right. I could not take Tréville's screams. I ran down the stairs, jumped on the first horse I could find and rode out of the garrison. Tala was desperate to run so I went to the safe forest. I hid the horse and made sure it would be safe and then walked off into the deepest part of the forest. I undressed and started to run slowly, and then stood still. I savoured the forest through Tala's eyes and could smell different scents on the air. I could feel the grass between my paws, and hear the rustling of leaves beneath the feet of other animals. I could also hear the chirping of many species of birds in the trees. Tala sees a rabbit, but leaves it alone. Then she runs, hard and fast for about an hour. When she stops her tongue is hanging out and she's panting heavily. We lay down to sleep. Two spirits sharing the same body, both minds operating as one. Tala was a primal creature whereas me, I relied on logic and reason. There was harmony and respect between both of us, but she also feels my distress, linked by my feelings.

Tala and I must have slept for hours, because when I woke the sun was high in the sky. I must get back to Tréville and hurriedly got dressed. I felt something touch my shoulder, and I turned to see my father. "Tala called to my spirit, my daughter, you are in great distress."

I looked at my father and smiled. "You called me daughter, Father."

"Well you are no longer a child now, as was told to me by your mother. Tell me what has you in so much distress?" he asked. I told him about Tréville. "This sounds bad, my daughter, I would need to see him. I think you and I can help him, but I cannot come until the moon is up."

"Oh, Father, what do I need to do?"

He told me I needed to be with Tréville on my own, and when I was, I had to say, "White wolf come to me," twice. I looked at him quizzically but I knew my father, then he vanished.

I found the horse and galloped back to the garrison. The Musketeers were on the balcony. "Lesley where have you been? You had us so worried," said Aramis.

I replied I just needed time and they accepted that. "How is Tréville?" I asked.

Aramis said Monsieur Verde had done all he could and now we had to wait. I quietly went in to see Tréville and was shocked by what I saw. There was a device in his back and another in his arm and blood everywhere. "Aramis," I shouted, "what on earth has he done?" Aramis explained the only way to get to the infection was to insert a tube in his back and then suck on the tube to get the infection to drain out of him, into the bowl on the floor. I also noticed a vein on his arm had been cut which meant Monsieur Verde had tried to bleed him, hence all the blood. I physically felt sick and could feel the bile rising. Aramis handed me a glass of water, and we went back outside. Looking at the sun, it looked like it was coming up to half the day. How on earth could I get Tréville on my own after the moon was up? Then I had an idea. I knew the four Musketeers were taking it in turns to stay with him, so I suggested I would take the night shift. They all said no, it was too risky. What if Tréville woke and started lashing out with pain? I then said they had all been looking after him for three days and nights, and could all do with a good night's rest. I would go back to the bakery and make bread, cakes and biscuits. They were only a shout away if I needed them. That went down well and they agreed. I returned to the bakery and between Catherine and myself we made what I had promised. As the moon was going up, I returned to the garrison and gave them the food and they all went off to Athos's room.

After the moon was up full, I went out onto the balcony and looked round. All seemed quiet, but just to be sure, I crept down the stairs and went to Athos's room and looked in the window. Looks like the wine had been flowing freely – they were all fast asleep. I checked around the garrison to make sure no one else was around. The only four Musketeers were the ones that were on guard duty at the gate. I'm glad to say they didn't see me. I went back to Tréville's room and said, "White wolf, come to me," twice, and my father appeared.

"My daughter, what has this doctor done to Tréville? This is a mess, we need to act quickly to save him."

"Save him? Father, is he dying?" I asked.

"He is gravely ill, Daughter, let us begin. I will need your help and I hope what I am going to try and do will work. A lot depends on you and Tala." What on earth had Tala to do with what my father was going to do?

He started chanting over Tréville and then took my hands and put them palm down just above his wound, but not on it. He then put his hands on the back of mine and I felt a heat running through me and a sort of light came out from the palms of my hands and glowed over Tréville's back. My father's chanting got louder as he called up to the spirits, but I knew it was only me who could hear him. I then heard other chanting but didn't look to see where it came from. I was too busy looking at my palms and Tréville's back. I was beginning to feel strange, as it was like I wasn't in my body. My father and the others stopped chanting and he took his hands away from mine, and then I felt faint.

"Come, daughter, you must rest and you need to heal."

"What did I just do, Father? I feel so weak."

"You must do something now that I have never thought would be possible; you must let Tala out so she can heal you."

"How can I let Tala out? I need to run first."

"No, my daughter, you have just shown me you have the gift to heal. Just sit on the floor and call Tala, she will come." I was scared, but I did as my father bade. I called Tala's name and seconds later I was looking at Tréville's room through Tala's eyes. She padded around, sniffing everything. She then went over to Tréville and licked his face!

"Tala return, Spirit of the Wolf appear," I heard my father say. I was back sitting on the floor and felt so much better.

"Well, my daughter, it looks like you love this man with all your heart," said my father.

"I love him as a brother, Father, there is no more for either of us," I replied.

"What you have just done proves you wrong, daughter. I wasn't sure if you had a healer wolf in you, but only a healer wolf can heal someone they love deeply and you, my daughter, have just healed Tréville." I looked at Tréville and no more yellow stuff was coming out of his back, no more blood from his arm and his colour was rising.

"Is this healing something I can do always, Father?"

"No, my daughter, only to someone you love deeply. Should you need to heal Tréville again, you must learn from Tala how to call her out and how to return. I called her to return this time, but you must learn to do it with your mind."

"Why am I a healer wolf, Father, and can I heal myself?"

He replied, "When you were born the spirits must have decided you would be a healer for the tribe, but alas, they did not know you would leave and come to a different world. I doubt you will heal again, but if you ever came across a wounded wolf, you would be able to heal it, without calling Tala out afterwards. No, you cannot heal yourself, you will need another healer to do that."

I was stunned by what I had just done and I didn't particularly want to call Tala again, I would be worried I could not return myself. "The sun is rising, Daughter," said my father, "and I hear footsteps, I must go," and with that he hugged me and vanished.

I quickly sat by Tréville pretending to be asleep. The Musketeers came in and quietly walked over to Tréville. I heard Aramis say, "Thank the lord, it's worked, the Captain has returned to us."

Athos gently touched me and I actually did jump. "He looks better, Lesley, look."

I looked at Tréville and his eyes were upon me and he smiled and said, "You lot not got any work to do?" We all laughed. Monsieur Verde returned and removed the devices and slowly Tréville returned to all of those who loved him.

Two weeks later Tréville was doing most of his duties as normal. Paperwork, attending to the King and Queen, stood looking out over his balcony, down on the garrison grounds telling the men what to do – nothing new there then. The King had demanded the Red Guards were to be brought to him and they were then questioned. Who did the dagger belong to? Each one blamed each other until the King said that if the culprit did not show himself, they would all be hanged for attempted murder. The Red Guard gave himself up and was then thrown in the Bastille, to await his hanging. Amanda had moved into Porthos's room but couldn't sleep very well on his bed, so I watched from the balcony one day as Porthos had her bed moved from the palace to his rooms. He would do anything for Amanda, but my heart went out to her not having much freedom anymore. How I hated Philip for what he was putting Amanda through.

I remembered I still had to go and get a bigger cabinet for my bedchamber, so on market day off I went. As I was walking down the lane I noticed how things had changed, since my arrival. The lane was cleaner and other businesses had arrived. There was now a butcher, a bookshop, a new tavern was being put up, and there were a couple of ladies who were seamstresses. I understood now what the word "developing" meant. The people seemed to be happier as well. I had a good look round the market and spotted a bigger cabinet that would do me nicely. I paid and the stall person said he would get his men to bring it round to the bakery for me. I found some other things I wanted and walked back quite happy. The men kindly delivered the cabinet for me, and I gave each of them a mug of hot chocolate.

They liked it, which is what I was hoping, so now hopefully news would get round the market people. Monsieur Rennard and I sat down at the kitchen table to talk about the opening of the new room. Catherine and I had managed to work out the correct amount of beans to make the chocolate, now we needed people to come in and try it. Monsieur Rennard said he would put a notice in the window. He had not yet tried the "hot chocolate" so I made us a mug each and we sat in the new room with a couple of pastries and talked. Quite a few people noticed – good sign? I asked him how he had become a baker.

"Alas, a short story to tell, Lesley. My father married twice and each time he had a son. My brother, who just died in Montmartre, was the one who became a baker. He was ten years older than me and his mother left my father and took him to England. There he grew up in a bakery and learnt the trade and then came back here and taught me. He learnt about a law that was passed called Assize of Bread and Ale. It was a list of large tables, which had size, weight, and the price of a loaf of bread was regulated in relation to grain prices. It was very confusing sometimes. Anyone found tampering with the weights would receive a severe penalty. You have heard the expression 'a baker's dozen'? Well, a baker would give 13 rolls for the price of 12 so they wouldn't be called a cheat.

"Bread was made very thin then and used as a plate. Other food was placed on the bread, which took in the juices or gravy and was then eaten as a cake. They were called Trenchers. The miller and baker were usually the same person and had an oven near the mill and baked the bread. There were different loaves – a Table Loaf was for the rich and the crusts were cut off for the ladies so they could dip them in the broth. Inferior loaves were for the servants, and were usually called common bread. Bread made with barley, oats or millet was coarse, and given to prisoners. Rye bread was for country people. In the end my brother met his beloved and they decided they wanted to live in Montmartre and so I took over the bakery."

"What of your brother's wife?" I asked. Monsieur Rennard said she passed two years before his brother and they had no children. We drank our mugs of the chocolate and then decided we would open the chocolate room on the Monday and see how it went.

On the Saturday I went to the garrison to see Tréville, who was now looking well, and asked if he would like to accompany me to the river for a picnic on the Sunday. He apologised and said he would not be able to do it this Sunday as he already had a previous engagement, but maybe another time. When I got back to the bakery I asked Catherine if she would like to accompany me and she replied she would be delighted to go. On the Sunday we both left in a carriage and went to Paris. We walked round and I pointed out special places to Catherine and then we decided to go for a drink and something to eat. We found a nice bakery shop and had hot chocolate and pastries. I had noticed they sold something called "pies" but made with meat. I bought two, we ate one and it seemed quite nice, the other we took back with us to the bakery to see how it was made. We then made our way to the park by the river.

I asked Catherine about her life before the bakery. She told me both her parents had died and she went to live with her aunt and only lived about ten minutes away from the bakery. Her aunt resented her because she was bringing no money into the home. She walked the lanes looking for work and that was how she met the other children and started begging for food with them. Then they started begging at the bakery and the rest I knew. I had only thought Catherine was about sixteen years old. In fact, she was twenty. Since she had been at the bakery and earning, her aunt treated her better. "Isn't that Captain Tréville walking towards us?" said Catherine. I looked in her direction and saw Tréville arm in arm with a very beautiful lady, dressed in the most gorgeous colour of blue I had ever seen.

Tréville noticed us and made his way over. "Lesley, Catherine, how lovely to see you," he said, doffing his hat. "May I introduce you to Michelle?"

We both curtsied at Michelle, who looked at us and put her hand to her nose as though we smelled and said, "Tréville, my darling, we will be late for the theatre, we don't have time to talk to servant girls," and with that she tugged on Tréville's arm and they both walked off. Catherine and I just looked at each other, stunned.

Catherine said, "What a rude woman, who does she think she is calling us servant girls?" I agreed with her, but then I suppose she was right. We both worked for Monsieur Rennard but he never treated us like servants, not like how I'd been treated as a servant back in England. We were treated more like family. I watched as they both walked away, laughing and talking, and when Tréville looked back I quickly turned my head away. So that was his previous engagement! Why didn't he just say, unless he had something to hide? Catherine and I carried on with our walk by the river and before the light started to fade we got a carriage back to the bakery.

Once back in the bakery, all thoughts of Tréville left me and I concentrated on how this "meat pie" was made. I went and looked through Katherine's cookbooks and found a rough recipe.

Meat be cooked in broth, take out and let go cold.

Into deep pastry dish put meat, cover with pastry, make hole in top, bake in oven.

They were called "coffins" as it was a dish with dead meat. I went to the butcher's and bought some mutton and beef mixed, and set about cooking these pies. I made about eight, tried one myself, seemed edible, and the rest I put in a basket and took them to the garrison. As I went to enter the garrison, I looked up to Tréville's balcony, and quickly stood back behind the wall. Tréville had his back to me, but he had his arm around the waist of Michelle, and she had her arm around his waist with her head on his shoulder, and they were talking with Athos and Aramis.

"Lesley, why are you hiding?" I turned to see D'Artagnan. "And what have you got there?" he asked pointing to the basket.

"I'm not hiding, I brought some pies for you to try to see if you liked them, but I see Tréville is otherwise engaged and I did not want to disturb them."

D'Artagnan looked and replied, "Ah, Lady Michelle, he has known her a long time. Come, we will go together."

"No, I would rather not intrude. Here, takes the pies and perhaps one of you could let me know if they are edible," I replied, and with that gave him the basket and walked away.

I went to visit Tréville quite a few times but every time I went, they were both on the balcony, in each other's arms. My heart ached, but really I should have been happy for Tréville – he did look so happy. As I walked back to the bakery I wondered if Tréville would marry Michelle, and there and then I decided I would visit him no more. I knew our friendship was over. Michelle would never let me see or talk to him again, and after all I was only a servant, according to her!

CHAPTER 11

Reunion and Philip

A couple of days later after I had decided not to see Tréville, Catherine told me that he was in the shop waiting to see me, so I asked her to tell him I was not at the bakery. She looked at me curiously, but did as I asked. She returned with the basket and told me that Tréville had said the pies were delicious and maybe we could sort out a weekly delivery for him and his men. We did, but I always got someone else to deliver them to the garrison, even though I missed him deeply.

The following weeks I threw myself into making the new chocolate room a success and making varieties of these new pies and other new pastries. Customers slowly started coming in, but being in a lane with a market, word soon got round and the chocolate room became popular. I was so pleased, as was Monsieur Rennard. Tréville visited several times and each time I had someone tell him I was not there. Tala was picking up on my emotions and so I went to the safe forest and we had some good runs. I had found my safe forest one day whilst out riding. Tréville had mentioned to me the forest not to go to if I was out alone because of the Red Guards, but I had spotted another one in a different direction, which was down by a river and quite dense with trees and shrubs, and quite large. I went there quite a few afternoons and evenings and just walked around, to see if it was safe, which it was, and also to practice letting Tala out and then me returning. The first time I did it I was scared I would not be able to return, but my mind commanded Tala to return and me to reappear.

All went well, and it got easier and Tala and I were both content.

One evening I heard a knock at the door and saw it was Athos. "Athos, how lovely to see you," I said. "Please come in by the fire."

Athos replied, "It's nice to see you again too, Lesley. We have not seen you at the garrison for a long time now. Something we said? Captain Tréville has asked me to call upon you, he has a delicate matter that he would like to discuss with you."

Was this to let me know about his intentions with Michelle? I didn't want to know about it. "Why did Captain Tréville not come himself, if it's such a delicate matter?" I asked. Athos replied that he was extremely busy at the garrison, and the palace as there had been talk of war. "Athos, please could you kindly convey my apologies to Captain Tréville but at the moment I am so busy with the bakery and the new room. We have at least three celebrations to bake for and poor Monsieur Rennard is staying at his friend's because he cannot go to his dwelling in the country. We are even working on a Sunday."

Athos looked at me and said, "Why not get more staff? You have a bigger kitchen."

"I have suggested that to Monsieur Rennard but he said that even though the kitchen is bigger, more staff would make it overwhelming and could lead to problems."

Athos replied, "I can see what he means. I will convey your message to Captain Tréville and now I will take my leave." It was lovely to see Athos – I did miss all of them, especially Amanda. For once, since I arrived in France, I felt very alone.

The following day was market day so I took a walk, mainly to cheer myself up, to see what was happening. I'm sure the market was getting bigger. Yes, I did buy some more things for my rooms, in particular a small cabinet that I could keep Katherine's cookbooks in, and a large jug and bowl for me to wash in, and that did cheer me up. On the Sunday I took myself off to Paris and walked by the river, then sat on a bench trying to read my book but my mind kept wandering to Tréville. What on earth was the matter with me? If Tréville was happy with Michelle then I should be happy for him. Neither of us had declared any intentions towards each other, we were like brother and sister. I decided I would go and see him at the garrison.

The following afternoon I took the basket of pies to the garrison, but as I arrived I saw a carriage pulling out with Tréville and Michelle inside. I quickly pulled my hood up and turned my head away and as the carriage stopped for a moment I heard Tréville and Michelle say they loved each other. The carriage then carried on with Athos, Porthos and D'Artagnan accompanying it. I went to take the pies to the garrison kitchen but a voice said, "Lesley, it's been some time since we last saw you, are you well?" It was Aramis.

"Aramis, I'm quite well thank you. I have brought the pies for Captain Tréville, is he here?"

"Alas, you have just missed him, he and Michelle have gone to the country for the wedding and he will be gone about a week. I have to catch them up so I will take the pies with me, they are far too good for the kitchen imbeciles," he said with a laugh. Aramis mounted his horse and I passed the pies up to him. "Lovely to see you, Lesley, must go," and with that he rode out of the garrison.

I walked back to the bakery in a daze. So Tréville and Michelle were getting married. I should be happy for him but my heart was far from happy. Tears welled in my eyes and I went to my bedchamber to compose myself. It was then two things shocked me. Was my father right, and was I in love with Tréville? I thought the world of him, but actually being in love with him, I didn't know, I'd never been in love before. The other, for me, was not nice – I was actually jealous of Michelle. I had never been jealous of anyone before, my father would be very displeased with me. I had to admit she was a beautiful woman; lovely figure, long flowing blonde hair and beautiful brown eyes, and extremely elegant. The dress she wore the day we met was exquisite, I could never see me wearing such a lovely dress. Now they were to be wed, would I ever see Tréville again? Would he move away from the garrison? No more Sunday picnics by the river or asking him for advice. That night I cried myself to sleep, as I had lost my best male friend.

About three weeks later after I returned from a day trip into Paris, I saw a note had been pushed under my door. It was from Tréville apologising for whatever he had done to upset me, and how much he was missing my company. He had wanted to talk to me about a delicate matter. Porthos had wanted to buy Amanda some undergarments and he wanted me to go to Paris with him, as Porthos wanted it to be a surprise for Amanda. D'Artagnan's lady friend,

Constance, went instead. I was shocked, Tréville was now married, why on earth would he want to be seen with me? It would be most improper. It did bring back memories of our happy times together though. After that I was very quiet in the bakery, which didn't go unnoticed. I just carried on with my work, encouraged people to have a hot chocolate, buy our pies and pastries, and went to bed and rarely went out. Apart from the day when I saw the carriage with Tréville and Michelle, I had not been to the garrison for over two months, and if the Musketeers visited I made myself scarce.

One day Monsieur Rennard stayed late and asked me to sit at the kitchen table with him. "What is wrong, Lesley, why are you so sad? I have noticed that you have not been to the garrison for some time, did something happen there?" he asked. I looked at him and the tears started to flow. "Lesley, please talk to me, maybe I can help." When I had composed myself, I told him about Tréville and Michelle in the park by the river and how she had spoken to myself and Catherine, what I had seen at the garrison, Tréville and Michelle declaring their love for each other in the carriage, and then Aramis telling me they'd gone to the country for the wedding and how much I missed him.

Monsieur Rennard took my hands in his and said, "Dry your tears, and cheer up, my dear. You are not about to lose Tréville and he certainly hasn't married Michelle. It was Michelle's cousin that got married. Michelle is one of Tréville's nieces, the other one being Aurore, and Michelle is married to Lord Jean de Siouville. Do you remember I told you Tréville's brother had passed and one of his nieces, Aurore, came to live here? She spends a lot of time away now, and it's said she does a lot for France, and she also visits Tréville now and then. Michelle visits Tréville once, maybe twice a year and stays for as long as she can. I can certainly see why you thought they were a couple, as they are very close but as uncle and niece, not lovers. If only you told me earlier. Is this why you have been avoiding Tréville when he's visited?" I replied it was and then showed him the note from Tréville. "Lesley, you need to go to him and tell him how you feel. I shouldn't say this but he's a man and would not have given it a thought and he probably would have explained to you about Michelle."

"Oh, how can I go to him, Monsieur Rennard? I would be so embarrassed to see him, especially as I've acted like an idiot."

Monsieur Rennard replied, "You're not an idiot, Lesley, you just didn't know the whole facts. Would it help if I went and saw Tréville and explained on your behalf?" I was reluctant but agreed.

The following day Monsieur Rennard went off to the garrison, and I felt so nervous. What on earth would Tréville think of me being so stupid? I never gave him the chance to explain. A couple of hours later Monsieur Rennard came back with Tréville and showed him up to my parlour. I made myself presentable and very nervously went up the steps to my parlour and my heart was pounding. Tréville was stood looking out of the window and as I entered he turned and said, "I like your new rooms, my dear, maybe one day when the weather is bad, we could partake of our picnic here." I smiled and thanked him, and said that would be nice. I stood with my head bowed and Tréville said, "Lesley." I looked up and he held his arms out and I went to him, and he hugged me so tight, and then kissed my forehead. "My dear I am so sorry, I never gave a thought that I would put you through so much anguish. I should have introduced you properly to Michelle when we met at the river. I apologise for the way Michelle spoke to you and Catherine that day, but we were going to be late for the theatre, and Michelle hates being late for anything. D'Artagnan told me he'd seen you outside the garrison and you wouldn't come in, and then he told you I'd known her for a long time, and then Aramis telling you we'd gone to the country for the wedding. I have been so busy with the King's affairs, Red Guards fighting with my men, and talk of war, I should have taken the time to either come and see you or written you a letter and explained. My dear Lesley, I have missed your company so much, how can I make amends?" He went quiet for a moment and then said, "May I make a suggestion? How about I return later after the bakery has closed and we partake of a meal at the tavern, like we used to do."

"Oh Tréville, I feel so stupid and I apologise for not seeing you when you came to the bakery, but I have learnt one thing – never to jump to conclusions, and yes, I would like to go to the tavern with you."

"Excellent, my dear, let us put the last months behind us, but I promise you in future to not let anything tear us apart again."

With that he released me from his hug, and saw tears had been rolling down my face. He cupped my face with his hands, moved my tears away with his thumbs and said, "No more tears, my dear." He kissed me on both cheeks and then made his way down the steps and back to the garrison.

I went back down to the bakery and Monsieur Rennard and Catherine both looked at me, and Monsieur Rennard said, "How did it go?" I smiled and said we were friends again and then they both hugged me. Tréville returned as promised and we went, arm in arm, to the tavern and had a lovely meal and talked like old times, as we had a lot of catching up to do.

When we went to leave, Athos, Aramis and D'Artagnan came in. I hugged all of them, and Athos said, "Hopefully this means we shall see you back at the garrison now?"

I nodded yes and as Tréville and I made our way to go I heard Aramis say, "Thank heavens for that, they're back together again, he's been like a bear with a sore head." I smiled at that thought. Tréville walked me back to the bakery and gave me a hug and kissed my forehead. That night I slept well, I had my friend back.

A couple of weeks went by and then Monsieur Rennard was called to the palace about a very important event that was to take place. The King and Queen were going to entertain some dignitaries, and the feasts were going to be held outside in one of the gardens, and he was asked if we could supply the cakes and pastries required, as the head pastry cook was ill. What an honour; he was delighted and accepted. Tréville was summoned and was informed that all the Musketeers would be needed for duty. All of us would be there, and something told me Philip would turn up, plenty of activities going on to distract people. I had three days to prepare the cakes, so it was a question of working all day and most of the night. I was pleased I was living at the bakery as I fell into my bed for a couple of hours' sleep each night.

The day arrived and everything was done; I was so tired. The carts transported all the cakes to the palace. I had a quick wash, changed my clothes, and made my way with Monsieur Rennard to the palace.

Tréville and the Musketeers were already there and kindly helped us offload the carts. I even got a wink from Tréville, which made me smile. Everything was laid out on the tables, and it looked splendid. Oh, please don't let it rain. I glanced around watching the guests as they arrived. I wondered where Amanda was so I walked round the gardens and then down the back of the palace. I saw someone near one of the pillars and as I approached he walked round the pillar as though trying to hide. I carried on walking but as I turned a corner my heart sank, it was Philip. I returned to the gardens to see if I could catch the eye of one of the Musketeers. I met Tréville's eyes and casually walked over to him, and went to stand behind a large shrub. Tréville followed me and I said, "Philip is at the back of the palace, hiding behind one of the pillars."

"Lesley, be careful. Have you seen Amanda?" he asked.

I said I hadn't but as I turned I spotted Amanda in the smaller garden. "Tréville, she's there in the garden."

"Quickly go to her, but please neither of you try and tackle him, promise me."

"I promise, my dear Tréville," and without warning gave him a kiss on the cheek, which made him smile.

I walked quickly over to Amanda and told her about Philip. "Time for a walk then, my dear Lesley."

Amanda and I walked arm in arm round the garden and slowly made our way to the back of the palace. I couldn't see any of the Musketeers or Philip. We turned to walk back when all of a sudden Philip lunged at Amanda and dragged her into the trees. I went after them, and Philip then recognised me. "You, you bitch, you're the one from the tavern. When I've done with her, you're next," he sneered. Where on earth are Tréville and the Musketeers? Amanda was struggling to get free of Philip and she kicked him and just for a second he let go of her. I lunged at him, but he sidestepped me, and grabbed Amanda again. This time he produced a knife and Amanda went rigid.

I just looked at him. "Philip, stop, I have something to tell you. I have just returned from England, I know about your mother and I've seen the poster. You don't need to do this."

Philip looked at me and laughed. "You daft bitch, do you think I'm stupid? I will plead innocence, I was away, no knowledge of my mother's death, and then I claim the inheritance once this one's done away with and you're in the frame for murder."

All of a sudden Musketeers surrounded us. Tréville told Philip to drop the knife. Pistols were pointed at him. "I can cut her throat quicker than you can shoot," said Philip.

Unbeknown to him Porthos had crept up behind him. "I'd do as he says if I were you, that's my woman you're holding a knife to," said Porthos, and he cocked his pistol at Philip's head.

Athos walked forward and took the knife and Philip released Amanda, who went straight into Porthos's arms. All of a sudden things went into a blur. As two Musketeers went to restrain him, Philip shouted, "I'm already going to hang, so one of you bitches will die with me." He grabbed a pistol and fired and time seem to freeze. There was a musket ball flying through the air, but who for?

I felt a thud, Tala howled in agony. I felt myself falling in slow motion, and there was a strange noise in my ears. I faintly heard someone screaming and then I heard Tréville shout, "Leessleeyy, noooooo!" and he rushed to me and caught me before I hit the ground.

I looked into his eyes, and put my hand on his face and said, "Tréville, look after..." and then everything went black... and my spirit along with Tala's rose...

CHAPTER 12

What Happened Next?

My eyes flutter open and I look around. I'm in a green field with a river flowing at the bottom, there is a wolf pack encircling me, and there's an Indian tipi to my right.

I try to sit up but the pain makes me gasp. I feel so light-headed. "Stay still, sister of the tribe, you are badly hurt," says a voice from somewhere. Two of the wolves have come to lie by my sides, I realise they are keeping me warm. I put my hand on my left side and it comes away red. Oh heavens, I remember Philip fired a shot and it hit me.

"Where is Tréville, Amanda, the Musketeers?" I ask.

"I know nothing of these people," came the reply.

I turn my head left, right, but I cannot see anyone, am I hallucinating? I then look towards the tipi and see an Indian lady coming towards me. She has a medicine pouch with her, so she must be a medicine woman. "Lay still, my friend, I need to tend to your wound, you are very badly wounded," she says. She kneels at the side of me and leans over the wolf, and starts chanting. I start to feel really strange and the next thing I know I'm on a bed in the tipi.

I feel a bit better and try to sit up; I still have pain but not as bad as before. I notice my gown has gone and I'm in Indian clothing. I see a movement and notice the two wolves are still with me, like they are guarding me. I try to stand but I'm too weak, so I stay sitting on the bed. The medicine woman comes into the tipi and sees me sitting up. "How are you feeling, Spirit of the Wolf?" she asks.

I look at her in shock, as nobody has called me by my Native American name since my father passed. "How do you know my name?" I ask.

"I know everybody who comes through my Reservation and I even know your father, White Wolf." Tears sting my eyes at the name of my father. I miss him and my mother so much.

All of a sudden I felt very sick and groaned in pain.

"Lay down, my child, your wolf is in grave danger, she too is badly hurt and I don't know if I can save her."

"No, Tala can't die, I can't live without her. Please do what you can to save her. I don't care how much pain I have to go through, I need her," I pleaded.

"Sshh, stay still, Spirit of the Wolf. I will do all I can to save her, and my name is Swallowtail."

I remembered hearing that name many moons ago; my father used to talk about a great medicine woman called Swallowtail. Her medicine was known all over the Indian nation, was this the same person? The blackness hit me again, and when I woke Swallowtail told me it was five days later. "Tala, is she all right?" I asked. Swallowtail looked at me and said it had been hard and she lost her. I gasped and tears fell down my cheeks, but Swallowtail told me not to cry, she lost her and then got her back with the help of a spirit chief dancing with his wolf and that was why I had been asleep so long, Tala was getting herself better. All of a sudden I felt a stirring – it was Tala and she was still weak. Now it was tears of joy.

"Come eat, my child, you are both weak and must be nourished slowly and often."

After what felt like weeks or months both Tala and myself were a lot stronger and Swallowtail told me it was time for me to go.

"Go where?" I asked.

It was then I realised I'd never been out of the tipi. Swallowtail took both my hands in hers, kissed both of them, then gave me a hug and told me to go outside. I went outside and to my surprise there was my father, his wolf and the two white wolves. "Oh, Father," I said and then ran into his arms.

"Oh, my daughter, what you have had to go through. You now feel better?" he asked. I told him I was and said I wanted to introduce him to Swallowtail. I turned but Swallowtail, the wolves and the tipi had vanished.

I looked at my father and said in disbelief, "There was a tipi there just now, I've lived in it for a long time, I don't understand."

My father looked at me and as usual told me to sit with him. He explained that Swallowtail only appeared to other Indians who were in desperate need of her medicine and she had chosen me. It was not my time to join the Reservation yet.

"But I never thanked her for everything she did for me, Father," I said.

My father smiled and nodded and replied, "You just did and she blesses you."

I sat and looked at my father and wondered how his life had been. "What is wrong, Daughter, are you in pain?"

"Oh no, Father, I was just wondering what your life was like when you were young."

He smiled and said, "I will tell you, my daughter.

"When I was born my parents lived on the Great Plains, mostly along the Mississippi River, and were farmers and hunters. When the settlers came they seized our lands, and then Indian enemies drove us out. We moved to South Dakota, but everything was green – we named it 'an ocean of grass'. Farming, forests and lakes were soon forgotten. The tribe was one of thirty tribes. Our community was made up of families. A family was father, mother, sisters, brothers, grandparents, cousins, uncles and aunts. When a newborn came along, only women relatives were allowed in the tipi, and the first four days the aunt feeds the baby, then the baby is put in a moss-packed buckskin bag laced to a cradleboard, so a mother can carry the baby around. Small boys had little bows and arrows and would try and shoot the birds, and gangs of boys would have mud fights. Girls played with dolls and tipis. We were ready to marry at the age of fourteen. Most Indian men are shy, and they would play love songs on a flute to a certain squaw, which carried hidden messages of where to meet.

"The buffalo were plenty and we used every part; one to two hundred uses were found for the parts. Tipis, blankets, clothes, ropes, shoes and other things. Stomachs were dried out and used as water containers. Before horses came we would wear buffalo skins to disguise ourselves, so we could move with them. As you know we tell time by the moon, not the sun, and life by the Great Circle of Life. This was divided into four seasons: Spring – started April. Families left winter camps and gathered food and hunted, but the buffalo were left to fatten up. Summer – men went on vision quests to seek personal guardian spirits. All the tribes got together and put all tipis in circles; four days they purified themselves, the next four days was for a tribal ritual. Fall – important hunting season but we only killed enough buffalo to last through a long, cold, frozen winter. Women made Pemmican. This was preserved deer meat that had been flattened and mixed with tallow (fat) and dried chokecherries. Winter – settled into winter campsites, men and boys repaired tools. Women and girls sewed, decorated clothing and made dolls. At night stories were told around each of the campfires.

"It was always thought that when a Chief passed his eldest son would take his place – not so. A Chief was picked by the tribe for his abilities and daring." He looked at me and smiled. "Does that help, my daughter?"

"Yes, thank you Father."

"How is Tala? I think maybe it's time for a run to see if she is fully fit again." I agreed and looked round to see where I could shed my clothes. Some trees had appeared so I went there and disrobed and started to run. Tala was faster than before, but it felt magical running with my father, his wolf and the two white wolves. After a couple of hours running we returned to the same spot and I went to put my Indian dress back on, but when I returned to my father he wasn't there, in his place was my mother.

"Oh, Mother, I'm so pleased to see you," I said.

"I was so worried for you, my dear daughter. How are you feeling now?" she asked.

"I'm fine now, Mother, thank you. It's so long since I last saw you, are you well?" I asked.

She replied she was and arm in arm we walked down to the river, reminiscing about the times we spent on the Reservation when I was little. I asked her if she'd ever heard of Swallowtail. "Oh yes, all the tribe knew her, she was a great medicine woman."

I told her what had happened before. "Tell me about her please, Mother," I said.

"I can only tell you what your father told me," she said. "Swallowtail, as I said, was a great medicine woman. She practised medicine all day to keep the well-being and emotional balance of the tribe, and in return we gave her food, shelter, whatever she needed to show her respect and honour. She was given the responsibility of making warriors shields, as it was believed special powers were put into them to give added protection.

"Sometimes your father would go out and gather certain plants and herbs for her. Tobacco was a most sacred plant and was used in nearly every cure. Sage was used to protect against bad spirits and draw them out of bodies they had gone into. It was also used for cleansing sweat lodges. It was used in healing for stomach problems, kidneys, liver, lungs, bones, burns and grazes, colds and fevers. She also learnt about healing powers watching sick animals. She performed rituals and ceremonies. As you know, Swallowtail has a medicine bundle that she always carries and in that are her medicine tools. The bundle is made out of hide or cloth and tied securely, and the contents are sacred. The medicine tools are made from nature – fur, bones, shells, roots, and feathers. These tools are also used to bring forth the spirit of what the tool has been made out of. For example, a small medicine drum was made of wood and animal skins, when played it would call up the help of the spirits of the tree and animals from which the drum was made. Others from the tribe would make their own personal medicine bundles which were private, and it was forbidden to ask them about their medicine bundles. Medicine pipes are made and represent the ebb and flow of life. Medicinal feathers are used to source energy in healing ceremonies, but are also linked to air and wind enabling birds to fly, so they can carry messages up to the Great Spirit. Eagle feathers are very powerful. I only met Swallowtail when I gave birth to you and I felt an inner peace."

It was lovely talking to my mother again; we laughed, we cried, and then she said it was time for me to go back. "Are we going back to the Reservation, Mother?" She took my arm and led me to a large shrub and there I saw my gown, covered in blood. My mother told me to change clothes. I changed and joined my mother and as we turned to walk away from the river, my father, the wolves and Swallowtail all stood there.

My father took me in his arms and said, "It is time now for you to return to your new people, they worry greatly about you, especially Captain Tréville. He was very distraught, and when I put my hand on his heart it was breaking, but I whispered to him that you would not die this day." I looked at my father, wondering how on earth he had done that. My father just put his finger to his lips. "My daughter, never forget that we both love you very much."

I looked at him and said, "I love you both too, but I can't return, I've been gone months."

Swallowtail came to me and said I'd only been gone but ten minutes of earth time. Reservation time was different, and as far as my loyal friends were concerned during that time my heart had never stopped beating. Tala was strong now and so was I. She also told me that when I returned to the earth plane some of the pain would return; for obvious reasons I could not return fully healed, but Tala was completely healed. I understood, and thanked her.

Swallowtail had made a sacred circle and I had to stand inside it. The wolves sat at either side of me but outside the circle. I looked at my parents and Swallowtail with tears in my eyes, wondering when I would see them again. Swallowtail started to chant and suddenly I felt a floating sensation.

CHAPTER 13

The Return

I slowly open my eyes and look around, and see I'm in a very plush bed in a beautiful bedchamber.

Amanda was with me and told me the King and Queen had been informed of the incident and the Queen insisted I was put in a spare bedchamber. I noticed my gown had been removed, and I had something like a long shirt on, which fell just below my knees. Amanda told me that along with two of the Queen's attendants they had got me out of my bloodied dress and made me presentable for the King's physician, Monsieur Verde. Apparently Amanda, Aramis and Monsieur Verde had worked really hard on me to stem the blood flow (I knew different) so I could be moved. Sheets had been placed to cover my modesty, so all that showed was where the musket ball had gone through my hip.

There was a knock at the door and Tréville slowly opened it, looking extremely worried, and said, "Is Lesley allowed visitors, Nurse Amanda?" We both smiled.

Athos, Porthos, Aramis and D'Artagnan walked in. I smiled and said it was lovely to see them. They all gave me a hug and a kiss on the cheek and then Athos suggested everyone stood around the bed. I looked at Amanda and she looked at me. Athos just put his hand out; my hand was placed on his, then Tréville's, then Amanda's, then Porthos and so on. All Athos said was, "You are both family now and we always watch one another's backs and we have a saying: 'All for one, one for all.'" I looked at them all, and I'm sure along with Amanda I felt honoured to have such wonderful, caring friends, brothers, or in Amanda's case, lover.

Porthos went over to Amanda and said, "You need to change your dress and you also need a bit of comfort, it's been a very hard, emotional day for all of us, and I imagine Lesley needs some rest."

Tréville said, "I will stay with Lesley until you return, Amanda."

Amanda thanked Tréville and with the rest of his men left the bedchamber.

"Tréville, what happened? Where's Philip?" I asked.

Tréville sat on the bed by my side, holding my hand. He told me it was all over, after he'd fired the pistol everyone concentrated on me, until Porthos saw him running away, and other Musketeers were sent after him. They caught him and tried to take him to the Bastille, but he fought, managed to get away again. He was warned to stop or be shot – he ran and was shot."

At long last Amanda was free – she had her life back. The shot I took was worth her freedom. "Oh, Lesley, you are so very lucky to be alive. If the musket ball had not hit the tree first, before going through you, you would have died, then what would I have done?"

I looked at Tréville and saw his eyes were full of concern but also had tears in them, and I put my hand to his cheek. "Oh, Tréville, I will be fine, please do not be upset," I said. I had slipped down the bed and tried to move.

"Lesley you cannot get up yet, you have to be very careful," said Tréville. I explained I was trying to sit up, so I would be more comfortable. "Put your arms around my neck and I will very gently slide you up," he said. Tréville put his right arm around the back of my shoulders, but his other hand went to my face, his thumb caressing my cheek, and then as I put my arms round his neck, and my face came up to his, he gently gave me a long, lingering kiss on my lips. As his lips left mine Amanda came in the door. It took me a couple of seconds to realise what he had done, I don't think Amanda saw the kiss. I smiled at him, put my hand on his face and looked into his eyes, which were now twinkling.

"Tréville," said Amanda, "do you need a hand there?"

Tréville replied that he was helping me sit up more comfortably. Between them Amanda rearranged my pillows and they sat me up.

"Tréville, I think Lesley needs to rest now and I also need to check her dressings."

Tréville kissed me on both cheeks and as I watched him leave, he turned, smiled and gave me a wink. I thought of his kiss.

"Amanda, did you...?" I then felt pain rip through me and the darkness came.

When I woke later on, Amanda was sitting at my bedside and told me Monsieur Verde had attended again, and had left me some medicine and ointment to keep the wound free of infection. Amanda told me that I could not have been moved straight away or I would have bled to death, and then explained what had happened after the musket ball hit me.

"Oh, Amanda, how on earth can I thank you and Aramis for saving my life?"

Amanda replied, "You would have done the same if it had been me, and I am just so pleased you are still with me, my friend." We both hugged each other.

"I don't need the ointment or medicine, Amanda," I said. She looked at me quizzically and I told her my story.

"Oohh, Lesley, how wonderful and how sad. I wish I had met your father, if he was as lovely as your mother you were blessed. I have contacted Monsieur Rennard and he looks forward to seeing you back at the bakery, but only when you are better. He said you must rest and not worry, oh, and the King and Queen were delighted with the pastries and other things you made, the event was a huge success.

It took about six weeks for me to fully recover, but when I'm tired my hip hurts and I walk with a bit of a limp. I stayed at the palace for about two weeks until Monsieur Verde told me it was quite all right for me to return to my own lodgings. Just as I was about to leave Tréville happened to appear and offered to accompany me back to the bakery, which I graciously accepted. The King and Queen visited me many times, and before I left the Queen came to me and I thanked her, to which she replied that four Musketeers and Amanda were very pleased I'd recovered from such an ordeal, but a certain

Captain was absolutely delighted I had survived; she had never known him be at the palace so much. I blushed as I thought of his gentle kiss.

Tréville arrived and took my face in his hands and kissed me on both cheeks, and then held me in his arms, and told me how pleased he was I was still with him, and then we walked arm in arm to the carriage and went back to the bakery, where he made me promise to not overdo things. When I was back in the bakery I had constant attention. Monsieur Rennard had Catherine looking after me day and night, poor girl. The Musketeers came when they could, as did Amanda. On one occasion Aramis popped in and I gave him such a hug and kiss on the cheek and thanked him for helping to save my life, first time I ever saw Aramis blush. Tréville would come and fill me in on what was happening. He even stayed some nights to give Catherine a rest, and would read to me, all the time holding my hand. It seemed strange to me that he held my hand, but it actually made me feel content.

Monsieur Rennard had a very large chair, which Tréville actually said was very comfortable. They moved it from Monsieur Rennard's parlour to my parlour. I had spare blankets so Tréville wouldn't be cold, but he kept the fires going so the rooms stayed warm. He always said goodnight with a kiss on my cheek or forehead but never on my lips. I was beginning to wonder if I had imagined the secret kiss. I was so pleased when Monsieur Verde said I could return to work. Monsieur Rennard had been at the bakery every day and was still staying at his friend's. I hoped he hadn't been overdoing things.

My first day back I was up bright and very early, eager to get back into work. The first thing I checked was the oven which was a brick clay oven (called a Wattle and Daub). It had two shelves, was doorless, with a fire underneath and a chimney. Once the ashes were raked out from the previous night, firewood was placed there overnight to help dry out the wood faster in preparation for the next day. Once the fire was lit it became very hot. Everyone had to be extremely careful.

I checked all the sacks of flour and sugar and salt were intact. Made sure all the pots, pans and utensils were spotless. At that moment Catherine appeared with two other girls, Francine and Matisse. She explained Monsieur Rennard had decided we did need extra help, as we were now very busy. Monsieur Rennard arrived with two men, Pierre and Laurens. They did all the heavy lifting, and used the paddles to remove the bread from the oven. The two girls were used to doing the loaves so I left them to it, but still keeping a wary eye, after all I didn't know them yet.

I decided to start by making sugar cakes, scones, and biskets of various flavours, and then countess's cakes. Catherine helped with weighing, kneading, adding fruit or flavours, then sorting into the various wooden hoops or round iron cake pans, or deep tins. The rest of the dough was made into small balls and then put on a flat tray, which was covered with buttered lining paper. They all went on the low shelf and the untinned cakes were turned just once. The bread was left upright and not touched. It was law that the bakery was only allowed to produce either brown or white bread, not both, until later on when a Royal Charter merged them both. We did brown bread, as it was natural, nutritious bread. The white bread was lighter with more flavour but a lot less nutritious.

Once the cakes were done they were left to cool, a mixture of boiled sugar and egg white was poured on some of them, left to set and then decorated with various fruits. All of these were then placed in the shop window, or put aside if somebody had asked for them. I had brought one of Katherine's cookbooks down with me and showed Catherine a recipe I wanted to try. It was called French bread. The recipe is as follows: -

Half a bushel of fine flower

Ten eggs, yolks and whites

One pound and a half of fresh butter

then put as much yest as into the ordinary manchet: temper it with new milk pretty hot, then let it lye half an hour to rise, then make it into loaves or rowles, and then wash them over with an egg beaten with milk, let not your oven be too hot.

The first results were dreadful, and they all got burnt. The fourth lot came out beautifully. I called Monsieur Rennard to see what he thought. "Lesley these are lovely, light and a new taste. Let's put some in the window and see how they go," he said. At first nobody bought them, they looked different to our normal bread, so I took some to the garrison to see what they thought. The Musketeers loved them and after that word soon got round and they sold. Actually, they sold quicker than we could bake them. After I'd been back a couple of weeks Monsieur Rennard decided it would be a good idea for me to meet the miller and farmer, as eventually I would be dealing with them. Monsieur Rennard was well liked and greatly respected and had the honour of having a really good miller and farmer.

We went first to the farmers. Monsieur Deloitte and his wife were very friendly. They showed me round the farm and explained how things were produced like cheese and butter. It was a very hard life for them, especially the wife. The water was not drinkable, so it had to be boiled and left to go cold. She had to brew beer, milk the cows, feed the animals, and grow herbs. On top of that she had to clean, cook, sell the produce at the local market (if needed) and do all the washing! If they were ill they called a wise woman for healing, only the wealthy could afford a physician.

Next we went to meet the miller, Monsieur DeGruchy and his wife – they were just as lovely. Again they showed me how the wheat was grown, cut down, threshed and made into flour. All in all a great insight into how our products were made. I hope I stay friends with both couples for a long time.

Amanda had been busy at the palace and also attending to wounded Musketeers, from rather harsh training, but eventually we met up, and went for our usual walk along the riverbank. "I have something to tell you, but it's a secret," she said.

She had my full attention. "And what might that be?" I asked.

"Well," she said, "I have found out that it is Tréville's birthday this weekend," she said, smiling at me.

"And?" I said.

"Oh, Lesley, you are working too hard. It's Tréville's birthday, so what are we going to do about it?" She was right, I had been overdoing it and I was tired and my hip and leg were hurting.

"Please can we sit for a while? My hip and leg are not very good today," I said.

"Of course, why didn't you say before? Come, there's a spare bench over there."

"So it's Tréville's birthday, is it? How about we surprise him? I could do a picnic," I said.

Amanda looked at me and shook her head and said, "I was thinking of something better than a picnic, what would we do if it was raining?"

"Give me a minute to think," I said. "All right, I have an idea. How about we somehow get Tréville away from the garrison and I will bake lots of different breads and cakes, and a special birthday cake, and we could set it up in his office. I'm sure the kitchen will help us at the garrison, and they could get fresh fruit in. The problem will be getting Tréville away from his office for a couple of hours."

Amanda pondered on that and then replied, "Don't worry about getting Tréville away, I'll have a word with Porthos and see what can be done."

We went back to the bakery first for a drink and then we walked back to the garrison, arm in arm, for which I was pleased, as I was in great discomfort with my hip and leg. The Musketeers were there, as was Tréville, duelling each other, and wrestling. Oh dear, D'Artagnan just slipped onto his backside and Porthos and Aramis are laughing. Tréville just sighed and rolled his eyes skywards. The sweat was pouring off them, not a nice smell and all were covered in dirt. Well I think it was dirt! Good grief, Porthos just threw a Musketeer over his shoulder, another casualty for Amanda. We both went and sat on the steps watching the perfect specimens of men trying to outdo each other. I noticed Tréville was ordering his men what to do, and not joining in. Perks of being a Captain, I suppose!!

After a short time of watching them, all stopped and the Musketeers made their way over to us. Porthos went to hug Amanda, but she was having none of it. She just looked at him and said one word, "Wash." They all looked at each other; Aramis sniffed his armpits and I think the look on his face was enough to say they stank!! They all went off to smell better! Amanda went with Porthos and I went to stand to talk with Tréville, but at that moment my leg decided what a good idea it was to give way and I fell flat on the dirt ground.

"Lesley," said Tréville. "Amanda, get back here please," he shouted. All the Musketeers turned around and along with Amanda came running back over.

"I'm fine, please don't fuss everyone, my leg is just tired," I said.

Both Amanda and Tréville looked at me and raised an eyebrow each. Tréville picked me up and carried me up to his office and put me down on his bed.

The other Musketeers came in and I put my hand to my nose. "Ooh, please go and wash. I'll be here for a little while," I said. They all shuffled out the door, then it sounded like they ran down the steps and across the garrison grounds.

"Captain, do you mind if Lesley and I have a bit of privacy? I need to examine her," said Amanda. Tréville sort of looked, coughed and walked out onto the balcony.

"Honestly Amanda I'm fine, I've been overdoing it at the bakery."

Amanda looked at me and replied, "And when did you become a physician? Please let me check it's nothing else." She examined my wound. "Your hip seems hot which to me means infection," she said. "The King's physician left you some medicine and ointment, have you used and taken it?" she asked.

"Umm... Sort of forgot," I replied.

"Oh Lesley, I'm really annoyed at you. Now as soon as you get back to the bakery take the medicine and apply the ointment as the physician told you to, and I'm going to examine you again in a couple of days."

At that moment it sounded like the whole garrison was running up the steps. Amanda opened the door and Tréville and the Musketeers came in. "Is Lesley well, Amanda?" asked Tréville. Amanda told them I'd forgotten to take my medicine and use the ointment. Tréville raised his eyebrow and a look that said, "I'll speak to you later."

The rest shook their heads and Athos looked at me and just said, "Why can't women do as they're told?"

I half smiled at Athos and was going to reply but Tréville put his finger on my lips and shook his head. "Ladies, I'm afraid I need to speak with my men, may I ask you both to take the air on the balcony? Lesley, please sit on the chair, and don't move. Porthos please take another chair out for Amanda, and when we have concluded our business, maybe we could all partake of a meal and drink at the tavern," said Tréville.

Aramis quickly replied, "Well Captain that would be nice, and on behalf of the four of us, we humbly accept your generosity to a free meal."

Tréville just looked at him, sighed, shook his head, and said, "Gentlemen, to business." Amanda and I stepped out of his office.

Amanda and I had been sat down for about five minutes when all of a sudden Catherine came running into the garrison. "Lesley, Lesley, come quick, it's Monsieur Rennard, he, he..."

"Catherine, calm down, whatever has happened?" I asked.

"He collapsed at the bakery. His physician is on his way, but he is asking for you," said Catherine.

"Amanda, can you help me down the steps and please can you apologise to Tréville for me? I must go at once," I said.

Amanda said of course she would and reminded me not to forget my medicine and ointment. Catherine and I walked slowly back to the bakery. Monsieur Rennard was sitting on a chair in the kitchen with his physician. "How is he, Monsieur Bernard?" I asked, quite concerned.

"If he would do as I asked him, he would not be in this state," he said very sternly. "He needs absolute rest and I am going to travel with him to his dwelling in the country and get a nurse to look in on him every day. He is going to stay with his friend tonight and we will depart tomorrow morning."

Monsieur Rennard looked at his physician and me and said, "I agree to go but I must speak with Lesley first." He told me how he did the ordering, there was a journal in his safe to show who got paid what and various other things of importance. He gave me his safe key, which I would put with my own. He then left the bakery with Monsieur Bernard and returned to his friend's. I went up to my parlour where I did as Amanda had asked and took my medicine and applied the ointment, smelly stuff. I went back down to the bakery, just as there was a knock at the door. It was Tréville checking to see how Monsieur Rennard was and to see if I still wanted to go to the tavern. I thanked him and said I needed to rest; we kissed each other on the cheek and said goodnight. I now had a cake to do for Tréville's birthday.

CHAPTER 14

End of an Era

The weekend arrived. The bread, pies, biscuits, and cakes were done, the "special" cake was ready. Monsieur Rennard had gone to the country and the bakery was now in my charge. On the Saturday, Amanda dropped in at the bakery and I showed her around and then we discussed how things were going to go. Athos had spoken to a friend of Tréville's who was going to ask him to visit him on the Sunday morning to discuss business. The garrison kitchen would be ready and more fruit had been ordered, they had also managed to get a small keg of ale, a small keg of brandy and flasks of wine – hope they manage to keep them well hidden from Tréville. The other Musketeers would drink any that was left. Amanda had to go to work at the palace and I had already arranged to go and see Monsieur Rennard.

When I arrived at his country dwelling, it was lovelier than I remembered, because my first visit was quick. It was a single-storey dwelling, with some sort of shrub growing up and across the building. The outside had a small pond with flowers and shrubs round it. There was a small shed and barn at the side. Inside everything was clean, in its place and fresh flowers in a container on the table. Even though it had only been a couple of days he looked better, obviously country air agreed with him. There were two bedchambers, each had a small fireplace, and the parlour was comfy with a small cooking area. Monsieur Rennard also loved to sit outside. There was a knock at the door and a lady appeared. "Ah, Lesley, please meet Madame Fleury, she has been looking after me with lovely pies and broth." We greeted each other and then she and Monsieur Rennard had a quick talk and she left. Monsieur Rennard apologised that Madame Fleury did not speak a lot of English. We then sat and talked about the bakery and then he mentioned Tréville. I told him about Tréville's birthday surprise and, being curious, asked what he knew of Tréville, as he had known him quite some years.

He replied he would give me a brief summary since he arrived, but it would be better to ask Tréville, in case he wanted some things to remain private. He didn't know much of his childhood. "When Tréville arrived in Paris," he said, "he was about seventeen, had no money, so he joined as a cadet in the French Guard. He was badly wounded at the Siege of Rochelle, but his bravery and good fortune helped him become what he is today. He is an excellent swordsman, understands war, has a rare gift of intrigue, is honest and admired, feared and loved by his men. Anyone at the palace will tell you he stood by the motto his father left him – Fidelis et Fortis (Faithful and Strong). When he was admitted to the household of the young King he made good use of his sword – faithful to his motto, that Louis would say that if he had a friend who was about to fight, he would advise him to choose a second, himself first and Tréville second, but sometimes Tréville first. Louis has a real liking for Tréville, a royal liking and a self-interested liking. Tréville was strong in body and mind as were many Musketeers, but few could claim faithful. When he became Captain of the Musketeers, it was one of his greatest achievements. He will parade his Musketeers in front of the Cardinal (total Musketeers were between two hundred and two hundred and fifty men) whose Red Guards are the enemy, and will always duel and fight with the Musketeers to get them into trouble. He always proves he has the upper hand, and in return his Musketeers obey and are ready to die for the cause. He is a father figure to his four elite Musketeers, gives them the missions, keeps an eye on their welfare and tolerates their skirmishes with the Red Guards, and his authority is unquestioned. He has a heavy responsibility that he must uphold, whatever the cost. He never shows sign of weakness, is good-humoured, but can be brusque – he does not suffer fools lightly, but deep down he has a good heart. There was a dark period in Tréville's time as a normal Musketeer but he never speaks about it and I will not betray his trust." As I listened, I got to know a little more of whom this Captain of the Musketeers was. I stayed with Monsieur Rennard for another couple of hours and then made my way back to the bakery.

Sunday morning arrived, and I heard a loud thumping on the door. I cautiously looked out of the window to see Porthos stood there grinning. "Morning Lesley. Come on, woman, there's work to be done, and we have about two hours." I went down the steps from my parlour and let Porthos in.

"Two hours, that's plenty of time," I said.

Porthos hitched up the horse and cart, and then we loaded everything on it, although I did notice he was eating quite a bit! One thing I had learnt – Porthos was always hungry and had a huge appetite. We arrived back at the garrison and had just put everything in the kitchen when Tréville came galloping into the yard. Porthos shot out and said, "Morning Captain, thought you were having some time away today?"

Tréville replied, "I am, but I forgot something. What's Lesley's horse and cart doing here? Is she all right, is there a problem?"

"Morning Tréville," I said, smiling as I emerged from the kitchen. "I have just delivered some pies for you and your men and then I'm... off to visit Monsieur Rennard." (He knew I usually walked to the garrison.)

He took my arm and said, "Let me help you up, my dear, do you need an escort?'

"No, I will be fine, thank you," I replied.

"Wait for me and I will go as far as the crossroads with you," he said, tying his horse to the back of the cart, and then went to his office. I looked at Porthos who just shrugged his shoulders and grinned. "Porthos, do something," I said.

"Captain's made his mind up, nothing I can do, I'll just stay around the garrison."

Five minutes later and we were on our way. We talked all the way to the crossroads, where he then gave me a kiss on my cheek, mounted his horse and rode off. I had asked him if he was going to be gone all day, to which he replied he hoped to be back in a couple of hours, he had lots of paperwork to do. When I eventually got back to the garrison, after leaving the horse and cart at the bakery, I found Porthos in the kitchen. "Porthos, there were twelve pies and now there is only eight," I said, rather annoyed.

Porthos looked at me, grinned and said, "Your pies are just so delicious, I couldn't help myself. Did you enjoy your ride with the Captain?"

For that comment he got a slap on his arm. "What was I supposed to do, Porthos? Now let's get to work before he returns."

Tréville's office and the garrison are situated at Rue de Vieux Colombier. As you enter through the arch into the garrison yard, there are three or four fires lit constantly in iron braziers. The left side houses the blacksmiths, the bayonet practice area, a door that leads to a large room which is used for informal meetings, meals for some of the other Musketeers, but if Tréville and his men entered and needed privacy, they would go out. At the back of the yard is a huge building, which is divided into the infirmary, Musketeers' sleeping quarters and where they eat their meals. Targets are put in front of this building for musket practice. To the right of the yard is a table with benches and stools, the kitchen rooms, and some steps leading up to Tréville's office. Behind the steps is an arch, down on the right is the huge stables and training areas, to the left takes you round the back of the infirmary and Musketeer quarters to another training area. At the very end there is a graveyard. The steps lead up to a balcony where straight in front of you is a door, which leads into a spare room, where a great friend of Tréville's stayed when he was badly wounded. Alas, he did not survive. This was also the room, used a lot later, for D'Artagnan and Constance's wedding night, after Amanda and I made it special.

At the far end of the balcony there was a small table and a couple of chairs, and a door. Through the door you enter into a small corridor, pass another entrance into the spare room, and when you reach the end, there is another door which opens to the right; go down a step and this leads into Tréville's office which is rather large and split into two sections. As you enter the door his desk, chair, bookcase and cabinets are to the left (this is where private and confidential meetings are held), and there are two windows, with shutters, which overlook the balcony. Straight ahead is his bed with a cabinet at the side, and another window. There is an iron divider at the end of his bed where he hangs his breastplate, sword, cloak and hat.

To the right, by his bedside cabinet, was another door that led into the bigger of the two rooms. This room was the armoury where extra muskets, pistols, halberd's, swords, helmets, uniforms, blankets, lanterns and other things were kept, and it had two large windows so plenty of light shone in. There was also a smaller room where barrels of gunpowder were kept. Two or three spare chairs were in his office, along with a medium-size fireplace. Tall candlesticks and lanterns were placed where needed and two lanterns were on the balcony, one between the windows and the other was by the door. The corridor had small, high windows that let lots of light in, night-time it was lit by four torches hung on the walls.

We were going to use his office to put the food in, so I carefully moved what was on his desk to the top of his bookcase and cabinets and the men from the kitchen carried another smaller table up. I laid out all the bread, pies, biscuits and cakes and in the centre I put his special cake. I had coloured the side in a blue covering and on the top, it was gold and had four fleurs-de-lis. The cake was quite large, as I know the Musketeers have good appetites. Another of the kitchen staff brought up two large bowls of various fruits. The table looked lovely, that's what I thought anyway. Porthos, who had gone to freshen up, arrived with Amanda, and then Athos, Aramis and D'Artagnan arrived and brought up the small keg of brandy and ale and flasks of wine and some spare stools. Now all we had to do was wait for Tréville to return. About ten minutes later we heard a horse gallop in, and then, "What the hell do you mean you haven't got any fruit? Do I have to do everything in this damned garrison?" He thumped up the steps and stood on the balcony with his hands tapping on the rail looking out at the yard. I peeked out the window, signalled to the others to be quiet, smoothed my dress down and made sure my hair was in place, and tiptoed out.

"You all right, Tréville? I was waiting to see you," I said.

"Lesley my dear, you made me jump. What can I do for you?" he said.

"It's rather delicate, may we go inside?"

"Of course," he replied and we walked down to his office, arm in arm.

As he entered his office he stopped and looked at everyone. "What's going on here, why are you all in my office?" he asked brusquely.

As they had been stood in front of his desk they moved and Amanda went to him, kissed him on both cheeks and said, "Happy birthday, Captain."

The look of surprise on his face was a picture, I then kissed him on both cheeks. He gave me a tight hug and said, "Thank you, Lesley, it looks wonderful." He stood there and smiled like he hadn't done in ages. "Well, looks like the paperwork will have to wait, who's hungry then?" he said.

After about half an hour Tréville looked at me and said, "Lesley, is Monsieur Rennard all right? Only you went to see him yesterday and again today." I looked at Porthos, who was grinning, and then Tréville said, "Aaahhh..." and rolled his eyes. "You had no intention of going to see Monsieur Rennard today, did you? I thought it strange you took the cart."

I put my hand on his arm, laughing, and said, "No." Porthos told the others the story. We ate, drank, laughed and had a thoroughly enjoyable afternoon and evening. I looked around at everyone and smiled to myself, my wonderful new family; each one of them held a special place in my heart, but Tréville more so.

A couple of days later, Tréville called on me at the bakery and said the Queen had asked to see me. "Have I done something wrong, Tréville?" I asked.

"Not that I know of, my dear, she was enquiring about your health, but I think she needs to talk to you about another matter. If you come to the garrison in about an hour I will escort you to the Palace."

I went to my bedchamber, had a wash, changed into a more suitable dress, re-did my hair, and then went to the garrison. Tréville was in the yard with his men, so I went over to them. "Morning gentlemen, how are we all today?" I asked. They replied they were quite well.

Tréville called for the stable boy to bring his horse. I looked at Tréville, the horse, then Tréville again with a quizzical look on my face, wondering where my horse was. "I thought... um... you could ride with me, Lesley, so you don't.... umm... crease your dress too much," he said quickly. I heard a noise behind me and turned to see his men were all stifling laughs behind their hands looking at each other. Tréville mounted his horse and then Porthos helped me up into Tréville's arms, giving me a wink! As we trotted out of the garrison I looked back at his men, who were still laughing, and Aramis and D'Artagnan gave me a little wave! Riding in Tréville's arms brought a small blush to my cheeks, but it also felt so natural.

When we arrived at the Palace, one of the guards helped me down, and a stable boy took Tréville's horse. I smoothed my dress out, made sure my hair was in place, and then the guard escorted Tréville and I to the room where I was to wait for the Queen. "When your audience with the Queen is over, the guard will come and find me and I will meet you in the gardens, my dear," said Tréville, and with that went on his way.

The door opened and the Queen entered. "Lesley, I am so pleased you could come and see me, please come and sit with me," she said.

I curtsied and replied, "It is nice to see you again, Your Majesty."

She asked me how I was now after the accident and I replied I would always walk with a bit of a limp and the pain comes and goes, but apart from that my life was good. She was pleased and then said, "The reason I wanted to see you, Lesley, is in a couple of weeks we have some very important dignitaries arriving. The King is taking the men on a shoot and I am to entertain the ladies, and I wondered if you would kindly do the refreshments for us. There will be twelve of us."

I replied, "It would be my pleasure, Your Majesty, to do this for you. I was wondering how I could repay you for all your kindness you showed me whilst I stayed at the palace."

She replied that she would let Tréville know the actual day, but would give me plenty of notice. "I saw you ride in with our Captain, you seemed both content in each other's arms," she said with a twinkle in her eyes and a smile. I blushed and replied we were very good friends. She stood, as did I, said her goodbye, and I curtsied and said my goodbye as she left me. The guard came in and told me he would show me the way back to the staircase and then go ahead and advise Tréville.

Due to my hip injury I walked down the steps one at a time. When I got halfway down I heard soldiers approaching me from behind. As the first soldier passed he turned and blocked my way. I recognised him immediately. It was Rochefort. Tréville had pointed him out to me one day. "And who might you be walking round the palace? I have not seen you here before," he said.

I curtsied and replied, "My name is Lesley, sire, and I have just had an audience with the Queen and I am now leaving."

He looked me up and down and then said with a smirk, "Lesley, now that name seems familiar to me... Ah yes... so you're Tréville's whore, prettier than I thought – for him."

My right hand clenched, but I knew better than to give this man a fist in the face. I stood defiant and replied, "I am nobody's whore, sire, and your remark is extremely insulting." I looked straight into his eyes, which were black, hollow, and full of contempt and hatred.

His face came to about an inch of mine, his eyes boring into me. "Remind me, it was your left hip where you took the shot, wasn't it?" said Rochefort. His guards roughly grabbed my arms and held them tightly behind my back, but one of them put his hand on my left hip and started putting pressure where my wound was. The pain shot through me, but I tried not to show Rochefort any pain on my face. Rochefort put one hand on my face and squeezed it tight on both of my cheeks, and with his other put his dagger to my throat and said cruelly, "Believe me, whore, if I insulted you, you would know about it. Perhaps you need to be taught a lesson on how to speak to me with respect." I could feel the blade of his dagger across my throat, and held my breath. He then pushed me back hard and the side of my head hit the pillar, his dagger cutting me as I fell back.

The guards released me but not before I slipped down the step, thank heavens I caught the rail or I would have fallen.

"Careful now, we don't want you falling down the steps, do we? May I make a suggestion? The next time you come to the palace, make sure you have an escort or I will personally throw you out, then we'll see how you walk, or maybe I'll just shoot you in the other hip. Oh dear, Tréville's whore a cripple, now that would be very amusing." He came to face me again, and then whispered in my ear, "Heed my warning if you know what's good for you." He looked at his men and with a shake of his head and a sneer said, "Come, we have important work to do, I don't want my reputation tainted seen talking to the Captain of the Musketeers' whore." They laughed as they pushed past me. Before Rochefort went out of my view he turned and said, "Oh by the way, give my kindest regards to Amanda, tell her I'll be seeing her soon," and with that he was gone.

I hadn't realised how much I was shaking. Where was Tréville, anyone? I looked around but nobody else was present. I put my hand to my throat but there was only a little blood. Slowly and painfully I walked down the rest of the staircase holding onto the rail, and out into the gardens. I saw a bench and went and sat there, my heart beating out of my chest, my head spinning, my hip in agony and then the tears started to fall, and that was where Tréville found me.

"Lesley, my dear, there you are. Did you have a good audience with the Queen?" he asked cheerily. I didn't reply, as my head was down. He put his hand under my chin and brought my face up to his. "Lesley what on earth...? You're shaking, and what's those marks on your face and neck?"

I looked at him and said quietly, "Please Tréville, can we go back now?"

"Not until you tell me what has happened, who did this to you?" he said angrily.

I replied shakily, "It was Rochefort."

Tréville paled and called for his horse. I went to stand but the pain in my hip was too much and I gave a low moan. Tréville called to one of the guards, who carefully lifted me up into his arms. We were about halfway back when I said, "Tréville... stop... feel... strange..." and with that the darkness came.

The next thing I heard was Tréville shouting, "Aramis, Athos, quickly, help me with Lesley." I felt someone's arms carefully help me down, and then being passed to someone else. I knew at that point I was in Tréville's arms.

"Captain, who has done this to Lesley?" asked Athos.

Tréville replied, "All Lesley said was Rochefort, halfway back she passed out."

Porthos roared, "Why can't that man leave our women alone?"

"Porthos, calm down," said Tréville. "Give me some time with Lesley and when I know what's happened I will talk to you all, now back to practice, and Porthos try not to injure anyone else. Aramis, I need you to check Lesley."

Aramis replied, "Of course, Captain."

Tréville carried me to his office and put me gently down on his bed, after Aramis had re-arranged the pillows so I was partially lying down. Aramis looked at my cheeks and neck and told Tréville the bruises would go and the cut on my neck was not deep. I had a large bump on the left side of my head, but no blood. Aramis put a cool cloth to my forehead and then had a quiet word with Tréville and left. Tréville came and sat on the bed and gently took my face in his hands and looked at my neck and face, bent over and very gently kissed the bruises, and then took my hands in his. "Lesley, do you need Amanda to look at your hip?" I replied that after a rest I would be fine. "Please, my dear," he asked me gently, but his voice was full of concern, "tell me what happened with Rochefort, what did he do to you?"

"May I have a glass of water please?" I asked. Whilst he got me the water, I put my legs back over the side of his bed so I was sitting upright, and Tréville put his arm around me. With my head on his shoulder I told him of my lovely audience with the Queen, how honoured I felt that she had asked me, and then the horrible encounter with Rochefort and his men. "Oh, Tréville I have to go back to the palace to do the refreshments for the Queen, what if he sees me? He could cripple me for life, or worse kill me. He frightened me, and I don't know what I did for his wrath," and the tears started to flow again. Tréville carried on holding me but went quiet and when I eventually looked at him, his eyes were wild and his face was full of anger. I had never seen him like this before. I put my hand to his face and turned it so he was looking at me. "Please Tréville, don't do anything to antagonise him, I don't want him to hurt you, or worse."

He looked at me and took my face in his hands and wiped my tears away, and said, "Do not worry about me, my dear, but I must make sure you are safe. When you go back to the palace you will have me and my men with you, let him try anything with the Queen present."

All of a sudden we heard a loud scream. Tréville went to the window and looked out. "Porthos, I told you not to hurt anyone!" he shouted.

"Sorry Captain, is Lesley all right?""

Tréville looked at me and said, "I need to tell them, Lesley," I agreed.

"All of you go and clean up and come to my office."

I looked at him and said, "Tréville, do you mind if I freshen myself up?"

"Of course not, my dear, I'll get you fresh water." He went and kindly brought me back a jug of fresh water. I stood slowly and went to Tréville's washbowl, and dabbed some of the cool water on my eyes, face and neck and tried to compose myself, but my head was still spinning and I felt a little faint. Tréville noticed and helped me back to sit on his bed. There was a knock at the door to which Tréville replied, "Enter," and his Musketeers walked in. Tréville looked at Aramis and a silent message was sent.

Aramis came to me and put his hand on my forehead. "May I, Captain?" he asked, looking at the washbowl. Tréville nodded. Aramis went to the washbowl and soaked the cloth and then put it back on my forehead. Aramis moved the pillows so I could still be sitting up but with my head back slightly. "I think it a good idea if someone stays with Lesley tonight, Captain, maybe Amanda or Catherine." Again, Tréville just nodded.

"Captain, may we know what happened?" asked Athos.

"Rochefort attacked Lesley at the palace, called her my whore," he said, and then relayed my story to them. The look of shock on their faces was apparent.

"We need to do something about him, Captain, he cannot attack our friends like this," said D'Artagnan, full of concern and looking at me.

"I know, D'Artagnan, I know," Tréville replied. I could see Porthos was seething, but I didn't know why. The rest of the men were now also watching him closely, obviously I was missing something here.

"Why are you all looking at Porthos, and Porthos why are you seething with anger?"

Athos looked at Tréville and said, "Captain, you need to tell Lesley about Amanda."

"What about Amanda? Is she all right? Has Rochefort done something to her?" I asked, extremely concerned. Tréville then told me about Rochefort harassing Amanda, and telling her she was his and he was going to steal her away from Porthos. She belonged to him and no one else. I couldn't believe it, we had got free of Philip and now my best friend was having more trouble.

"She's my woman and I want revenge," said Porthos, banging his fist down hard on Tréville's desk, which made me jump and I put my hand to my head.

"Porthos, calm down," snapped Tréville.

"Lesley, are you all right?" asked Tréville, who came to my side immediately. I replied I was fine. My head had calmed down slightly but with Porthos banging the desk and me jumping, it had started again.

"Lesley, I apologise, I didn't mean to frighten you. Are you all right?" said Porthos.

I stood slowly, with Tréville's help, and went to Porthos and took his face in my hands. "I'll be fine Porthos and I know how you feel. Please, my musketeer brother, don't do anything that would take you away from Amanda, it would kill her to lose you, and me as well. Listen to what Tréville suggests and hopefully he will be dealt with." I turned and looked at the rest of them and said, "And that goes for all of you, I don't want to lose any of you, I look upon you all as my brothers now." They all smiled.

"Gentlemen," said Tréville, "we will talk about this and other matters later, but now I am going to escort Lesley back to the bakery, she needs to rest."

Each one of them gave me a hug and very gently kissed my cheek and Porthos whispered, "Thank you for your words, my sister."

As his men left, Athos turned and said, "Lesley, do not worry, we will always be there to protect you and Amanda, and this is a promise none of us will ever break."

I smiled back at Athos and said, "Hopefully it will never happen again."

As Tréville and I walked back, arm in arm, my head started to feel better. Tréville thanked me for calming Porthos. I smiled at him, and then paled. "Lesley, what is it?" he said.

"Oh Tréville, I didn't tell you the end, Rochefort asked me to give Amanda a message, I have to give her his kindest regards and he would see her soon."

"Don't worry, Lesley, I will look out for Amanda, and as soon as the Queen gives me the day for you to go to the palace, I will personally escort you and then your Musketeer brothers will meet us – you will be protected at all times. Neither Rochefort nor his men will hurt you whilst I have breath in my body." He took me upstairs to my parlour and said to give him a minute. When he returned he told me he had asked Catherine to stay with me until he returned later. He would stay the night in case Rochefort tried anything, or if I was taken ill, and with that gave me a hug and kiss on my forehead and left. I retired to bed early and when I woke the following morning Tréville was asleep in the chair, I never heard him arrive.

Tréville walked me to the garrison. Aramis checked the side of my head and said the bump was going down, which was good news.

The day arrived when I had to return to the palace. Porthos drove the cart, Tréville and Athos on their horses rode at our sides. Aramis and D'Artagnan had gone ahead to see where Rochefort was. As we neared the palace I started to shake and paled. Tréville noticed immediately and leant over and placed his hand on my shoulder and said, "Lesley do not worry, we are all with you." I gave him a nervous smile. Porthos looked at Tréville and then gave me a quick hug and a wink.

At the palace entrance Aramis rode over to us and told Tréville that Rochefort was just mounting his horse, he was being sent on an errand for the Cardinal, and would be gone for most of the day.

"Porthos, help Lesley onto my horse, then you and Athos carry on to the entrance at the back of the palace. We will wait out of sight until Rochefort leaves." Quickly, I got onto Tréville's horse and we rode to a copse of trees where we were totally hidden but Tréville had clear sight of the palace. I was still shaking and Tréville said, "My dear, please calm, I promise you Rochefort is not going to hurt you." I went to say something but Tréville put his finger to my lips and I followed his eyes. Rochefort rode past us with six of his men. Relief flooded through me. I looked at Tréville and my smile returned and we went to the entrance. With the help of a couple of maids, the refreshments were laid out in the room where the Queen and her guests would return.

As I went to leave I saw Amanda. She came over and hugged me and asked if I was all right after my horrible ordeal with Rochefort. I told her I was well, but she could still see the marks on my face and neck, even though they were fading. Tréville came to see where I was and Amanda asked him if we could have some time together and we would go to her bedchamber. Tréville said he would send his men back with the cart and he would wait for me. Amanda and I talked for a long time, and I totally forgot Tréville was waiting for me. Amanda told me when she was in Tréville's office talking about Philip, from nowhere the name of Georges D'aubigne came to her. She told me he was Philip's brother. I had never met him and I hoped he wasn't another Philip. Tréville and his men tracked him down, and he was a Red Guard! It turned out that their father was a Red Guard, but he was also a spy for the Musketeers. Tréville and Porthos would be with her when they arranged for a meeting at Tréville's office. Then she told me everything that had been happening with Rochefort and how frightened she was that Porthos might do something rash against him. I told her what I'd said to him and she hugged me and then we walked back to where Tréville was waiting. I apologised to him but he said it made a change to relax in one of the gardens and he had been keeping his eyes on the door. He lifted me up onto his horse and then once he was at my side, his arm went round my waist, and my arm went round his; I laid my head on his shoulder and this time I left the palace happy. I looked back and waved to Amanda hoping she would be safe from Rochefort. At least I would never see him again, as it was very rare that I went to the palace.

A couple of weeks later I was busy in the kitchen when Catherine came to me and said Monsieur Bernard was here to see me. I tidied myself and went out to greet him. "Monsieur Bernard, how lovely to see you again."

"Nice to see you again, Lesley, but is there somewhere private we can talk?"

I showed him upstairs to the parlour and we sat at the table. "What's wrong? Is it Monsieur Rennard?" I asked, not wanting to know the answer.

"I'm sorry, Lesley, I'm the bearer of bad news. Monsieur Rennard passed away this morning, peacefully in his chair in the garden." The tears welled up in my eyes and started to fall. "I will contact his solicitor, and no doubt he will be in touch with you soon, there is a lot to be sorted."

"Thank you for coming to tell me personally, Monsieur Bernard," I said.

We talked for a bit longer and then he left me to my grief. I went back down to the kitchen and called all the workers together and broke the sad news. Like myself they were all heartbroken. I told them to go home, as I now had to close the bakery until the solicitor advised me as to what would happen with the premises. Before they left I gave them what they were owed and a bit extra and told them to divide up we had baked between them. The fire was doused, and everything cleaned and put away. I put a notice on the door advising our customers that we were closed due to the death of the owner, and a piece of black fabric was put up against the shop window to show respect.

I went up to my rooms and cried like I did when I lost my father. I felt Tala stirring and knew she wanted to run, as she was feeling my distress. I took the horse out of the stable and rode out to my safe forest. There I let Tala run for a good hour – we hadn't run for quite some time. I returned to the bakery, all now dark and grim. The next morning, as usual, I was up early. I walked round the bakery which should now be bustling with activity, but lay quiet and dejected, feeling like the life had been taken out of it. I heard a knock at the door and saw it was Tréville.

"Oh my dear Lesley, I am so, so sorry for your loss," he said. I burst into tears and we went into the kitchen. "Is there anything at all I can do for you?" he asked. I said nothing. I was probably now jobless along with the rest of the workforce, would have to find new lodgings, basically start all over again. Tréville hugged me and I sobbed so much I must have soaked his shirt. When I calmed a bit Tréville said to me, "Lesley this is just a suggestion. You have funds, why not buy the bakery? I will come with you to the solicitor and see what he advises, after all it is a thriving business."

"Tréville, you know I cannot, women are not allowed to buy property," I replied.

Tréville looked at me, kissed me on my forehead and replied, "No problem there then." I wasn't quite sure where he was going with this, was he going to try and buy it and I work for him!

A couple of days later, Monsieur Rennard's solicitor Monsieur Ogier, and Tréville came to the bakery. I showed them up to the parlour, and we sat around the table. I quickly put wine and food out for them to partake. Monsieur Ogier looked at me over his glasses as he read Monsieur Rennard's will. He quickly went over what Monsieur Rennard had decided to leave to friends and then read, "The property I own is the bakery on the outskirts of Paris and my dwelling in the village of Plemon. This I leave to my very special friend, who came into my life just at the right time. With determination, love, sincerity, and more than anything else, trust. I know, under the guidance of this person, that the bakery will carry on and thrive. Hopefully the country dwelling might become a marital home one day. I feel like I have known this person all my life, but in fact it's been a short time. I hereby bequeath the bakery and the dwelling, and any funds that remain, to the one I call daughter, even though she is not. That person is Lesley. May God bless you and watch over you like he watched over me."

I looked at Tréville and the solicitor in absolute shock. "No, this cannot be. He has family, what of them?" I asked.

Monsieur Ogier replied he did have family, but they had gone to England and all perished with the plague. "You have just become a very rich lady, Lesley, and personally it was an absolute delight for me to give you this good news. Monsieur Rennard has also stated in his will, that should you marry, the bakery and dwelling are to remain in your name, not your husband's, unless you decide otherwise. You do not have to worry yourself about the funeral, as he had already made the arrangements before he passed. Now if you will excuse me I have other duties I must attend to, but I will be in touch." I shook his hand, curtsied and Tréville showed him out.

Tréville took me in his arms, kissed my forehead and said, "My dear, you look exhausted, maybe you should rest a while and let this news slowly come to you. I think it a good idea if Amanda comes to stay with you, tonight at least."

I said I would be all right, and after Tréville left, I went to my bedchamber and cried until I fell into a sort of sleep. I dreamed of my father and mother, Katherine, the wolves, money, it was all mixed up. I woke with a start and decided I needed a calming drink of mint leaves and went into my parlour. All of a sudden I felt a presence and turned and saw Monsieur Rennard stood by the table.

"Please Lesley, do not be afraid, your father told me I should come to you. I hope you are not too distressed that I left you my world. I loved you like my daughter and it could not be in better hands."

The tears welled in my eyes again and I walked to him and hugged him, the only thing that would come was, "Thank you."

"I have to go now, I'm going to see my wife again and our daughter, and if I may be so bold a piece of advice for you, my dear Lesley. You may not realise that Tréville thinks the world of you, he would make an excellent husband."

"Husband? But he's..." I said, shocked, but he had vanished.

CHAPTER 15

Tréville's Story

The bakery stayed closed until after Monsieur Rennard's funeral, which I attended with Tréville, the workforce, a few of his friends and the villagers. He was buried in the church graveyard where the dwelling is at Plemon. At least I could visit his grave when I went to the village. The solicitor called upon me a couple of times, upon where I had to sign papers with regards to the bakery and the country dwelling. Everything was now in my name, but it had come to me through someone I looked upon as a father figure, and that made me sad. Tréville had kindly taken time out to be with me when the solicitor came, helped me with the paperwork and checked everything was in order before I signed anything. I was so pleased that I had him as a close friend. He showed me a quicker way to do the ordering of produce and other things. Over the next month I didn't see as much of Tréville as normal, the Red Guards had been fighting the Musketeers, seeing to the King's business had taken up most of his time. I had also been extremely busy at the bakery. In fact I was shattered. Thank heavens I was taking the weekend off. I must tell Tréville I'm going to be away.

All that were under Monsieur Rennard, I'm glad to say came back – my second family. I had promoted Catherine to be under me, so if I was away or ill, she could step in. When I eventually caught up with Tréville, I noticed how tired he was looking. "You look like you could do with a rest, Tréville," I said.

"I agree, my dear Lesley, and I'm glad to say I have this weekend free."

I thought for a moment and then said, "Please do not think me being too forward, Tréville, I was going to let you know, but I am going to the country dwelling this weekend. Would you, maybe, like to accompany me?" He looked at me and sort of frowned. I said, "Please Tréville, if you have made other arrangements it will not be a problem, I understand."

He said, "It's not that, Lesley. I was thinking of the... um... um... Is there a tavern nearby where I can stay?"

I smiled and replied, "Yes there is a tavern at the other end of the village, Tréville, but the dwelling does have two separate bedchambers."

He looked at me and smiled and replied, "In that case, my dear Lesley I would love to accompany you. I will come for you, say, mid-morning on Saturday."

"I look forward to it," I replied.

I packed a small case, a picnic, and took other food for us, and we departed at the time Tréville suggested. He had decided to take a carriage, as I wasn't sure where we could leave the horses. As I went to get into the carriage my left leg buckled and pain hit my hip. Tréville grabbed me before I actually fell. "Lesley my dear, are you all right?"

"Tréville, I'll be fine, can you just help me into the carriage please?" Once I was sat down, the pain subsided quite a bit. I looked at Tréville and said, "I think, like you, Tréville, I need to relax. I have been so busy, I have been ignoring the pain, and before you reprimand me, yes, stupid of me, I know." Tréville looked at me, shook his head and then kissed my forehead. He put his arm around me, where it stayed until we reached the dwelling. In fact I was so comfortable I nearly fell asleep! By the time we got to the dwelling the pain in my hip and leg had gone. I pointed out the tavern to Tréville as we passed it. At the dwelling I noticed the garden was overgrown, and to me, the cottage looked sad. I wondered what the inside looked like. This was my first visit since Monsieur Rennard passed, as I just had not had the time before. "Tréville, I have no idea what it is like inside so please forgive me if it is a mess or dusty," I said as I alighted from the carriage, with his help. Tréville spoke to the carriage driver. I assume arranging for our return. I opened the door and my mouth dropped – it was spotless. Who had done this? I did not think anyone else had a key.

Tréville carried our bags in and said, "What dust?" We both looked at each other and laughed. I noticed that Monsieur Rennard had made some alterations to the inside. The parlour fireplace had been made bigger, as had the cooking area. There was a new table and chairs, and a couple of new cabinets. The floors had new wood on them, in every room. There were new shutters on new windows, which could be left open to let the light in, and when the windows were open you could hear the songs of the birds and smell the fresh country air.

We had been there a short time when there was a knock at the door. It was the neighbour, Madame Fleury, who I had met briefly before when I visited, and at the funeral. "Ah, bonjour Lesley, comment ca va?" she said.

I replied, "Tres bien, Madame Fleury. Merci."

I introduced her to Tréville who she looked at and said, "Aahh, vous êtes un mousquetaire?"

Tréville replied, "Non, Madame, je suis le Capitaine."

Madame Fleury looked at me, smiled and winked. I smiled back and felt myself blush. I hope she would not think it inappropriate if Tréville did decide to stay. They talked for a short while. I had learnt a little French but not enough for a full conversation. Tréville told me later he had explained why he was there and would be staying at the tavern, but Madame Fleury suggested he stay with me in the spare bedchamber. I would be in a strange dwelling with strange noises, and knowing a friend was staying would calm me. He told her he did not want my reputation tainted.

She then explained to me in half English, half French that there was a well at the back of the dwelling, but there was already two buckets filled with water in the parlour. She said that Monsieur Rennard had given her a key and asked her if she would keep an eye on the dwelling until I arrived. She also told us that the field opposite was where we could let the horses run, the barn had been made bigger to take three horses with a cart or carriage, and he had made a doorway from the second bedchamber into what used to be the shed, and what was in there was new. Monsieur Rennard had made arrangements that once he passed, the beds were to be taken away and new ones put in their place. There was a big four-poster in the main bedchamber and a smaller one in the second bedchamber, along with tall cabinets. In the cabinet in the main bedchamber there was new pillows, blankets, cloths and soap. She gave me the spare key, said her goodbyes and left, but I did notice she gave Tréville a wink!

"Would you like to walk round the village, Tréville? We can go to the tavern and get you settled in, but you are more than welcome to use the other bedchamber. We could then have our picnic and later on in the evening partake of a meal and drink at the tavern."

"Thank you, Lesley, I would like to take you up on your kind offer and stay here with you. I would worry about you being on your own in a strange place, and what an excellent idea. Shall we, my dear?"

Arm in arm we walked round the village, and visited Monsieur Rennard's grave. I had picked some flowers from his front garden and with tears in my eyes placed them on his grave. Tréville and I sat talking on a bench overlooking the stream, had our picnic and eventually I think our stressful lives were left behind and we relaxed in each other's company. It warmed my heart to see Tréville laugh. The meal at the tavern was delicious; chicken with local vegetables, and the pudding was fresh fruit. It also gave me the chance to meet some of the other villagers, who were very friendly and welcomed me to the village. After we arrived back at the dwelling, we talked for some time and then Tréville retired for the night. I was pleased he had decided to stay.

Tala was restless, as she could smell the forest. I very quietly tiptoed to Tréville's door. Let's just say snoring was well loud. My bedchamber was at the other end, so I opened the window, which was fairly low, climbed out, pushed it to from the outside, looked around and ran towards the forest. Minutes later, after I had undressed, I started running and Tala came forth. Tala was running free and did she enjoy it. She rolled in the long grass, played with the leaves, quietly sat and watched small creatures at play, and listened to an owl. I realised I'd been gone for a couple of hours, so changed back, re-dressed and noticed my hip and leg was stronger, and made my way back, Tala now content. I was still looking everywhere. No one was around. I climbed back in the window and again crept towards Tréville's door, still snoring. I would come here as often as I could, just to give Tala a run. The new bed was really comfortable and I soon fell into a long deep slumber.

The following morning Tréville had awoken before me and gone for a walk. When he returned he told me he had watched the sunrise and all the beauty that went with it, but even more pleasing was to relax and breathe in fresh air. He had also met and talked with some of the villagers. We had a hearty breakfast, and then he suggested we look at what was behind the door of the bedchamber he was using and the barn. I opened the door and gasped. There in the middle of what used to be the shed was a huge tub. Tréville looked at me and said, "I don't remember Monsieur Rennard being a large, tall man." I just smiled, not sure what to say. A large fireplace had been built along with a cabinet. Inside the cabinet were more cloths of various sizes and soap. The floor was stone and there were a couple of rugs. The original shed door had remained and the key was in the lock, and again new shutters at the windows. I took the key from the door and put it in the cabinet. I noticed something in the wall that was round with a covering and asked Tréville what it was. He told me it was something called a tube so the water could be poured down it to the outside. Monsieur Rennard had thought of everything. I looked at the tub and thought of being able to bathe in front of the fire – wonderful, but that would have to be when Tréville was not around.

The barn was indeed big, as Madame Fleury had told me. There were three separate stalls for the horses and a large area where a cart or carriage could be left. There was a stack of logs neatly piled up. Next time I could ride, so much quicker than a carriage. There was a small cabinet, which held tools for the garden in it. We went outside and I saw Monsieur Rennard had started what looked like a vegetable patch. I saw where the tube came out of the wall and a solid structure had been built around it to protect it, and it looked like the tube went under the ground. I had never seen the back of the dwelling, but it was lovely. Large trees were at the bottom of a small garden along with a stream, and the well was at the top of the garden, by the door. The birds were singing, the sun was shining; oh, how I wished both of us could stay longer. Maybe next time when I came, I would be lucky enough for Tréville to accompany me again.

At that moment we heard a noise and went back to the front of the dwelling to see the carriage arriving. Alas, too soon we had to return to the bakery and garrison. We got our bags and I locked up the dwelling and got into the carriage. Tréville had a word with the driver and then we departed. Madame Fleury was in her garden as we passed and she waved. As we travelled back I looked at Tréville, the worry lines were gone and he looked so relaxed. I got the spare key out of my bag. "Tréville, I would like you to have this. You can go whenever you like, especially if you need to relax, or just want to go somewhere quiet for a couple of hours."

He looked quite surprised then smiled. "Lesley, how kind of you, but I will check with you first and maybe we can go together again?" I smiled and replied that would be a lovely idea.

On one such occasion, Tréville and I decided to go on horseback and have a look at the countryside around the village and take a picnic. We rode for some time and then came upon a ruin of what looked like an old house of nobility. There was a stream and plenty of trees for shade. We dismounted, Tréville took the horses to the stream for a drink and then tethered them to a tree, in the shade, whilst I laid out the blanket under a large tree and put the picnic out. I had also brought a flask of wine, but in my rush I had forgotten to bring something to drink out of. Not very ladylike swigging wine from a flask! Tréville thought it hilarious.

We had our meal and wine and then we heard voices. I looked and saw two small children were playing in the stream, so another village must not be far away. They were splashing, laughing and having a lovely time, and my mind started to wander back to my childhood on the Reservation.

"Lesley... Lesley." My mind came back to the present. I looked at Tréville and he said, "You looked like you were elsewhere, does it bring back memories?"

I replied it reminded me of my time on the Reservation when I was small, and told him quickly about my childhood. I looked into his beautiful blue eyes and said, "What about your childhood, Tréville, and how did you get to be Captain? If you don't mind me asking."

Over our times at the dwelling Tréville and I had learnt to relax in each other's company, so when he put his arm around my shoulders and I rested my head on his shoulder, it was the most natural thing to do, and that's what we did now.

"From the very beginning?" he said.

"Of course," I replied.

"Well, first of all I was born," he said, laughing, and for that he got a gentle slap on his chest. "My father and mother were Jean and Marie, and before he passed, my father was also Comte de Troisville."

My head shot off his shoulder and I said, "You are the Comte de Troisville?"

Tréville smiled and said, "I have the title, nothing else." His hand put my head back on his shoulder. "From my father's first marriage I have two half-brothers, Pierre and Arnaud, and two half-sisters, Jeanne and Marie. I have no idea what happened to them. From my father's second marriage I had a brother, Pierre, and a sister, Louise. I was the eldest of the three of us. My mother was only seventeen when she married my father, who was thirty years older than her. My mother had a very hard life, as she was no more than a child herself. As children life was hard; we worked on the lands sunrise to sunset, worked in the mill, slept on the stone floor, and washed in the stream. Not much fun in the cold winters. You know my brother Pierre was killed and the story of Aurore and Michelle. My sister passed at the age of three. My father was a soldier and served under the King's father, Henry IV, but he was classed as a favourite soldier, and because of his loyalty Henry IV bestowed a great matter of honour upon him – a coat of arms. It's a golden lion passant upon gules with the motto Fidelis et Fortis – Faithful and Strong. (Lion passant is walking with right forepaw raised, others on the ground.)

"My father left his young wife and my brother Pierre at the dwelling but took me to Paris with him. He stayed at the palace so I had access to the Royal Court and that was where I met our King and we became friends. I was three years older than him. When I was nine years old my father and I left Paris and went back to the dwelling. It was whilst he was there, he bought three very small villages and called the area Troisville. When Henry IV heard of this he made him a Comte, hence Comte de Troisville. Later on, my father changed our name to Tréville, so my proper title is Comte de Tréville. Three years later came the sad news that Louis's father had been assassinated. Louis became King Louis XIII at the age of nine. His mother Marie de Medici became Regent. It was a very turbulent time and his mother agreed to an arranged marriage between Louis and Anne of Austria, who was the daughter of Philip III of Spain – they were the same age and were betrothed at twelve and married at fourteen. Neither of them met until the day of the wedding ceremony. A year later my father passed and left my mother penniless, and me a Sword and a Motto – Fidelis et Fortis. My brother and I worked hard to try and get some coins for my mother; we turned our hands to anything that came our way, and somehow we survived. About two years after my father passed, my mother was courted again and they married a year later. I did not get on with her new husband and a year later I decided to leave. Pierre left two years later, eventually married and had a family.

"I travelled to Paris with nothing but the clothes I stood up in and joined the French Guards. I was seventeen. I lost contact with my mother but heard later on she had passed in childbirth. I stayed in touch with Pierre until he was killed. Two years later the King took power from his mother and exiled her to a chateau in Blois after an attempted coup to kill him. During the siege of Montauban, I met the King again. The King's father had a regiment of Carabiniers and when our King decided to give them muskets they became known as Musketeers. As you know the Cardinal had his own guards called the Red Guards. We are all supposed to be on the same side, but the Red Guards try everything to goad the Musketeers into fighting, brawling in the taverns, anything to get them in trouble, and I don't trust the Cardinal at all. Both the King and I fought in battles; the infantry were on foot and the dragoons were on horses. The King had already set up a Junior Unit of the Musketeers, which was not closely linked to the Royal Household, but it opened the way for the lower classes of French nobility or younger sons of noble families to join, and because my father became nobility, that was how I entered the regiment. The unit gained a reputation for boisterousness and fighting spirit because the only way for social and career advancement was to excel at their tasks as mounted light dragoons. Later on they were seen at Court and in Paris. I was lucky enough to have an excellent tutor who showed me how to fire a musket and pistol with accuracy and also how to become an excellent swordsman, amongst other things.

"After a year I advanced from the French Guard to become a Musketeer and started my difficult social climb. I was appointed Horn Bearer in the Musketeers after my contributions at the sieges of St Antoin and Montpelier. This was a part of the military branch of the French Royal Household. I met two other Musketeers and we became blood brothers, we went everywhere together, our own small elite band – both have since passed. I was appointed as Lieutenant of the Musketeers after leading a group of Musketeers and ended up capturing a Spanish General. I also became a Gentleman of the King's Chamber. Unbeknown to me the King had been watching my difficult climb of the ladder called Court Favor. I was badly wounded in the Siege of Rochelle and have a long scar on my leg. My men and I were blown up by cannon fire, all I remember was flying through the air and waking up in a tent, and someone telling me they might have to take my leg off. I pleaded with them not to, and I passed out, and when I came round I was told they had saved my leg, I was so relieved. The next chapter in my life turned out to be a dark time for me."

I looked at Tréville and he seemed sad. I took his face in my hands so he was looking at me and said, "Tréville, you do not have to tell me anything you do not want me to hear, and I do respect your privacy."

He looked at me, his hand placing a lock of my hair back behind my ear, and said, "I have only ever told one person about this before, but I know you will understand why I don't mention it. King Louis's mother (Marie de Medici) had Cardinal Richelieu working for her at this time, but she was growing weary of his close friendship with her son, so she decided to try another coup, but this time to kill Richelieu. As I was Lieutenant of the Musketeers she ordered me to carry out this killing, along with six other Musketeers, but at the last moment Marie de Medici told the King we had plotted murderous intent and we were all thrown into the Bastille for a month, where all of us were brutally tortured." Tréville's voice went quiet and his face paled, and his eyes had a distant look in them.

I took him in my arms and held him tight, tears running down my cheeks. "Oh Tréville, I'm so sorry for your pain," I said.

Tréville held me for some time and then when he released me he realised I had been crying. "My dear, dry your tears, it was not you that sent me to the Bastille." Again, I put my head on his shoulder and then he carried on with his story. "Once the King had realised what had been plotted and what had happened to me and the others, and eventually got the truth from his mother, we were released immediately. The King exiled her back to Blois, never to return, or she would be killed on sight. I believe she ended up going to Holland and then England.

"After that attempted coup, the King decided he needed extra security for himself and the Queen, and during the following year the King asked me to create a unique band of men to act as his personal guards and they would be called The King's Musketeers. I had the honour of being the first King's Musketeer. I then watched and waited for my elite band of men but they had to prove to me, beyond doubt, that they were worthy of the honour. I had already seen Aramis in action at Montauban, Athos and Porthos were in other regiments and came to my notice. I did know Porthos when he was small but I'll tell you that story another time. I introduced them to the King. Each of them was told to kneel and the King put his sword to each of their shoulders and welcomed them into his regiment. Each one was given a pauldron (badge of honour), decorated with the fleur-de-lis, and put onto their right arm. As you know D'Artagnan came along a lot later and was also honoured. Two years later I was greatly honoured by the King, when he bestowed me with the title Captain Lieutenant of the Musketeers, but everyone calls me Captain." He put his hand under my chin so I was looking at him and said, "And then a couple of years later a very special lady entered my life," and kissed my forehead. I smiled and kissed his cheek.

We just sat there, under the shade of the tree, with our own thoughts, arms around each other. A little bit later the horses started to move around uneasily, as if they had sensed something. I noticed storm clouds were forming and looked at Tréville and suggested we make our way back to the dwelling before the storm hit. We gathered everything up and had just got back to the dwelling when the skies opened and heavy rain fell. Tréville and I sat by the log fire and I thanked him for telling me his story. He smiled and said it was his pleasure, but he would appreciate it if I did not mention to anyone his dark period. I smiled and said, "What dark period? I have no knowledge of what you are talking about, Tréville."

CHAPTER 16

Rochefort

One day I was sitting quietly in my parlour at the bakery, relaxing, when I heard a light tapping on the door. I went down and was delighted to see it was Amanda. "Amanda, how lovely to see you. Please come in." We went to my parlour where Amanda put her cloak on the back of a chair and then surprised me by holding her arms out for a hug. Something was not right. "Amanda, what's wrong?" I said as I hugged her back.

She replied, "Everything." I looked at her and could see she looked quite upset.

"I think this calls for a hot chocolate, sit by the fire and warm yourself," I said. I returned with two cups of hot chocolate and gave one to Amanda. "Amanda, tell me what's wrong and do not say nothing."

Amanda replied looking into her drink, "What did I do wrong?"

"What do you mean 'what did I do wrong'?" I asked.

She looked at me and sort of smiled. "I'm being silly, Lesley, probably seeing things that aren't there, just ignore me." I knew from that remark something was troubling her deeply.

"Amanda..."

All of a sudden someone was banging the door so hard I thought it would break. I went down the steps, shouting, "I'm coming, I'm coming, stop hammering the door down." I slowly opened the door, and saw Athos standing there. "Athos, good to see you but did you have to frighten me with that hammering? I thought it was the Red Guards," I snapped. He looked at me and mumbled something about Amanda. Was he drunk again! I took him up to the parlour and was surprised to see Amanda had her cloak on. I looked at both of them and knew something wasn't right. "What's going on with you two?" I demanded.

Amanda replied, "Time for me to go, Lesley. I gave Athos and Remy the slip to come and see you and because of that I have upset Athos. As you know I am not supposed to go anywhere without an escort."

I looked at her and raised my eyebrow. Amanda hugged me and said her goodbye, but as Athos went to go I put my hand on his arm to stop him, "Athos, what has happened? You and Amanda usually get on well." Athos glared at me, grunted and walked out. Charming! I watched the carriage pull away and Amanda waved.

The following evening I heard a knocking at the door. "Who is it?" I asked.

A voice replied, "It's all right, Lesley, it's me." I opened the door to see Tréville.

"Oh, Tréville, come in and dry yourself, what a dreadful night."

Tréville replied, "As much as I would love to, unfortunately, I am on a mercy mission. I need you to come back with me to the garrison, it's Amanda."

I looked at him and said, quite concerned, "What's happened? She wasn't herself the other day, is this to do with Athos?"

Tréville looked at me and said, "Athos, no, hopefully that has been sorted. It's Isabella. Athos took Amanda to Claudette's yesterday, as Isabella was very ill. Alas, she passed away. Amanda ran and Athos could not find her, so he rode back to the garrison to get Porthos, and together they searched for her. They found her this morning curled up in a field, soaked to her bones. Porthos brought her back, has given her a bath to warm her up, and hot drinks. She seems to be in denial and Porthos wondered if you could help." I grabbed my cloak and went down to the door, still pouring with rain. "Lesley, I brought an extra one. Here, wrap this round you... um... on second thoughts…" and with that Tréville picked me up in his arms. I looked at him and he had a twinkle in his eyes. I wrapped my arms around him, he covered us both with the waterproof cloaks, but more me than him, and took my key and locked the door, and then we rushed back to the garrison.

Tréville knocked quietly on the door and Porthos opened it. "Thank you for coming, Lesley, I don't know..."

"Hush, Porthos, I am here now."

Tréville said he would wait in his office and just Porthos and myself entered the room. I saw Amanda was in their bed. I went to her and wrapped my arms around her. "Oh, my dear Amanda," I said.

Amanda looked up and said, "Lesley, what has happened? Why are you here?" She apologised for not being dressed and told Porthos off, and tried to get out of bed.

"No Amanda, please stay where you are, you've had a traumatic time."

She just shook her head, so Porthos went and sat at the other side of her. "I don't understand why you are here, I am not having a traumatic time. I sneaked out whilst Athos and Remy slept, and came to see you. I am fine... I am fine," said Amanda.

Porthos looked at me and said, "You see what I mean, Lesley, she is in denial."

I took Porthos's hand and replied gently, "It's fine, Porthos, leave it to me. I see you brought some flowers, how about you place them in some water and put them in the spare jug on the window sill?"

I looked at Amanda and took her hands in mine and said softly, "Amanda, you did come and see me two days ago. Yesterday Athos took you to Paris to see Isabella, do you remember?"

Amanda replied, "Of course I do, that's when I slipped out on Athos and Remy when they slept and I..." Amanda's eyes glazed over and she was staring at something. I turned and saw the spirit of Isabella, she was saying something to Amanda and then she faded. Suddenly tears started flowing down Amanda's cheeks and she looked at me and said, "Oh Lesley, my Isabella is dead, I could not save her. I tried so hard, it was too late... I was too late." She started sobbing uncontrollably and Porthos came to her and held her in his arms.

Porthos looked at me and said, "Thank you Lesley." I put my hand on his shoulder and left, with tears in my eyes. I went to Tréville's office and he took me in his arms, whilst I cried for Amanda's grief. Isabella had been so young. The rain had stopped and Tréville walked me back to the bakery.

The day of Isabella's funeral arrived. I told Amanda I would meet her at Claudette's, but not to worry if I was slightly late as I had already made an appointment to meet the merchant, who sold the cacao beans, used to make the hot chocolate. He only came once a month. I had asked Tréville if I could borrow a horse and he had agreed, and at the same time he told me he was going to be away with his men for four days. The King had requested them to escort him to a secret meeting, where and with whom, he did not tell me. I always missed him when he was away. I asked him who would escort Amanda to the funeral, he replied she had met Georges and he was going with her. I looked at him with concern, but he assured me Georges was totally the opposite to Philip – not only that he had grilled him! He would leave the details for Amanda to tell me. They all left the day before I went to Paris. I let Catherine know where I was going and went to the garrison, got a horse and rode off.

It was a lovely sunny day, but it was going to be a sad day, especially for Amanda. I didn't like wearing black so I had dressed in a dark blue summer dress, with short sleeves, the neckline a little bit off my shoulders and not too low on my chest, and taken a shawl for later on. I arrived in Paris and left my horse at one of the stables, which Tréville had suggested. I had a look at the markets to see what new produce was around, the new fabrics, looked at the cafés for ideas, even had a look at the upmarket dress shops. I then went to see the merchant, but unfortunately he had been delayed and was over an hour late. I agreed a suitable price for two bags of cacao beans, which he would deliver the following week. Alas, with him being delayed I had missed Isabella's funeral, I was so upset not to have been there to support Amanda. I walked back to the stables to get my horse, but I had a strange feeling of being watched. I looked around but saw no one acting strangely. I rode back thinking of Amanda and Claudette.

I got as far as the crossroads when four men with their faces masked stopped me. "Gentlemen, I only have a little money on me if that is what you want." One of the riders came alongside me and quickly put something over my nose. I tried to push him away but the darkness hit me. When I came round my head was hurting, I was gagged tightly, which was hurting the sides of my mouth, and tied to a wooden pillar. Thick rope was round my shoulders and chest, my arms were at the side of me and the rope was around my wrists and body, and also my ankles. The only part of my body I could move was my head, and my fingers. The room was small and empty, dimly lit, and felt damp – where on earth was I? I listened for any noises – all I heard was scurrying of feet – rats! After some time I heard a door behind me open and someone removed my gag. "Please, where am I? What have I done?" The stranger, who was still masked, I could only see his eyes, did not speak, stood at the side of me and gave me a drink of water, which I gratefully accepted.

Someone else entered and said angrily, "Where have Tréville and his men gone?"

I did not recognise his voice. "I do not know," I replied. The stranger at the side of me looked behind me, nodded and then slapped my face so hard it split my lip. "Please, I don't know anything, he does not tell me of his whereabouts." I received another slap, on the other side.

The voice behind me said, "Put pressure on her left hip." The stranger put his hand on my hip so hard I screamed in agony. "Please," I pleaded, "all I know is he is away with the King. Where, he did not tell me." The stranger removed his hand, re-gagged me, and then they left the room.

I didn't know if it was day or night – there were no windows. How long had I been there? I was getting cold, as my dress was only thin. Surely Catherine would have missed me by now and they were looking for me. Stupid, how would they know where to look? I assumed they had brought my horse with them. Tréville and his men were gone, I was feeling frightened and the tears came. Tala, my spirit wolf, knew I was in grave danger and was willing me to bring her forth. "Hush, Tala," I said silently, "I cannot bring you forth, we would be shot on sight. I will be all right – I hope."

Later on the door opened, and my gag was removed. Another lantern was placed on a hook. I looked at a young woman, who was covered in bruises, and very pale. "I have brought you food and water, lady, and have to tend to your wounds," she said.

"Where am I? What do they want with me? I do not know anything."

"Please eat," she said.

I took tiny bites of the bread she gave me, but it hurt to chew. She gave me sips of water and then put a damp cloth gently over my face and wiped the blood away from my lips. The pain in my hip had slowly calmed down, but my arms were now starting to hurt and were going numb. "Please can you slacken the ropes? I cannot feel my arms and my back feels like it's being stretched."

She looked at with me with such pity in her eyes. All she said was, "I am sorry, lady," pulled the gag back up, took the lantern and left. That was the last food and water I was offered. I tried to move, but the more I moved the more the ropes cut into me. My mind started to wander and my head kept dropping down. *Oh, please, someone help me.* I must have closed my eyes and drifted. The next thing I knew I had frozen water thrown in my face and a voice said, "Wake up, whore."

That was a voice I knew and my blood ran cold – it was Rochefort.

"Well, well, Lesley," he spat. "We meet again. I see you are still Tréville's whore and that is why you are here. You will tell me where Tréville and his men have escorted the King to and then I might just let you go. If you do not answer my questions Tréville will receive your crippled body. Now we don't want to upset the Captain, do we?" I froze, how could I tell him what I did not know? "Take her gag off," he said to another man behind me. "Well, you have something to tell me, whore."

I looked into his cold eyes and said, "Go ahead and cripple me, Rochefort, because all I know is Tréville has gone somewhere, but where, I have no idea. He does not tell me his secrets. I am only a friend. You are at the palace, I'm sure the Cardinal will know where the King has gone." The last bit I said with venom in my voice. His gloved hand came across my cheek and I felt the studs rip my skin open, and then he did the same to my other cheek. I was seeing stars and I could feel the blood trickling down my face, then blood flowed from my nose, down my face and the back of my throat. He nodded to someone behind me, who punched me so hard on my left hip, I felt sure the shot wound had re-opened. I tried not to scream, but I did. As I took the punch so the ropes went deeper into my body. My head went down and I could see my chest and dress was covered in blood, the rope across my shoulders and chest had opened my skin and was also bleeding. My wrists, tops of my legs and ankles felt the same.

Someone else came in the room and I heard him say to Rochefort, "Sire, we have made secret enquiries around the garrison and taverns, no one knows where they have gone."

Rochefort replied, "Someone must know something. How can the King disappear and the Cardinal not know?" He then came back to me and threw more freezing water over me. I was soaked through, and he said, "Oh dear, now don't catch cold will you? After all I don't really want to kill you, you can still be useful to me in the future. Don't bother gagging her, no one will hear her screams," and with that walked out the room. The men left and the candle was doused so the room was pitch black.

I drifted in and out of trying to stay awake. Nobody came, time dragged by, I felt I had been there for an eternity. I was feeling weak, I could taste blood in my mouth, my hip was in agony, and I was getting colder and colder, and shivering. The water had made the rope restraints even tighter and I could feel them cutting deeper into my body. Suddenly a brilliant light appeared before me. I had to turn away, it hurt my eyes.

"My daughter, what have they done to you?" It was my father. "Tala has been calling to me with her distress," he said.

"Father, am I dying, I feel so cold and my is life ebbing away. I cannot swallow. Have you come to take me to the Reservation?"

"No, my daughter, it is not your time yet. You must survive, but you need to cough. The back of your throat has filled with blood and it is staying there. You need to cough it up, my daughter." I coughed slightly, nothing happened. "Cough harder," my father said. Disgusting as it was, I coughed harder, and felt something come up into my mouth and I spat out a huge lump of blood. Now I could swallow. "I have found Tréville and his mission with the King has been concluded, and they are back at the garrison. You are in the basement of a derelict building about ten miles east of Paris. I will try and communicate, somehow, with Tréville and get him to you. Now close your eyes, my light is going to get brighter to warm you inside." I closed my eyes and I felt his warmth go over and inside of me and felt my blood pulsing through my body again.

"Thank you, Father."

"Someone is coming but I will be near," he said and left. The room was now a lot darker but I felt a little warmer.

The door opened, the candle was re-lit and Rochefort stood in front of me. "Glad to see you are still with us, whore," he said. "Now again, where has Tréville gone?"

I replied, "Please, I do not know." He grabbed the front of my dress and ripped it down the middle, exposing my petticoat beneath. I watched, eyes wide, as he took his dagger out, and pointed it at my throat and very slowly dragged it down towards my chest. He looked at me and sneered. "Oh, sorry Lesley, I didn't realise how sharp my dagger was – at least the cut is in a straight line." I glanced down to see he had cut me all the way down to the top of my chest, and my blood was trickling down my petticoat. "You're a stubborn whore, aren't you?" he said, seething. "I don't like asking the same question over and over, so be a good whore and tell me where Tréville went."

"I honestly do not know," I said. The dagger slashed down my right arm, I screamed.

"You know I will get the truth out of you in the end so why prolong the agony? You will answer my question. Again, where is Tréville?"

I was sobbing. "I cannot tell you what I do not know."

His dagger then slashed down my left arm, and again I screamed. Blood was pouring down both of my arms. "I will ask you one last time, whore, and if you don't give me the answer I want, this dagger will be plunged into your right hip, but then... maybe it would be better on the left... Umm... yes, let's re-open your shot wound and then when your end is near I will get you thrown into the garrison yard and Tréville can watch your last moment of life."

Rochefort made a sob sound. "Oh, forgive me Lesley, I am filling up with remorse here. You're not exactly ugly, I could actually take a liking to you, but alas, I have my mind set on someone else. Years I have wanted to get revenge on Tréville and now... well, I've got you."

I could feel his anger and his eyes were full of rage. I felt the dagger on my left hip. "Do it, Rochefort, I can take no more, my life is already ebbing away, I have lost so much blood. I cannot tell you what I do not know. Forget my hip, just plunge the dagger through my heart," I screamed at him.

"Oh, do not tempt me, whore," he replied, and he slapped me so hard, my nose started bleeding again, so bad I felt it pour down my face and down my chest. It also felt like every tooth in my mouth had shattered. "You must care more for Tréville than I thought, I will cut you everywhere if I have to, to get the truth out of you. I know you know, most men tell their whores everything, apart from me, I'm not that stupid."

I looked at him with contempt and shouted with anger, "I do not know of his whereabouts, and I am not his whore." He plunged the dagger into the wood pillar, just missing my face, and then his hands went round my throat and I felt him squeezing the life out of me. My eyes closed and I could see the Reservation.

At that moment the door creaked opened and a voice said, "Sire, a word please."

"What?" snapped Rochefort.

"We are too late. The King is back at the palace and his Musketeers have returned to the garrison. They will soon find out she is missing." I heard Rochefort take a deep breath in and then exhale, and take his hands away from my throat.

"The Cardinal is going to be most displeased. Get rid of her, but don't kill her. Take her, if you wish, maybe she might learn what a real man feels like inside her." Rochefort came to me and put his hand on my bloody cheeks and said, "Tell Tréville I did this and it will be your word against mine. I will deny everything, I was never here." He retrieved his dagger and walked out the door. It was all I could do to breathe, but I did. The stranger cut my ropes, and I fell to the floor. He pulled me back up and then re-tied my hands in front of me. I looked down and saw I was covered in blood from all my wounds. Where the ropes had been had totally ripped my skin to bits. I also noticed the stranger had removed his mask, but it was too dark for me to see his features. He then blindfolded me so tightly I could not open my eyes, and gagged me. He pushed me forward; I tripped a couple of times, and then I felt the air. I knew it was night as it was cold, and then I stumbled and fell.

He roughly turned me over and I felt his hand go inside my petticoat and roughly squeeze my breast. "Perhaps you should feel a real big man inside of you," he said. He moved his hand from my breast and started moving my skirt up. I froze for a second. *Please no, no.* I tried to get up but he pushed me back down, pressing hard on my shoulders; the pain was unbearable. He tried to move my legs apart but I fought him, my hands thumping into his chest, with what little strength I had, tears flowing down my face. He then tried to turn me back over, pushing my face and shoulders down in the dirt, but I managed to kick him, where I don't know, so he pushed me back onto my back and then punched me in the stomach. I doubled up in pain and Tala howled. He grabbed my arms and pulled me up and said, "No... bitch... kicks... me," and with every word he said he slapped me hard across my face and then kicked my ankles away so that I fell backwards onto the stony ground. It felt like tiny knives entered my back. My head went into what felt like a shrub. "Get up, you filthy bitch, you're not worth it. I like my women to be ready and willing, but I will give you something to remind you of me, my whores love it."

I was still on my back when I felt him push my skirt up quite high, and he then saw I had an undergarment on, which finished just below my knees. "Ha, you don't think these are going to stop me, do you bitch." I felt the fabric being ripped half way up my left thigh and then my leg being lifted in his hands and then he was kissing the inside of my thigh. I cringed. I then started screaming over and over, the pain that shot through my leg was immense, but as I was gagged it came out as a small shriek, and I felt like I was going to pass out. At that moment I wished death would take me. He had sunk his teeth into me on the inside of my thigh and was shaking his head side to side, like a rabid dog. I could now feel blood going down my leg. My hair had come down in the affray, he grabbed my plait (which came down below my waist) and tied it round my neck, then grabbed my arms and pulled them over my head and dragged me over the rough stony ground to where the horses were. He then picked me up and more or less threw me on a horse, yanked my legs over the saddle and put my feet into the stirrups. He re-tied my tied hands to the saddle, covered me over with something, took my horse's reins, and we rode but I didn't know where.

As my clothing was still wet, I was absolutely freezing, and the cold was seeping deeper and deeper into every part of my body. My stomach hurt and my thigh was hurting where he had bitten me, as it was rubbing against the saddle. I could feel my heartbeat getting slower and slower. As I could not see where I was going, I felt something hard hit my forehead and saw stars for a moment, and then I felt blood dripping down my face. "Mind the low branches, you stupid bitch," he said. Twice more he did that, each time branches hitting my face. Every time he laughed. My face felt like it was totally gone, and I didn't hear so well anymore. Then suddenly he stopped, and said, "You're on your own now, bitch. Pleasant memories of me now I've marked you, oh and by the way, I like the taste of your blood." He laughed and then slapped my horse's rump and the horse went galloping off.

I was falling in and out of consciousness. My head was slumped down, and then I faintly heard my father's voice. "My daughter, I'm here, I'm guiding the horse to the garrison. I am with you. Breathe, my daughter, breathe." The next thing I knew was the horse was neighing, and going round in circles like it had been frightened and was trying to rear up. I couldn't move, as I couldn't control it. I felt my feet slip out of the stirrups and if my hands had not been tied to the saddle I would have just fallen.

"Whoa, boy. Whoa." I immediately recognised the voice. I was at the garrison. "Captain!" he shouted. He brought the horse to a standstill.

"What is it, D'Artagnan? What's the matter and who's that?" I heard Tréville say.

D'Artagnan removed the covering from my body and then I heard him gasp. "What the...?"

"D'Artagnan?" said Tréville. I could feel him at my side.

"Whoever it is has been tied to the saddle, gagged and blindfolded. Her face is badly beaten and she's covered in blood and dirt. She is barely breathing. I don't recognise her."

I felt the ropes being cut and at that moment the horse moved, and I slid off the horse. "D'Artagnan, look out!" shouted Tréville. Luckily I fell onto loose straw, and moaned in agony.

I felt someone's arms go round me. "It's all right, you're safe," said D'Artagnan gently, and then he removed my blindfold and gag.

I slowly opened my eyes and looked at a blur and said very quietly, "Tréville." My head fell down again.

"D'Artagnan, who is it?" said Tréville.

D'Artagnan replied, "She asked for you, Captain."

"It's too dark here, someone bring a torch," said Tréville. I saw a dim light and then felt a hand under my chin and tip my face up. "No, no, it can't be. Oh dear God, no," said Tréville, his voice full of emotion, and then shouted, "We need help here, **now**."

D'Artagnan said, "Captain who is it?"

Tréville replied, "It's... it's Lesley."

CHAPTER 17

After the Incident

I hear D'Artagnan say, his voice full of emotion, "Captain, I'm sorry I didn't..."

Tréville replied, "It's all right, D'Artagnan. Quickly, get me something to cover Lesley, her dress is torn."

I feel a blanket going round my body. I hear men running and then Aramis say, "Gently, gently, gentlemen, she looks to be badly injured."

Tréville shouts, "Porthos, get Amanda; D'Artagnan, go and get Catherine and tell her to bring clothing and things."

I feel myself being lifted and then a bright light hits my eyes; it hurts, so I close them. I hear furniture being moved and other strange noises.

"Put the straw pallet on the large table and place her down very, very gently," said Aramis.

Tréville said, "You two, go get a bed, pallet, blankets, pillows and cloths of various sizes from the stores quickly. Athos, could you get more logs?" I couldn't see him but I hear the emotion in his voice when he said, "Oh my dear, what has been done to you?"

My whole body was in agony, and I was so – so cold.

I open my eyes slowly and through the blur I see I am in the meeting room. A huge fire is roaring, warming up the room, but not me. I faintly hear a voice speaking to me. "Lesley... Lesley, it's Tréville, can you hear me?" he said gently.

I lift my hand up slowly and he takes it. Tears sting my eyes. I say quietly, "Tréville, I'm..."

"Hush, Lesley, rest now. I have sent for Amanda and Catherine."

I put my hand up to touch his face, even though it pains me. "Can't see properly, Tréville, eyes hurt."

He takes my hand and kisses it and says, "Hush now, my dear, we are all here, you are safe now, give your eyes time."

At that moment Amanda came in the room with Porthos, and I heard her sharp intake of breath. "Oh Lesley, what...?" Her voice sounded on the brink of tears. She took my hand and quickly looked under the blanket at what injuries she could see. "Tréville, I need to get Lesley out of these wet clothes, she is very cold and getting colder by the minute and I worry we will lose her. Porthos, I need the tub from our room, **now**. Can someone please start getting the water warm?"

I was drifting with the pain. I heard Porthos, Athos and others come back and put the tub down and then the sounds of it being filled. The two men came back with what Tréville had asked for and I heard him say, "Thank you, men. Put it all over there. What you have all seen here this night, I do not want to go any further, and for reasons I'm sure you understand."

"Captain, you have our word this will go no further," one of them said and then they left. I think there were six of them that had helped me.

D'Artagnan came back with Catherine. When she saw me I heard her gasp. She had been going out of her mind with worry, as I had just disappeared. Tréville and his men were not around, she didn't know when they would be back or who to turn to, and this was the fourth evening.

There was a knock at the door and Athos went to answer it. When he returned he went to Amanda and whispered something. Amanda's hands went to her face, and she paled and looked at me with such sorrow in her eyes. Tréville said, "What is it? What's wrong?"

Athos looked at his Captain and said, "Remy tended to the horse that brought Lesley here, he has just informed me it's not one of ours. He has looked to see if there were any markings on the saddle, but none. He also said, as we all know, Lesley's horse never has a saddle. A loose horse was in the stable four days ago, everyone thought it had just got out of its stall." His voice then changed and he said with emotion, "Remy also told me there was blood all down the saddle and on the horse." Nobody spoke. I saw Tréville put his arm across his chest, the other resting on it with his head in his hand. "No, no, wasn't..." I said, but too quietly.

Amanda said, "Gentleman, I need you all to leave. Aramis, I will leave Lesley's face for you to tend to, is that all right?"

Aramis replied, "If you can just put a warm cloth over her face to remove the blood and dirt, I will then tend to her." As they went to leave, each one of them came to me and kissed my hand. D'Artagnan had tears in his eyes. I so wanted to put my hand on his face and tell him it was all right. Must have been a huge shock when he realised who I was. I knew they were all upset. I whispered to Amanda. "Lesley said you're not to worry, she's back with her brothers now." I heard them all leave and Amanda say, "Tréville, that includes you as well. Don't worry, I will look after her, I promise."

Tréville came over, took my hands in his and kissed them, and said, "Will you be able to manage getting Lesley in and out of the tub? I could help if you wrapped her in a cloth?" Amanda replied they would be fine. "I am just outside the door. You are safe now, my dear Lesley. Thank you, Amanda," and he put his hand on her shoulder and left.

I looked at Amanda and said, "How bad am I?"

"Hush, Lesley, I need to wash and examine your injuries first."

Catherine said, "Would you like me to leave, Amanda? I don't want Lesley to be embarrassed."

Amanda looked at me and I held my hand out to Catherine, who took it and I said quietly, "She can't do this without you, Catherine. Amanda needs you, it's all right." I noticed how shallow my breathing was.

When they removed the blanket, my torn dress and petticoat and ripped undergarment, they saw the full extent of my injuries. They both gasped though when they saw where I had been bitten, on the inside of my left thigh, and Amanda said, "Oh Lesley, what animal has done this to you?"

They carefully lifted me into the tub and very gently washed away the blood and dirt that totally covered me. Catherine told me to close my eyes whilst she very carefully put water over my face and then dabbed it dry. The warm water felt good, even though it was stinging me, but it did nothing to warm me up inside. I knew the only one who would warm my soul was my father, but unless I was left on my own he could not appear.

Whilst I soaked in the tub, Amanda and Catherine moved the bed as near to the fire as was safe, put the new pallet on, laid large cloths over the top, and then some pillows. When they came back to me I was trying to rub the soap hard over my breast. "Lesley, what are you doing?" said Amanda.

"Dirty... dirty," I replied. Amanda gently took the soap and told me it wasn't dirty. I was clean. "Dirty, he put his dirty hand on me," I said, tears falling down my cheeks.

Amanda and Catherine just looked at each other as they realised what I had said. "Lesley, I have to ask you a question, and I apologise for asking – did this brute touch you anywhere else?" asked Amanda.

I shook my head and replied, "No."

I heard Amanda's sigh of relief. "Lesley, do you think you could stand just for a moment whilst Catherine and I dry you?" I said I would try. They both helped me stand and then Catherine held on to me whilst Amanda dabbed me dry, being very careful of my wounds. I then painfully put my legs outside the tub, again Catherine holding me, especially when I wobbled, and Amanda finished drying me off. Whilst I was standing Amanda put ointment on my back, legs and round the top of my legs where the rope marks were, to help heal the cuts and bruises. Then between them they put a short-sleeved nightgown on me, which laced up the front, and got me onto the bed. They left the top of my nightgown at my waist, as they needed to tend to my shoulders and chest. Amanda put ointment on the cut from my throat down to my chest. Again, I was drifting in and out with the pain. Amanda had checked my hip – the shot wound had not re-opened, but a huge bruise was forming – and checked my stomach, which was really tender and bruising. There was no movement from Tala.

Amanda showed Catherine how to put the ointment on the rope wounds on my shoulders, chest, ankles and wrists. Amanda then started working on my bite wound. I winced, as it hurt so much. She apologised for the pain she was causing me, but the bite was deep and she had to make sure it was totally clean and slowly poured some alcohol on it. I screamed and nearly passed out. The door burst open and Amanda shouted, "**OUT**." I heard Tréville say they had heard me scream, was I all right? Amanda replied she would explain later. She cleaned my arms in the same way, then put ointment on and bandaged my thigh and arms. They then pulled my nightgown up and laced it so I was decent, and put blankets over me, but left my arms out. Another blanket was placed over my chest and arms, but my hands were left out. Catherine had brought quite a few nightgowns but they all had long sleeves, so she cut some of them short so when my nightgown was changed Amanda, Aramis or Tréville would be able to check and change the bandages round my arms when needed. Amanda would check everything else.

"Lesley I need Aramis to help me with your face now, is that all right?"

I replied, "It hurts... feels on fire." My eyes were clearing very slowly, but they still hurt. My hearing was better, but I was getting no warmer.

Aramis came and looked at my injured face and Amanda told him what I had said. They just looked at each other. Aramis then said, "I need to get some more supplies, I will be but a moment, and Tréville is wearing out the yard pacing up and down." As I was decent and had blankets over me, Amanda said it would be all right for them to come in, as it was a cold night.

Tréville came to my side, I was pleased to see him, but for some reason he didn't look at me, and said to Amanda, his voice shaky, "Was she... the blood on the saddle?"

Amanda replied, "No, Tréville. I'm glad to say she was spared that, the blood was from where she has been brutally bitten."

"What?" they all said together.

I sort of saw Tréville raise his eyes up and sigh in relief, and quietly say, "Thank heavens," but his face went pale at the bite news, and he said, stunned, "She was what?"

"Bitten, Tréville, she was badly bitten. I had to put alcohol on the wound to clean it, as it is deep, that's why Lesley screamed. That's not all, as you can see her face is badly injured, she was punched in the stomach and her left hip and huge bruises are forming, both her upper arms were slashed, she has been cut, not deeply, from her throat down to her chest, she has cuts and bruises down her back and legs, rope marks on her shoulders and across her chest, ankles, wrists and the top of her legs and someone had tried to strangle her – she has the marks on her neck. She was also... touched... here," and she pointed to her chest. "She is so very cold, her heart rate is getting slower and she is in shock, and I am deeply concerned for her." I could see Amanda was distressed and crying. Porthos came to her and took her in his arms, whispering something to her.

D'Artagnan, now full of rage said, "Who was it? I'll kill them!"

Athos looked at D'Artagnan and said quietly, "Calm, D'Artagnan, for Lesley's sake. When we find out who it was, we will all get our revenge for what's been done to her."

Tréville turned, again without looking or saying anything to me and said, "I really can't take this in," and went and sat at a table on his own and put his head in his hands. None of them knew what to say to him. The room was totally silent except for the crackling of the logs on the fire. At that moment I felt like I'd lost Tréville; he couldn't look at me, wouldn't speak to me.

A bit later Tréville called Catherine over. I could not hear what they were saying. Aramis had come back and was gently cleaning the wounds on my face and forehead. Whatever he was putting on my wounds, it was cooling. He touched a part of my face and I winced. "Sorry Lesley, this is going to be a bit painful, I'll be as gentle as I can."

Amanda, who was holding my hand, said, "What has Lesley ever done to anyone, to deserve this? Who would do this to her?"

I looked at her and quietly said, "It was Rochefort and then one of his men."

Everyone in the room fell silent, and in slow motion they all looked at me in absolute shock. Athos actually dropped his tumbler of wine! Tréville walked over to the fireplace. I put my hand out to him, he ignored it, glanced quickly at me, and then looked back at the fire and said, with what sounded like anger in his voice, "Lesley, what did you say?"

"It was Rochefort, wanted to know where you and the King went. I could not... could not tell him what I did not know... So he kept hurting me. He gave me to one of his men who tried to... He bit me instead. I'm sorry, I tried to fend him off..." I said, my breath labouring even more, tears again falling down my cheeks. Tréville turned and looked at me; his lips were tight, his face full of rage, and I had never seen such utter hatred in his eyes before, but I did now and he really frightened me. He went back to the table, put his hat on, sheathed his sword, clipped both muskets on his belt and went to march out of the room.

"Captain, Captain, where are you going?" said Athos.

"The palace. Rochefort has gone too far this time, I need to face him," replied Tréville brusquely.

D'Artagnan went and stood by the door, shaking his head.

Porthos said, "Captain, please don't go there, you know what you have told me, and I am taking your advice. Please, you need to calm down."

Tréville put his face as close to Porthos as he could and shouted angrily, "Don't you **dare** tell me to calm down, Porthos. I am sick to death of the way Rochefort's treated Amanda and now this." I saw he was pointing at me.

"I'm sorry," I said.

Tréville turned and snapped at me, saying nastily, "Did you say something, Lesley? Just look at the state of you, you were unmarked. Well now you look like you'll be marked for life. Everyone will stare at you and no one will want you."

Even with the pain I was enduring, his look and words made me crumble. I rolled onto my side and curled into a ball and sobbed. Amanda looked at Tréville and said furiously, "How dare you speak to and treat Lesley like that? You apologise, Captain, and you apologise now." Tréville turned his back on her and went towards the door.

"Captain, why are you being like this? It's not Lesley's fault," snapped D'Artagnan.

Angrily, Tréville replied, "Isn't it? Why the hell didn't she take an escort with her? All she had to do was ask."

Athos put a hand to Tréville's shoulder and said calmly, "Perhaps because Lesley was never told to."

"Oh, so it's all my fault now, is it? D'Artagnan, unless you want a court-martial, get out of my way," he shouted and then slammed out the door.

Athos came to my side and put his hand gently under my chin. I looked at him and he said, "Lesley, he is in turmoil, don't take his words or actions to heart. I have never seen him react like this before, and we all know you mean the world to him."

I looked at Athos and quietly said, "I wish my father would come and take me to the Reservation, I don't want to be on this earth anymore." Athos gave me a quizzical look. Amanda told him when my people died they went to the Reservation. His face paled when he realised what I had said. "Lesley, that would kill him, and us, and you are going nowhere. You are going to get well. I... we... would all miss our sister, so please no more talk about leaving us."

He looked at Aramis who said, "You need to go if you're going to catch the Captain, I will stay with Lesley."

They left and I heard their horses gallop out of the garrison. "Aramis... please... stop... him." My breath rasping, gulping for air. "It is no use... Rochefort said he will deny all knowledge... it will be my word against his... Please, Aramis, I feel a bad foreboding... Tréville must not see Rochefort this night," I said.

"Hush, Lesley, hush. Try and breathe," said Aramis.

"Aramis, go to Tréville. Catherine and I will look after Lesley," said Amanda.

"If you are sure. Amanda, you will need to put more ointment on Lesley's face, her tears have washed most of it away. Thank you, ladies," he said and left.

I slowly and painfully uncurled so Amanda could carry on gently tending to my wounded face and forehead and Catherine held my hand, trying to calm me down. "Amanda, how bad are my wounds, will they heal?"

Amanda looked at me and said, "Your face and forehead are a mess, but not as bad as we first feared. With time you will heal, your arms will have scars. The rope marks, the bruising, the cut down to your chest will go, as will... the bite. You need complete rest and I am going to suggest to Tréville you stay here for at least a week, if not longer, then if I'm not here Aramis will be, and then go back to the bakery. Your bed there I would imagine is far more comfortable than this one."

I looked at Amanda with tears in my eyes and said, "Can I go to the bakery now? It's obvious Tréville doesn't want me here... he couldn't talk to me, he can't even look at me... and when he did the hatred in his eyes frightened me so much. The way he pointed at me, I felt humiliated... I didn't ask for this and the last thing I want to be is a burden to him." My breathing was getting a lot worse. "An escort would not have helped, there were four masked men... then Rochefort. The escort probably would have been killed. Please, Amanda, let me go home... Catherine can stay with me." By now I was sobbing my heart out, gasping for breath and painfully struggling to get out of the bed.

Amanda put her arms around me and replied, "Lesley, please stay in the bed and calm. Tréville is in shock, like all of us. You know he wouldn't turn his back on you, and he thinks the world of you. Do not take what he said to your heart. Remember all the lovely times you've had together at the dwelling. Remember what Athos just said. In my heart I know Tréville loves you and I know you love him, one day you just might tell each other. Anyway, you are too badly hurt to be moved at the moment, and we need to get you warm; your heart beat is too slow, your breathing is laboured and it is worrying me." Amanda was now the third person to tell me they thought Tréville loved me, surely he would have said something. Well, not anymore, by the look and way he was with me now, he absolutely hated me for the trouble I'd caused. I would never forget the look of hatred in his eyes for me. Hopefully Tréville would stay away, and even if I was in agony, I would try and get back to the bakery, even if I had to crawl.

Later on Catherine had to go and said, "I will come and see you every day, Lesley, don't worry about the bakery. I'm sure Tréville didn't mean to upset you and he will make sure you are well looked after."

I took her hand and said, "Thank you for helping Amanda. Please, Amanda, don't let Catherine go back on her own, I fear for her. What if Rochefort or his men are watching?" Amanda went to the door and looked out and spoke to someone and Catherine left with two Musketeers.

My mind drifted to Tréville, I hoped nothing had happened between him and Rochefort. I knew he hated me now, but I didn't wish him any ill will. My body was in such agony, my eyes still hurting, but as long as I didn't move I was comfortable, but I was still so cold. Amanda sat at the side of me and took my hand. "Don't worry, Lesley, they will stop Tréville going in the palace."

"Oh Amanda, I hope so. I would hate for anything to happen to him because of me. I feel so ashamed and embarrassed."

"You have nothing to feel ashamed or embarrassed about, Lesley."

"Why did that... that thing bite me? He was like a wild animal." Tears were flowing down my cheeks. I could see the tears in Amanda's eyes, as my ordeal must have brought back her bad memory of Philip. "Oh, Amanda I'm sorry, I didn't mean..."

"Lesley I'm fine, I'm just worried about you. Now, you must get some rest, try and sleep."

I closed my eyes, and all sorts of images were going through my mind. I put my hand on my stomach. Tala had been quiet, had that brute hurt her? I tried to communicate with her, but all I got was a whimper, and then I drifted away.

I woke some time later and my eyes went wide. Rochefort was sitting at the side of me. I looked around. Where was Tréville and his men?

"Ah, there you are, I was wondering when you would wake. Tréville and his men stupidly left you unattended to go and eat. You honestly didn't think I'd finished with you, did you?" he said with venom in his voice. I couldn't speak. "Time for you to tell me where the King went, I'm sure Tréville has told you by now, and then... it's time for my revenge on Tréville... you die." Rochefort put pressure on my arms, the pain hitting me, and the blood flowing again. I didn't want to die, so I found what little inner strength I had and started fighting for my life. I felt my right fist connect with his face.

I was shouting, "No, no, I don't know, don't hurt me anymore."

His hands went round my throat and he started squeezing. I felt Tala rising and then she appeared. She lunged at Rochefort's throat and sunk her teeth in deep. Rochefort screamed in agony but he had pulled his dagger out and rammed it into Tala's heart."

"Tala no. Tala noooooo..."

Tala howled in agony and then fell silent. My body went limp, and my eyes closed. I heard my Indian tribe wailing in grief; wolves were howling in lament, my mother and father sobbing. "No, our daughter, no!" The moment Tala died, I died.

I'm floating and look at the scene below me. Tréville is cradling me in his arms and calling my name over and over, his voice full of emotion. "Lesley, no. Oh, my dear Lesley no, I never told you..."

Aramis was feeling for my pulse but there was none. Aramis looked at the Captain and shook his head.

"Sorry Captain, Lesley's gone, she is with her Great Spirit now."

D'Artagnan ran out of the room sobbing, Athos went after him. Tréville gently laid me down, and Aramis put his hand to my forehead and did the sign of the cross, at the same time kissing the cross round his neck. I had kicked the blankets off, and they saw the extent of my injuries on my ankles and shoulders. Both my arms had been bleeding badly. Tréville picked a blanket up and put it back over my body, took my face in his hands, kissed my forehead and lips, and whispered in my ear, "I love you so much, my dearest Lesley, and yet I never told you, and now I never will."

My body was turning blue. He left my arms at my side and then put another blanket over my chest and face, then went and sat at a table, and wept. Aramis said a prayer and then went and sat at a table opposite Tréville.

Athos and D'Artagnan came back, and had Amanda and Porthos with them. Amanda went to go to Tréville but Aramis put his hand out and shook his head. Porthos took Amanda in his arms as her grief flowed. The rest of them all sat there in total silence, at different tables, and then their tears and grief flowed. Athos went and got a bottle of wine but ended up throwing it against the wall instead. I had never seen grown men, Musketeers or not, break down like they did now. I never realised, until that moment, how much I had been deeply loved. Tears were flowing from my eyes. No longer would I feel Tréville's arms around me, or kiss my forehead, no more visits to the dwelling. No more telling my brothers off or cooking pies for them. No more walks and laughs with Amanda. Rochefort had won and got his revenge on Tréville. I was dead. I then realised Rochefort was nowhere to be seen, strange, yet Tala had savagely ripped his throat. At least he would not be allowed into the Reservation. I closed my eyes, and felt myself floating up and out of the room.

When I open my eyes I see I am sitting by the river on the Reservation and Swallowtail is walking towards me.

"Spirit of the Wolf, what are you doing here?" she asked with concern.

I tell her what had happened.

"It's not your time yet, you must go back."

I look at her, confused, and said with tears in my eyes, "What do you mean, 'go back'? Tala is dead, Rochefort stabbed her through her heart. She died, I died."

Swallowtail put her hand on my stomach and replied, "Tala has not died, but she is injured and in pain, and she will remain so until your father can come to you, but she will not die. Your father is away from the Reservation at the moment, but he knows what has happened, he knows I can help you."

"I don't understand, Swallowtail. If Tala has not died why am I here?"

"Come, let's go to my tipi and I will make you a calming drink and explain what I think has happened." She helped me up as I was very weak and we walked back to the tipi, where she then made me lay down on the bed. Swallowtail made me a drink of herbs, which I drank and it did calm me. "What I think has happened, Spirit of the Wolf, is this. You had a dream but a very real dream. You know you and Tala are linked by life. When you thought this Rochefort had stabbed Tala, and killed her, your spirit thought it too, and left your body to be with Tala. Does this make sense?"

I replied, "It was just a dream? Oh no, the grief I am putting Tréville, Amanda and my brothers through, they really think I've passed. Oh Swallowtail," I said with such emotion in my voice. "How do I go back?"

"It will be very painful, and your body is already in turmoil. I need to give you a mixture that will give you extra strength or you will not survive. You will need to hold my hands, you will feel strange as your spirit goes back into your body. It will happen quickly, and then I will breathe life into you. I will not leave you. One thing though, when you awake from a deep sleep, and you will sleep, you will remember none of this."

I looked at Swallowtail and said, "Nothing at all?"

"No nothing, why do you ask?"

I replied, "Tréville whispered he loves me."

"Ah, I see. Give him time, Spirit of the Wolf. The Great Spirit has put you together but that is for another day and your loyalties to each other will be tested even more before declarations are made." Swallowtail made another drink for me, which tasted bitter, and then told me to lie back down and close my eyes. "Are you ready, Spirit of the Wolf?" I nodded. Swallowtail took my hands and started chanting and suddenly I felt a rushing, my head spinning, I was spiralling down and something slam into me hard – I was back in my body.

I opened my eyes but couldn't see, it was dark, and then I remembered Tréville had covered me with a blanket. I could hardly move, how could I tell them I was there? I heard them still sobbing with grief. Reservation time was different to earth time. I had been gone less than a minute. Swallowtail was at my side and understood so she gently put my arm out from under the blanket and told me to move my fingers.

"Look... look... her arm and fingers, they're not blue anymore and they're moving," said D'Artagnan. Suddenly I heard a noise sounding like a chair crashing to the floor, and the blanket over my face was removed. I opened my eyes, blinking a couple of times as the light hit me and looked at Tréville and then closed them.

"Lesley, open your eyes, please," said Tréville who had taken my face in his hands. I opened my eyes slowly and looked into his blue eyes, and slowly lifted my hand to his face, which he took and then I closed my eyes again. My eyelids felt so heavy. I felt so drained; the pain was intense, but I did not sleep.

I felt Aramis check my pulse, but it was very, very slow and heard him say, "It's a miracle, she's back with us. Thank you, Great Spirit." I felt the relief in the room at that moment and it was immense.

I heard Porthos's voice say with worry, "Amanda, Amanda."

Athos said, "What's wrong?"

Porthos replied, "It's been too much for her, she's fainted."

Aramis told Tréville they needed to tend to my arms, so between them they took the bandages off, put new ointment on and re-bandaged them, and then put the blankets back over to try and keep me warm. I was still very cold. Aramis told Tréville he would stay with him just in case. I heard someone put more logs on the fire. Tréville asked Amanda if she was all right, she replied it was all too much to take in. Tréville then told Athos, D'Artagnan, Porthos and Amanda to go and rest, and if they were needed he would let them know. I heard footsteps moving, then D'Artagnan said, "We love her too, Captain."

Tréville replied, "I know you do. One thing before you all go and rest, I think it best if none of what happened here be mentioned to Lesley." I heard them all agree. Tréville kissed and held my hand and then I remembered Tréville had told me he loved me. My heart was full of joy.

At that moment I felt a hand on my heart and heard Swallowtail whispering, "Sleep, Spirit of the Wolf, sleep," and I drifted away into a deep, deep slumber.

CHAPTER 18

Recovery

When I woke the sun was just rising but I still felt so cold, but at least my eyes had cleared, and didn't hurt anymore. I felt Tala stir just slightly. Did something happen last night? Something told me it did but I couldn't remember. I looked around and saw Tréville asleep in a chair, at least nothing had happened to him. I wondered when I could make my escape and get back to the bakery, as the less time I was here the better. I tried to move but my body did not respond, my arms felt heavy and I moaned in pain.

Tréville woke immediately and came to my side. "I'm here, Lesley, I'm here."

I looked at him and said, "Sorry Captain, I did not mean to wake you. I am still cold, do you have another blanket please?" I noticed he had some deep scratches and a large bruise on his left cheek and wondered what had happened. He must have fought with Rochefort. I also noticed he raised his eyebrow when I called him Captain. If he went out now, I knew where the blankets were kept, and hopefully someone might keep him talking. I would try, somehow, and get out of the bed and get to the bakery. Instead of going himself, Tréville went to the door and said something to someone and came back and then put more logs on the fire to get it roaring again. There was a knock at the door and a young Musketeer came in with about four blankets; Tréville thanked him and the lad left. Looks like I will have to wait until later – perhaps when whoever was sitting with me that night fell asleep, hopefully not Tréville.

Tréville came back to me and said, "Here you go, my dear," and draped two more blankets over me, but left my hands out, and sat beside me on the bed. He tried to take my hand but I moved it away, and put it on my stomach. "How do you feel? Do you think you could eat something and drink? You need to get your strength back." Then I remembered my face and bite and turned away from him. "Lesley, what's wrong?"

"My face, it must be horrible, I know you cannot bear to look at me and I feel ashamed and embarrassed," I said.

"Lesley look at me, please," he said softly.

I turned slowly to face him and he gently took my face in his hands. I flinched and said, "Please, don't touch me." He dropped his hands and I saw the pity in his eyes. I didn't want his pity.

"Your face will heal, it's looking better already, you have no reason to feel ashamed or embarrassed. Please, Lesley, my dear, don't ever turn from me again," he said gently. "I'm always here for you." I sort of smiled but for once I was unsure of him.

At that moment Aramis came in. "And how is my favourite patient today?" he said. I noticed a look between both men and Aramis nodded. Something I should know? Tréville went to get me food and drink. Aramis came and sat at the side of me.

"What happened, Aramis?"

Aramis replied, "We caught up with the Captain just as he was about to enter the palace and talked him out of going in. Rochefort will slip up and say something, especially if the Captain does not go to him as he thinks he will. He apologised to all of us for his behaviour, but then we berated him for the way he had treated you. He went quiet and we rode back to the garrison in silence. When we arrived we were surprised to see him go to his office. Athos, Porthos, D'Artagnan and myself came to you. Porthos went to Amanda and eventually persuaded her to go to his room; she didn't want to leave you, but you were asleep. I slipped out later, after I had checked you, and went to Tréville's office. He didn't see or hear me as I went to enter the office door, and for the first time ever, in all the years I have known him, I saw the Captain sitting on his bed with tears flowing down his face. He was totally distraught. I crept back to the balcony door and re-entered making a noise. I called out to him, and as I entered his office he was stood with his back to me, obviously trying to compose himself. We talked about you and I told him you would recover, maybe left with a few scars though. I could see he was fighting to compose himself, and I had never seen such emotion in his eyes before, but the tears came. He slumped in his chair and put his head in his hands. He told me he was struggling with what he had said to you, and hoped you would accept his apology. I wasn't sure what to do so I just put my hand on his shoulder. He apologised and I told him he had nothing to apologise for.

"A little while later, after he had composed himself, he came back with me and told all of us to go and rest for the night, he would sit and be with you. You must have been having a nightmare, you started saying, 'No, no, I don't know, don't hurt me anymore. Tala no, Tala noooooo...' The Captain went to you and cradled you in his arms, talking to you quietly, but suddenly your arms came up and you were fighting him, your legs kicked the blankets off."

Aramis then gave a slight chuckle and I looked at him and said, "What did I do?"

He replied, "You gave him a fist in the face and he nearly fell off the bed, and then you... passed out in his arms. Your arms were bleeding badly so between the Captain and myself we re-did them. I said I would stay with him in case I was needed. Athos and D'Artagnan went to leave and D'Artagnan said, 'We love her too, Captain.' Tréville replied, 'I know you do.' Then Athos said, 'Well, that's two of us Lesley has given a fist in the face. Wonder when you two will get it, and believe me it hurts, wouldn't you say, Captain?' Tréville smiled and put his hand to his face, rubbing his cheek and replied, 'For someone so frail at the moment, yes, she hits hard. I don't think I would ever want to be on the end of a fist in the face when Lesley is strong again.' We all smiled at that. Some time later you were resting well so Tréville told me to go and rest, he would get word to me if there was a change in you."

I had tears in my eyes. Tréville really did care for me after all. "Oh Aramis, I must apologise to Tréville for hitting him, did I do him any damage?"

"Aaahhh... best not. He made us all promise to keep quiet about that, and no, you only hurt his pride. I wouldn't have told you but I saw the hurt in your eyes when the Captain snapped at you last night. Don't take it to heart, I know he feels very deeply for you. This must be our secret, promise." I nodded my head slowly. "I am curious about one thing though, who is Tala?"

I thought and replied, "A very close lady friend I knew at the Reservation, and heaven knows why she was in my nightmare." I didn't like lying but I had to keep Tala a secret. Aramis then gently applied new ointment to my face. When he took the bandages off my arms I gasped. They were yellow. Aramis said, "It's all right, Lesley, it is just the colour of the ointment. I need to wash this off and re-do them. At least the cuts weren't as deep as we first thought, so you didn't need my special sewing."

I tried to smile at him, and said, "Thank you, Aramis." Tréville returned. He had gone to the bakery to get some pies and a hot mint drink. He then helped Aramis wash my arms in warm water and put new ointment and bandages on.

Between Tréville and Aramis they gently helped me to sit up. Aramis held me whilst Tréville put pillows behind me, and then they wrapped a couple of blankets round my shoulders and chest to keep me warm. Aramis kissed my hand and left. Tréville sat with me and because it was still painful to lift my arms he had to feed me and held the tumbler whilst I drank my mint drink. He was such a gentle caring man. From nowhere the tears and turmoil inside of me started to flow, and Tréville went to put his arms out and then stopped. I looked at him and said, "Please." He took me in his arms very gently, so he didn't hurt me, and I sobbed uncontrollably on his shoulder. He just held me. I heard Amanda come in. Tréville turned and said something and Amanda left. I looked at Tréville and still sobbing said, "You haven't asked me what happened, why could you not look at me last night? The way you pointed at me, the hatred in your eyes, I didn't ask for this to happen to me. I suffered four agonising days with Rochefort, am I not your friend anymore, now I'm... marked?"

Tréville replied, "Oh Lesley, never think that. I care for you more than you know. I did not ask because I knew when you were ready, hopefully, you would tell me. I didn't want to upset you anymore by asking, you have suffered enough, but it might help to ease your memories, if you want to tell me. I was in turmoil and I apologise if I upset you last night, none of my actions were against you. How could they be, my dear? You did nothing wrong. I never thought Rochefort or any man would cause such injuries to a woman, or should I say lady." He smiled at me, but I could see the concern in his eyes. How could I have misjudged him so? I smiled as best as I could at him and told him everything.

Tréville just held me in his arms quietly listening to the whole incident. I could feel his anger welling up in him, but he didn't say a word. When I had finished he said, "When you are well enough the first thing we are going to do is go to the dwelling, breathe in the fresh air and relax. After that if you need to go anywhere, Paris, the dwelling, wherever, I will always accompany you, and if I can't one of your brothers will."

"Oh Tréville, I'm so sorry to cause you so much trouble, you have enough looking after Amanda."

He looked into my eyes and said, "You both mean the world to all of us. None of this is your fault, it's Rochefort's, and that's a problem that will be dealt with. Now, I can feel you getting cold, so under the blankets you go and rest," and with that he helped me to lay down, put my pillows flat and pulled the blankets around me and kissed my forehead.

As he bent over to kiss my forehead, I put my hand to his cheek and said, "Tréville, what happened to your cheek? You have quite a bruise and scratches."

He replied, "Oh that, nothing for you to worry about, my dear, now hand under the blanket." He put more logs on the fire, and then came and sat at the side of me holding my hand, under the blanket. I closed my eyes and thought of happier times with Tréville at the dwelling and drifted into slumber. When I woke Amanda was there and said she'd returned about an hour ago, but didn't want to wake me. I noticed Tréville had gone. She then re-applied the ointment to my face, as I had washed most of it away with my tears. Amanda and Aramis checked me four times a day, worried that infection might set in, but luckily it didn't. Tréville stayed with me every night. The rest of them were in and out and they did cheer me up, but it did hurt to smile or laugh.

A couple of days later there was a knock at the door. Tréville, who had been putting ointment on my face, as Aramis and Amanda were busy, went to answer it. "Monsieur Verde, what can I do for you?" I heard Monsieur Verde (the King's physician) reply he had come to see me. Tréville let him in and he came to my side.

"Good heavens, Lesley, what on earth has been done to you?"

I could see the concern in his eyes. I looked at Tréville and held my hand out to him, which he took. Tréville holding my hand made me feel safe. Tréville said, "If you don't mind me asking, Monsieur Verde, how did you know about Lesley? I ordered all my men for it not to be mentioned." Monsieur Verde told him he had been in a tavern a couple of evenings before, but on the other side of Paris. Some Red Guards were there, but one in particular was bragging about assaulting a woman who belonged to a higher up Musketeer, and how another had cut her up. He had noticed at the palace, that Amanda had seemed pre-occupied about something and he knew Rochefort had already attacked me. He went to the bakery and was told I was indisposed. He had put the scenario together. He assumed I would be at the garrison and that was why he had come to see if he could help.

Monsieur Verde looked at me and said, "Lesley, do you mind if I check your wounds, just to make sure all is well?"

I looked at Tréville and glanced down to my leg. Tréville understood and nodded to me. Tréville showed Monsieur Verde my wrists and ankles. He took the bandages off my arms and then rebandaged them. Tréville told him about my shoulders and chest. Monsieur Verde asked if I would mind him looking at those as well. That would mean unlacing my nightgown. Even Tréville had not seen that cut. I tried to put my hand up but Tréville said gently, "Would you like me to do that for you, Lesley?" I nodded. Very carefully Tréville unlaced it but only a little way, he knew I would be embarrassed. Both of them took a deep intake of breath and looked at each other; I felt tears stinging my eyes. Tréville re-laced my nightgown, tucked the blankets round me and held my hand again. Monsieur Verde said what an excellent job Amanda and he assumed Aramis had done. He was, however, concerned at how cold I was. He promised Tréville he would tell no one, but if he was needed, he would come immediately. I thanked him, he kissed my hand and Tréville walked out with him. I could see them through the window and saw Monsieur Verde's face pale. I knew Tréville was telling him about my other injuries and the bite. Tréville came back, saw I was upset, memories had come back, sat at the side of me and cradled me in his arms, talking to me softly, until I drifted off to slumber.

Every time Tréville's men came to me I knew D'Artagnan wanted to say something, so one day when he was on his own, he said, "I'm so sorry I didn't recognise you that night, Lesley."

I saw he had tears in his eyes. I put my hand to his face and said, "Hush, D'Artagnan, you have nothing to be sorry for. I was rather a mess, still am. I probably would not have recognised me. Now gently give me a hug." He did and I kissed his cheek. He might be a Musketeer, and engaged to be married to Constance, but he was a lot younger than the rest of them, I called him my baby brother.

"Ahem.... not interrupting anything am I?" said Porthos. I looked at Porthos and sort of raised my eyebrow. "The Captain needs us, D'Artagnan." I smiled at D'Artagnan and then they both left, but not before Porthos came to me, asked me if I needed anything, then kissed my hand, gave me a smile and a wink.

Tala remained quiet and I feared for her. It was not like her to not communicate with me, but then my body was still not warming up. I felt guilty being in the meeting room, so after a week Tréville and Aramis carefully carried me up to Tréville's bed in his office. He made sure I was always comfortable, had plenty to eat and drink, had his meetings elsewhere, made sure I rested. He was really strict as to how long his men stayed with me. They did cheer me up so much though. If all of them had to go to the palace, Tréville made sure one of the garrison Musketeers kept watch over me. They had been told I had been attacked, but not all the extent of my injuries. They had all been shocked and I know Tréville and my brothers had had to calm them; they wanted whoever was responsible to be strung up. Catherine came nearly every day and filled me in with regards to the bakery. Naturally Amanda and/or Aramis tended to my wounds. It was during one of those times when I asked Amanda to tell me all about her meeting with George. She relayed her story to me. I was surprised he was now a Musketeer, must talk to Tréville about that. I was so pleased everything had turned out well for her, and looked forward to meeting him.

Another bed had been brought up and was kept in the armoury. At night time Tréville would put it at the side of mine, in case I needed anything, and he would sleep holding my hand, which made me feel safe. I did notice that a couple of nights my brothers were away, but he had stayed. I never asked him if he had told the King what had happened, but he did spend a lot of time with me; he didn't go on any missions with his men, so I could only assume he had. One night when Tréville was on the balcony talking to Athos, I heard Aramis call to him. As the balcony window was slightly open I heard Aramis say, "Captain I'm worried, Lesley's wounds are healing nicely but she is not getting any warmer, her body is still cold and I'm at a loss as what to do, as is Amanda."

Tréville replied, "Do you think Monsieur Verde might have a remedy?" Aramis said he would ask him but he was away until the following day.

At that moment I felt a hand on my shoulder and turned, it was my father. "My daughter I cannot stay long, you need somehow to get Tréville to leave you for at least a very short time, I need to heal you inside, as well as Tala, she is in pain and struggling."

I heard Tréville's footsteps coming down the corridor and enter into the office. "Tréville, I know it's a bit late but I wondered if it would be possible for me to have a hot mint drink, please?" Tréville replied he didn't think the garrison kitchen had any left, I suggested the bakery. He said he didn't want to leave me, and Catherine might have retired for the night. I said I would be fine, it wasn't like he was going to be gone a long time, and I was sure Catherine would still be up. Tréville gave in, put some more logs on the fire, and went off to the bakery.

My father appeared immediately. "Well done, my daughter, now I need you to lay down and close your eyes." I did as I was told and then a bright light shone over me, I could feel the heat going deep and deeper into me, and I could hear my father chanting. I felt Tala stirring and then she communicated with me, I was so relieved. I could slowly feel the blood starting to pulse round my body and my heart rate seemed to beat faster.

"Captain, could I have a word please, maybe in private?" said D'Artagnan. Tréville suggested the meeting room.

My father took the light down to a dim light, worried it would be seen. After a little while longer my father said, "I'm sorry, my daughter, I could not get to you before, but Tréville never left you alone. I will go now. Tala is now better, and your heart rate will get better each day. Let the physician give you a remedy, it will help. Now I must go, Tréville will be here any second." With that he gave me a hug and kissed me on my cheek and was gone. Tréville walked into the office with my hot mint drink, and closed the door.

The following day Aramis came to the office and told Tréville he had seen Monsieur Verde and he had given him a remedy, and I was to take it three times a day, and this time I did. Well, I should say Tréville made sure I did! They all thought the remedy worked, but I knew different. After twelve more days I moved back to the bakery, where Catherine looked after me and Tréville came and stayed every night so Catherine could rest. The ointment worked well and within another month my wounds were healing well. Both my arms though, carried the scars, which would be a permanent reminder. Amanda told me they would fade with time. The bite mark was also healing. I felt sick every time I looked at it. Catherine gave everyone my apologies and just said I was indisposed. After the incident I only ventured as far as the garrison, or the tavern with them all. Tréville knew the time I left the bakery with their pies, and, surprisingly, escorted me most of the time, there and back.

As Tréville had suggested when I felt like travelling we went to the dwelling for a very long weekend. We rode on one horse. I was astride the horse with Tréville's arm around my waist and I snuggled my back into him, my hands holding the saddle. I still didn't like riding on a saddle – so uncomfortable. When we got to the crossroads I felt a shiver go through me, remembering this was where it had all started. I had not ridden or been here since my kidnapping. Tréville said, "It's all right Lesley, no one is around and if they are my men will deal with them," and held me tighter.

"Your men are not with us, Tréville, I would have heard or seen them," I said, looking at him.

Tréville grinned, kissed my cheek and said, "Look behind us." He turned the horse slightly and I saw my four brothers were riding behind us, but at a distance. I waved to them and they acknowledged. They left us as soon as we got to the village outskirts. When we got to the dwelling, Tréville dismounted and then helped me down. Madame Fleury was in her garden and came over. My face still had marks, as did my chest and arms, but I did not hide them. She looked at me, then Tréville and said, "Cieux, ce qui sur terre est arrivé à toi, mon ami?"

Tréville replied, with his arm round my waist, "Malheureusement, Lesley a été sérieusement agressée et j'ai pensé que l'air frais, et un repos relaxant serait bon pour elle."

Madame Fleury hugged me and said, "Yes, fresh air and a rest will be good for you. If you need me, please mon amie, come to me." I thanked her. Tréville and Madame Fleury carried on talking whilst I unlocked the dwelling. I opened the shutters and windows and let the air in and then sat down on the chair in the parlour. Suddenly I felt tired and closed my eyes.

When I awoke I was in my bedchamber, on my bed, covered with a blanket. Oh, how unladylike of me to fall asleep, I must find Tréville and apologise. He wasn't in the dwelling so I looked in the garden. There he was, jacket off, sorting the garden out.

"Tréville," I said, "I am so sorry, I did not..."

Tréville came to me and put his finger on my lips and said, "This was the idea, to make you rest. No apologies needed, my dear. I'm not having you cooking either so I suggest we go to the tavern for an early dinner, after I've had a wash, then we can sit on the bench and talk, it's such a lovely evening." I looked at Tréville and smiled to myself. What had I done to deserve such a lovely man? During my recovery from the assault I had come to rely on Tréville greatly, if nothing else, he made me feel safe, my protector.

The villagers, as usual, welcomed us with open arms, and we had a lovely evening. When we returned to the dwelling I was so tired, so Tréville kissed my forehead and I retired. That night I had a nightmare, Rochefort invaded my dreams and the next thing I knew Tréville was saying, "Lesley, Lesley, wake up, my dear." I opened my eyes and without thinking sat up and put my arms round him. He held me so gently and said, "It's all right, Lesley, and I'm here."

Suddenly I realised I was in my nightgown and blushed. "Oh Tréville, forgive me, I forgot myself for a moment."

Tréville tilted my chin up so I was looking at him and said, "If I can't hug my special lady when she needs me, then I am no gentleman. Would you like me to make you a mint drink to calm you?" I replied I would be fine and went to apologise again for waking him, but Tréville said gently, "Don't you dare apologise, if you do I won't stay here with you anymore." I looked at him, but he had a twinkle in his eyes, smiled, took my face in his hands and kissed both my cheeks, gave me a wink and went to his bedchamber.

I closed my eyes and thought about Tréville. That was twice now he had called me his "special lady" and I was sure he kissed my lips the day I was shot. I thought back to our other visits and everything that happened to me lately. He was always with me, in fact he hardly left my side, he was so gentle, loving and caring. Was my heart going to be broken? I knew I could always speak to Amanda, but maybe I could have a word with Madame Fleury, she had got to know both of us well now.

The following morning I heard a tap on my bedchamber door. "Are you awake, Lesley?"

I made sure I was decent and said, "Yes, come in Tréville." He entered and came over to me and kissed my forehead.

"I trust you slept the rest of the night well, my dear. I hope it is all right, I have just filled the tub for you to bathe, put soap and cloths out as well. Whilst you bathe I will go and get us something to eat."

I was surprised at this lovely gesture and said, "Oh thank you, Tréville, what a lovely thought, you are so kind to me."

Tréville smiled and said, "Only the best for you, my dear. I have already washed so you need not rush. I will leave you now and be back later. Do not empty the tub, I will do that," and with that he left and I heard the main door close. I went into the parlour and looked out the window to see Tréville walking towards Madame Fleury's. I looked into the room with the tub, and true enough, it was as Tréville said, and it brought a tear to my eyes. I bathed, then went back to my bedchamber and tended to my hair and dressed.

All of a sudden I could smell fresh bread. I went out into the parlour and Tréville had put fresh bread on the table with cheese and fruit. He had made both of us a mint drink and in the middle of the table was a tumbler full of water with yellow and red flowers in it. I went to him, gave him a hug and kissed his cheek and said, "Thank you." Now I knew why he had been going in the direction of Madame Fleury's. I must go and thank her.

Later in the morning I went to see Madame Fleury. I thanked her for the bread, and we talked. I told her about the incident and she was horrified. She came to me and gave me such a hug, and then she looked at me and said, "Something else is troubling you, mon amie." I looked at her and blushed. "Ah, le Capitaine," she replied. She looked at me and then said worriedly, "He hasn't tried..."

"Oh no, no, he has been a perfect gentleman," I replied and then from nowhere my whole story came tumbling out. She sat and listened patiently until I finished.

"Oh mon amie, you have never been in love before, have you? Well from what you say, you are now. Listen to your heart, it will guide you, although I think you already know you love Tréville, but you're not sure of him. I have seen the pair of you together, you are made for each other, but at the same time he is the Captain of the Musketeers and, maybe, he is a little hesitant because of his loyalty to his men and the King. Men are not good at telling us what they feel, some find it hard and try to show us in different ways. My late husband would always bring me flowers. From what you have told me the pair of you have been through some bad times, and yet, you are still with each other.

"I will be honest with you, mon amie, Tréville has spoken to me about you, only in a caring way, but the light in his eyes, when he speaks of you, tells me he cares for you deeply. When we spoke yesterday he had already decided you would do nothing but relax. He asked me if I would kindly cook some bread for you, and naturally, I agreed, and will do it each day you are here. Give him time, mon amie, just remember to invite me to the wedding." We laughed, hugged and kissed each other's cheeks and I went back to the dwelling.

Tréville was nowhere to be seen; maybe he had gone for a walk, which he liked to do. I decided to get a book and go and sit on a blanket at the back of the dwelling, under the big tree, as it was such a lovely sunny afternoon. I had only been there a short while when a voice said, "Ah, there you are my dear." I looked at Tréville and smiled.

"What have you got there?" I asked, looking at a basket.

"A picnic," he replied. He came and sat at the side of me and brought out chicken, ham, bread, fruit, cheese and a flask of wine.

"Now you are spoiling me, Tréville. I was going to cook some pies for us."

Tréville replied, "I told you no cooking, now eat and I will go and get us a couple of tumblers for the wine."

When he returned he rested his back against the tree. We ate, drank, laughed and talked, and then he put his arm around me and I put my head on his shoulder and my arm across his waist, and he held my hand with his other hand; slowly I felt my eyes close and drifted away. When I woke later, I looked at Tréville, and he too had closed his eyes and drifted off, so I just closed my eyes again.

The rest of the weekend went by quickly. We had our meals at the tavern, went for walks, had a meal with Madame Fleury. Madame Fleury told me that she had come round to the dwelling the afternoon after we had talked, and had seen the pair of us asleep under the tree, and said how contented we both looked in each other's arms.

I did have to admit the rest and the fresh air did me a power of good. Life was good again.

CHAPTER 19

Betrayal

Several weeks after Tréville and I had been to the dwelling, I was at the bakery waiting for him when there was a knock at the back door and Athos walked in. "Athos, lovely to see you, have you come to escort me to the garrison?"

"Yes I have, unfortunately the Captain has been called to the palace."

As we entered the garrison, Tréville rode out, gave me a lovely smile and a quick wave and, naturally, I smiled and waved back. Tréville had always been there for me after the incident with Rochefort. I tried to get my life back to normal. I knew I always had Amanda and Catherine, but I always seemed to break down when Tréville was with me. Memories kept resurfacing, especially at night. Tréville would take me in his arms and I would sob on his shoulder. One day I was in his office, as we had arranged to go for a picnic, and Athos said something which triggered a memory, and the tears flowed down my face. Athos came to me immediately and put his arms around me. "I don't know what I said Lesley, but I apologise," he said. All of my brothers looked after me, as they did Amanda.

"Let's all go and have a picnic," said Tréville, and with that we left the office. Tréville told his men to mount up, I rode with Tréville, and we all rode down to the river. We had a lovely picnic and my brothers had me laughing so much, the memory soon went away. Would have been ever better if Amanda had been with us.

After Athos and I entered the yard, I went and had a talk with my brothers and then went to the kitchen and gave Pascal the pies. I was explaining about making pies when Athos came in.

"Lesley, I'm sorry, we have been summoned to the palace and must leave immediately."

"That's all right, Athos, I will go back to the bakery now, I am quite busy. You need not escort me, you can see me walking back. I will talk to you another time, Pascal." Athos thanked me and I saw them all mounting their horses and when I got to the bakery I turned and waved. They put their hands up to acknowledge my wave and then rode off.

The rest of the week one of the garrison Musketeers came and collected the pies, which I thought strange, but Tréville must have his reasons. I wondered if there was trouble with Rochefort. I decided I would go to the dwelling at the weekend, so when the Musketeer arrived that morning, I walked back with him to the garrison so I could arrange to borrow a horse and an escort to accompany me. My Musketeer brothers were there and all looked a bit uncomfortable when I asked about a horse and escort. Athos looked at me, with downcast eyes and said, "I'm sorry Lesley, you will not be able to go this weekend, we have orders to... keep you here."

I looked at all of them, stunned, and said, "You have orders to what!! Where is Tréville?"

Again, they all looked at each other, D'Artagnan scuffing his boots in the straw. "He's not here, Lesley, he can't see you and that's all I can say," said Athos.

I went to go up the steps but Aramis caught my arm and said, "Honestly Lesley, the Captain is not here."

Porthos said calmly, "Let Lesley go to the Captain's office so she can see for herself."

I looked at all of them and walked off back to the bakery. Why was Tréville ignoring me? He always told me if he was away on a mission, why were my brothers being so strange with me? Then I realised what it was – it was my ordeal with Rochefort. I was right, he couldn't bear to look at me with my scars, and my brothers were covering for him. I put my hand to my face and could still feel the ones that hadn't healed yet. I looked at the scars on my arms and tears welled in my eyes. At the dwelling it must have all been an act. How could I have been so stupid!

The following weekend I wanted a rest and whether Tréville liked it or not, I was going to the dwelling. I hadn't seen him or his men at all, for nearly two weeks. I asked Pierre and Lauren if they knew where I could borrow a horse. Pierre said he knew of someone who owed him a favour. I knew I would need someone to ride with me so Pierre offered, went and got the horses and off we went. As we passed the garrison I glanced in, none of them were there. When we rode through the village, about mid-afternoon, quite a lot of the villagers gave me a strange look. Was it because Pierre was with me instead of Tréville or a Musketeer? When I arrived at the dwelling I kindly asked Pierre to come back for me the following afternoon. Pierre replied he would and rode off. I put the horse in the barn and then entered the dwelling. The first thing that hit me was the smell of a strong rose perfume. Someone had been here. I noticed things had been moved and were not where I had left them. At that moment there was a knock at the door, it was Madame Fleury. "Ah Lesley, it is you, are you all right?"

"I'm not sure, Madame Fleury, I do not wear rose perfume and yet the dwelling smells of it, do you know if someone has been here?" I asked.

"Mon amie, I think it's time you called me Helene. Leave the door open and come back with me."

I walked back to Helene's dwelling, and we sat in her parlour. She took my hands in hers and said, "Do you know anything of Tréville bringing another lady here, Lesley?"

I looked at her in absolute shock. "Tréville brought another woman to my dwelling? When?" I asked.

"Oh, mon amie, I am so sorry, I thought you must have known. Tréville rode in about twelve days ago, with a lady. They stayed here until early this morning and then left. I did see Tréville ride off and come back quite a few times, usually early morning and late evening, but the lady did not venture out at all. The villagers, like myself, were quite shocked. I went and knocked on the door but neither of them answered." Tears welled in my eyes; how could Tréville do that to me and in my dwelling? I would never forgive him, no wonder the villagers looked at me strangely. Helene gave me a hug and I broke down, my heart totally shattered by his open betrayal. Now I knew why his men had stopped me from coming the weekend before – they knew, another betrayal. I wondered if Amanda knew. Well, on my way back I was going to the palace to find out.

I left Helene's, and went back to the dwelling. I opened every window and left the door open. I went into my bedchamber but everything seemed to be in place. I grabbed the blanket and put it to my nose – no smell of perfume. I did the same with the cloth and pillows. I went to the spare bedchamber, again smelling the blanket, cloth and pillow – they all smelled of the rose perfume. Obviously, this is where they had both laid. I grabbed the blanket and cloths and tore them to bits. His betrayal was ripping me apart, tears flowing down my cheeks. I opened the door to the tub room and the rose smell hit me. It was so overpowering I felt sick. I opened the windows, unlocked the outside door to let the smell out. I started the fire, threw the pillow, cloth and blanket on it, warmed the water, and then scrubbed the tub until my fingers bled. That night I did not sleep, as I spent the time scrubbing the dwelling. I was so distraught to think Tréville had done this to me. So much for having a relaxing weekend!

Pierre came back in the afternoon. I locked up the dwelling, now without a trace of rose perfume, went to see Helene and said I would see her soon. She gave me a hug and said, "I am always here for you, mon amie. Try to let him explain and then take your action."

Yes, I could feel "a fist in the face" coming.

I was going to go to the palace on my way back, but decided not to. I went straight to the bakery so Pierre could return the horses. Then I walked to the garrison. When I got there all my so-called brothers were sitting at the outside table eating. "Lesley, how lovely to see you," said Aramis.

I glared at each of them. "Something you need to tell me, gentlemen, like your **betrayal**?" I snapped.

Aramis said quietly, "I think she knows."

I went to Aramis and said, "Knows what, Aramis? Do tell."

"Lesley have you been to the dwelling?" asked Athos.

I replied, "And what if I have, Athos, what has it got to do with you?"

"I cannot believe you went to the dwelling without an escort, Tréville will be furious," said Athos angrily, banging the table with his fist.

"Oh will he, Athos? I'm sure your Captain has got other things on his mind, like his new lady love, and how **dare** he take her to **my** dwelling? Just to ease your conscience I did have an escort, Pierre escorted me there and back. Now are you going to tell me what the hell is going on, and where is Tréville? I want an explanation **now!**" I said, raging with anger.

"He's at the palace," replied D'Artagnan, who got a thunderous look from Athos. At that moment I noticed Remy bring out an unsaddled horse and leave it by the steps. They all just looked at each other and hung their heads. Without a second thought I made my way up some of the steps, grabbed the horse, got on its back and rode out of the garrison.

I heard Athos shout, "Lesley, stop."

I rode to the palace as fast as I could. I knew I had no hold on Tréville, but to take another woman to my dwelling was unforgivable. How dare he? As I neared the palace I remembered where Tréville and I had hidden when Rochefort was there. Oh heavens, I hadn't given Rochefort a thought, I would have to be careful. I reigned the horse into the little copse, so I could look and see who was around, and then to my dismay I saw Tréville and his woman, arm in arm, walking round the gardens looking extremely at ease with each other, and then she kissed his cheek. I was just about to ride out to confront Tréville, when I heard horses galloping towards the palace. Oh what a surprise, it was his men!! They rode into the palace, dismounted and went straight to Tréville. Aramis escorted his lady away. I could see Tréville shouting and shaking his fist at them, he looked absolutely furious. He strode off and went to get his lady. The four of them re-mounted and rode out of the palace, but two going in the direction of the dwelling, the other two back towards the garrison. I waited a while longer, dismounted my horse and left it tied to a tree, in the shade. I carefully weaved my way through the gardens hoping no one from the palace would see me. Time to find Tréville.

As I rounded a corner I saw Tréville and his woman sitting on a bench and my anger got the better of me. "Captain Tréville!" I shouted at him. He could see the anger in my body as I approached them.

"Lesley, my dear, I didn't expect..." he said, surprised, as he stood up.

"No, obviously you didn't expect me and don't you dare 'my dear' me. How dare you take... **that**... to **my** dwelling? Give me the spare key now," I said angrily.

"Lesley, can I...?"

"**Key, now,**" and I held my hand out. He took the key from his pocket and placed it in my now shaking hand. "Thank you." I went to walk away but turned full of rage and said, "One other thing, Captain Tréville," and with that I hit him so hard with my "fist in the face" that he fell down on the ground and I noticed I split his lip. I also forgot I had the key in my hand and that cut his left cheek, the blood flowing down.

"Je n'ai jamais, jamais souhaitez vous voir ou tes hommes à nouveau. Je pensais qu'ils étaient mes frères, pas non plus maintenant. J'ai été assez stupide pour penser que vous soigné pour moi, surtout après Rochefort's attaque sur moi, et vous pouvez aller à l'enfer. Comprendre? Bon."

His woman went to go to him and said to me, "You've really hurt him, you stupid woman."

I turned to leave but she caught my arm and turned me round and went to slap me. I caught her arm, looked her up and down and replied angrily, "I wouldn't if I were you, and oh, what a shame, that's nothing compared to what he's done to me." I looked at Tréville who was getting to his feet, holding his elbow and said, "At least she's not... **marked**... like I am. Enjoy your life together, you deserve each other."

I started to run back to my horse, but as I did I heard Tréville shouting, "Lesley, Lesley..." When I reached my horse I was shaking with so much with anger, I needed to calm down. I found a tree stump to stand on and mounted the horse and then rode back to the bakery and asked Lauren to return the horse to the garrison. I went to my room and sobbed my heart out. I didn't want to see anyone so I stayed in my rooms for two days.

Catherine came and knocked on my door at least three times a day and I politely told her to go away and leave me in peace. My heart and my dreams were shattered. I was in utter turmoil. How much more could I take? My nightmares of Rochefort had returned. I had lost my protector and my brothers, and I hardly slept. I decided I needed to get far away from the garrison, so maybe it was time for me to go back to England. I would see my solicitor and legally put Catherine in charge of the bakery and also ask him to sell the dwelling.

Eventually I let Catherine in. "Oh Lesley, I have been so worried about you. What has happened? You look so ill. Athos has been round numerous times and today Tréville came to see you twice." I told her what had happened. "I can't believe it. Tréville wouldn't do that to you, Lesley. He was so upset at what Rochefort had done to you. Did you do that to Tréville's face?" I nodded. "Heavens, half his face is badly bruised, and, he has a very deep nasty cut."

"No more than he deserved, Catherine. I thought I meant something to him, but obviously I was wrong. It was the fact that he took her to the dwelling and lay with her there that has upset me so much. That is my dwelling, not his. I berated him as well, told him I never want to see him or his men again. I thought they were my brothers but they weren't, then I'm embarrassed to say I told him to go to hell. Anyway, I have come to a decision, but you must tell no one. I am going back to England. I will see my solicitor and sign the bakery over to you, so you can run it legally, the dwelling will be sold. I will not go back there again. I will go and stay with my friend, Liz, and when I am settled I will write to you so you know where to contact me." Catherine burst into tears and I put my arms around her.

The following morning I took the horse and cart and went to see my solicitor, Monsieur Ogier. "No, Lesley, I will not sell the dwelling," he said. "You are not selling the bakery, so why sell the dwelling? Monsieur Rennard would be heartbroken to think you let it go. I think it best you leave things as they are, you do not need to sign anything over to Catherine. I will keep an eye on both properties for you, for when you return, and return you will. You will not settle in England, you have made your life here now. Yes, you will see Tréville and his men around, but you do not have to associate with them. I could look for another bakery for you, maybe the other side of Paris, where there is no garrison. Why not just go away for some time instead? Relax and think things through."

I smiled at him and had to agree; maybe time away would do me good, but where? I thanked him and left. I went to a stable I knew well in Paris and bought a horse and saddle, tied the horse to the back of the cart, and then went to the market and bought provisions for the bakery. As I drove back, I thought about the past events. I put both horses and cart in the barn, then went to my parlour and wrote a letter to Amanda.

My dearest Amanda,

I am going away, where or for however long, I do not know, but I know I can no longer stay here. At the moment my mind is in turmoil. I will probably go back to England and stay with Liz. Monsieur Ogier, my solicitor, is going to keep an eye on the bakery and dwelling, but Catherine will be in charge of the bakery. He would not let me sell the dwelling, in case I ever decide to return. At the moment that is highly unlikely. He kindly said he would keep an eye out to see if another bakery, the other side of Paris ever came up for sale, and would let me know, once I had contacted him as to my whereabouts.

The reason I'm leaving is because of Tréville's betrayal. He took another woman to my dwelling, and they stayed together for nearly two weeks, and he lay with her, and it has ripped my heart out, and I cannot stand to see him, or his men, who were in on the betrayal. I'm sure Porthos will explain their reasons for their betrayal. I thought they were my brothers, obviously not. In my heart I believe you knew nothing, you would have told me, but even if you did I would understand your loyalty to Porthos. You are, and always will be my best friend.

Not that he will, but please Amanda, if Tréville asks you where Liz lives in England, do not tell him or anyone else. I will contact you and Catherine when the time is right. Don't worry if you don't hear from me for some months, I promise you I will keep myself safe.

I am so pleased you have Porthos and George to look after you, and I know you and Porthos will always be together.

Until, hopefully, we meet again my friend, take care of yourself.

Lesley xx

Very early the next morning, I left the letter for Amanda and one for Catherine on the kitchen table. I asked Catherine to give Amanda her letter by her hand only. I saddled the horse, attached a couple of bags to the saddle, one of which had a false bottom where I hid my extra money, and rode off down the lane. As I passed the garrison I saw Tréville stood on the balcony, he looked straight at me; tears welled in my eyes. As I arrived at the crossroads, I heard a horse galloping fast behind me. I looked around and saw a small copse of trees, and quickly dismounted my horse and led him there and stood quietly stroking the horse's nose to keep him calm. I heard the other horse stop and a voice shouted, "Lesley, Lesley, where are you? Damn it, where the hell did she go?" It was Tréville.

After a couple of minutes he turned his horse round and went back in the direction of the garrison. I was surprised to see he rode with no saddle. I got on my horse and took the right fork. I had decided to go and visit Monsieur and Madame DelaCroix on the outskirts of Chartres. I didn't rush. I had plenty of time. It took me two days to get there. I remembered the tavern I had passed before and stayed there. This time as I rode down the avenue of trees to the large gates, I could see how magnificent the castle was. The sun was shining and the water in the moat around the castle was shimmering and even had some wild ducks on it. The forest behind looked bigger than I remembered, and the trees and shrubs were all in full bloom. I hoped Monsieur and Madame DelaCroix would forgive me for my impromptu arrival as I had not written and asked their permission to visit.

I rode up to the main door, dismounted, brushed my dress down, tucked a few strands of hair behind my ears and knocked on the large door. A man opened it and said, "May I help you, Mademoiselle?" I replied I was passing by and wondered if it was possible to see Monsieur and Madame DelaCroix, I was an old friend. The man replied, "I'm very sorry, Mademoiselle, but they are away in England at the moment, and will not be back for some time."

"Oh, oh well never mind, thank you."

A voice I recognised said, "Lesley?"

"Theresa?" I replied.

"Oh how lovely to... heavens, what on earth has happened to you? You look so ill. Come in, come in." We both hugged each other. She looked at me and said, "You were just passing? I do not think so. Come, let's go to my parlour and I will make us a drink and you can tell me the real reason why you are here. Raoul, please take Lesley's horse to the stables and bring her bags in." I walked through the great hall with everything covered in large cloths, down the steps to the servants' quarters and into Theresa's parlour.

Theresa told me the DelaCroix's had gone to England for six months and still had four months to go. She asked me how my life had been and I told her most things that had happened. She was absolutely shocked at the way I'd been treated by Rochefort, and was disgusted with Tréville. "Was he the Captain who came and escorted you back when you were here?" she asked. I replied that it was. "I remember talking to him, he was very taken with you, that was obvious. I had a feeling then you two would be together, but to do this to you is inexcusable. Is that why you came here, to get away?"

I replied, "Yes it is, it was the only place I could think of, apart from going back to England. I couldn't go to the dwelling, Tréville would find me there, and it was the last place I wanted to be. Do you know of a tavern I can stay at in Chartres for a couple of weeks, Theresa?'

"You can stay here, Lesley, if you don't mind being in the servants' quarters. I can easily make a bed up for you. There is only Raoul and myself, no need for the rest of the servants to be here."

"Are you sure, Theresa? I don't want to cause you a problem."

"And how are you going to be a problem? Actually, I'm delighted you're here, we can spend time together which we could not before. Come, I'll show you to one of the rooms," she said. Between us we made the bed up; I unpacked my belongings, had a wash and went down to the kitchen for dinner.

Raoul was quite a character. He was from London, employed as the Head Butler and very English, so I talked to him about old times, and he had the pair of us laughing until we cried. When I retired for the night, I realised I had left my ointment behind, I would have to ask Theresa if there was a physician I could see in Chartres. I actually slept well that night, with no nightmare. The following morning I asked Theresa about seeing a physician and she replied, "No need, Lesley, I have an excellent ointment here. Monsieur DelaCroix had a nasty accident whilst out riding, and had deeper cuts than yours, and this worked really well." With that she gave me a jar, which I used.

During the time I was there, Theresa, sometimes Raoul, and

myself went into Chartres, or other nearby places. We would ride out into the countryside, which was beautiful, and have picnics.

I went and walked round the grounds and down to the lake, where Tréville had found me that day. Memories invaded my thoughts and I sat down and sobbed. One day I managed to walk right around the lake; it took me over three hours, due to my hip hurting, but the views at the end were magnificent and all the wildlife and birds – wonderful. I could stay in this forest forever. About twice a week, during the night, I would quietly leave the castle and then Tala and I would run, free of any danger. For once in my life I was totally relaxed and had no worries.

Raoul took me round the whole of the castle explaining everything. It certainly was a large castle. One of Theresa's friends had a celebration, and she asked us to provide all the food. I enjoyed cooking again, making the bread, pastries, pies and special cake. Before I realised it two months had passed. My face, forehead and chest marks had all healed and gone. All I was left with were the scars on my arms, but even they seemed to have faded slightly. Even the nightmares had gone. I had to decide what to do or where to go next. As much as I loved it here, I couldn't stay. When I thought about how long I had actually been away from when I first found out, apart from seeing Tréville and his men twice, it was nearly three months. I still thought about going to England, even though it would be a long trip, but I was actually missing being at the bakery, and seeing Amanda and Catherine. My thoughts never went to Tréville or his men.

A couple of days later when Theresa, Raoul and I were returning from another day out, as we approached the gates, I noticed a familiar horse. "Oh no," I said.

"Lesley, what is it?" said Theresa.

I looked at her and said, "The horse, it's a Musketeer's horse and that means it's either Tréville or one of his men, but where is he?"

Theresa looked at me and said, "Don't worry Lesley, quickly get off the cart, follow the left wall, it will lead round to a path. Follow the path and it links up with the path that takes you down to the lake, you know your way back then. There are plenty of large trees and shrubs you can hide behind, especially if it is Tréville and he has walked down to the lake. Let yourself in by the servants' kitchen door, I will keep whoever it is in the great hall. I will tell him you were here but left days ago. Now go quickly." With that, I made sure whoever it was had not come back to his horse and got off the cart. As Theresa had said I followed the wall, and then onto the path, but decided to stay off the path and went from tree to tree just in case. Good job I did as I saw Athos passing the stables. He must have heard the horse and cart arriving.

I made my way back to the kitchen door and entered. I quietly went to the top of the steps and heard Athos saying, "You're sure you have absolutely no idea where Lesley has gone? I am here on behalf of the King, who needs to see her immediately." My heart started thumping, what had happened?

Theresa gasped and said, "Oh dear, I hope nothing untoward has happened to any of Lesley's friends, she would be most distraught."

Athos replied, "As far as I know all of Lesley's friends are well. This is a personal matter."

That got my curiosity going. Raoul said, "Lesley did say something about going to England, if that helps?"

"England, are you sure?" said Athos.

Theresa replied I had mentioned it. Athos thanked them both and left. I stayed at the top of the steps until I saw Athos had ridden out of the gates. "Did you hear all that, Lesley?" asked Theresa. I nodded.

"I don't understand why the King wants to see me on a personal matter, I've done nothing wrong, apart from giving Tréville a "fist in the face", but that was between him and me."

"Maybe Athos thinks you're still here and is trying to see if you flee," said Raoul. "I think you should stay here until the end of the week, but not go out, and I will look around the castle and the grounds every day."

I replied, "I'm sorry, I did not want to bring any trouble to your door. I think it best if I leave very early in the morning, I would go tonight but only if someone was riding with me. I know these Musketeers, the last thing I want is this going back to Monsieur and Madame DelaCroix, and you both getting turned out of your positions. Theresa, do you mind if I make some bread and pies to take on my journey with me, in case I don't pass a tavern?"

"Lesley, of course you can. I will make a basket up and you can take fruit, cheese, whatever you need with you. Where will you go?"

"I have no idea, wherever the road takes me. I still have a lot of France to see. If Athos tells Tréville I'm on my way to England, they know short cuts and would get to Calais before me." I went to the kitchen and started baking, with Theresa's help. Raoul went to put the horse and cart away.

Very early the following morning, before the sun was up, I washed, dressed, had something to eat, and Theresa put everything in a food basket for me. Suddenly Raoul came to us. "Quickly, we need to hide Lesley, there are five Musketeers coming down the drive." My heart sank – it had to be Tréville and his men.

"Raoul, get Lesley's bags and basket, Lesley follow me," said Theresa. We went into the great hall, where she pressed something at the side of the huge fireplace. A panel clicked open, Raoul put my bags and food basket in there and Theresa said, "You'll be safe here, I found it one day by mistake, even the Master and Mistress don't know it exists, and I keep it clean." There was a loud banging on the door. "Quickly, in you go."

The area was small, but big enough for me not to be cramped up; the panel closed. I heard Theresa say to Raoul, "Calmly, Raoul, don't rush." I heard the swishing of her dress as she went back towards the steps. Thank heavens I had stripped the bed in the room I had stayed in and covered everything with cloths, like the rest of the servants' quarters.

"Good morning gentlemen, how can I help you? Oh, Musketeer Athos, I did not see you there, please enter," said Raoul. There was a small hole in the panel and I put my eye to it. There stood Tréville, Athos and Porthos. D'Artagnan and Aramis must be looking round the grounds. Tréville removed his hat and said, "Apologies for our early morning call, my name is Captain Tréville of the King's Musketeers. May I speak with the Master on an important matter?" My heart missed a beat when I heard his voice. Raoul replied the master was away in England.

"What is going on here, Raoul?" I heard Theresa say with authority. I saw her approach Tréville and say, "May I be of assistance? I am Madame Theresa Guillichon, Head Housekeeper and in charge of the castle whilst Monsieur and Madame DelaCroix are away. You seem familiar to me, have we met before?"

Tréville replied he had visited before to escort myself back to my bakery, after a wedding. "I understand from Athos that Lesley is or was staying with you. Myself and my men have come, hopefully, to escort her back to Paris, where the King requires an immediate audience with her."

Theresa replied, "Heavens, what on earth has Lesley done for the Captain of the King's Musketeers and his two men to ride down here to escort her back? Lesley would not harm anyone." I could see all three of them were looking round the hall.

Tréville replied, "We were actually in Chartres on the King's business and a friend of mine advised me he had seen Lesley at the market a few times. I knew she had been here before, and Lesley has been missing for quite some time now, and we are all very concerned for her welfare, and that was why I sent Athos yesterday to see if she was here. The King wishes to see Lesley on a very personal matter, and as we are her friends, it would be safer for her to ride back with us." Did he just say "concern" and "friends"? I nearly burst out from where I was and gave him another "fist in the face", but I stayed still and quiet.

Theresa replied, "As we told Musketeer Athos yesterday, Captain Tréville, Lesley was staying with us, but left a couple of days ago. She did mention going to England. She was very distressed, wounded and ill when she arrived. She told me she had been having very bad nightmares and was also desperately upset about another matter, of what she did not say, but as the weeks went by she seemed to relax, her wounds healed and her nightmares left her. Then Lesley decided it was time to go. She thanked us and left, again, in which direction I have no idea. I apologise I cannot help you more." Tréville walked towards the fireplace and asked Theresa if the painting above it was Monsieur and Madame DelaCroix. Theresa replied it was. I could make out the remains of a huge bruise on the left side of his face, and a deep cut. No wonder my hand hurt afterwards. My heart was beating so loud, I was sure he would hear it. Seeing him again made me realise how much I had missed him. His blue eyes always used to twinkle, but now they were dull and lifeless. Tréville walked round the great hall, his eyes looking everywhere. I had totally forgotten about his friend we had visited in Chartres.

I heard footsteps coming up the steps from the servants' quarters. Aramis and D'Artagnan both appeared and said, "Nothing, Captain."

Theresa turned and said, rather annoyed, "If you wanted to search the castle and grounds, Captain Tréville, I would have been agreeable. How dare you do it without my given permission?"

Tréville replied, "I apologise, Madame, I had to make sure."

"Well in that case you had better search the rest of the inside of the castle, to make sure Lesley is not here," replied Theresa curtly. "I can offer you refreshments if you require them."

Tréville replied that refreshments would not be necessary, but thanked her for the offer to search the inside of the castle. Tréville, D'Artagnan and Athos walked away to search. I think they just wanted to look around. Theresa and Raoul went back to the servants' quarters. Porthos and Aramis walked towards the fireplace. I held my breath. Suddenly Porthos started banging on the panels, and made me jump. "What are you doing, Porthos? I do not think the owner of this grand castle would be happy to see you have punched holes in these lovely panels."

Porthos said, "I had a friend who lived in a castle and it was full of secret passages and hideaways, especially round fireplaces. Anyway, I think we just missed Lesley."

"And how do you know that, my friend?" said Aramis.

"As soon as we entered I could smell Lesley's pies."

"How on earth do you know the smell of Lesley's pies?" said Aramis.

"It must be an ingredient she puts in it, no other pie smells like it," said Porthos. What I didn't see was Porthos wink at Aramis, nod his head and point towards the panel. "I just wish to God the Captain would find Lesley and tell her the truth, that he didn't betray her, and neither did we. We were only doing what the King had ordered all of us to do. He is missing her dreadfully, but the stubborn fool won't admit it though. I haven't seen him smile or laugh since the day she left, he's so brusque with everyone and was furious with himself for missing her at the crossroad. Not only that, I really miss her as well," said Aramis.

"We all really miss her, Aramis, it's not the same at the garrison without her. I'll never forget the day she came to us and accused us of betrayal, that hurt. I so much wanted to tell her the truth then. I don't understand why the King didn't summon Lesley to the palace and explain the reasons why the Condesa de Barros Hernandez had arrived in secret; Lesley wouldn't have said anything. In fact it would have been better if Lesley had been at the dwelling with her. Tréville now saying the King wants to see her on a personal matter would probably frighten the life out of her. Also the fact that Tréville told us she ranted at him in French and told him we were no longer her brothers, now that really hurt," said Porthos.

"Yes, I think Lesley and Amanda understand more French than we realise. I must say Elisabet was a very, very beautiful woman... for a French spy," said Aramis."

"Aramis," said Porthos.

"What? You know I can't resist a beautiful woman. I thoroughly enjoyed our talks in the palace gardens before she left. At least she is now safe in England where her husband cannot find her. Fancy trying to execute such a beautiful woman?" He sighed. "Mind you, I did have to chuckle at the Captain's face, Lesley really did hit him hard." They both chuckled.

Porthos replied, "I would love to have seen that, apparently she knocked him to the ground, split his lip open, cut his cheek and he still has faint bruises. Then she told him to go to hell. That was nearly three months ago now, and she hit him twice within a couple of months so he took a double blow. Athos told me Tréville had told him that the Condesa went to slap Lesley, but Lesley stopped her, hate to think what Lesley would have done to her."

Aramis replied, "Love a woman who can stand up for herself, that's our Lesley."

Porthos replied, "Amanda is really missing her, but knows in her heart she will return, and would be very surprised if she went back to England permanently. Why can't the Captain just tell Lesley he loves her? Life might go back to normal then. We all know Lesley loves him, her love for him shines out of her eyes. Why can he not see it?"

Aramis replied, "Because he is who he is and stubborn, and possibly frightened to tell her how he really feels in case he thinks she will reject him, which we know she wouldn't. By the way how did Amanda know?"

"Lesley left her a letter explaining why she left, including our so-called betrayal."

"Oh, that didn't bode well for you then, my friend?"

Porthos replied, "Let's just say activities were stopped for a while." Aramis slapped Porthos's shoulder and laughed.

I slid quietly to the floor not believing what I was hearing. Tears flowed down my face. I heard footsteps. Tréville called to Theresa. "Time to go, gentlemen, Lesley is not here." I can hear the sorrow in his voice. "Madame Guillichon, I thank you for your time in letting us search the castle and grounds, and apologise if we have inconvenienced you," said Tréville, "but if Lesley should return, please, ask her to... come home. I will mention nothing of our visit here, I would not want any misunderstanding to reach your master and mistress."

Theresa thanked him and said she would convey his message, if I returned. I heard their footsteps go out the door and then the sound of the horses galloping away. Theresa opened the panel and found me in a crumpled heap. "Oh, Lesley, what's wrong? Come, let's go to the kitchen and I will make us a mint drink. Raoul, please can you bring Lesley's bags?"

Theresa made the drink for which I was grateful, as my throat was so dry. She put her arms around me and said, "What has upset you so much?" looking worriedly at Raoul.

I told them what I heard Aramis and Porthos say to each other.

"A French spy," said Raoul. "That would explain all the secrecy, she must have been closely linked to the King."

Theresa said, "So that is why the King wants to see you, to explain why Tréville and his men acted the way they did. What are you going to do, Lesley?"

I looked at them both and said, "The only thing I can do – go back. I actually miss all of them, including Tréville."

CHAPTER 20

Leaving Chartres

A couple of days later, I said my goodbyes to Theresa and Raoul and thanked them for everything they had done, I would never forget it, and would keep in touch by letter. On my way back from Chartres, again I stayed at the same tavern. That night the heavens opened and the rain was torrential, deafening thunder and huge streaks of lightning hit the night sky. I could hear the horses whinnying from fright in the stable. In the morning as I was having something to eat and drink the tavern owner came over to me. "Which direction are you heading, Mademoiselle?" he asked. I replied I was heading to Paris. "The bridge by the crossroad has been washed away in the storm, you have two options. If you take the right fork it takes you through a very dense forest, which I would not advise. There has been talk, let's say, of men you would not like to be associated with, but the journey will only take you an extra two days, and there is a village with a tavern. The left fork, takes you through two or three small villages, but is longer and will take you about four days, and there are taverns."

I went back to my room to decide what to do. I would make my mind up at the crossroad. I thanked the tavern owner, paid my debt and went to the stable to get my horse. I put my bags on the saddle, and then rode off to the crossroad. Now I had to decide which direction to take – right or left.

I decided to take the right fork, after all it was only two days, and now I really wanted to get back home and see all my friends, including Tréville. At the castle I had totally put him out of my mind, but the minute I heard his voice, all the lovely times we had spent together came back to me. Yes, he had a lot of explaining to do, as did his men, but from what Porthos and Aramis had said he was following the King's orders. I rode for about an hour before the dense forest appeared in front of me. I felt no foreboding as I entered, but did not take it slow. I actually found the forest calming. Tall and short trees, shrubs all in bloom, different scents, birds singing, and the odd stream here and there, where I let my horse drink. I saw lots of wildlife. In fact I could have been in the castle forest at Chartres. Eventually I could see the end of the forest and was pleased I had come this way. After I had left the forest I saw the tavern and stopped.

The tavern was nearly full, which seemed strange as it was in the middle of nowhere, but the owner said he had a room. I noticed a group of men sitting at a table, playing cards. All of a sudden a shot rang out and one of the players lay dead upon the floor. I gasped. The man who had shot him raised his head and looked at me. I looked at the most handsome man I had ever seen. He had long, dark, unkept hair, a rugged face with a short beard and moustache, couple of scars on his forehead, and was about six feet tall with a strong body, but it was his dark eyes that transfixed me. My heart was beating so hard, my breath rapid and my body felt like it was fluttering and I actually felt faint. I blushed and turned away. The tavern owner asked me if I was all right, and I sort of replied what had happened shook me for a moment. He escorted me up the steps and showed me to my room, which was acceptable. I felt the dark stranger's eyes on me all the way up the steps.

"I hope you don't mind me asking but are shootings in your tavern frequent?"

He looked at me and replied, "Did you just come through the forest or are you just going to go through it?" I replied that I had come through it and was on my way to Paris. "You are a lucky lady then, those men downstairs believe they own that forest and would take someone like yourself hostage. I suggest you do not venture out of your room until you leave in the morning. I will put your horse in the stable, and bring you a meal later on. I also suggest you put that chair against the door handle." I thanked him, but I was still thinking of the dark stranger, all I wanted to do was see him again. All thoughts of Tréville left my mind. I went and lay on the bed and must have drifted into slumber. I heard a knock at my door and asked who it was. It was the tavern owner. He had brought me a meal of chicken with vegetables, bread, cheese, fruit and a small flask of wine. I thanked him and he left. Again, my thoughts wandered to the dark stranger. Who was he? Where did he come from? What was his name? Was he still downstairs? I desperately wanted to see him again. I realised I had only brought one bag up with me. I needed the other one. I remembered what the tavern owner had said, was it really that dangerous? I quietly opened my door and crept to the top of the steps and glanced down. The tavern was empty.

I walked down the steps, out of the door and into the cold night air. I quickly made my way to the stables, found my horse and saw where the saddle and bag was. Suddenly I knew I was not alone and turned slowly. The dark stranger was leant against the side of the stall with a smile across his face. "So we meet again," he said. His voice was husky and welcoming. The stable was not that well lit, so hopefully he did not see me blush.

"Monsieur," I replied.

"Where is such a pretty creature as you heading?" he asked.

"I am returning to Paris, after spending time with friends in Chartres," I replied.

"Chartres, you say, did you take the wrong turning at the crossroad, or did you know I would be here?"

I looked at him, surprised, and replied, "The floods washed away the bridge, the tavern owner advised me this was the quickest route, and as I have never met you before, Monsieur, how would I know you would be here?" He walked towards me and I froze. His eyes were drawing me in, I wanted to be in his arms with him kissing me, I wanted to be naked with him and laying with him, feeling his hands and kisses all over me. Heavens, what was wrong with me? I had never had thoughts like this before. The dark stranger was now stood in front of me, his face coming closer and closer, and then his lips were on mine. His kiss was soft and welcoming. He drew me into his arms, my arms went round him and our kisses deepened. I heard a moan in my throat. My body felt like it was on fire. I felt him unpin my hair and then he started to undo the buttons on my dress. Slowly he pushed my dress down and it fell to the ground. He then started undoing the buttons on my petticoat. My chest was rising and falling, his kisses trailing down my neck to my chest.

He was about to remove my petticoat when I heard a voice behind us say, "Get your hands off her, **now**."

I heard a pistol being cocked. The dark stranger let go of me, put his hands up and turned slowly. "Who are you? I've not seen you before. You want her first? Well you can watch, if anyone is going to break her in it's me, then you can have your turn. What do you say?"

"You have exactly one second to move away from her, and keep walking unless..."

Suddenly I came out of the trance I was in. I looked at the state of me and my hands went to my face, I grabbed my bag and dress and ran back sobbing, passing the tavern owner as I went up the steps to my room. The following morning the tavern owner asked me if I was all right. I replied I was deeply ashamed of my actions and what could have happened. He replied, "It wasn't your fault, the dark stranger cast a spell on you, which drew you to him. He has done it before, and then after he gets what he wants, he passes the woman round to his men. Good job for you, the other stranger came along. I did warn you to stay in your room."

"What are the names of these strangers, especially the one that saved me?"

He replied, "The dark stranger has no name, the other one sounded like... Tréville?"

Suddenly I heard a loud banging and opened my eyes. "Mademoiselle, the sun is just rising."

I looked around and realised I was still in bed, in my room at the tavern. The dark stranger had all been a dream!! I was so relieved, but it made me wonder what had put such wicked thoughts into my dream. Was it seeing Tréville again? I blushed deeply, and then I remembered he had come to my rescue. I washed, dressed, went down and had a meal and drink, paid my debt. I asked the tavern owner where the right and left fork went at the crossroads. He told me both of them just went through villages, with a couple of taverns, but both would be three days longer. I went to the stable, got my horse and rode to the crossroads, where the bridge was intact, and rode over it.

About midday I rode into the village and went to the dwelling. Helene saw me pass and came straight to me. "Oh, mon amie, I have been so worried about you. I even went to the bakery to see if there was any news of you. Tréville saw me and came rushing over, the look on his face when I said you had not come back, so upset."

I hugged and kissed her cheek. "I have missed you too, Helene." I saw to my horse, then made us a drink and told her where I had been and what had happened. "I now, somehow, need to get a message to the King, see him, talk to him, but all without Tréville knowing."

Helene told me to write my letter and she would be back in a couple of moments. When she returned she had a man with her. "Lesley, this is Gillius, he works at the palace as one of the King's Guards.

"Gillius, qu'il s'agit de Lesley, désireuse de voir le roi. Prenez cette lettre à lui, mais en aucun cas faut Capitaine Tréville ou ses hommes savoir à ce sujet. Comprende?"

Gillius took my hand and kissed it and in broken English replied, "Letter, King, no Tréville, understand."

"Merci Gillius," I said.

"Maintenant, allez, allez," said Helena, and with that he left us.

A couple of hours later he returned, with two guards and a spare horse. He spoke to Helene and she told me what he had said.

"The King is pleased you are back and wants to see you straight away. You must put these guard's clothes on so no one will recognise you. Gillius also said the King wondered how you knew he wanted to see you, so Gillius told the King he had told me as I was a close friend." I hadn't thought about that. I looked at the clothes and wondered why on earth the King was being so mysterious. Was this not about the Condesa? Had what I heard from Porthos and Aramis been a lie? No, they didn't know I was behind the panel. I must remember as well not to mention the Condesa. I did as he asked and dressed in the guard's clothes. The trousers and shirt were too big, so I put a belt round them, put the cape round me, pulled the hat down well over my head, making sure most of my hair was hidden but leaving the ends down so it looked about the right length for a guard.

Gillius nodded and off we rode. As we entered the palace gates, Tréville and his men were riding towards us, I put my head down until they had passed, but still glanced at Tréville. I turned back to look at them, the same time Porthos turned to look at me, and he winked! The guards took me to an entrance at the back of the palace, I was shown up some back steps and then we entered a room. Gillius told me to wait.

The door burst open and the King entered. Without thinking, I curtsied! "Well at least I know which one you are, Lesley," said the King, smiling. "The rest of you may leave us, Gillius, stay outside the door."

"Your Majesty, I understand you wanted to see me urgently, but this..." I said.

The King said, "I think it suits you, Lesley, maybe better without the hat. Come and sit with me, I think I have some explaining to do. The disguise was, hopefully, so Tréville did not recognise you. I wanted to see you first. Lesley, some of the things I have to do, as King, must be kept secret, and if I tell Tréville and his men to keep quiet, unless they want to go to the Bastille, they will keep quiet. Do I make myself clear?"

His voice was full of authority. I looked at the King, who was not now smiling and replied, "Yes your Majesty, but if I may be so bold, what does this have to do with me? I am annoyed with Tréville, not with you, Your Majesty."

The King looked at me and raised his eyebrow, and said, "Do I know it? Since you left, Tréville has been beside himself, I even thought he was going to burst into tears at one point, when I shouted at him. You have had a profound effect on my Captain." I blushed.

"I understand your actions, Tréville should not have taken the Condesa to your dwelling."

"Condesa, what Condesa?" I said, hopefully looking confused.

"Ah, you have no idea. I assume you thought Tréville took just any woman to your dwelling, so I must make amends. My distant cousin Condesa Elisabet de Barros Hernandez is French, but was married off to a Spanish Conde, as no one else would have the poor girl. Her loyalty to France has never been compromised until recently. Her husband is high up in the Spanish government and Elisabet, let's say, has a way of extracting information from people. Over two months ago she turned up here fearing for her life; she had passed a note to my emissary, who was later caught and executed. I sent for Tréville, explained the situation, asked him where I could hide her, knowing full well her husband would come here. Tréville suggested a few places but they weren't secret enough. He then, hesitantly told me of your dwelling and he had a key. It was perfect, and away from the palace, so I ordered Tréville to take her there. In Tréville's defence he did say he wanted to ask you and I said no. I sent for his men and they were told to keep quiet as well. I knew you always borrowed a horse and had an escort because of Rochefort, but I did not want you going to the dwelling. For this I apologise, I should have taken you into my confidence. Elisabet's husband came here and searched for nearly two weeks, threatening war, but he never found her. When he left I had already made arrangements for Elisabet to go to England. Tréville brought her back here the day before you turned up." The King then laughed and said, "You really must teach me how to hit someone like you did Tréville. I have never seen anyone with such a bruised face, and you knocked him over. I should charge you with affray on my Captain, but, my dear Lesley, that was the best entertainment I'd seen for weeks. I did worry when I saw Elisabet go to strike you, she was very upset, but I think I'll let Tréville tell you that story." I was curious as to what he meant.

I looked at the King and said, "I apologise, Your Majesty, I was so angry. I know Tréville and I have no connection, it was just the idea of him taking another woman to my dwelling, and breaking my trust in him, but now I understand."

The King took my hands in his and said, "You think you and Tréville have no connection? Anyone can see you're both besotted with each other, heaven forbid even I can see it in your eyes now." Again, I blushed. "Now Tréville and his men are due back here any minute, but I don't want you to confront him, I want to see the look on his face when he knows you're back and I have a plan," he said, smiling. "Gillius, enter!" he shouted. Gillius entered. "Go in there, my dear, hopefully everything you require is there. I hope the dress and other garments fit, I got Amanda to get them. Oh, and that reminds me, Amanda knew nothing of this event, and I know how much she has missed you since you've been away – how long have you been away?"

"I haven't seen Amanda for nearly three months, Your Majesty."

"Good heavens, there will be a lot of talking then," he said, and pointed to a door. Gillius opened the door for me and I entered – it was a bedchamber. There was a beautiful fireplace, chairs, and a table with a mirror, washstand, and a lovely dress lay on the bed with other garments. I quickly washed, looked at the dress and decided to do my hair differently.

I brushed my hair from just above my ears and took it back. I then plaited it and secured the bottom of the plait with a ribbon. I then brushed the rest of my hair so it fell in huge ringlets down my back, with the plait in the middle. I put the dress on which laced up the front, and blushed at how much cleavage was on show. When I'd finished I looked in the mirror and didn't recognise myself. I noticed I had lost weight, which made my figure look a lot better. I don't know why but when I looked in the mirror, a smile of satisfaction appeared on my face.

I went back out to the King, just as there was a knock at the door. Gillius went to the door, opened it, nodded and re-closed it. "Who is it?" asked the King.

"It is Captain Tréville Your Majesty, and your Musketeers."

"Lesley you look beautiful, I hardly recognised you, now if I didn't have my Queen..." he said, smiling. "I can't wait to see his face." I noticed the King's eyes went to the scars on my arms. I tried to pull the sleeves down. "Lesley, forgive me, I didn't mean to stare. I should apologise for what Rochefort did to you."

I looked at the King in shock. "Your Majesty knew of the incident?"

"Not at first. I found Tréville and Rochefort about to duel each other and stopped it. I ordered Tréville to tell me, which he did, and I told him to be with you as much as possible. I had his Musketeers if I needed them. I am pleased you are now well, but I promise you Rochefort will get his comeuppance for what he did to you. Now put your hand on mine and I will escort you out," he said, smiling and his eyes twinkling. "A carriage is waiting to take you back to your dwelling."

I curtsied and said, "Thank you, Your Majesty, it's been a pleasure to see you and talk everything out. I will have the dress cleaned and returned," and I put my hand on his.

"The dress is yours, Lesley, by way of an apology."

I thanked His Majesty.

Gillius and another guard opened the door and we walked out. Tréville and his men bowed to the King, then they looked at me in shock. I heard Tréville say, "Lesley?" Our eyes met briefly.

"Gentlemen, it is not nice to have your mouths open whilst I escort a lady to her carriage," said the King. "I will be but a moment. Come, my dear Lesley," and with that the King and I walked out of another door, with Gillius closing it behind us. The King laughed and said, "Oh, the looks on their faces, magnificent. Try not to hit Tréville too hard when he turns up, Lesley, or if you do, can you do the other side so it matches?" The pair of us laughed, the King returned to his chamber, I went to the carriage and then back to the dwelling, just as the heavens opened and the rain poured.

The night was drawing in and I didn't think Tréville would turn up, but he did. He knocked on the door and I said, "Who is it?"

"It's Tréville, may I speak with you please, Lesley?" I opened the door but did not ask him in. We just stood and looked at each other. Tréville made a move to take my hand but I put my hand out and stopped him. "I think you have some explaining to do, Captain Tréville," I said coldly.

Tréville replied, "Where would you like me to start?"

I raised my eyebrow and said, "The beginning might be a good idea, and if you're expecting an apology from me, you'll have a very long wait."

"You have nothing to apologise for, Lesley, but I do."

I replied, "I'm sorry, Captain Tréville, but I'm rather weary, maybe this conversation can be spoken about another day." I said, "Goodnight," closed the door and left him standing in the pouring rain.

The following day, I saw Helene, and asked her to thank Gillius, and then told her what had happened. "I thought I heard Tréville arrive and then leave. Are you staying or going back to the bakery?"

"I'm going back to the bakery, I will make amends with his men but Tréville can wait a little while longer," I said, smiling. We hugged each other and I rode back to the garrison. Tréville's men were sitting at the table.

"Lesley, lovely to see you back," said Athos.

I raised my eyebrow at them. "Nice to be back, and I have something to say to you all. I was so desperately upset by your betrayal, but the King has explained it all to me. I now understand why you could not tell me. I would like to think you are still my brothers?" I said, and then smiled at each of them. Porthos came and helped me off my horse and hugged me so tight he nearly broke my ribs, and then the rest of them hugged me. I got the feeling they were all pleased to have me back.

"Athos, would it be possible to stable my horse? Only I don't have enough room at the bakery, in fact I probably won't be using him that much so if you want to take him, he could join the garrison horses, if not I'll sell him."

A voice from above said, "Of course we'll take him."

I looked up and said, "Thank you Captain Tréville, he's a good horse. Well, I must be on my way, I presume pies tomorrow would be in order." They all agreed to that.

Tréville was walking down the steps. Athos took the horse, gave me a knowing look and whispered, "Interesting, looks like the horse from the Chartres castle stable." I looked at him wide-eyed, and he smiled and kissed my cheek.

"I'll accompany you back, Lesley," said Porthos. He got my bags and I put my arm in his and walked off. I turned to look at Tréville. He looked so downhearted.

"You two going to be friends again?" said Porthos. "He's like a bear with a sore head."

"Should have thought of that before he took another woman to my dwelling," I said.

"I assume you heard what Aramis and I said at the castle?"

I looked at him surprised and said, "How did you know I was at the castle that day?"

"I think I mentioned it was the smell of your pies, plus I know a dodgy panel when I bang it. Athos noticed your horse straight away, as it was different to the others. That's how we knew you were there. If you and your friends had arrived a little earlier, Athos would not have looked in the stables. Tréville knew you would not ride in the dark, hence the early arrival. Like I knew it was you on the horse yesterday, your eyes gave you away when you glanced at Tréville, and then you turned and looked."

"Why did you not tell Tréville?"

"The King had his reasons to see you, it was not up to me to interfere. I must say how beautiful you looked yesterday, and you should wear your hair down more often, the Captain was totally speechless, which is unusual for him!!." I laughed. Nothing gets past Porthos. "At least you're back now and he knows you are alive. There were times when he was convinced you had either gone to England or had been killed by Rochefort." In all the time I'd been away I hadn't given Rochefort a thought, now I was back... I opened the bakery door and Catherine came out.

"Lesley, Lesley you're back. Oh, my friend, I'm so pleased to see you," she said, hugging and kissing my cheek. I thanked Porthos and told him to tell Amanda I would see her soon.

Catherine brought me up to date with what had been happening and I told her what had happened regarding Tréville, the King and my adventure. It might only be late afternoon, but I was shattered, and my hip was hurting. I told Catherine no visitors. I was going to rest. When I woke the moon had risen, so I just went back to sleep. In the morning I felt refreshed and ready to start a new day. It was good to be back in the bakery and with my workforce. Catherine told me Tréville had called twice, whilst I was resting.

The pies were made for the garrison and I took them, but not before I did my hair as I had at the palace. If Tréville didn't like me walking with no escort, then that was his problem. I entered the garrison and said, "Good morning, my brothers."

Porthos said, "Mmmmm I can smell those pies from here, let me at them."

I smiled and said, "No, there won't be any left for anyone else," and took them into the kitchen. When I went back to them I timidly asked, "Is your Captain here?" Athos replied he was at the palace. "That's all right then," I said. I sat down with them and we talked and laughed like I'd never been away.

Later, Porthos came out of the kitchen with four pies. "Porthos, put them back," I said.

"Not a chance, and no disrespect to Catherine but they taste so much better," he said.

"Well in that case," said Aramis, and he went to the kitchen and brought the lot out, all thirty-two of them! I always baked thirty-six pies.

"Well I'm glad I was missed for something," I said.

Aramis put his arm round me and kissed my cheek and said, "Lesley, we have all missed you, and when I say all, I mean all." I raised my eyebrow at him.

At that moment Tréville rode back in. "Time for me to go," I said.

Athos put his hand on my shoulder and said, "You're going nowhere until you two have sorted your differences out. You've forgiven us, why can't you forgive the Captain?"

I looked at Tréville, and he nodded, said nothing and went to his office.

"Perhaps the Captain would like a couple of your pies," said D'Artagnan, with a questioning look. "He was obeying the King's orders, Lesley, as we all were. Yes, I understand how betrayed you felt, especially with him taking the Condesa to your dwelling, without your consent, but the future of France was at stake, it could have meant war. You must see it from his point of view. He did nothing to hurt you. When he found out you had left he was beside himself and he has been a different man, he is totally lost without you," said Athos. Tears welled in my eyes. I was lost without him too.

"Go to him, Lesley, make our lives normal again, please," said Aramis.

I stood up, taking the pies from D'Artagnan, who winked at me. Porthos gave me a wink as well. I walked up the steps, through the door then down the corridor to his office. The door was closed, which was unusual, as it was always open. I hesitated for a moment, made sure my hair was tidy, smoothed my dress down, and then knocked on the door. "Enter," said Tréville. I slowly opened the door and he had his back to me. "Put the orders on my desk and leave," he said brusquely.

"I apologise, Captain, I have brought you pies, not orders."

Tréville turned round so quickly he nearly fell over. "Lesley, I'm sorry, I thought it was a courier from the palace. Please, please take a seat," which I did.

"I thought you might like some of these before they were all eaten," I said.

"Thank you, I love your pies," he said, and took them and put them on his desk. I really didn't know what to say so I stood to leave but Tréville said, "Please Lesley, don't go." I sat back down. Tréville leaned against his desk and said, "I understand the King has told you what happened?"

"Perhaps, Captain, you would like to explain to me why you did what you did," I said, rather curtly. He more or less repeated what the King had told me.

"I'm so sorry, Lesley, I was wrong to suggest your dwelling, but once I had, I had to obey the King's orders, as did my men, who by the way, could hardly speak to me afterwards, because they thought they had lost you forever. Amanda was absolutely furious with me until I explained. I wanted to take you into my confidence but I was not allowed, and then after I'd found you had gone, all I wanted to do was find you to explain. I tried to catch up with you at the crossroads, but you'd gone." I looked at Tréville, and there was such sorrow in his eyes but other things had to be explained.

"I burnt the bedding from the spare bedchamber, you obviously got to know her quite well?" I said. The look of surprise on his face even surprised me.

"Oh no, Lesley, no, no. I can assure you nothing happened between the Condesa and myself. I didn't feel it was right for her to use your bedchamber so I asked her to use the spare bedchamber, and I slept in the parlour. I will replace whatever you had to burn. I only have eyes for one lady, and she is sitting in my office." My heart missed a beat.

He bent down and took my hands in his. "I'm so pleased you have come back, we have been through so much together. You have no idea how much I have really missed you since you left; the garrison seemed empty. I kept looking for you to turn up, but you never did. Thank heavens the King sent us to Chartres or I would never have found you. When I saw you with the King, you took my breath away. You looked absolutely beautiful. I think the world of you and I know I have no right to ask you, but please, my dear Lesley, don't leave me again." He pulled my hands and I stood up but my head was down because tears were flowing down my face. Tréville put his finger under my chin and lifted my face up and saw my tears. "My dear, dear Lesley," he said. He put his hands on my face and wiped away my tears. We looked into each other's eyes and Tréville's lips came towards mine, but he kissed my cheek instead. He took me in his arms and held me so tight. "I have missed you so, so much, mon très cher, très cher amour," he said, and gave me a couple of kisses on my neck. Those kisses took my breath away.

"Thank you for explaining and I understand you were under the King's orders. You obviously saw I was nearly slapped by the Condesa, thank heavens I didn't slap her back, I thought she was... well, never mind."

Tréville smiled and said, "You should have waited. After you had gone the Condesa demanded to know who you were and your connection to the dwelling and me. When I told her she was furious, she said she understood why you were so angry. Then to my surprise she slapped me hard, on the same cheek you hit me."

I laughed. "Oh, sorry Captain, you had a really bad day that day, didn't you? Why did you not try to get rid of the rose smell? It was so strong, you knew I would smell it as soon as I opened the door."

Tréville replied, "I went to the palace early to see what was happening. The King told me to bring the Condesa back immediately, her husband had departed, and he was sending her to England. I rode back to get her and was going to go back later on, and explain to Madame Fleury, but the King assigned my men and myself to stay at the palace. The following day you found us in the garden. Under cover of darkness the Condesa left that night with the Red Guard protecting her." Tréville put his hands up and put some of my hair back that had fallen around my shoulders and said, "I love your hair like this. I wanted to explain everything to you when we were on our own, Lesley, I never meant to hurt you so badly."

I looked at Tréville and could see sincerity in his eyes. I put my hand to his cheek and said, "I think I need to apologise for my fist in the face. Is it still painful? I saw I had split your lip and cut you deeply with the key I forgot I had in my hand, and I noticed you were holding your elbow."

Tréville looked at me, smiled and said, "If I'm honest, my dear, yes, for a couple of weeks it really did hurt. My lip is healed, the bruise and cut are nearly gone, and my elbow was fine. It was nothing more than what I deserved. I would hate to think what damage you could do if you ever got really, really angry." I smiled. I took his face in my hands and kissed his bruised cheek, and we just stood there with our arms wrapped round each other. It felt so good to be back in his arms again. "Lesley, do you think you could call me Tréville again? Captain Tréville sounds so formal."

I looked at him and said, "Of course, Tréville." He smiled, and trailed kisses down my neck. It was all I could do to breathe.

A lot later, after I had refreshed myself, and Tréville and I had talked honestly about the past events, Tréville went out to the balcony and said, "Anyone fancy a meal at the tavern, on me, or are you all full with Lesley's pies?" His men looked at him, rather surprised, and said what a good idea. "Gentlemen, would you mind if I brought someone else with us?" and held his hand out to me, which I took.

"No problem, Captain," said Athos, and they all smiled.

When I went back down the steps, Tréville went back to his office to get his jacket. Athos said, "Dare I ask, is everything all right between you two again?" I replied it was, and they all hugged me and gave me a kiss on my cheek. Athos and Tréville took an arm each as we walked to the tavern. We had a great time at the tavern, ate, laughed, and talked, like we had done many times before. Once the wine started flowing, and his men were very merry, Tréville and I left. He walked me back to the bakery, kissed me goodnight on both cheeks, and gave me such a tight hug and said he would see me in the morning.

"Tréville, I think you need this back," I said, and held the dwelling key out to him. He looked surprised but I insisted he took it. He smiled and kissed my forehead. As he went to leave I said, "Tréville, there is one other thing I need to say to you." He turned and looked worried. "I missed you too, goodnight." His smile radiated and I watched him walk back to the garrison and smiled. I was back home with Tréville and my brothers. As I went to shut the door I heard his men staggering back from the tavern.

Aramis said, "A toast to our Captain, who hasn't stopped smiling all night, and to him and our sister Lesley who are back together again."

"I'll... to... dat... drink," said Athos, slurring his words. Porthos and D'Artagnan roared laughing. I heard the clink of bottles and a huge cheer. I laughed, closed and locked the door and went to my bedchamber.

As I laid in my comfy bed I thought of everything that had happened, but as I was drifting off to slumber I suddenly remembered what Tréville had called me before he kissed my neck – "My dearest, dearest love."

CHAPTER 21

Meeting George

Days later, after I had delivered the pies to the kitchen, I went to see Tréville in his office. He told me he was about to leave for the palace, and I asked if I could go with him. I had not seen Amanda since my return. "Of course you may come with me, my dear." As we walked down the steps a Musketeer rode out of the yard fast. "Where's he going?" asked Tréville. Porthos shrugged his shoulders. "Porthos, could you kindly send someone to the bakery, just to let Catherine know Lesley is with me?" Porthos nodded his head. Tréville helped me up and I sat astride his horse, then Tréville got on and sat behind me. His arm went round my waist and he pulled me into him, and my hands held the saddle. It felt good to be back with him.

With a wink at me Porthos said, "Have a nice ride, you two." I smiled, Tréville coughed.

As we were riding along, not in any hurry, Tréville said, "May I ask you something Lesley?"

"Of course, Tréville, what is it?"

"I was wondering now we are together again, may I be allowed to accompany you to the dwelling, the next time you go?"

I turned my head and looked at him and put my hand up to his cheek and said, smiling, "I think that would be a lovely idea, Tréville. Mind you, you will have to sort the bedding out in the spare bedchamber."

He took my hand and kissed my neck, which is something he had taken to doing lately, not that I was complaining, and replied, "I will replace everything, my dear."

Since my return it was like Tréville and I had turned a corner, we were more relaxed, and we were both slowly opening our feelings for each other. Tréville was more attentive to me than he had ever been before, and my heart was falling deeper and deeper for him.

As we entered the palace gates there seem to be a lot of activity. Tréville brought his horse to a standstill to see what was happening, just as a rider rode by. Tréville asked him what was going on. The rider informed him it was something to do with Rochefort and the King. I looked at Tréville and he could see the fear in my eyes. "It's all right, Lesley, I will protect you," and with that he reined his horse down another path, which came round the back of the palace. Tréville dismounted and then helped me down. He took my hand and held me close as we entered the palace. We could hear Rochefort shouting somewhere.

"Tréville, Lesley," someone said quietly. It was Amanda. "Quickly, come this way," she said. We followed her and then entered her quarters. "Oh, my friend, it's so lovely to see you again, I have missed you so much," she said, hugging and kissing my cheek, as I did her.

"What's going on, Amanda?" said Tréville. She replied she wasn't sure, but the King was absolutely furious about something that had happened a short time ago, and had ordered Rochefort out of the palace. She had seen us ride in, from the upstairs window, and knew where Tréville would enter the palace.

"I had better go to the King and see what is happening," said Tréville. "Amanda, you and Lesley stay here and do not let anyone, and I mean anyone, into your quarters until I return." He walked round the room and closed the shutters on the windows. I looked at him curiously. "I want you both safe from prying eyes," he said. He took me in his arms and kissed my neck – every time he did it, it took my breath away. He opened the door slowly and looked out, and then said, "Lock your door. Remember, don't answer it to anyone but me. I'm sure you both have lots to talk about so I will return in a couple of hours."

Amanda looked at me, and smiling, said, "I assume you two are friends again?" I smiled radiantly and told her we were. We both had lots to tell each other and neither of us realised how much time had gone by until there was a loud banging on the door. Hours had gone by. Amanda was about to ask who was it, but I stopped her by putting my finger to my lips. I knew Tréville would call to us. We both held our breath. Again, the door was banged upon and then the handle was being tried. I glanced round her quarters and saw a tall cabinet, which had a lock on it. I looked inside and it was nearly empty. I took the key out, and pointed for her to get in, I followed, closed the cabinet door behind me, and locked us in. There were a couple of gaps for air to come in, and we could just see out. At that moment the door crashed in and three red guards entered. I could see them looking everywhere. One of them said, "Rochefort will not be pleased, he was told they would both be here, I reckon that Musketeer was lying." They left. I put my finger to my lips to tell Amanda to stay quiet.

About a minute later we heard, "Amanda, Amanda," it was Porthos's booming voice.

Again, I told Amanda to keep quiet. Then I heard Athos say, "Tréville's going to be furious, they're not here, Rochefort must have them."

At that moment I unlocked the cabinet door and Amanda ran into Porthos's arms. Athos came and put his arms round me. "Thank heavens, you are both safe," he said. "Why did you not come out when Porthos called?"

"I didn't know if Porthos had been captured and they were trying to lure Amanda out," I said. Athos smiled. At that moment Tréville arrived.

"Are you both all right?" said Tréville with a worried voice, taking me in his arms and holding me tight, kissing my forehead. We both nodded. "We have to get you both out of the palace immediately. Rochefort tried to attack the Queen, and the King, naturally, is enraged. Rochefort knows you're both here and is threatening to take one or both of you with him."

"No, no, not again please," I said, holding Tréville tighter.

"Hush, Lesley, hush. Trust me, you and Amanda will be safe. We have a plan. Here, put these cloaks round you. I have Musketeers outside who will take you both back to the garrison, which is on full alert. Lesley, if you need to rest, please make yourself comfortable in my office. I don't know when we will be back, but our loyalty is to the King and Queen at the moment," he said. "Please, Tréville, I'm frightened, what if Rochefort should see us," I said.

"Athos, return to the others, Porthos and I will catch you up. Lesley, Amanda, put your hoods up."

As we left the room, there were six Musketeers waiting outside Amanda's door. Porthos and Tréville walked Amanda and myself out to the entrance where Tréville and I had entered earlier. Tréville then took my arm and Amanda's and moved us to the side. "Stay here," he said and a couple of the Musketeers stood with us. Two other Musketeers appeared covered in long robes and hoods and took our places. I carefully looked out the window to see a carriage waiting. Tréville and Porthos hugged the two Musketeers covered with hoods, who got in the carriage. The other four mounted their horses and positioned themselves round the carriage. Tréville shouted, "Quickly, get them to the garrison." The carriage and Musketeers galloped out of the palace grounds. Tréville and Porthos came back to us. We waited about a minute and then to mine and Amanda's surprise about six red guards galloped after the carriage.

I looked at Tréville and said, "You set a trap?"

Tréville looked at me and said, "Yes, you and Amanda are precious to all of us, your safety is paramount. Now go with these two Musketeers, they know a more secretive route to get you to the garrison."

The Musketeers came back with two spare horses. "Amanda can ride with me, Tréville."

Amanda looked at me and said, smiling, "Whilst you were away I have learnt to ride."

"Oh Amanda, that's wonderful, now you and..."

"Lesley, you and Amanda can discuss this later. Now on your horses, quickly," said Tréville. Porthos kissed Amanda deeply and helped her up. Tréville gave me a tight hug, took my face in his hands, kissed my cheeks and helped me up. "You'll be safe, Lesley, the Musketeers will protect you both."

I put my hand on his cheek and said, "Be safe, all of you, please."

Tréville took my hand and kissed it. "Go quickly, and whatever you do make sure they're safe," said Tréville to the two Musketeers. As we rode off through the trees, I glanced back and was stunned to see Rochefort with another man, in a Musketeer's uniform, at one of the windows. Luckily they didn't see us, but I worried for Tréville and my brothers. We must have been about halfway back when we heard shots. The two Musketeers looked at each other.

"Ladies we need to gallop fast, will you be all right?" I saw Amanda pale. I took her reins and said, "Amanda, hold your saddle tightly, like this. Keep your head down so the branches won't hurt you. We all galloped back as fast as the horses would take us. When we arrived at the garrison it was the first time I had ever seen the garrison gates closed. Once inside the two Musketeers dismounted and helped us down. Pascal came to us and told us to go to the meeting room and he would bring food and drink for us both. The Musketeers who escorted us then returned to the palace on fresh horses, Remy took the other horses to the stables. I made sure Amanda was fine, as she seemed a bit shaken. I would have to give her galloping lessons. Amanda and I sat by the fireplace and Pascal gave us a lovely meal, and wine. There were only a couple of Musketeers eating, as the others were guarding the gates and other areas.

Amanda went over to speak to one of them about an injury he sustained, after we had finished our meal. The door opened and a Musketeer entered, he had his back to me. I kept my eyes on him as I watched him approach Amanda. I saw him put one arm round her shoulder and the other round her waist. Amanda jumped and shrieked. I moved quietly up behind the Musketeer and grabbed his pistol. I cocked the pistol and put it to his head, and said threateningly, "Take your hands off my friend now, and if you know what's good for you, with your hands above your head, very slowly turn round."

"Lesley, it's all right, put the pistol down, it's a misunderstanding," said Amanda nervously. I looked at her and raised my eyebrow. The Musketeer slowly turned to face me. I caught my breath. Oh no, he looked like the man I had seen talking to Rochefort!!

Suddenly a voice said, "Lesley, it's all right, put the pistol down." It was Aramis who had entered with D'Artagnan. I glanced at

Aramis, but kept the pistol aimed. "Lesley, let me introduce you to Amanda's brother, George. George, this is Lesley," said Aramis. This was Amanda's brother!! I lowered the pistol and Aramis took it.

"My apologies, Monsieur, I have never met you before and with the trouble at the palace..."

George smiled and said, "It's all right, I understand your worry and I'm pleased to see you defend my sister so well, if needed. So, you are Lesley, Rochefort... Interesting. Pleased to meet you at last." Why did he mention Rochefort and say "interesting"? "Who taught you to hold a pistol like that?"

I replied, "Tréville."

"He taught you well," said George.

"Good job we arrived when we did, Lesley doesn't miss her target," said D'Artagnan.

I looked at them all and George said, "I think we all need a drink."

We all went and sat at the table; Pascal brought more food and wine and slowly I got to know George. He seemed to be the total opposite of Philip, and I could see in his eyes Amanda meant a lot to him. Perhaps I had made a mistake, but I was sure I had not.

"Where are Tréville, Athos and Porthos?" I asked. Aramis told us things had calmed at the palace, the King and Queen were both well. Rochefort had talked his way out of the trouble, as usual, and said it had been a huge misunderstanding, but the King had asked him to leave the palace until tomorrow. No one knew where he was. The King asked the Captain, Athos and Porthos to stay longer until his guards had been sorted. The garrison was going to stay on full alert, and that was why they had come back, mainly to protect Amanda and myself. I asked about the other Musketeers who took our place. D'Artagnan said all were well, but the red guards were dead. Later on I was growing weary and decided to retire for the night, and asked Aramis if I could go back to the bakery. He said the Captain suggested I stay at the garrison, as it was safer than the bakery, so I asked if a note could be sent to Catherine so she would not worry when I was not there in the morning. I said my goodnights and again apologised to George and made my way up to Tréville's office.

I heard someone running up behind me and turned quickly, with my fist up.

"Whoa, it's all right Lesley, it's me," said D'Artagnan. "Tréville said you would need this," and handed me his office key.

"You frightened me, D'Artagnan."

"Sorry Lesley. If you need anything I will be in the spare room until the Captain returns."

I looked at him and said, "You'll be in the spare room, why? Are you guarding me?"

He raised his eyebrow and said, "Do you honestly think the Captain is going to leave you unguarded now he's got you back?"

I smiled, thanked him, he kissed my cheek and I went into the office. Tréville had left a note on his bed saying the cloths, pillow, blanket and nightgown were all fresh and if he returned, he would stay in the spare room. I wondered how he knew that I would be staying. All I could think of was that Tréville had ridden back to the garrison, whilst I was with Amanda, put it on full alert, discussed events with his men and sorted out various things, including his bed. I closed the windows and shutters, lit a candle, undressed, had a quick wash, put on the nightgown and got into Tréville's bed. Tréville must have put a new straw pallet on the bed, as it was lovely and comfortable. I read for a short while, and then blew the candle out.

A lot later I faintly heard the door open and there was a dim light. I turned to see who it was. "Tréville is that you?" I asked sleepily.

"Sorry Lesley, I didn't mean to wake you, but I needed some papers."

"Is everything all right?" I asked.

"Yes, everything is all right, now close your eyes and go back to sleep."

He made sure I was covered with the blanket, and then kissed my cheek. When I awoke the sun was just rising, so I washed, dressed and went to find Tréville. He was in the spare room and suggested we went onto the balcony, where food and drink had been left for us. We sat at the small table and as I was eating I saw George walking across the yard and watched him intently, totally unaware that Tréville was watching me. "Lesley my dear, what's wrong?"

"What do you know of George?"

"Why do you ask?"

"I'm sorry, Tréville, I have a feeling something is not right. Amanda is my best friend and has been through enough. I don't want her hurt again. Perhaps it's because I don't understand why he left the Red Guards so suddenly to become a Musketeer."

Tréville took my hands and explained George's story to me, including his father, who was a spy for the Musketeers, as a Red Guard. Tréville told me George was outraged at what Rochefort had been doing with Amanda and just wanted to protect her, and that was why he asked to become a Musketeer. "My dear, I can assure you I have uncovered everything about George, along with your brothers, and believe me when I say he is no threat, but to keep you happy I will keep an eye on him." That made me feel better, but in my mind something still wasn't right. Tréville then walked me back to the bakery. I told him I was thinking about going to the dwelling at the weekend and we agreed we would go together.

A couple of days later, after I'd given Pascal the pies, I thought I would go and see Tréville to see if he wanted to go to the dwelling on the Friday or Saturday. As I neared his office I could see someone was there, looking through his papers. It wasn't Tréville. I quietly made my way back to the spare room and let myself in. A couple of minutes later I saw Tréville come out of the meeting room and make his way up the steps. Luckily there were two doors into the spare room. I opened the door onto the balcony, grabbed him and pulled him into the room. "Lesley, what...?" I put my finger to his lips, he understood immediately. We waited a few seconds, and then I heard the man in his office walk past and out onto the balcony. As he passed the window he looked in, so I put my hands on Tréville's face and went to kiss his cheek, but Tréville moved and I kissed him on the lips instead, but at the same time glancing quickly at the stranger. Afterwards we both looked at each other, stunned, and I blushed, but I did notice Tréville's eyes were twinkling, and he had a smile on his face.

"My apologies, Tréville, can we go to your office?"

We had just got there when Athos appeared. "Athos, could you leave us for a moment?" said Tréville.

"Tréville, I'd like Athos to stay," I said as I closed the door.

"What's going on, Captain?" asked Athos. He replied he had no idea and looked at me. I walked over to the window, closed it and sat down on the chair.

"Tréville, please don't be annoyed with me, but are you absolutely sure you checked everything out about George?"

Athos looked at me and said, "You don't trust him, do you?"

I replied, "No."

Tréville said, "Lesley, I told you before, myself and all my men checked George out thoroughly, we know everything about him, why do you not trust him?"

I replied, "The day we went to the palace, there was only Porthos sitting at the table. Who was that Musketeer that galloped out? No one else was around. How did Rochefort know I was there? Only Amanda saw us, you said Rochefort was in a part of the palace with no windows, remember, and the trouble had only just started. Was this a trap to kidnap us? The Red Guards who broke in said something about the Musketeer lying. When we left the palace I saw a man in a Musketeer's uniform talking to Rochefort at one of the palace windows. Just now a man was looking through your papers on your desk, and when he looked through the window of the spare room, I went to kiss your cheek, but you moved and I kissed you instead.

"You kissed the Captain?' said Athos, stunned, to which I blushed again. Tréville looked at me, smiled and gave me a wink. Athos looked at the pair of us and smiled.

"I'm sorry, Tréville, that man was George. He doesn't know I recognised him as the man from the palace. I was stunned when he turned and I saw who he was when I had a pistol aimed at him, when I thought he was hurting Amanda. He knew there was only Aramis guarding Amanda as D'Artagnan was guarding me. He could have kidnapped her."

Tréville and Athos looked at each other with great concern on their faces. "Is anything missing from your desk, Captain?" Tréville had a look and frowned.

"Captain, what is it?" said Athos.

"There was an order outlining the route the King is going to take to another secret meeting – it's missing. I can't believe this, as we checked everything about him. Just now as I went to the meeting room I noticed George hanging around by the steps, and it was George that rode out of the garrison. We need to decide what to do next; if he is working for Rochefort, Lesley and Amanda are in great danger. We've let him into our lives as a friend, how could I have missed something?" said Tréville, banging his fist hard on his desk.

"Breaking your desk will not solve the problem, Captain. My main concern is, do we tell Porthos and Amanda?"

"I don't know about Porthos, but if anyone tells Amanda it's going to be me. Please, Tréville," I said as I walked towards him.

Tréville took my hand and said, "We'll do it together, my dear, when the time is right. Athos, just for the time being let Aramis and D'Artagnan know, leave Porthos in the dark. No one else must be told. The only way to find out is to set a trap, we'll discuss this later between the four of us." Athos nodded and left. Tréville and I went to the tavern for something to eat, and then he took me back to the bakery. Tréville wanted to stay at the bakery with me, but I said it would bring attention to the fact he was guarding me. He gave me one of his pistols to keep at my side, just in case.

CHAPTER 22

Sadness, Love and Laughter

At the weekend I met Tréville at the garrison and I rode the horse I had bought, but this time unsaddled. Tréville told me he would keep him at the garrison, but he would always be mine as I had bought him. I was pleased and decided to call him Sunkwa. Tréville's men made sure one way or another George was never alone. They had something planned, but over the weekend the order that went missing re-appeared on Tréville's desk. As we rode into the village, quite a lot of the villagers looked surprised. As we passed Helene's dwelling, I noticed the door was closed, which usually meant she was out. We got to the dwelling, dismounted the horses and Tréville took them to the barn. I unlocked the dwelling. Tréville came in and put the bundle he carried in the spare bedchamber – it was a pillow, cloths and blanket – and made his bed up. It was a hot day so I decided to go to the tavern to get a picnic. As I entered everyone went quiet. "What's he doing here, Lesley?" asked Patric, the tavern owner.

"I assume you mean Captain Tréville. Is there a problem?" I asked, looking at the villagers that were in the tavern.

"We know what he did to you, Lesley, it was wrong," said one of them.

"I think maybe Captain Tréville should explain what happened. I'm surprised you remembered, it was months ago."

Patric replied, "You are one of us, Lesley, we look after each other, we need to know you will be all right." I assured them I would be, but for all the villagers to attend tonight, and with that I got the picnic, a flask of wine and left.

Tréville was tending to the garden at the back of the dwelling. "Tréville, we have a problem."

Tréville looked at me and said, "The villagers?"

I nodded. "I have asked them all to attend the tavern tonight so you can explain. I hope I did the right thing?"

"Of course you did, I had a feeling this might happen. I am more than happy to tell them, but names will not be revealed."

I got a blanket and laid it under the big tree, set out the picnic, got some tumblers and we sat, ate, drank and enjoyed each other's company. Later in the evening we entered the tavern, which was full, and it went deadly quiet. Tréville took my hand and led me to the front. "Ladies and gentlemen, if I may, I believe I have some explaining to do. First of all, I have apologised to Lesley for the event that took place here. Yes, I did bring a lady to Lesley's dwelling without her consent."

"Shame on you," said someone in the crowd.

"Let him speak," said Helene forcibly. I looked at Helene and smiled.

"Just to clarify who I am for those of you who do not know me, I am Captain Tréville of the King's Musketeers. I naturally take my orders from the King, and, unfortunately, this was one order I had to obey, or go to the Bastille. Shall we say a certain lady of royalty had to be hidden quickly, and stupidly I mentioned Lesley's dwelling. As you know I brought the lady here; if she had been found at the palace, war would have been declared on France. She has now departed from France to another country. I am a soldier and my loyalty is to France. I tried to find Lesley to explain before she rode away, and for that I humbly apologise to Lesley again, but when she returned she had an audience with the King who explained everything to her. I would never bring any shame on Lesley, she is a very special lady to me, as she is to all of you." Tréville then kissed my hand, and I smiled.

The tavern remained silent for a couple of minutes and then a voice from somewhere said, "Drinks on you then, Captain?"

Tréville replied, "Of course."

Helene came up and hugged us both. "Nice to have you back, my friends," she said.

The villagers all talked to us and we ended up having a lovely evening. Patric put bread, cheese, and fruit on the tables, and a couple of the men played their musical instruments; some of the villagers started dancing. By the time we returned to the dwelling I was shattered. Tréville gave me a tight hug and kissed my cheeks and I retired to my bedchamber. After that evening the event was never mentioned again and Tréville was always welcomed at the village. We enjoyed the rest of the weekend together, just as it had always been before.

Tréville left me at the bakery and took my horse to the garrison. Much to my surprise Amanda was waiting for me. "Amanda, how lovely... What's wrong, why are you so upset?"

Amanda told me she was in turmoil over George. She had been at the palace when she accidentally came upon Rochefort and George. She hid behind a pillar and told me she saw George hand Rochefort a parchment. He told Rochefort it was the secret route the King was going to take. Rochefort was delighted and then they walked off together.

"We need to see Tréville now," I said, and with that we both walked to the garrison and went to his office.

Tréville looked at me and said smiling, "Missing me already, my dear?"

I smiled at him and replied, "Of course." Amanda just looked at the pair of us. "Seriously, Tréville, Amanda has something to tell you."

Amanda relayed to Tréville what she had told me. He went to the window and called for his men to come up.

"Captain?" said Athos.

I looked at Amanda, who went to Porthos and held him. "It has to do with George," I said. "Porthos, Amanda, I'm sorry but I have been keeping something from you," and I relayed what I had seen.

Suddenly Porthos changed – he was absolutely furious. He grabbed my arms so tight and started shaking me roughly, and said with hatred in his voice, "Why are you doing this to Amanda? I thought she was your best friend – are you so jealous that she's got a brother and you haven't?"

"Porthos, please stop, you're hurting me," I pleaded.

"**Porthos!**" shouted Tréville. "Let Lesley go **now**, we all knew about it. Amanda, you need to tell him what you saw and heard."

Porthos pushed me away so hard I fell backwards, hitting my left arm and hip on the edge of the desk and I screamed in pain. Athos moved towards me but it was Tréville who got to me first. **"Lesley!"** said Tréville, catching me just before my head hit the stone floor. "**Get out, all of you, get out of my office now... I said... GET OUT!**" roared Tréville as he gently picked me up and put me on his bed. The whole garrison must have heard him. Porthos was beside himself, he didn't want to go, but Amanda and Aramis persuaded him, and they all left.

"Lesley, you're bleeding. Stay still whilst I see to it." I had a long cut down my left arm in exactly the same place of my scar from Rochefort. Tréville washed, cleaned, put ointment on, and then bandaged my arm. "You look pale, you hit your hip. Are you all right?"

"Tréville, I'm fine. Please get them back, we must sort this out. I'm sure Porthos didn't mean it. I can understand why he's upset, we should have told him."

Tréville held me in his arms and then said, "I agree, it must be sorted. Are you sure you're all right?"

I didn't dare tell him the pain in my hip was agonising and had gone down my leg, across my back and up to my shoulders, and my neck was hurting. I would see Amanda later. I said I was fine. There was a knock on the door and Tréville said, "Enter." It was Athos.

"Captain, we are all very concerned about Lesley, especially Porthos. I have explained everything to him again and Amanda has told us what she saw and heard." Athos looked at me and said, "Lesley are you all right?" I looked at Athos, and he was a blur. I faintly heard Tréville say, "Lesley what's...?" Suddenly everything went black.

When I opened my eyes Monsieur Verde was there with Tréville. "Lesley, do you know where you are, and who we are?" asked Monsieur Verde. I replied I did. "Tréville, could you kindly leave us please? I need to examine Lesley." Tréville kissed my hand and left, he looked so concerned.

Luckily I had an undergarment on, as I had been riding, so I unzipped my skirt, and gasped. I was covered in blood. "May I?" asked Monsieur Verde. I nodded. He gently pulled my petticoat up and pushed my undergarment down, just a little way, so he had access to the wound. It was a long deep gash just below my left hipbone and would need stitching. He warmed some water, washed the area, and then poured alcohol on it. I passed out. When I came round he had just finished the last stitch. He gave me some ointment for my cut and bruised arms and scar, and medicine to take, then asked me if I had pain anywhere else. I told him my neck was hurting. He called Tréville and between them they gently sat me up with pillows behind my back. He examined my neck, said all seemed fine, but I'd to make no sudden movements. He said it was hurting due to being shaken so hard; the pain and shock had made be pass out. He also suggested I stayed in bed and not put any weight on my leg for at least three days, when he would see me again.

Tréville said he would make sure I followed his orders, as I was staying where I was. He went and got me a fresh nightgown, which I put on when he went to the meeting room to see his men and Amanda. I struggled to undress but did it; the scar looked awful, and the bruise was spreading all over my hip. I unpinned my hair and left it in a long plait. I couldn't understand why I had got such a bad injury, but when the sun shone on Tréville's desk I could see there was metal on the edges. All of a sudden I heard, **"For God's sake, Porthos, what got into you? You could have killed Lesley."** When Tréville roared – he roared. I must have drifted off as when I opened my eyes Porthos was sitting at the side of me, holding my hand, tears rolling down his face. Tréville was sitting at his desk, and Amanda on a chair, both looking extremely concerned.

"Lesley, I am so sorry, I wouldn't hurt you for the world. You're my sister, now look what I've done to you," he said.

I put my hands to his face and wiped his tears away. "Porthos, it was wrong of me to keep what I had seen from you and Amanda, but

I knew you would probably tackle George. We needed signs of his betrayal, and now Amanda has that. I will be up and around in a couple of days, and then look out, you just might get a fist in the face." We both laughed and hugged each other, and I kissed his cheek. Amanda came over and hugged me and I said, "I'm so sorry about George, are you all right?" She replied she was shocked, but she had Porthos, Tréville and her brothers and me to look after her, and that was all she needed. I hugged her so tightly, and my heart went out to her. How many more times would her heart be broken?

Tréville said, "I think Lesley needs to rest now," and with that Porthos and Amanda left. Amanda took my dress and other belongings to be cleaned.

"I'm sorry, Tréville, to take your bed, I can sleep in the spare room and then your office is free."

"You'll stay exactly where you are, and that's an order," he said, but he was smiling. "I'm getting used to you being in my bed." I blushed slightly. He came and sat at the side of me and took me in his arms, kissed my forehead, whilst placing some long strands of my hair behind my ears. His eyes showed the deep concern in them. "Can I get you something to eat, drink?" I replied that would be nice.

The next thing I knew it was dark and someone was holding my hand. I went to move, but pain shot through me and I moaned. A voice said, "Are you all right, Lesley?"

I realised it was Tréville, and said, "I wondered where I was for a minute. I have some pain, but I will be all right." He helped me to lie down, made sure I was comfortable and the blanket was wrapped round me. "Tréville, please go and lay down in the spare room, if I need you I will call out."

"Not a chance, my dear, I'm staying right here. I still have the spare bed in the armoury room. I will bring that in here and sleep on it. Now close your eyes and sleep." He kissed my cheek and I closed my eyes.

I stayed in bed for three days. Amanda brought my dress and garments back. Monsieur Verde came back, said everything was healing nicely, took the bandage off my arm which just looked like a red line, and helped me get up. I still had pain, but I could walk very slowly again. Tréville, however, would not let me walk up or down the steps, so he carried me up and down to the meeting room, so I could eat – any excuse to hold me close. Tréville insisted I go to the dwelling for as long as was needed to get better, which I did. He could not stay but I had Helene, and the villagers. Within two weeks, and with Swallowtail healing me, I was ready to return.

When Tréville returned to bring me back, the hugs and kisses I got made me think he had missed me. I prepared a picnic, which we ate in the back garden. Afterwards Tréville took my hands in his. "Lesley, I am afraid I have some bad news to tell you with regards to George. He was killed trying to protect Amanda, by a Red Guard."

I paled and said, "Oh no, what happened? Is Amanda all right?"

Tréville replied, "I thought it would be a good idea to change Amanda's routes, but this day George grabbed Amanda and told her to leave France, to get away from Rochefort. Suddenly two Red Guards appeared, as did Remy and Rousseau, and a sword fight broke out. Remy and Rousseau thought they had killed the guards, but one of them was alive long enough to throw his dagger, which hit George in the chest. Porthos, Aramis and myself came upon the scene, and George told us that he did take the King's route from my office, but had given Rochefort a fake one leading them in the reverse direction. Rochefort had forced him to do it, by saying he would kidnap Amanda and take her to Spain, where he would wed her. He also left a copy of the fake route in my office, explaining what it was. Aramis and Amanda did all they could, but he died where he fell."

Tears fell from my eyes. "Oh, Tréville, this is all my fault, if I had not said anything George would still be alive. Amanda will never, ever, forgive me."

Tréville took me in his arms and said, "Dry your tears, my dear. None of it was your fault. You must not repeat this to anyone, but when I told the King, he told me George was a Red Guard and was working with Rochefort. They had done many missions together. The trouble was when George met Amanda he wanted to protect her at all costs from Rochefort; he loved his sister very much, but Rochefort had the lever he needed. As soon as George went against Rochefort, he would have been killed." Tréville took my face in his hands and kissed my cheeks and said, "Now if you're ready, I know four Musketeers and a certain lady who are eagerly waiting for you at the garrison."

Tréville had only brought one horse, so I locked up the dwelling, said my goodbyes to Helene and we rode back together. Tréville held me so tight and I was lucky enough to get kisses on my neck.

When we entered the garrison I saw Sunkwa was being taken out for exercise, and I patted him as he passed us. The first one of my brothers to come to me was Porthos. He helped me down, hugged me and kissed my cheek. "Lesley, are you all right?" I told him I was a lot better. "But you're sure, Lesley, if you need me to do..."

"Porthos, my brother, I am better and if you don't behave, I won't be responsible for my right fist."

Porthos laughed and then said, "If you don't mind me asking, I'm curious, what does Sunkwa mean?"

I replied, "Thunder Horse."

Porthos looked and said, "Why Thunder Horse?"

I grinned and said mischievously, "Well I could hardly call him Tréville, could I? Imagine your comments every time I said, 'I'm going to ride Tréville today.'"

Porthos and the rest of them roared with laughter and Aramis said, "Lesley's back."

I looked at Tréville and smiled – he had gone absolutely crimson! The rest of them all hugged and kissed my cheek. I took Amanda in my arms and hugged her and said how sorry I was about George, and we went off to Porthos's room so I could share her grief.

A couple of months later, after Tréville and I returned from a very long weekend at the dwelling, we rode into the garrison to see lots of Musketeers around, drinking, laughing, staggering. Tréville did not look happy. He helped me down from my horse and was looking around. "Athos," he shouted, "what the hell is going on?"

Athos strode over and said, "It's all right, Captain, it's good news, Amanda and Porthos have announced they're going to be wed."

"What?" we both said together.

Amanda and Porthos made their way over to us and I hugged and kissed them both. I was so happy for them. Tréville hugged and kissed Amanda, hugged and shook hands with Porthos, and then took him to one side. What he said I couldn't hear, but they both laughed and hugged again. Amanda and Porthos had already decided that they didn't want to wait and were going to sort the church and everything else straight away. Naturally I said I would do the wedding feast.

"Tréville, may I have a private word with you please?" I asked. We went up the steps, stopped on the balcony and looked down at everyone and then went to his office, and a short while later we joined in the celebrations, and what celebrations they were!

Four weeks later the day of Amanda and Porthos's wedding arrived, and it was a glorious sunny day. I stayed at the palace the night before, after the King and Queen had invited me. As I went to Amanda's room, the maid arrived at the same time with some food for her. I knocked on the door and Amanda said, "Come in." I looked at Amanda and she seemed sad. I asked her if all was well. She replied she was happy, but sad. I asked her why. She replied she was upset her father was not there to give her away, and now she had no one to do it. *Hmmmm.* I had a thought. I left Amanda to go and get ready and luckily bumped into Athos. I told him about Amanda's dilemma and he said to leave it with him. I washed, did my hair, dressed and then went to see if Amanda was ready.

As I entered into the corridor the King and Queen appeared. "Your Majesties," I said as I curtsied.

"Lesley, you look lovely," said the Queen. I thanked them and knocked on Amanda's door. The door opened and we all walked in. Amanda looked absolutely stunning, and her dress was gorgeous. She had not told me what her dress was like, but gave me an idea of what to wear.

It was made with the most delicate silver damask with a rounded neckline that rested on her shoulders, with the softest lace around its edge. The puff sleeves reaching the elbows in the same damask material and white lace was attached to this. The dress was covered in small pink and silver stones, which sparkled with the light as Amanda moved around. The V-shaped bodice was covered in pink stones only, and had the fleur-de-lis symbol of the Musketeers. It had a fitted waist with an overskirt attached, which gathered at each side, held in place with silver and pink stoned bows, which then fell into a long train. The Queen asked her where it had come from. Amanda told us it was her mother's wedding dress. She had left her hair down and wore a beautiful necklace and matching earrings, also her mother's. The Queen told Amanda she had something for her from Porthos, and held out a small box to her. The King started clapping and was desperate to know what was inside. Amanda unwrapped it and inside was a gorgeous fleur-de-lis brooch, and she actually had a tear in her eye. The Queen pinned it to her right sleeve. The King and Queen walked with us to the entrance and wished Amanda well as we took our seats in the carriage. We had a four-Musketeer escort.

My dress complimented Amanda's. It was in grey damask, with a square neckline with a lace pattern around the outside, which had pearls on the design. The bodice was in cream silk and it had long sleeves. On the shoulders were small silk bows. The V at the waist was embroidered with pearls. I decided to have my hair up, and wore a pearl necklace and earrings. Whilst we were in the carriage Amanda told me what she had bought Porthos. I knew he would be delighted. Tréville had mentioned to me that Amanda, Athos and himself were going into Paris and would be staying at Claudette's. I assumed Amanda wanted to talk to Claudette and I knew she would go to Isabella's grave.

At the church Athos and D'Artagnan are waiting outside, everyone else is inside. Athos tells Amanda that D'Artagnan is going to walk her down the aisle. She is so pleased. D'Artagnan takes Amanda's arm, I straighten her train out and then take Athos's arm, and we head inside the church, first Amanda and then me. The church is packed and everyone looks resplendent. Tréville and his men are all in full uniform, with cloaks. They all look extremely handsome. The last time all of us were in church was for D'Artagnan's wedding to Constance, such a lovely day.

"Lesley, are you all right?" said Athos.

"Sorry, I was thinking of the past. I still can't believe everything that has happened to Amanda and myself since coming to Paris. Both of us have gained brothers, who watch over us at all times. Look at me, who would have thought I would inherit the bakery and the dwelling, even though I lost a very dear friend? Amanda found both her brothers and then lost them, but she has a splendid job at the palace and is now marrying the man of her dreams. The pair of us have caused you all so much trouble, mainly Philip and Rochefort."

Athos studied me for a moment, then put his hands on my face and kissed my forehead and said, "The past is the past, Lesley, forget it. Hopefully our futures will be a lot better now." I smiled and we hugged each other. Just lately Athos and I had got very close to each other.

The music began and Amanda and D'Artagnan started to walk down the aisle. Porthos moved out to meet her and gave her one of his "winks". I smiled. Tréville was stood at Porthos's right side. D'Artagnan placed Amanda's hand in Porthos's. D'Artagnan, Athos and myself then joined Aramis. The wedding began, the vows were read and Amanda and Porthos were married. What a lovely couple they made. Amanda and Porthos walked towards a side door, along with D'Artagnan, to sign and witness the agreements. The priest asked everyone to remain seated. Tréville then walked over and joined Athos and Aramis. I made my way towards the back of the church, where there was another room and entered. Catherine was there waiting for me with my wedding dress, which, with her help, I carefully changed into. Catherine knew my secret.

My wedding dress is a cream fitted three-quarter dress over a full light peach underskirt, with a small train. The neckline is square with peach lace edging. The bodice has two sections with the fleur-de-lis of the Musketeers in peach stones on each. Peach rosebuds are across the front of the bodice and then all the way down both sides of the dress to the bottom. The bottom of the underskirt has cream lace with pearls attached all the way round. The sleeves are straight to the elbow and then fluted with the peach lace attached inside. I wore Katherine's diamond necklace and earrings. I unpinned and unplaited my hair, brushed it, then brushed a section from just above my ears and plaited that, leaving the plait hanging down in the middle of my long hair that fell in large ringlets.

When Amanda, Porthos and D'Artagnan returned from signing the agreements, they joined Aramis. Tréville had gone back to where he stood before, along with Athos, and then the priest announced a wedding blessing was to take place. Murmurs went round the church. Apart from Catherine, one other person and the priest, no one had any idea. Again, the music started and Catherine escorted me down the aisle to where Athos and Tréville were standing. Athos moved out to my side and said, "You look beautiful, Lesley." I looked into his amazing green eyes and smiled. "Are you happy?" he asked. I replied I was very happy, and placed my hand in his.

Amanda looked at Athos and me and said, "Blessing, what blessing? When... when did you marry Athos? Why didn't...?"

Porthos put his fingers to Amanda's lips and whispered, "Hush, wife."

I smiled and said we'd got married four weeks ago in the village church where the dwelling was. The rest of the Musketeers looked on, stunned. The priest started the blessing by saying a few words and explaining what would take place. He then asked, "Who comes to give this woman's hand away?"

Athos then said, "I have that very great honour."

He then takes my hand and places it into Tréville's hand, and then goes and joins Amanda and my brothers. I look into Tréville's gorgeous blue eyes, so full of love and devotion, the man I had loved since the day I met him.

Tréville looked at me and said, "My love, again, you look absolutely exquisite." My smile radiated my happiness. The priest blessed our marriage and our rings, which we had left off, and were now replaced on our fingers, which both had the fleur-de-lis etched on them.

When the blessing finished and to everyone's amusement, Porthos roared laughing and said, "Well how about that then? A double wedding."

The four of us walked down the aisle and out into glorious sunshine and a Musketeer's salute. I'm not quite sure who the Musketeers were more surprised at. Porthos had picked Amanda up and was kissing her deeply, or the fact their Captain was married and kissing his bride. As we walked to our separate carriages I heard D'Artagnan say to Athos, "You can keep a secret then." I turned and went to Athos, and gave him a hug and a kiss on the cheek. I looked at D'Artagnan and Aramis and gave them both a wink. I then returned to my husband.

We all returned to the garrison for Amanda and Porthos's wedding feast. Everything had been arranged before we left, all the food had been set out by Catherine and the other girls, Pierre and Lauren helped with the ale and wine, and all had been set out on tables in the garrison yard. Tréville and I went to Amanda and Porthos and said we hoped we had not spoilt their day with our blessing. They both said they were delighted, and Amanda whispered to me, "I want, and I mean want, all the details of your secret wedding."

I laughed, hugged and kissed her cheek. "We must meet up for a meal and I'll tell you everything. Well, more or less everything," I said.

Aramis and D'Artagnan hugged Tréville, and me. They were so happy. Some of the Musketeers were musicians and so the music started and we all danced with each other. When I danced with Porthos he literally picked me up and whirled me round, he was so happy for his Captain, and me, as I was for him and Amanda. We had been there quite some time, and everyone was having a wonderful time, Amanda and Porthos had just cut their wedding cake, when all of a sudden a rider came galloping into the garrison. "Apologies, Captain Tréville, the King requests your immediate presence at the palace, on an extremely important matter." Tréville apologised, kissed me and left. We all stood looking at one another, wondering what the urgency was from the palace.

"Come, everyone, the festivities must continue," I said, and they did. Athos, Aramis and D'Artagnan took turns in dancing with me and generally keeping me company. Amanda and I must have danced with nearly every Musketeer in the garrison.

CHAPTER 23

Happiness

I was sitting on the garrison steps, having a rest, when Tréville returned hours later, and the first thing he did was drink a huge tumbler of wine, and then he grabbed my hand and we went up to his office. "Tréville, what's wrong?" I asked.

"Hush, just let me kiss you and hold you," he said. Straight away I knew something was terribly wrong. He held me so tight, and kissed me so passionately. When we parted he had tears in his eyes. "Are your brothers merry?" he asked. I replied they were very merry. He looked at me and said, "I have some grave news to tell them, but perhaps not tonight."

"What grave news, Tréville? Please my love, tell me?"

He took my hands in his and said, "The King has just told me war has been declared on Spain." I paled and then I held him tight. He told me the King had bestowed the title Minister for War on him, and Athos was to be the new Captain. Tréville then tilted my head up and kissed me deeply. "Did I tell you how beautiful you look? Je t'aime, mon très cher amour," he said.

I looked into his eyes and replied, "And did I tell you how wonderful you look? Je t'aime trop, mon beau Ministre de la Guerre." We kissed again, our arms going round each other, our passions rising, and I said, "My love, I think we had better make an appearance." He smiled and we went back to enjoy the festivities. A lot later I noticed Amanda and Porthos had slipped away, so Tréville and I did the same.

That night as I lay in Tréville's arms, after our passions had been fulfilled, all of a sudden I felt he was never going to come back and tears fell from my eyes.

"Lesley, my love, I will return to you, I promise. We both have so much to live for, we have only just got wed, and nothing is going to happen to your brothers or me. We have had outbreaks before, maybe not as serious as this, but hopefully within a couple of months we will all be back." I looked at him and hugged him so tight. "We do need to talk about you being safe, here at the bakery though," he said.

I leaned over him and said, "I don't think we should waste any more time talking, my Minister for War, I have yet to congratulate you," and with that brought my lips down to his, our kisses deepening, our passions riding to another realm. We then fell asleep entwined in each other arms.

In the morning, as the sun was rising, Tréville and I washed, dressed and then made our way to the garrison. There were about four Musketeers clearing up the remains of the night before. "Remy," said Tréville, "will you please tell my men I need them in my office now?"

"Yes Captain, and if you don't mind me saying, congratulations to you both," replied Remy.

I went over to him and thanked him and gave him a quick kiss on his cheek. Never had I seen a Musketeer blush so red. I personally did not have a lot of dealings with Remy, but I knew he would fight to the death, if needed, with regards to Amanda. About five minutes later his men entered his office.

"Morning Captain and Madame Tréville," said Aramis. I smiled.

"Where is Amanda?" asked Tréville. Porthos replied she had already left for the palace. "You will have to tell her this news later on then," he said. He looked at each one of his men and said, "There is no easy way to tell you all this, war has been declared on Spain."

The room went quiet, and his men looked at each other. Tréville then said, "The other news is I'm no longer your Captain."

"What?" said Porthos.

Tréville put his hand up and said, "The King has honoured me and I am to be his Minister for War. Athos is now your new Captain."

Athos looked stunned and said, "That is great news, Captain – sorry, Minister – but me as Captain, surely someone else would be better than me?"

Tréville replied, "I think everyone here will agree that the men respect and look up to you, Athos, and I can think of no one better than yourself to have as my Captain."

I went to him, curtsied, smiled, hugged him and said, "Congratulations, Captain Athos," and kissed his cheek.

Athos said, "Thank you, Minister, and Lesley please don't curtsey to me again, embarrassing." I giggled. Both men shook hands. Porthos, Aramis and D'Artagnan were delighted with the news and congratulated both men. Tréville asked Porthos to call all the Musketeers together in the yard. They all then went and stood on the balcony, I stood in the doorway.

"Gentlemen," said Tréville, and the yard went quiet. "As you know I was summoned to the King yesterday and the news I have to give is grave. As of last night we are now at war with Spain. We have at least four weeks before we have to leave for the border, and in that time, obviously, all leave is cancelled. Those of you who have wives and children, you need to get things sorted before we leave. Intense training will start as of now. You also have a new Captain."

"You're our Captain," someone shouted, and the men started murmuring.

"Please, gentleman, please. As of yesterday I was honoured by the King to be his Minister for War, and Athos is now your Captain. I hope you will all give him the same respect that you gave me." The mood changed and everyone seemed happy with the news.

As Tréville and I returned to his office he called Porthos in. "Porthos, I'm sorry this has come on your wedding time, but I am prepared to let you and Amanda go away and celebrate your marriage. You may take a week away, as of today, and then I need you both back."

Porthos replied, "Thank you, Minister," and Tréville grinned. Porthos gave me a hug, kissed my cheek and went to find Amanda.

Tréville took me in his arms and kissed me deeply; I told him I had to go back to the bakery, to tell my workforce, and would see him later. He walked me to the gate, gave me a quick kiss and then watched me walk back to the bakery.

When I got to the bakery I called the workforce together and told them the news. Catherine broke down into tears, and I later learned that her young man was a Musketeer. Both Pierre and Laurens knew they would have to go to war but they didn't want to, and I needed them. I would talk to Tréville. I needed to get my head round things as well. The first thing I did was go and see the farmer and the miller, with a Musketeer escort of two men, and arrange to have as much flour, salt, cheese, whatever, as I could store, and in return if things got bad I would make meals for them and their families. They both said they would send as much as they could when they could and not to worry, they would survive. Within a couple of weeks the dry storeroom was full and the rest was stored in the small parlour upstairs. I even got them to deliver supplies to the dwelling, where the barn was totally safe, secure and dry, in case the villagers needed food. The second thing was logs. Laurens knew someone who could help us stockpile logs for the ovens, and these were piled high up in the bakery barn. I still had my funds hidden away in the safe, if needed.

A couple of days later, Tréville came to the bakery and told me we had both been summoned to the palace. I rode astride his horse with him behind me, his arm tightly round my waist holding me close, and we talked and laughed all the way, but as we neared the palace I got worried. Tréville saw the change in me and said, "It's all right, my love, I'm with you, and Rochefort would never try anything, especially as we have an audience with the King and Queen." I smiled and sort of relaxed.

We were escorted to where the King and Queen awaited us. When we entered Tréville bowed and I curtsied. "Your Majesties," we both said.

I heard a door close and my eyes were looking around when the King said, smiling, "Lesley, he is not here." I smiled and lowered my eyes. "Minister Tréville, I am most displeased with you," said the King, who stood and walked over to him. I glanced at Tréville who had paled.

"Sire, I apologise, how have I displeased you?"

"You have done something so bad I can never forgive you, Tréville, I thought we were friends. I had to hear this news from someone else and I am deeply hurt to the quick that you did not confide in me," the King said angrily. Now I was getting worried and I looked at the Queen, as she also walked towards us.

"Louis, stop teasing Tréville, Lesley is looking so worried."

The King looked at both of us and then with a huge smile on his face said, "Tréville, why did you not tell us of your marriage? We are both delighted for you and Lesley, and wanted to give you our blessing."

I think the relief from the pair of us was apparent. "Sire," said Tréville. "I..."

The King put his hand up to stop him and said, "Tréville, we are going to war soon, but before we do, I want you to take Lesley away, so you will go now, take a week off, and that is an order."

Tréville looked at the King and then me and said, "Thank you, sire, but I cannot accept. As you know Amanda and Porthos married and I have given them both a week's leave."

The King looked at Tréville and said, "I trust Captain Athos is still at the garrison along with my other Musketeers?" Tréville replied they were. "Then I do not see a problem, Tréville. Now go before I change my mind."

The King and Queen went to leave, again Tréville bowed and I curtsied, but before they walked out of the door, the King turned smiling and said, "Oh, Tréville, one other thing and this is most important – have fun." I giggled. We left and returned to the garrison.

"Will Catherine be all right with the bakery?" I replied she would be fine, but I did have some things I needed to do. Tréville said he had a lot of paperwork to get through and other things so we arranged to meet at the garrison later. He reminded me to make sure if he wasn't at the garrison to get an escort to ride with me to the dwelling. I had the most stressful and irritable afternoon ever. I couldn't wait to leave. Catherine went out to do an errand, and seemed to be gone ages, and when she returned I left. I went to the garrison, but Tréville had been summoned back to the palace. I found Sunkwa and rode off to the dwelling with my escort.

As I was riding my thoughts wandered as how to relax before Tréville arrived. I decided I would have a relaxing time in the tub, peace and quiet. Oh yes, just what I needed. When I arrived at the dwelling, I thanked the escort, who rode back, and took Sunkwa to the barn. Oh no, Tréville was already here!! I saw to Sunkwa and then went into the dwelling. "Tréville, I'm here."

"I won't be long, my love. I'm in the tub." I sighed deeply. *Typical. Oh well, another day,* and went to our bedchamber. I undressed, and only had my petticoat on when Tréville called me. "My love, can you help me?"

Now what? I thought to myself, and went to him. As I walked through the door I stopped in absolute amazement. The shutters were closed, a roaring fire going, the tub was half full and everywhere was lit by candles in lanterns, and Tréville just had a cloth wrapped round him from his waist downwards. I looked him up and down and smiled. "Oh, Tréville, it looks wonderful, and so do you," I said.

"It's all for you, my love," he said.

"How did you know when I would be here?" I asked, surprised.

"I saw Catherine and she told me your afternoon had not gone well, so..." And with that he scooped me up in his arms and put me in the tub.

"Tréville, I've still got my petticoat on."

Tréville laughed and replied, "Not for long, my love, not for long," dropped his cloth and got in the tub with me. We kissed each other deeply, my petticoat soon went flying across the room and as we gently soaped each other, our passions rose and were fulfilled.

As I got out of the tub, Tréville smacked my backside, a little bit too hard. "Ouch!" I said, and looked at him. He was laid there with his eyes twinkling, watching me and grinning.

I wrapped a large, long cloth round me, from under my arms, went to our bedchamber and unpinned my hair, brushed it and then re-plaited it. I had a small mirror and looked at my backside to see a large red mark on it. No wonder it hurt. I went back to see if Tréville would like to go to the tavern for a meal. He was still in the tub, eyes closed, and then I noticed a spare bucket of water, and a mischievous grin came on my face. I picked up the bucket, with water now cold, and stood behind him and said, "You relaxed, my love?"

Tréville just "uummed". I poured the cold water over him. He spluttered and said, "Oh, wife, this is war," and jumped out the bath. I dropped the bucket and ran giggling into the spare bedchamber, and hid at the side of the tall cabinet. I saw he had grabbed a cloth and was putting it round his waist, as he made his way to our bedchamber. I went back to the tub room to get another large cloth and hid behind the door.

When he came in I threw the cloth over his head saying, "I think your hair is wet, my love." I then ran out, still giggling, again through the spare bedchamber, then the parlour and into our bedchamber, trying to avoid him catching me, but he caught my plait and slowly reeled me in.

He unplaited my hair and spread it out with his fingers. Then he took me into his arms, and gently threw me onto the bed. "Now, what is a suitable punishment for someone trying to drown their husband?" he said, as he removed my cloth, trailing kisses down my neck.

I took his face in my hands, his blue eyes ablaze with passion and said, 'I don't know, my handsome husband, but I do know one thing."

"And what is that, my love?" he said, gently kissing my lips.

I replied, "I surrender." My arms went round him and down his back; we deepened our kisses, my hands went to the edge of his cloth. I stopped and gasped.

"My love, what's wrong?"

"Tréville, have you hurt your back lately?"

"Not that I know of, why?"

"You have a small lump in the middle of your back. Sit up, put your back to me and drop your cloth." He looked at me and smiled. I took his hand and put it on the lump.

He paled and did as I asked. I couldn't believe what I saw. "Oh, Tréville," I said with concern in my voice, "I think Aramis should see this, it's most unusual, but I think I can sort it out for you." It was all I could do to not burst out laughing. I have no idea how it got there but a small piece of soap was stuck to a couple of small hairs in the middle of his back, just above his buttocks, and obviously, the cloth had kept it in place. I gently put my fingers round the soap and made sure I had a bit of skin and pulled.

"Ouch! What have you done, Lesley?" He turned and looked at me and I burst out laughing. "It's not funny, my love, that really hurt."

"Oh Tréville, you are fine. This was your... lump," and I showed him the small piece of soap, with the small bits of hairs stuck to it.

"What...? Oh, double war now, wife, for putting me through that," he said. With that, he gently pushed me back on the bed. Our arms went round each other and our passion rose to its height, and then we lay entwined in each other's arms. "Don't think I've let you off, my love, my revenge will be oh so sweet," he said, smiling. I saw mischief in his eyes. Hmm, I had better watch out.

"Tréville, I was told at the garrison you had been summoned back to the palace?"

"Ah, yes my love, I was." Tréville got up and went to the cabinet and brought back a box. "It's a wedding present from the King and Queen." I unwrapped it and inside were six beautifully decorated glasses for wine with the fleur-de-lis etched on them.

"Oh Tréville, what a beautiful present, we must not forget to thank them." Tréville put them back on the cabinet and then got back into bed; our arms went round each other and after goodnight kisses we both slept.

The next couple of days we spent lazily, went horse riding in the countryside, had picnics and just absolutely loved each other, in and out of the tub, and as the King had ordered, we had lots and lots of fun. One day we revisited the spot where Tréville told me about his childhood, and how he became Captain. We sat under the same tree, arms wrapped round each other. Tréville started kissing my neck and at the same time unpinned my hair. "I want to see your hair blow in the breeze, I love it when it's down," he said. I remembered what he had said about "revenge" but I saw no mischief in his eyes. He unplaited my hair and let his fingers comb through it. We walked down to the stream, hand in hand, and then Tréville put his hand in the water and splashed me.

"Tréville, you're getting me wet," I said.

Another handful of water came at me. Now I saw mischief in his eyes. I splashed water back at him. I saw both his hands go in the water and ran, giggling. He missed. As I ran so my hair blew in the breeze. Eventually he caught me and we showered each other with kisses, our passions rising. Later on as we went to leave, I went to plait my hair. Tréville said, "Leave it, my love," so I did.

When we got back to the dwelling my hair was in such a tangle. I had removed my dress and was sitting on the bed in just my petticoat trying to brush it when Tréville came in. "Let me do that, my love," and he started brushing. Suddenly I noticed a couple of long black hairs fall onto my petticoat and then some more. "Tréville, is my hair coming out?"

"Yes, quite a lot, but with beautiful long hair like yours I thought it was normal." He showed me the brush and it was full of my hair.

"What? I must go and see the physician, something is wrong with me, I never lose my hair," I said, extremely concerned.

All of a sudden I heard him laugh. "Sweet revenge," he said. It wasn't my hair at all, as he had carefully cut some hair off from one of the horse's tails!! I pushed him down on the bed, his head went on the pillow, and I sat astride him.

"Oh, sweet revenge is it, my love? We will see about that, my Minister for War," I said and leant down and kissed him.

What he didn't know was I knew this "revenge" would come soon. Our bed was a four-poster and unbeknown to Tréville I had tied pieces of thin rope around the top posts (obviously hidden them). One of the first things I was taught on the Reservation was how to tie knots and do it quickly. I pulled his shirt out of his breeches. "Now I need to remove this, so arms up." I distracted him with feather like kisses, and as my hair was loose it also covered most of his face. I quickly got his arms out of his shirt and then secured both his wrists. I left his shirt round his neck and over his face.

"What the...?" he said as he tried to move his arms. I pulled his shirt down and grinned at him, gave him a deep kiss and put the shirt back over his face. I then got off him and went into the parlour. Hidden in a corner was a bucket of water with a cloth in it. I went back to Tréville, replaited my hair, then removed his boots, undid his belt, unbuttoned his breeches and helped him out of them, but left his undergarment on. "What are you up to?" said Tréville.

"Well, you have not washed so I thought I would do it," I said.

Tréville replied, "So far, my love, I'm liking your revenge." I put my hand in the water, wrung the cloth out a bit, and slapped it on his chest. "Good grief, woman, that's absolutely freezing."

"Oh, is it?" I said in all innocence. I carried on washing his chest and arms with the freezing water.

When I'd finished my hands, obviously, were so very cold. I pulled the shirt over his head, kissed him and said softly, "My hands are so cold, my love, I wonder where I can warm them?" I was then looking down his body.

Tréville looked at me and said, "Oh no, don't you dare." I raised my eyebrow and smiled, as my hands went down to the top of his undergarment, and unlaced some of it. Tréville was trying to wriggle his legs, so I sat astride them. As he tried to unbalance me, he gave me an advantage and I slipped my hands into his undergarment and put my two freezing hands on his buttocks. "Aaahhh, that's better," I said, moving my cold hands all over his buttocks. He still tried to unbalance me and nearly succeeded but I grabbed his buttocks a bit harder than I thought.

"Ouch!" said Tréville.

After my hands had warmed up slightly, I moved them up his back and then round to his chest, and moved up and sat astride his waist and said, "Yes, my love, I agree with you, revenge is oh so sweet," and then I took his face in my hands and kissed him deeply. I felt him shivering. Without him realising, for a couple of minutes, I had released his arms.

As soon as he realised he was free, he turned and I was flat on my back. Stupidly I had not moved the bucket with the cold water and Tréville saw it. I followed his eyes and said, "I knew I forgot something." Tréville had mischief in his eyes. He then sat astride me, with his knees on both my hands, unbuttoned my petticoat and pushed it down to my waist, and then reached in the bucket and got the cloth and slapped it on my chest. All I could do was giggle, even though it really was freezing.

I freed my hands and wrestled him for the cloth and then said,

"Tréville, do you want to sleep in a wet bed?"

He raised his eyebrow, got up, picked up the bucket and said, "I think this needs to be moved."

As he went to walk out the door I said, "Tréville, don't forget your undergarment is..." Alas, too late. His undergarment fell to the floor and he nearly tripped over it. Luckily he was by the door and stopped himself falling. He glanced at me and I was doubled with laughter. What he couldn't see was on each buttock he had five fingernail marks that looked like a smile!! The only way he could stop me laughing was to kiss me.

"Now I think we both need to warm up," he said, and pressed his cold chest against mine. I gasped at how cold he actually was. Our arms wrapped around each other, our kisses deepening with every kiss, we both could see the passion in our eyes and then our hearts entwined in absolute love.

CHAPTER 24

Death

The following day, Tréville was up and dressed when I woke. He loved going out and walking before anyone was around. I washed, dressed and saw him talking to Helene, and Helene was pointing out a direction. When he returned to the dwelling he took me in his arms and kissed me and said, "After we have eaten, I have a surprise for you." About an hour later, Tréville saddled his horse, attached a picnic basket and another bag, helped me up, and then he got up and put his arm round my waist and I snuggled into his front, and we rode off. Helene waved as we passed her.

We must have been riding for a good half hour when a large forest appeared in front of us. "Tréville, where are we going?" Tréville just smiled as he guided his horse down a trail, which had tall and short trees either side. Suddenly I said, "Tréville, stop."

"Lesley?"

I looked behind me and could have sworn I saw a red cape. "Tréville, I have a feeling we are being followed." Tréville turned his horse but neither of us saw anything untoward.

"I can't see anyone Lesley, are you sure it wasn't an animal you saw?"

"Maybe," I said, and we carried on. At the bottom of the trail, which was a gentle slope, the view was wonderful. Straight ahead of us was a waterfall that cascaded down huge rocks and then went into a lovely lake, not too big. All various sizes and different types of trees and rocks surrounded most of the lake. On the right the lake cascaded over smaller rocks and then carried on as a stream through the forest. On the left, there was an area of green grass. There were various small slopes that led down into the lake.

Tréville unsaddled the horse and then led him down for a drink, and then tied him to a tree. "Tréville this is lovely, why have we never been here before?"

Tréville replied, "I was talking to Helene and she told me about it. Apparently years ago some of the villagers thought swimming in the lake brought good luck, others thought it was cursed. I thought it would be nice to see it for ourselves."

I looked around and felt a calm and said to Tréville, "I can tell you it's not cursed."

"Well, how about we go for a swim then?" he said.

"What a lovely idea, but I have brought nothing to put on."

"We can swim in our undergarments," said Tréville.

"Tréville, the sun may be out but it's not hot yet, and if we swim in our undergarments we will both get cold, trying to dry out."

Tréville opened the bag and produced three large cloths, one of my petticoats and another undergarment for him.

"Well, my love, you thought of everything." I looked around and saw behind us two large clumps of trees. "Tréville, look at those trees, we could tie your horse there so when the sun is high he will be in the cool shade. The other clump we could put the picnic basket, blanket, saddle, our clothes to keep them out of the sun." Tréville agreed it was a good idea.

We undressed down to our undergarments, and I unpinned and unplaited my hair. Hand in hand we walked down and got into the lake. The water, to me, was cool and refreshing; Tréville found it a bit cold, but he soon warmed up. I liked to swim deep under the water and look around, so I always saw where Tréville was. My father always said I swam like a fish. Quite a few times I grabbed his waist and made him jump. I would swim underneath him on my back and then surface and kiss him quickly and then swim down again. Both of us were good swimmers and ended up racing each other; alas,

Tréville won. We went and stood under the waterfall, arms entwined and kissing each other deeply and passions rising. Afterwards, hand in hand, we walked back to where our clothes were and Tréville got the three large cloths. We undressed each other out of our wet clothes. Tréville put one of the large cloths round me, as I did him, and we dried each other bodies. The other one I wrapped my hair in it, and twisted the cloth to get most of the water out and then plaited it. Then I heard the noise. "Tréville, can you hear that?"

"I can hear nothing, my love. Come here, I have something in mind." I could see what he had in mind!!

"It's horses, and a lot of them, coming this way," I said. We quickly put our undergarments on, grabbed our clothes, cloths, blanket and saddle and moved up to where the horse was. The only weapons we had were two pistols. A couple of minutes later about twenty riders came down the trail. They were Red Guards.

"Well, where are they then? You said you followed them here and they were in the lake?"

I knew that voice well, as did Tréville – it was Rochefort. Tréville held me close.

"We did follow them here, sire, we saw them turn down, I sent Berg back to tell you, and I followed them down the trail. I saw both of them in the lake and then I returned to meet you. This is the only trail back to the road, if they had passed me I would have seen them."

"Well they're not there now, are they? Perhaps you're blind as well as being stupid?" snapped Rochefort. "This would have been an excellent spot to get rid of both of them, such a tragedy, both drowning in the lake. I never knew this lake was here, so it probably would have been months before anyone found them. Spread out and see if you can see anything."

The Red Guards dismounted and started searching round. Two of them made their way to where we were hiding. I stroked the horse to keep him quiet. One of the guards said, "I'm new, what problem does our leader have with these two people?"

The other one replied, "Tréville is the Minister for War, the woman is his wife."

The other guard said, "The Minister for War? We can't kill him, we would all hang."

The other guard replied, "There has been a long term of hatred between the two men, Rochefort even kidnapped his wife before they wed and tortured her. He gave her to my brother who tried to take her, but she fought well. He took her through the forest and made sure she hit her head on every low branch. She was at death's door, but somehow she lived. I have no desire to kill either of them, and if you repeat that to Rochefort I will deny it, so if you know what's good for you, my friend, say nothing of this. Come, let's get back, there's no one here."

They both left and returned to the rest of the Red Guards. "Nothing, sire," said someone.

"Typical. No matter, soon they will all be going to war, so I can wait. Now move, this detour has cost us time getting back to the palace," and with that they all mounted their horses and rode off back up the trail.

Tréville and I stayed where we were until we were sure they had gone, and then moved back down. "Tréville, we had better go," I said, shivering, but with cold, not fear.

Tréville replied, "I must remember to listen to you in future. Rochefort could have had both of us, but there is nothing we can do. I will consult with the King when I return. The sun is hot now and you are shivering, so let's put the blanket out, lay down and both of us get warm again." He was right, there was nothing we could do. If Tréville confronted Rochefort he would deny all knowledge. We left the horse where he was, picked up our belongings and went back to where we were originally. Tréville laid the blanket out, the other side of the clump of trees, where the sun was now shining brightly, and put our wet undergarments and cloths on a couple of branches to dry. We both lay on the blanket, holding hands, and looking up into the blue sky.

"I wonder if he would have drowned us one by one or together?" I said.

"My love, don't think about it," said Tréville, gently pulling me on top of him and kissing me deeply. "You are still cold, I think I need to warm you up, but first, can you hear anything?"

I looked at him and smiled and said, "No, my love, all I can hear is the birds singing, the rustling of the leaves, the..." Tréville's lips were on mine, the passion was in both our eyes and our undergarments were soon gone, and our passions fulfilled. Afterwards we put our undergarments back on, just in case, had our picnic and wine, and later on Tréville started kissing my neck again, which led to our passions being fulfilled again. We then got fully dressed, packed everything up and rode back to the dwelling. Apart from Rochefort, it had been a beautiful day.

Our last full day, we decided to ride into Paris, and I rode with Tréville. We both loved Paris, as it held happy memories for us. We walked down by the Seine, partook of a lovely meal at the tavern. We went and sat in the public botanical garden, which had opened a couple of years before, and had something called a conservatory which held plants for medicinal research, whatever that meant. We relaxed, talked, our arms around each other, snatching the odd kisses here and there. Many people walking by glanced at us and smiled. We visited the places where we went the day after our wedding, even going back to the upmarket hotel for a late tea/early evening meal. We were both surprised that the people working there recognised us. We rode back to the dwelling, our arms around each other's waists and my head on his shoulder. Later on when we were in each other's arms, after our passions had been fulfilled, we talked about various things and then Tréville mentioned the bakery. He needed to know I would be safe and secure, not just from the Spanish, but the Red Guards as well. I explained that Pierre and Laurens didn't want to fight, but stay with me.

"The Red Guards will not come during the day, it will be night-time when you are alone and vulnerable."

I sat up and looked down at him and said, "Tréville, do you not think I can handle a couple of Red Guards? After all, you have taught me how to shoot and how to point and thrust a sword."

Tréville sat up alongside me. "My love, if you deal with them like you do me I have every confidence in you," he said, smiling, "but you don't know these Guards, they can be very ruthless and I don't want you hurt." I replied I would think of something. With a twinkle in his eyes, Tréville looked at me and then took me in his arms and kissed me deeply and slowly we both laid back down, eyes again ablaze with passion and he said, "Umm... maybe I should show you the more gentle way about pointing and thrusting, but not with a sword," and started kissing my neck.

I ran my fingers through his hair, giggling and said, "And how do you intend to do that, my love?"

"Well, my beautiful wife," he said, "We start like this..."

The following morning we walked round the village, talked to the people, partook of a meal at the tavern, walked to the bridge, sat on the bench, and then later we went to the church, where we married. All of the villagers were there and the priest blessed us all for what was coming. Helene came to us and told Tréville to be safe, and gave him a hug and kissed his cheek. Tréville in return kissed her hand. I hugged her too. She told us not to worry about the dwelling, as everyone would look after it. We left late Saturday afternoon as Tréville had to be back at the garrison. I loved our village, as did Tréville, and wondered when we would go back again, if ever. Should the Spanish invade, it would all probably be razed to the ground. That was something I didn't want to think about, we had so many friends there.

When I woke Sunday morning, the sun was high in the sky. Tréville was not there, obviously gone to the garrison, so I decided I would take some pies and cakes and do us a picnic in his office. I washed, dressed and went down to the bakery and put everything in a basket. I went into the lane – all was quiet. Something didn't seem right, and was that smoke I could smell? As I neared the garrison the smell of smoke got stronger. I entered the garrison yard, all was quiet. Strange, where were the guards? I stood and felt a bad foreboding awaiting me, and shivered. I decided I would put the picnic in the meeting room, so I went in and laid it all out on one of the tables, with a note telling Tréville's men if any of it was eaten there would be trouble, from me! As I left the meeting room I heard a crackling noise from the Musketeers' quarters, infirmary and eating area, so entered through the door. I could not believe what my eyes were looking at. The back half of the building looked like it had been blown up, remains of bodies all over the floor, blood everywhere, and that was where the smoke was coming from as fires had started. There were mangled beds and tables and broken stones everywhere. I could even see the graveyard through the smoke. Was that the loud noises I thought I heard in the early morning? My stomach churned and I could feel the bile coming up into my throat. I left the building and made my way around the back of the garrison yard to where the training grounds were, and the sight and smell made me retch.

The training ground was a battlefield. There were all the Musketeers, shot, stabbed (some still had the Spanish swords in their bodies) or blown to pieces and blood flowing from their wounds, and as the sun was really hot the stench was awful. I carefully walked round them, with my hand over my nose, looking for Tréville and my brothers, but they weren't there. Lots of blood was flowing from the stables but I didn't dare go and look, I assumed all the horses had been slaughtered. I thought of my beautiful horse, Sunkwa. Even the lovely big trees had been damaged – one was totally black, and others had their branches ripped off them, splinters of wood everywhere. I looked down at my shoes, they were now red, and as was the bottom of my dress and petticoat; as I walked so my dress and petticoat soaked the blood up. At that moment the sky went dark and it started raining heavily, the blood was now running like a stream, and the field became mud and it was hard to lift my feet in and out and I kept getting stuck. I walked past the arch that led into the garrison yard, and came to the other training ground. Quite a few Musketeers were there, well, the remains of those blown from within the infirmary. Again, no sign of the loved ones I was looking for. The only tree that was there had fallen and had completely smashed the water well. As I turned to walk back to the yard I heard horses trotting through the yard. I expected to see Tréville and my brothers, but looked straight at Rochefort and about twenty Red Guards on horseback instead.

"Well, well, looks like one of the vermin survived, but seeing as the Spanish have done the job for me, I'll let you live," he said. "Alas, I couldn't find your husband, but Amanda is now mine," and with that remark, they turned their horses and rode out of the garrison.

After the encounter with Rochefort, I returned to the yard and looked in the garrison rooms. D'Artagnan's room – he wasn't there, Porthos's room – the same, Aramis's room – the same. Last was Athos's room. They were all there lying on the floor looking like they were asleep, except they weren't from the wounds inflicted and the blood-red floor. Tears started to fall down my cheeks. I then walked round to Tréville's office, past the kitchen; same there – all the men slain. Slowly I walked up the steps to Tréville's office. I winced and looked down and saw somewhere I had lost my shoes and I was barefoot, splinters entering the soles of my feet, and I was soaked through to my skin. My hair had unplaited and as it was below my waist it was plastered around my face and body, my dress was heavy and clinging to me as well. I stopped on the balcony and looked down. The ground now looked like a red pond. Red water was flowing in every direction. I then noticed behind the garrison gate the bodies of the two guards. I went through the door, the slabs ice-cold to my feet. The corridor was dim, no torches lit. I looked in the spare room, nothing. I went to Tréville's office and opened the door and went down the step. Tréville was not at his desk, but there were signs of a violent struggle.

I noticed the door to the armoury was closed. I walked over and tried to push it open, it was heavy and as it slowly opened it moaned and creaked. Tréville was not in there; I noticed all the halberds, muskets, pistols and gunpowder were gone, but as I turned to walk out my eyes noticed a rope wrapped around the middle pillar, about four times and blood on the floor. Slowly I walked round the pillar, stopped and looked on in shock and horror, my hands went to my mouth, my heart beating so fast and my breathing so erratic, and my eyes wide.

There was Tréville tied to the pillar. He had been stripped of his uniform and only had his lower undergarment on, which was soaked with his blood, and his body looked like it had been used as bayonet practice. Deep cuts, mixed with smaller ones, were across his chest, stomach, arms, legs, every wound was dripping blood, down his body and pooling on the floor. His head was hung down so I went over to him, walking through his blood on the floor, and slowly lifted his face up to mine. His face had the look of excruciating pain, his eyes were open and his face was badly bruised and cut. A note was attached to the ropes around his waist and arms and it said, "Here is the Musketeer's Minister for War, their deaths are at his hands."

I saw a dagger on the table and cut Tréville's ropes and his limp body fell forward and hit the floor with such a thud, it sounded like every bone in his body shattered. I knelt down beside him, rolled him over and cradled him in my arms, tears flowing down my face, and tried to close his eyes, but they would not close. I kissed his cold lips.

Whoever had done this had murdered the love of my life. Tala let out a loud mournful howl, as she knew my alpha was dead. I could hardly breathe, my throat felt like I was being strangled and then suddenly from nowhere I heard something, it was very loud... It was a scream... and it was coming from me. I saw the dagger at my side, looked at Tréville and knew I could not live without him. I picked the dagger up, held it in both of my hands above my head and swiftly brought it down, plunging it into my heart. My limp body fell over Tréville's.

CHAPTER 25

War

I faintly hear a voice calling to me. "Lesley, Lesley my love, please wake up."

I slowly opened my eyes, and saw I was sitting up in bed, and looked at Tréville, who looked like a ghost. "Tréville," I said quietly, "is that you?"

"Yes my love, it's me, you were having a bad dream and you were screaming. What made you scream so?" Tréville moved to hold me, I put my hands up to stop him and just looked at him, eyes wide, and said with panic in my voice, "No, no, you're a ghost, you're not here, you're dead, my brothers are dead, the garrison is dead, I'm dead."

"My love, please listen to me," he said gently, "none of us are dead and neither are you. Let me hold you to prove I'm here and alive, feel my heart beating."

I cautiously put my hand out and touched his face, I put my other hand on his beating heart, he wasn't a ghost, and he was real and with me. I flung my arms round him and held him so tightly saying, "Oh my love, you're alive, you're alive," and then the tears started flowing and slowly, through my sobs, I told him about my dream. There was a knock at the door, and it was Catherine asking if everything was all right. Tréville said all was well, I had had a bad dream and he would be down later.

Tréville put his arms around me, holding me so tight, and we lay back down in the bed, Tréville kissing my forehead and then my lips. "Oh my love, I'm here, I'm here," he said softly. I held him so tight, frightened to let him go in case he vanished. After I had calmed, Tréville told me unfortunately, he had to go to the palace and then the garrison to see the King and then his men, as it was his first day back.

My eyes went wide and I looked at him. "Lesley, everything is all right, I'm here, you're here and so are your brothers," he said. "I will go to the palace first and then come back for you and, if you feel up to it, we will go to the garrison together so you can see for yourself, my love, I promise you no one has died at the garrison." Tréville kissed me deeply, got up, washed, dressed and went down to see Catherine. He came back with a hot drink for me that I drank, and then, after another kiss, he left. Catherine came up to make sure I was all right and I told her my dream. She gave me a hug, and like Tréville, told me nothing had happened.

When Tréville returned later I had decided to go with him, I had to do it, but as I went outside I said, "Tréville, what's all that black smoke rising from the garrison?"

Tréville suddenly looked worried. "Whatever it is, I'm sure it has nothing to do with your dream, my love," he replied. I stopped at the garrison gate, my heart beating so fast, my breathing heavy and the smell of the smoke made me feel ill. Tréville put his arm round my waist and held my hands with his other hand, and gave me a gentle kiss.

As we entered the yard, thick black smoke was rising out of the kitchen. I saw his men handing buckets of water into the kitchen. I was relieved, especially when Aramis said, "Ah, the other newlyweds. Good afternoon, Madame Tréville, Minister."

Aramis looked at me, and came straight over, "Lesley, are you not well? You look quite distressed." He looked at Tréville and said, "May I be of assistance, Minister?" Tréville explained quickly about my dream and Aramis took my hand and placed it inside his shirt.

"Forgive me, Minister, for being so bold, but Lesley now knows that my heart is beating and we are all here for her. Obviously the fire in the kitchen has not helped."

I smiled, removed my hand, and replied, "Thank you, Aramis."

Aramis hugged me and kissed my cheek. Tréville and Aramis nodded a silent look between each other. It had just been a horrible dream and I hoped I never, ever, had another one, but it was a dream I never forgot. Athos came over, as did Porthos and D'Artagnan, and all gave me a hug and a kiss on the cheek. "Is Amanda here, Porthos?" I asked. Porthos replied she was already at the palace. I'd forgotten how late it was.

I looked at Tréville and said, "Tréville, I will wait for you in the meeting room, as I'm sure you have private matters to discuss with my brothers, and also the kitchen fire."

Porthos looked at me and said, "Any spare pies going, Lesley? I'm starving."

I replied, "Is Amanda not feeding you?"

He replied, "Of course, but, how shall I put it..."

Athos slapped Porthos on his back and said, smiling, "He means he's getting rather a lot of exercise!"

I laughed, glanced at Tréville, who winked at me, and said I would go and get all of them some more pies. Tréville gave me a quick kiss and then they all went up to the office. Remy escorted me to the bakery and back. I filled a basket full of pies and other pastries. I gave Remy a couple of pies, just for him – he was happy. As I entered the meeting room there was about eight Musketeers there playing cards. I went to sit at another table so as not to interrupt them, but they asked me to join them, so I sat with them, partook of a drink, had some fruit and was being shown how to play with the cards, when Tréville came for me. "Careful men, Lesley will end up beating you all," he said, smiling. I thanked them and we walked out into the yard, where my brothers were sitting at the table.

"Here you go, my brothers, and Porthos... share."

Tréville and I then walked back to the bakery with our arms wrapped around each other. I felt so safe when he was with me, and my love for him was overwhelming. Unbeknown to me, my screams had been so loud half the people in the lane had rushed to the bakery, as they thought murder had been committed. Catherine explained I had a bad dream and everyone was well. The garrison kitchen was down for about a week. Pascal had let the broth overflow and some fell onto straw, which had been accidentally covered in oil, which caught fire. I made the hot broth, and the pie orders more than doubled, along with the bread, and then a cart would come and collect it three times a day from the bakery. Certainly kept us all busy.

When we got back to the bakery, Tréville whispered something to Catherine, who blushed deeply. "What on earth did you say to Catherine? I've never seen her blush like that before."

Tréville said, "I told her we were going to our bedchamber, and not to be disturbed, as I was going to show you I was still alive." I looked at him, stunned, then burst out laughing – poor Catherine.

Tréville took me in his arms, kissed me deeply, and slowly we undressed each other; as usual Tréville unpinned and unplaited my hair. We caressed and kissed each other's bodies, like it was our first time together, and slowly our passions were reached. I looked at him, smiling, as I trailed my fingers down his chest, and said, "Well, now I know you are alive, my love."

He gently pulled me on top of him and put his arms around me and looked into my eyes and said, "Yes I am, I'm very much alive, my love." He rolled me back over and I could see the passion in his twinkling blue eyes, and he started trailing kisses down my neck.

The following two weeks I hardly saw Tréville. Everything was now about the onset of going to war. We did spend our nights together though, and even spent a few nights at the dwelling, when an unexpected guest arrived. Athos was more than content to stay in his rooms, so Tréville still used his office. Tréville had spoken to the King about Pierre and Laurens, and the King agreed they could stay but they must have intense training so they could protect me, and Tréville made sure they had intense training!! He gave me more pistol and sword fighting lessons, along with how to throw a dagger, and I was as good as any Musketeer now. My brothers didn't believe Tréville, so one morning we had a competition and I came second, after Tréville, in the pistol shooting. Athos was the only one to beat me at sword fighting and I beat all of them, including Tréville, at throwing the daggers. They all agreed they were glad I was fighting for France.

One day, after Tréville had left for the garrison, I went and sat at the parlour table, where I had put paper, quill and ink. This was going to be hard, I had never before in my life written a letter to a loved one, who was going to leave me to go to war. I dipped the quill in the ink and wrote:

My beloved Tréville,

This is a letter I never thought I would have to write and it is so hard for me to do. Just to say "I love you" doesn't seem enough, I've said it to you so many times, and I hope you understand what I really mean when I say it. How can so much feeling and intense loving fit into those three little words?

You are my life and my only true love, and I love you with all of my heart and each day you are away will seem like an eternity, until you return. I will miss not waking up with you in the mornings, feeling your arms around me, watching you sleep and feeling the beating of your heart with the palm of my hand, or listening with my head on your chest, and your gorgeous twinkling blue eyes that always captivate me every time I look into them.

Since the day we met I knew you were the only one for me. My most beautiful memories are the ones we have shared together, and, hopefully, there will be many more. Without you I would be so lost. Whilst reading one day, I came across this poem:

It was a short time

When I became yours

And you became mine

And we will always be together

Until the end of time

I promise to stay strong and keep myself safe, along with Amanda. You have taught me well how to use the pistol, sword and daggers.

I will pray, every day, to The Great Spirit to guide and protect you and my brothers. Our hearts are entwined and always will be until we leave this earth. When you return, maybe, The Great Spirit will bless us with the one thing we both want most – a child or children.

I have put in five eagle feathers, one for each of you, keep them close to your hearts, the eagle is a great protector in war, and they are a symbol of bravery and strength.

Take care my dearest love,

Je t'aime mon bien-aimé Tréville, et comme vous le dites, je vais toujours jusqu'à mon dernier souffle de vie.

Your beloved Lesley

xxxxxxxxxxxxxxxxx

At the same time I wrote a letter to each of my brothers, just simply saying:

I will be thinking of you every day my brother, take my sisterly love with you and I will await your return to me.

Your loving sister, Lesley xxxxxxxx

During the week, when I went to the garrison, Tréville introduced me to Gaston, who was going to look after the garrison whilst they were gone, along with about twenty men. Men who wanted to fight from the villages or outskirts of Paris would be brought to the garrison where they would be trained, and then replace the men who didn't return. Anything I needed I had to see him, especially if there was any trouble; I knew he meant Rochefort. With Tréville and my brothers going to war, that meant Rochefort was staying – Amanda and I would have to be very careful, but Amanda more so. Why could Rochefort not leave her alone! Tréville advised me never to go out without a pistol on my person, and maybe a dagger. He showed me where to hide them so they weren't on show. A cloak came in handy now.

Tréville and my brothers had already decided that on the last night we would all go to the tavern and have a meal together. When we arrived there must have been about fifteen Red Guards sitting and drinking, they looked at us and then turned away. "Gentlemen, please, no trouble tonight," said Tréville. We went and sat at a table, and enjoyed a lovely meal with wine, we laughed and talked about everything, except the war. Not once did the Red Guards make any attempt to rile us, this was most unusual.

After they had left, Aramis called to one of the wenches he knew and asked her if something was wrong, as the Red Guards had been quiet all night. "Have you not heard the news, my handsome?" she said. "Rochefort was killed early this morning, along with three of his men, and they're all mourning him. I, for one, am not. He was an evil, vicious man and I'm glad I won't ever have to see him again. I am also delighted 'biter' is dead too."

"Biter?" said Aramis.

"A nickname we gave one of his men; every time he went with a wench, which thankfully wasn't many, he would bite them somewhere and would say it was a reminder of the best lover they'd ever had." The tumbler of wine in my hand fell to the ground as a memory came flooding back.

"You all right? You've gone very pale, deary. He didn't..." she said.

I looked at her and apologised and said the tumbler just slipped from my hand. She walked round and picked the tumbler up and then walked back to the bar. Tréville's arm went round my waist and he held me close and kissed my cheek. Amanda asked me if I was all right, I smiled and nodded.

We all looked at each other in stunned silence. Athos then said, "You have heard nothing of this, Minister?" Tréville replied he had heard nothing, but then he had not been at the palace that day.

Something told me he knew more, and then I remembered the remark the King had said to me, "Rochefort would get his comeuppance." They were all off to war tomorrow and somehow Rochefort gets killed before they leave, this was more than a coincidence, but I kept my thoughts to myself. Amanda and I had our freedom back.

"Well I'm glad he's dead, at least Lesley and Amanda will be safe now," said D'Artagnan.

Porthos went and got me another tumbler, and then filled all the tumblers with wine and said, "Ladies, gents, a toast to Rochefort. May him and his men rot very, very slowly in hell." We all drank to that.

When we went to leave, one of the King's guards arrived and gave Tréville a written message, then bowed and left. Tréville read the message and said, "It is from the King confirming Rochefort's death. For reasons unbeknown to the King, Rochefort and three of his men had left the palace before the sun rose, but out of uniform. About a dozen men wearing the Spanish uniform attacked them. Apart from one Red Guard, who made it back to the palace, then passed of his injuries, the rest of them died. The King sent some other Red Guards to retrieve the bodies, which they did, and Rochefort's was one of them. He is sad at Rochefort's passing, but quietly relieved that Amanda and Lesley will now be safe. He also hopes all will go well with what we are about to face. Apparently we are his Champions." I looked at Tréville; maybe he didn't know anything, and he actually looked surprised at the news.

"Wonder what he was up to?" said D'Artagnan.

Aramis put his arm round D'Artagnan's shoulder and replied, "That, my friend, we will never know." We all said our goodnights and parted company.

After Tréville and I retired for the night, I thought our passions had been intense and passionate before, but this night we went to different levels of passion that neither of us knew existed. I actually felt our hearts entwine. Afterwards Tréville wriggled down the bed and put his head on my stomach. "You prefer my stomach to my arms?"

Tréville looked up at me, smiling, and said, "No, my love, I was thinking if one day we were honoured and you carried my child, I would be the most happiest and contented man ever."

I looked into his eyes and put my hands on his face and he came back up the bed, kissing my stomach and upwards until he met my lips. I kissed him so gently and said, "Tréville, if the Great Spirit grants our wish I would be happy and contented too, our child would be ours to cherish forever more." He wound his arms around me as I did him, kissing each other deeply, until our passions for each other had been reached again and then we slept entwined in each other's arms.

I woke later but my eyes deceived me. I was floating, looking down at myself and Tréville; for some reason I had rolled over onto my back. Was this an omen that he was not coming back and I would be on my own? We always slept in each other's arms. I felt strange and Tala was yapping, but I felt she was contented, I'd never known her like that before. I carried on slowly floating up into the night, the bakery and garrison getting smaller and smaller, slowly passing the full bright moon and the many hundreds of stars, which, as a child I was told were my tribe's ancestors, and then I entered a new dawn. I recognised where I was, I was floating over the Reservation. Suddenly I was concerned, had I passed?

A voice said, "Fear not, my child, you have not passed, you are here for another reason."

"If I may, what reason?" I asked. I got no reply. The sky was a brilliant blue, the sun shining brightly, fields green with different coloured flowers, the river looking cool and inviting. I could hear wolves howling in contentment, and Tala had joined in, the beating of the Indian drums and chanting – but I saw no one.

I felt a powerful heat on me and when I looked I was covered from head to foot in the most beautiful colours of a double rainbow, and Tréville was entwined in my arms. I saw both of our hearts rise for the Great Spirit to bless, and then return. Tréville and I looked into each other's eyes and we kissed each other with such a passion that I actually felt our heart's beat as one. We basked in this light for a time and then Tréville was gone and I started to float down. As I descended I saw a movement, it was Motomo and his mate with four young cubs by the river, at least they were on the Reservation. That was a great honour for Motomo. It had been so long since I had seen him. I waved, he howled back and Tala howled as well. Slowly I carried on floating down, the full moon now brighter than before and every star brightly twinkling in the night sky. The bakery came into my view, as did the garrison. I was then back with my love and I rolled over to face him. Tréville must have felt me move and said sleepily, "You all right, my love?" I replied I was fine, we kissed each other deeply and then our arms entwined around each other. I put my head on his chest, listening to the gentle beat of his heart, and we both drifted back off into slumber.

The following morning, Tréville and I looked at each other, the day we dreaded was now here. He took my face in his hands and kissed me so tenderly, I felt tears in my eyes. Our arms went round each other, our kisses deepening, our eyes showing our love for each other and slowly our passions were reached, maybe for the last time, but hopefully not. We held each other so tightly. Afterwards we washed and dressed, then went down to the bakery. The entire workforce wished Tréville, and his men, well. Once outside, we were just about to walk to the garrison when suddenly Tréville said he had forgotten something and went back. He said he had forgotten his gloves. I could have sworn they were in his belt, as usual. As we entered the garrison, all the Musketeers and horses were ready. Tréville and I went to his office. My brothers were there, sorting out their armoury, weapons and everything else. The time had come for them to go. Amanda and myself said a tearful farewell to our Musketeer brothers, and then Athos put his hand out and we all followed.

We looked at each other and Athos said, "All for one..."

We all replied, "One for all."

Amanda and the rest of them left.

Tréville took me in his arms and kissed me deeply. I couldn't help it, the tears flowed down my face, and there was an ache in my heart I had never known before. I took his face in my hands and looked into his now sad blue eyes and said, "Remember, my love, my heart is entwined with yours and I will always be with you and I love you more than life itself. May the Great Spirit guide and protect you all." We just held each other so tightly that neither of us wanted to let go.

Tréville took my face in his hands and wiped away my tears. "My dearest love, I love you so much, and I will always love you until my very last breath and my heart will always be with you." He sighed and said, "My men await me, and it's time for me to go." We walked out of his office and stopped on the balcony and looked down at the Musketeers, and then for my eyes only I noticed my father, mother, the wolves and Swallowtail were there. My mother was stood to one side with the wolves. Swallowtail and my father were dancing and chanting around my Musketeer brothers, doing a protection dance. I stood back behind Tréville.

Tréville then said, "Gentlemen, the time has come for us to go and fight for France. In the past some of us have fought many battles, and we showed that France were the victorious. We are to defend the northern borders of France from the Spanish. Listen to your Captain Athos, and follow his orders. Most of the time I will be with you, some of the time I will be away from you. We do not know what we are going to endure in this battle – watch your comrades' backs. My wish would be for all of you to return safely, but we know some of you will not. You are all brave Musketeers in my eyes, so let's ride and defeat the Spanish and victory."

A loud cheer went up from the Musketeers. I looked at Tréville's back and could feel my tears forming, but I must not cry, and swallowed hard and took a deep breath. Swallowtail and my father were now throwing protection dust over the rest of the men. My mother beckoned me down, so I went to Tréville and we walked down the steps, holding hands, to his waiting Musketeers.

Tréville went over and spoke to my brothers and at the same time Swallowtail chanted round him, throwing the protection dust over him. "**Musketeers,**" shouted Athos, "**mount your horses**." The Musketeers mounted their horses, apart from Tréville and my brothers. We all hugged and kissed each other on the cheeks again. Porthos took Amanda in his arms and kissed her deeply, Tréville held me so tight and then kissed me deeply, and whispered, "I love you so much, my beautiful wife. Please stay safe."

I took the letters from my skirt pocket and said, "Tréville, I have written a letter for you, and one each for my brothers," and gave them to him. He put them in his inside pocket, next to his heart and said he would hand them out that evening. He and my brothers then mounted their horses, and in front of the other Musketeers, rode out to heaven knows what might befall them. Amanda and I stood there holding each other with tears rolling down our faces. We didn't know when we would see them again, if ever. Unbeknown to Amanda, my father, mother and Swallowtail had their arms round both of us. After they had ridden out, the garrison fell silent. My father, mother, and Swallowtail said their goodbyes to me, after Swallowtail said she would see me later – I wondered why – and with the wolves faded away. Amanda sadly returned to work at the palace and I walked back to the bakery. All of a sudden I felt so lonely. Catherine came to me and we both wept for our men together. We then started baking the pies for the men left at the garrison, and fulfilling other orders.

It was late when I went up to my parlour and the first thing I noticed, after I had lit the candles, was a large water-filled fleur-de-lis tumbler with a bunch of red roses, a letter and a small box. I took the box and letter and sat on the bed. I opened the letter and it read:

My dearest love,

Leaving you is the hardest thing I have ever had to do, especially when I do not know when I will return, and so I thought you might like these gifts to remind you of how much I love you, and I love you so deeply. We have only been married a couple of months but always remember, you captured my heart from the first moment I saw you. You are the one thing in my life I can count on, and at the end of every day it's only you I want to hold in my arms. I know when I'm away from you I will miss you every minute of every day. We have been through such a lot together and survived and I hope we will be together at the end of this too.

I want to promise you we will all return, but I cannot, and that saddens me. Should the worst happen to me, and I pray it won't, my love please do not grieve for me for too long. Hopefully, happiness will come to you again, please consider it. It would sadden me greatly to think you were not happy.

The gift in the box I had specially designed and I hope you like it.

I have never told you this before, but I am so proud to be your husband. My heart will always be with you, and, as I always say to you, Je t'aimerai toujours jusqu'à mon dernier souffle de vie.

Stay safe my beautiful wife.

Je t'aime, mon très cher amour.

Tréville xxxxxxxxxxxxxxxxx

I opened the box and tears fell from my eyes; inside was the most gorgeous necklace I had ever seen. It was in the shape of a hollow heart. In the middle was a solid amethyst heart surrounded by tiny pearls. Each side of the amethyst heart had a fleur-de-lis, in small pink stones. The outside of the heart was in tiny amethyst stones. Suddenly Swallowtail appeared. "Spirit of the Wolf, may I have your necklace please?" I gave it to her and she chanted something over it, and then gave it back to me. "Now you can put it on, Spirit of the Wolf," she said. I took it and put it round my neck. The minute I put it on, I felt a calming, and I could feel the solid heart beating. "Spirit of the Wolf, as you know, both of your hearts are entwined. Tréville was guided, unbeknown to him, as to how the necklace was to be made. As long as this heart beats you will know Tréville lives. It will only stop beating the day he leaves this world."

"Oh Swallowtail, thank you so much." We hugged and she left. From that moment on I never took the necklace off.

CHAPTER 26

Reminiscing

The worst time was when I retired to bed and Tréville was not there to hold me; I cried myself to sleep most nights. I'm sure it was the same for Amanda. About five to six weeks went by before I met up with her. "Oh Lesley, what a lovely necklace." I told her it was a gift left from Tréville along with a letter and roses. (As the rose petals fell I carefully put them into a book to keep forever, along with Tréville's letter.) I asked her to come to the bakery for a meal, so we made arrangements for the Sunday. Amanda arrived just before the middle of the day. After we had finished our meal, I made us some hot chocolate and we sat by a roaring fire. We talked about our husbands, of whom we had heard nothing. Amanda then asked me why I had kept my marriage a secret. I explained I hadn't, it just didn't seem right to spoil their engagement and wedding. She wanted to know what happened and what our wedding was like. "I will tell you everything, but it's a long story, so tell me all about your honeymoon first," I said. Amanda then told me all about she and Porthos's honeymoon.

Amanda told me how Claudette had given them the run of her home whilst she was away, and how excited she was to see that a tub had been put in one of the rooms for bathing. I noticed her blush slightly, obviously remembering a private moment with Porthos. She told me of their days out, and how Porthos taught her to fire a pistol so she could protect herself. They had cooked together, but now it all seemed like a distant memory. She told me of the gift that Porthos had made for her by the blacksmith and she would show me the next time I was at the garrison.

I then relayed my story to Amanda.

"Going back to the beginning, you knew straight away that I liked Tréville, as you did with Porthos, but to start with I saw him as more of a brother than a lover. Then when I was left the dwelling I decided to give Tréville a key, so he could relax. Both of us did go separately, but as you know we mainly went together. Naturally, like you and Porthos, I got to see him in a non-working light and I liked what I saw. All the troubles we went through seem to bring us closer; I knew how I felt, but still wasn't sure of Tréville. The turning point was when I returned after being away for those three months. After that, it was like Tréville was a different man.

"One weekend at the dwelling, about two months ago, Tréville seemed to be deep in thought. I did not ask what worried him as I thought it might be something I didn't want to hear. We went for a meal at the tavern and then he asked if we might go for a walk and then sit on the bench by the stream. Our walk was quiet, neither of us spoke, I was getting really worried as to what was wrong with Tréville, then we sat on the bench. 'Lesley, I must speak to you of a... um... a private matter, and I am worried about how you will receive it,' he said. 'Tréville, please tell me what is wrong, you have not been yourself since we arrived.' He looked at me with such a serious expression, and then took my hands in his. 'I hope what I have to say does not shock you too much, but I can keep quiet no longer. The day Philip shot you I thought I had lost you and then something strange happened. I felt a hand on my heart and a voice whispered, "She is a survivor, she will not pass this day." (I knew that was my father.) After both incidents with Rochefort I had never wanted to kill anyone as much as I wanted to kill him. Then the Condesa arrived, and you rode out of my life, and I thought I would never see you again, and for the first time in my life I knew real heartache. We have been through so much together, and yet we are still with each other. I have tried, on many occasions to tell you, but, if I'm honest, I was actually scared.'

"Tréville took my face in his hands and looking into my eyes said, 'Lesley, I can hold back no longer. I love you with all of my heart. I have been in love with you since the day we first met, and I would like for us to wed. I know I should have told you my feelings long ago, but I worried you might not feel the same, and there is the fact that I am four years older than you.' I looked at Tréville, into his gorgeous blue eyes, and before I could say anything he gently kissed my lips with such tenderness.

"My heart was beating so fast I thought it would come out of my chest. Tala was feeling my emotions but in a different way. She didn't want to run, she was enjoying what was happening between Tréville and me. Our lips separated, and in that moment I knew my father, Monsieur Rennard and you had been right. I loved Tréville with all of my heart, and I had never felt safer and loved than when I was with him. 'I love you too, Tréville, I always have. To me your age does not matter,' and I placed my hand on his heart. 'In here you are young and I thank the Great Spirit for sending you to me, and my answer is yes, I will wed you,' I said. Our arms entwined around each other as we embraced our next kiss, which seem to go on forever, and I felt as if the heavens had opened and encircled us with all the love possible. As we walked back to the dwelling I asked Tréville if he had kissed me the day I was shot, or had I imagined it? He looked at me and said, 'Yes, I did kiss you, I couldn't help it. I had to know you were breathing life and had not left me, if that makes sense.' I replied by gently taking his face in my hands and kissing him. When we arrived back at the dwelling, we curled up together on the long chair in front of the fire, his arm around me, with my head on his shoulder and reminisced about when we had first met, and after.

"Tréville said he noticed me the minute I walked into the Paris tavern, and knew I was from England as soon as I spoke to the tavern owner, but he also noticed I wasn't pale like most English ladies, and had said to Porthos he was worried for me being on my own. Porthos apparently raised his eyebrow and said, 'Someone catch your eye, Captain?' Paris especially after dark was not a good place for a lady to be on her own. (Unfortunately they were not staying at the same tavern as me. I told him what had happened that night, with the Red Guards.) The following day, the other three normal Musketeers went on their way, and then he and Porthos saw me out walking and that's when they followed me to the square. He was stunned when I told him I was looking for you. If that wasn't fate he didn't know what was. Whilst I chose my ball gown he had already decided I would ride with him. When Porthos helped me onto his horse and I was in his arms he just knew I would always be with him. When he saw me in my ball gown, his heart missed a beat, and he said I looked so beautiful. When I stayed at the garrison, in his office, it somehow felt right. The way I had helped him tidy things up, and then helped in the kitchen and various other help within the garrison. He was worried about the relationship of you and Porthos but over time he saw you were meant for each other, and if you were at the garrison he knew I would be there as well. When I used to go walking or riding he would worry and was relieved when I returned. The day I moved into my lodgings he felt a bit lonely again, but knew I was at the bakery and hoped I would visit the garrison.

"He so looked forward to my visits, and was annoyed with himself if he had missed me. He thought I would stay in England and was so happy when I returned and told him I had decided to stay in France. He was furious with himself over the Michelle and Condesa incidents and felt he had lost me forever. I told him from the first moment I met him, I felt a stirring in my heart and when I rode back with him it felt so natural to be in his arms. My heart had melted when he had been stood on the balcony, after I had hit Athos, and he had smiled. He asked me why I had hit Athos, and I told him that was one secret I could not tell, but all had finished on an amicable note. He understood. Same as him, I thought I had lost him forever when Michelle arrived, and the Condesa incident. He also told me, as well as our brothers, all the Musketeers in the garrison had taken both of us to their hearts and looked upon us as their sisters. Tears welled in my eyes at that.

"Looking back to that night, both of us poured our hearts out to each other and we never looked back. Both of us had been through so much together, and so far survived. I made myself a hot chocolate, Tréville had some wine, and then as we kissed each other goodnight Tréville said, 'Lesley, may I... umm... ask you something?' I replied, 'Of course, Tréville, what is it?' He looked at me and seemed hesitant. 'You know I am a gentleman, Lesley, and would never do anything to embarrass you, but I wondered if... um... I may lay with you this night?' That was not what I was expecting and felt my face go crimson. 'Please forgive me, I should never has suggested it,' said Tréville. 'Please, Tréville, I would like you to lay with me, but I cannot until after we are wed, it would bring dishonour to myself, my family and my tribe.' Tréville took my face in his hands and kissed my lips gently and said, 'And I honour that. I love you and just want to sleep with you in my arms, I have waited so long for this moment.' I trusted Tréville and knew he would keep his word so I agreed. We went to our separate rooms to wash and undress and put our night garments on. When Tréville knocked on my door I was sitting on the bed brushing my hair and told him to enter. I turned to look at him and my heart missed a beat and I blushed, he stood there with just his undergarment on. I took all of him in slowly and felt very hot all of a sudden. I looked away and carried on brushing my hair. 'Forgive me, I do not sleep in a night garment, do you have one I could borrow?' I replied I didn't.

"He came and sat on the bed and said, 'May I?' He took the brush and gently took my hair in his hand and brushed it for me. 'I used to brush my mother's hair, but it was never as long as yours or as soft, and I love the way it looks like long curls. Do you sleep with it like this?' I replied I didn't, night-time I put it into one plait, and during the day I did three plaits and then put them into one, rolled and twisted it up and pinned it to the back of my head. When I washed it I re-plaited it and let it dry. He finished brushing and quickly I plaited it. We both looked at each other and I shivered. 'My dear, you are getting cold.' I was far from getting cold, but I could not tell him that. I got into the bed and Tréville asked me again if it was still all right. I replied by moving the blanket so he could get in. It felt so strange to me to have him in my bed, but at the same time safe. Tréville wrapped his arms round me and we kissed each other, but kissing more deeply each time. My hands roamed over his chest and back and then I felt his manhood pressing against me. Tréville broke our kisses, and with arms still around each other, I laid my head on his shoulder. My whole body felt on fire and every nerve end was tingling. I drifted off to sleep hoping I didn't have too long to wait to marry my handsome Captain. In the morning I was awoken with a gentle kiss and still wrapped in Tréville's arms – we both felt so content with each other. Once we had lain with each other we wanted to be together every night, but that was impossible. When we were at the dwelling though we did share my bed, but nothing untoward happened.

"The following day we went and saw the priest who said he could marry us in just over three weeks. After seeing the priest we went to see Helene, who was delighted for us. By the end of that day the whole village knew, and we were invited to the tavern for a surprise celebration. Four weeks after we found out how much we were in love with each other we married and on the Sunday night we returned to the garrison to tell all of you our news and to arrange a celebratory meal, and then Athos told us your news. Luckily both of us were wearing gloves so no one saw our rings. Tréville and I went up to his office and watched the celebrations from the balcony, and then slipped into his office. We removed our wedding rings and I kept them in a pouch around my neck. Neither of us wanted to spoil the brilliant news of your engagement. We then went back and joined in with the celebrations. Athos looked at me curiously and said, 'Something we should know about you and the Captain? You both look as though something has happened between you.' I replied there was nothing, we were just good friends, who had both enjoyed a break away from our busy lives. Athos seemed to accept that, but for some reason stayed close to me all that night. Instead of being drunk he was charming, witty and I saw him differently; he was also very caring. Tréville glanced over to me a couple of times and smiled and winked. Apart from Helene and the villagers, the only other person I confided in about our pending marriage was Catherine and she was then sworn to secrecy. After we were wed, the only way Tréville and I could be together was at the dwelling, so we always arranged to meet there, whenever we could. We had moments together in his office when we could and yes, twice in his office Athos or yourself nearly caught us, when we were in a passionate embrace. It was so hard to keep our secret from you.

"A week before the wedding my mother and Swallowtail visited me. They were both delighted with my news. My mother said it would be nice after our church wedding to have an Indian wedding. She explained to me what would happen, and the dress to wear, how to do my hair and what Tréville could wear. I was to wear full Indian outfit, along with my tribe markings on my face, but Tréville could not. Swallowtail told me she would return two nights before the wedding and bring my dress, feathers and the shirt for Tréville, which he would wear over his breeches, as she would have done a special blessing on them, sacred only to us. My hair had to be braided into two plaits, with sacred feathers, which would hang either side of my face. My mother then explained, albeit embarrassingly, what would happen on my wedding night. At least I wouldn't have to show my

Indian tribe the proof that Tréville was my first. Swallowtail gave me the sayings for Tréville and me to learn. We married in the village church; Tréville came the night before but stayed at the tavern, all the villagers attended. Catherine gave me away, and then afterwards, in the tavern, we told the villagers there would be a special ceremony taking place in the evening, and all were welcomed. I then explained briefly about my upbringing.

"Later on Tréville and I went back to the dwelling to change. He took me in his arms and kissed me so deeply, I could see and feel the passion within him. 'Tréville, can we wait? I know it seems stupid, but I want to have our Indian wedding first and then I'm all yours.' Tréville smiled and said, 'My love, of course and then I am all yours as well.' Our arms entwined around each other, kisses deepening until we released each other. Tréville went to his bedchamber and changed, I changed in mine, soon to become ours. Tréville left before me, so both of us would have a surprise when we saw each other. Even though Swallowtail had brought our clothing, neither of us had seen them. Tréville's shirt was put in his cabinet, and my dress in mine.

Tréville's shirt had actually belonged to my father, which was a huge honour on the part of my father and mother. I told Tréville I had brought it with me from the Americas. My dress was white – for purity. A white belt around my waist had blue beads hanging from it. Around my neck was a blue beaded necklace. A headband made from various coloured wampum beads was secured round my forehead, with five eagle feathers attached at the back. I had white moccasins with blue beads attached, on my feet. I then put my tribe markings on my face and when I was ready, I left for our Indian Wedding. It was called The Rite of Seven Steps.

"Both bride and groom take seven steps sun-wise (clockwise) around a sacred fire. For each step taken, each says a vow. The groom makes one step forward and says a vow, and then the bride takes a step to join him and says her vow until one round, around the fire, is completed. The villagers and Catherine joined hands in a circle around the fire. They had no idea what was going to happen, and when I arrived they all gasped. They had never seen an Indian before, but the smiles told me they approved. Tréville was already there and the smile he gave me was wonderful. 'You look absolutely beautiful, the markings on your face are lovely, you must tell me what they mean, and the coloured feathers in your hair are amazing. I look forward to unbraiding them later, my beautiful Indian bride,' he said with a twinkle in his eyes. I replied how handsome he looked in his shirt. All of a sudden I could hear the beat of the Indian drums and chanting. I looked in the distance and to my surprise there was my father, mother, the wolves, and other Indians of my tribe. My father and the Indians were dancing a ritual with the wolves, to the sound of the Indian drums, and it was good to see them there. Of course no one else could see them. I then looked at the fire and Swallowtail was there, chanting her own songs and completing various wedding rituals, to make the fire sacred. I looked at my mother and nodded thanks, and she smiled. Tréville grabbed my hand and said, 'Are you all right, my love? You look far away. Is something wrong?' I replied, 'No, my love, everything is now perfect, so let's get married again, the Indian way.'

"The ritual began.

"Tréville Step 1: O my beloved, our love has become firm by your walking one with me. Together we will share the responsibilities of the lodge, food and children. May the Creator bless noble children to share, and may they live long.

"Me Step 1: This is my commitment to you, my husband. Together we will share the responsibility of the home, food and children. I promise that I shall discharge all my share of the responsibilities for the welfare of the family and the children.

"Tréville Step 2: O my beloved, now you have walked with me the second step. May the Creator bless you, and I will love you and you alone as my wife. I will fill your heart with strength and courage, and this is my commitment and my pledge to you. May the Great Spirit protect the lodge and our children.

"Me Step 2: O my husband, at all times I shall fill your heart with courage and strength. In your happiness I shall rejoice. May the Great Spirit bless you and our honourable lodge.

"Tréville Step 3: O my beloved, now since you have walked three steps with me, our wealth and prosperity will grow. May the Great Spirit bless us. May we educate our children and may they live long.

"Me Step 3: O my husband, I love you with single-minded devotion as my husband. I will treat all other men as my brothers. My devotion to you is pure and you are my joy. This is my commitment and pledge to you.

"Tréville Step 4: O my beloved, it is a great blessing that you have now walked four steps with me. May the Creator bless you. You have brought favour and sacredness in my life.

"Me Step 4: O my husband, in all acts of righteousness, in material prosperity, in every form of enjoyment, and in those divine acts such as fire sacrifice, worship and charity, I promise you that I shall participate and I will always be with you.

"Tréville Step 5: O my beloved, now you have walked five steps with me. May the Creator make us prosperous. May the Creator bless us.

"Me Step 5: O my husband, I will share both in your joys and sorrows. Your love will make me very happy.

"Tréville Step 6: O my beloved, by walking six steps with me, you have filled my heart with happiness. May I fill your heart with great joy and peace, time and time again. May the Creator bless you.

"Me Step 6: O my husband, the Creator blesses you. May I fill your heart with great joy and peace. I promise that I will always be with you.

"Tréville Step 7: O my beloved, as you have walked the seven steps with me, our love and friendship have become inseparable and firm. We have experienced spiritual union in the Great Spirit. Now you have become completely mine. I offer my total self to you. May our marriage last forever.

"Me Step 7: O my husband, by the law of the Creator, and the spirits of our honourable ancestors, I have become your wife. Whatever promises I gave you I have spoken them with a pure heart. All the spirits are witnesses to this fact. I shall never deceive you, nor will I let you down. I shall love you forever.

"As we said each step the drums and chanting got louder and louder. We then hugged and kissed each other, and the villagers showered us with different coloured petals. When the ceremony was over I looked over to where my father and mother stood and there was just them, Swallowtail and the wolves had left. They bowed and waved. I told Tréville we had to bow and we did, and then they were gone. The fire was doused and we all went back to the tavern to continue our wedding feast.

"Tréville and I had already decided to have a wedding blessing so all of you could attend. The village church was too small and Tréville needed to be near the garrison. When we heard you were getting married we decided we would like to celebrate with you, but still keep it as a surprise, and because of that Tréville took Athos into his confidence. After Athos knew, he took my arm one day and said, 'So nothing happened at the dwelling then? You convinced me that night he was a brother, when he was actually your husband.' I looked at Athos and smiled and said, 'A lady must keep her secrets close to her chest.' He replied, 'I'll never understand women, but you have made him happier than he's ever been and anyone can see how much you love each other, and about time too,' and with that he kissed my cheek and walked away."

"What about the wedding night, Lesley?" Amanda asked, with a glint in her eyes. "Did you have a ritual Indian night?"

I felt myself blush slightly and smiled. "As you know, I had not given myself to another man and was rather shy and worried I would not perform as a wife should, but Tréville was so gentle and patient. He asked me about my face markings, before I washed them off, spent time unplaiting and brushing my hair and carefully putting the feathers into a basket, so they would not crush. He took me in his arms and kissed me and went to remove my dress. I stopped him and said shyly, 'I have no petticoat on under my dress, Tréville.' He removed his boots, shirt and breeches and then blew the candles out. He slowly undid the four-bead fastening at the back of my dress, kissing me deeply, and then put his hands on my shoulders and gently pushed my dress down, which slid to the floor, and I carefully unlaced his undergarment, which also fell to the floor. He picked me up in his arms and gently laid me down on the bed, my hair fanned out around me. I could see his eyes were full of passion and we deepened our kisses. My hands roamed over his chest and back, holding him so close. He was kissing my neck, which always took my breath away, and then his kisses went lower. When his hand went up the inside of my left thigh though I froze, it brought back the memory of Rochefort's man biting me. Tréville looked at me and said softly, 'It's all right, my love, it's me, no one else,' and then he gently kissed where I had been bitten. I will not go into detail, my dear Amanda, let's just say, the clouds disappeared and the bright moon shone down on both of us, and our love for each other was overwhelming. We slept entwined in each other's arms. At last I had my handsome Captain.

"In the morning, after a passionate embrace, Tréville moved the blanket, to go and get us something to eat and drink. I had never seen him naked, or any other man fully naked before, and I lowered my eyes and blushed so red that Tréville smiled. He put his hand on my face and said, 'My love, there is no need for you to blush, after all we got to know each other's bodies intimately last night, and we slept naked.' I look at him and said, 'I know... but it was dark." He kissed me and went to the parlour. When he returned, yes, I blushed again. I saw the long scar on his leg, and when he sat next to me I ran my hand over it. 'Does it hurt you at all?' I asked. He replied not anymore. I sat up and looked at him. 'Lesley, are you all right?' There was one question I wanted to ask him. 'Tréville, may I ask you a very personal question?' He replied, 'Of course my love, you can ask me anything.' I lowered my eyes and said, 'I know I should not ask, but did you have many loves before me?' Tréville smiled and said, 'You are my one and only true love. When I was about twelve, my father introduced me to a wench he knew well, who in my father's words "broke me into a man – eventually." I can't say it was a pleasant experience, but I learnt what I had to do. Yes, I have had wenches now and then, but they always reminded me of my father's wench, and I had to have a lot of wine inside me first. I have escorted ladies out, but nothing untoward ever happened, but that all changed when I met you.'

"I could see the sincerity in his eyes, so I knew what he was saying was true. I smiled and kissed him. 'Your blushes seem to have gone now,' said Tréville. I looked at him curiously. Tréville took me in his arms and said, 'When you sat up the blanket fell, leaving me with a lovely view.' I blushed slightly. I could see the passion in his eyes, and put my arms round his neck and kissed him deeply. We slowly lay back down in the bed, our lips never parting and slowly we were both taken over by our passions for each other. Food, drink and blushes were soon forgotten. Afterwards we washed each other in the tub, dressed and decided to go into Paris. We had a picnic by the Seine, we watched a puppet show, and then went to a coffee shop on Rue des Bucherie, where I had a lovely hot chocolate and Tréville had wine. We walked round admiring the architecture of Paris, then a meal in one of the rather upmarket hotels. By this time evening was drawing in. We went back to the dwelling and packed our bags as Tréville had to return to the garrison. It was a beautiful weekend, one I will never forget. We are both so in love with each other, as you and Porthos are, and now both of them have been wrenched from us."

Tears welled in both of our eyes.

CHAPTER 27

Surprise

All of a sudden Catherine came through the door breathing heavily. "Catherine, what's wrong?"

"A rider has come saying that some of the Musketeers are on their way back and some are badly wounded, they need Amanda," she said. All three of us went as fast as we could to the garrison and as we entered the gate, we heard a noise and turned and saw horses and carts coming towards us. There must have been at least forty Musketeers, but no Tréville or our brothers. There were about fifteen wounded so Amanda went straight to work. Catherine went to see if her Musketeer had returned; he had and he was well. I glanced over to the garrison kitchen and saw Pascal who looked rather anxious. I went over to him and asked him if all was well. "Got nothing to feed 'em with, only got bit of cold pig and chicken."

"Have you not been getting supplies from the palace?" I said.

"Hardly any, half of 'em gone, don't know who's coming back, or when. Now they're 'ere, got nothing to give em."

I thought for a moment. "Pascal, get some broth going and I will be back shortly." I looked for Gaston and asked if he could spare us a horse and cart and a couple of men to get more supplies.

I found Catherine and we all went back to the bakery and loaded the cart with pies, bread, cakes, anything that was baked. The farmer had started growing things called artichokes, carrots, onions, cauliflower, leeks and chicory, so I took those as well. I went to the fruit seller and got apples, grapes, oranges, whatever they could spare. Everything was put onto the cart and then into the garrison kitchen. Pascal had got the broth going, I added the vegetables, just as the farmer's wife had shown me. The men looked starved and cold, but once they had a large bowl of broth with bread and whatever afterwards, they were soon well fed and warm and then made their way to their families or rooms. I asked Catherine to go and see Amanda, to see what could be given to the wounded. A bit later I heard more horses galloping in and I looked up to see Porthos, Athos, Aramis, and D'Artagnan all come riding in. "**Amanda!**" I shouted. They all looked battered and bruised but alive.

Amanda ran to Porthos, I ran and hugged the rest of them. I looked out of the garrison but no other riders were there. *Please no, not Tréville.* "Where is Tréville? Please, he's not?" I asked with tears welling in my eyes.

"Lesley, calm yourself; he is with us, he has gone to the palace, and thank you for your letters and eagle feathers, it meant a lot to all of us," said Athos. I was so relieved I nearly fainted but D'Artagnan caught me. I was having a few fainting spells – I put it down to my emotions, and not eating properly. My brothers went and sat at a table in the back of the meeting room. I cut up what was left of the pig and chicken and put that in the middle, along with some broth and bread. I also put pies, pastries and more bread on the table with wine, but kept some to one side for Tréville.

Afterwards Porthos, who would have eaten everything in sight, given the chance said, "That was delicious, I've been wasting away. Now where's that wench of a wife of mine gone?"

I looked at him and said, "She is not a wench, Porthos. Amanda is your wife and she's tending the wounded."

"My apologies, Lesley, it was meant as an endearment," and with that gave me a hug and kiss on my forehead, winked and walked off.

A voice behind me said, "Anything left for me?"

I turned and looked into Tréville's eyes and tears of joy welled up. I ran into his arms and kissed him so long, that Aramis said, "Think it's time you two got a room." That made me smile.

After Tréville had eaten I told him about the supplies that had not been received from the palace. Tréville had a talk with Gaston and Pascal and then we said our goodnights and walked arm in arm back to the bakery. Once in our bedchamber, our kisses for each other were deep and passionate. Tréville said, "Oh my love, I have missed you so much. I see you liked your necklace." I never got chance to reply, within seconds our clothes were on the floor and our passions were intense as ever, maybe more so. Afterwards as we lay in each other's arms, Tréville told me how much my letter meant to him and he would carry it always, at least until after the war finished.

He wanted to know how the bakery was going and then I said, "We talk too much, my love," and kissed him deeply. Our passions rose again and then we slept entwined in each other's arms. It felt so good to have him back.

In the morning I asked Tréville about the war and if he had to go back. He replied, "I have an audience with the King later on to talk strategy and how this can, hopefully, be concluded, on the northern borders. The biggest war is on the southern French-Spanish border and I wonder if we will be sent there next. Where we have been, so far, even though it's only been six weeks, has been tough; lots of our men have been killed, as well as the Spanish, and we could not bury them, we had to leave them where they fell. The fights were long and bloody, and the men were soon starving, we had hardly any rations. The weather didn't help either, torrential rain, non-stop and everywhere was nothing but mud, which men got stuck in and were easy targets for the cannon or musket fire. Our wagons with gunpowder, rifles, muskets and bombs got held up. I won't say any more, my love, I don't want you having another nightmare and me not be here to hold you. I know we all have to return but for how long I have no idea, maybe another month or two."

My thoughts went to him and his men. *Please don't let anything happen to any of them.* We held each other tight and then he started kissing my neck and our passions led to him nearly being late for his audience with the King. Little did I know then it would be over seven months before I saw Tréville again!

Three days later they all left the garrison again, back to the northern borders with new recruits. The war there had flared up worse that what it was before. Amanda and I carried on with our lives, but four weeks later, three Musketeers arrived back at the garrison with Porthos, who was badly injured. Amanda was already at the garrison and attending to Porthos's injury when I got there. Catherine had told me who it was. He had been badly slashed across his stomach and even though Aramis had done his best to patch him up, infection had set in. Porthos was on a table thrashing around and sounded delirious. Amanda was distraught and crying. "Amanda, let me help Porthos, please," I said.

"What can you do, Lesley? You're not a physician," she replied, and then apologised for her sharp tongue.

"Amanda I have to take you into my confidence, you know I have a spirit wolf inside me and I have to run. Quite some time ago I found out I was a healer wolf; if you would let me try I might be able to help, but you must not breathe a word of what you will see and neither must you be frightened."

"Why on earth would I be frightened of you, Lesley?"

"Because once I've finished, Tala, my spirit wolf, will surface to heal me. My eyes also will change colour. They go from my normal dark brown to grey with yellow flecks in them. Also if I go to howl just say, 'Tala, no.' She will understand."

Amanda looked at me in disbelief, but nodded. I told her under no circumstances must anyone enter the room until I was back as myself. Amanda closed the door and I asked her to put something at Porthos's side to catch the infection as it came out of his wound and also to try and secure his arms down. I would have to re-open his wound and once I had finished Amanda would have to clean it and re-sew it up. Amanda tore up some blankets and tied them round Porthos's body including his arms. I went and stood over Porthos and put my hands on his face and chanted, slowly Porthos calmed and slept. Then I put my hands above the wound and started chanting for the light to appear. At first nothing happened, was it because I didn't love him with my whole heart like Tréville? I did love Porthos and the rest of them. They were my brothers.

Suddenly I felt the warmth from my hands come out and the light shone over his wound. Very, very slowly the wound opened and the infection and blood started to trickle out, which had a foul smell. After a short time I knew the infection was out and I could feel myself getting faint so I moved my hands away and quickly undressed, much to Amanda's amazement, and said, "Tala appear." Seconds later I was looking at Amanda through Tala's eyes. Amanda stood absolutely still, but I sensed she wasn't frightened, just curious. I padded over to her and nudged her hand with my nose, and she patted my head ever so gently. Amanda had never seen me as a wolf before. I then jumped onto the table and looked at Porthos, who just seemed to be sleeping, gave him a sniff and smelt no infection in his body. I jumped back down and padded round the room, looking at everything, and then went to where my clothes were. My mind started chanting, "Tala return, Spirit of the Wolf appear." After about a minute I re-appeared and dressed, but still felt drained, so I sat on a spare chair.

"How, what?" said Amanda, as she was sewing Porthos's wound back together again.

At that moment the door burst open and one of the wenches from the tavern stood in the doorway. "Wanna... hic... know how... hic... lovely Porthos is?" she said, quite drunk.

Amanda told her it had been touch and go, but once she stitched him up he would make a good recovery. She staggered out the door talking to herself. I looked at Amanda; that had been too close.

"How's Porthos, is he all right?"

Amanda told me he was a lot better and then looked at me and said, "Your eyes, they are so beautiful, I've never seen your eyes like that before." I was stunned.

"Are you saying my eyes are still grey and yellow?"

Amanda replied they were, but now they were going dark brown. Something was wrong with me, my eyes always changed more or less immediately. Amanda looked at me, as something registered within her, and said, "You healed Tréville when he was stabbed, didn't you?"

"Yes, along with my father, and that was when my father realised I was a healer wolf."

"Oh, Lesley, how can I thank you for saving my beloved?" she said.

"Amanda you saved my life after Philip shot me, and the incident with Rochefort, no thanks are needed. All I ask is please keep my secret."

"Oh, my friend, I will always keep your secret," she said, and we hugged each other. After a week of lots of tender loving care, Porthos returned to the war.

With the war in full flow, life was not so good. Our lovely lane was now a dirty alley. The miller and farmer could no longer send me supplies, as it was too dangerous, not from the Spanish, but the Red Guards who were pillaging everything. Animals were being slaughtered for food. The butcher, a couple of fruit sellers and the bakery got together and gave food to the men in the garrison when they returned, but even our supplies were going down. All we baked now was bread. We still had some customers, but people didn't have the coins anymore, as taxes were now very high, even some of the King's buildings were being sold off, noblemen were going bankrupt. None of the workforce now, except Catherine, had families so they stayed at the bakery and slept on straw pallets on makeshift beds in the tea room. Catherine decided she wanted to stay with her friends at the bakery, at least they were warm and dry. We put up a large piece of fabric, so the men and girls would have privacy. We all ate together, but smaller portions; others were not so fortunate. The poor people in the villages were foraging in the forests for fruit and nuts, even eating moss and dirt to survive. No more runs for Tala, and me, too dangerous. Cheese was made in two rounds, the first called "Le Bloche", the second "Re Bloche". The poor were given the Reblochon, which had a very, very low cream content. Any villagers lucky enough to have a cow could use the milk for butter or cheese. Hardly any of them had livestock. Vegetables were added to broth to make it thicker and were served with black bread. Wine was watered down and ale was stopped, as the grain was needed for food. Conditions for the poor became very harsh indeed. I heard some villages had been totally wiped out due to epidemics and famine. I hoped our village wasn't one of them.

I decided I would go into Paris, to see if anywhere had any sort of supplies I could have. I took the horse and cart but when I was on the outskirts of the city a feeling of foreboding told me to go no further. I had also forgotten to get a Musketeer to escort me, but I had two pistols, a sword and daggers. The smell from the city was stinking, smelt like rotting flesh. I looked through the large gates and saw four people running in my direction. I could see the shops were all barricaded up. There seem to be a huge fight taking place. The people who were running reached me. It was a family of father, mother and two children. "Don't go there, Madame, you might get out alive, but your horse won't."

I looked at the man who spoke. "What's happening?" I asked.

The man replied, "Thought we were at war with the Spanish, not each other. There's no food, people are starving and when someone finds a scrap of food, they're fighting each other to get it and it's brutal. Just yesterday a man of wealth rode through, within seconds he was dragged from his horse, killed and robbed. The poor horse was shot. People hacking the flesh from the horse's dead body and eating it." I felt the bile rising within me.

"Get in the cart," I said. "Where are you heading?" He told me they were going to try and get to his sister's in a village about two leagues away. I took them to the crossroads where we said our goodbyes, now they only had about half a league to go. I was relieved when I got back to the bakery.

I was glad the workforce had decided to stay at the bakery, as one night the Red Guards came banging on the door, there was six of them. "Good evening, gentlemen. What can I do for you?" I asked very politely.

"We have orders from the King to confiscate all your supplies."

I looked at them and said, "I find this very surprising. Are you sure? As now and then I receive a request from the King and Queen to supply them with extra supplies for guests who have arrived unexpectedly. Of course, if this is what the King has requested, please come in, I will not stand in your way," and moved to the side of the door to let them in. My heart was beating so loudly I was surprised they didn't hear it. Pierre and Laurens had pistols at the ready. The Red Guards looked at each other, and the one who had been talking beckoned to another of the men, had a conversation and then he replied they would check this with the King before removing any supplies. They never came back!

One day when I was in the bakery, my back and hip were really hurting and I didn't feel right. In fact I hadn't been feeling right for some time, and Tala had been very quiet, which was most unusual. Catherine looked at me and said, "Lesley, are you all right? You look ill, and you have not seemed well for some time. Maybe a visit to your physician would be an idea, he might be able to give you a remedy?"

I agreed and went to see him. When I left I was in shock. How would I cope with this news? I knew Tréville was alive because of my necklace, but I could tell no one. It felt like a lifetime since I last saw him, and now I desperately needed him. Would I see him again before my condition took me over? I had to talk to Amanda and Catherine straight away. I went to the garrison and saw Gaston. "Morning, Madame Tréville," he said.

I raised my eyebrow and looked at him. "Gaston, please call me Lesley, everyone else does." He smiled and asked me how he could help me. I asked him if he could spare a couple of Musketeers, my horse Sunkwa and another horse, as I wanted to go to the palace, along with Catherine, to see Amanda. (Tréville had left orders that Amanda and I were to be escorted at all times in case of trouble.)

Gaston replied, "Sunkwa, which one is that?" We walked to the stables, but I could not see Sunkwa. "**Remy!**" shouted Gaston. Remy came running, and Gaston asked him where Sunkwa was. Remy looked at me and lowered his eyes and said, "I'm sorry Madame Tréville, Sunkwa has gone to war, and he was taken by mistake."

"What?" I said. Remy replied he had left orders that Sunkwa was to remain separated from the rest, but when he arrived back from the palace, Sunkwa had gone. I was so upset, but what had happened, had happened.

"It's all right, Remy, it wasn't your fault, let us hope he returns."

Gaston then said, "I'm so sorry, Lesley, I had no idea. As to Amanda, she will be here soon. I have two injured men that need tending to and have despatched two Musketeers to escort her to the garrison."

I smiled and replied, "When Amanda has tended to your men, please can you ask her to come to the bakery? It's very important." Suddenly I felt faint and Gaston made me sit on the steps. He asked me if I was all right and I replied it was the heat, but he still insisted on walking me back to the bakery.

Once back Catherine came to me. "Lesley are you all right, what did the physician say?" I told her I was waiting for Amanda to arrive and then I would talk to both of them. I then went up to my parlour to rest.

Some time later Amanda arrived and came up to the parlour with Catherine. "Gaston said you had important news, is it our husbands?" asked Amanda. I stood and paced up and down and said I had heard nothing about them.

Catherine then said, "Lesley please tell us, what did the physician say, are you ill?"

Amanda looked at me and said, "Physician, why have you been to see him, are you all right?"

I looked at both of them and replied, "Oh, how I wish Tréville was here."

"Lesley, what's wrong? You must tell us," said Amanda.

I took a deep breath and said, "The physician told me that I have maybe five months left and..."

Both of them paled and Catherine burst into tears and said, "Oh, my friend, what will I do without you?"

I looked at them and said, "Oh no, my friends. The physician told me the reason I have not been feeling well and I have so much hip and back pain is The Great Spirit has blessed me and Tréville – I am with, not one, but two children, and have about five months to go. He also told me my labour would be intense as I am not young. How can I bring children into this world? We are at war and for all I know Tréville could be dead." My tears started to flow. Both Amanda and Catherine sighed with relief, and took me in their arms to comfort me.

"Lesley, this is delightful news, I am so happy for you but you must put all thoughts of Tréville being dead out of your mind, but I hate to be sad. If anything has happened to Tréville, you now have two little Trévilles to care for, and as to the war, well, other women are with child. They will manage and so will you, and you will always have us to help you, and you are young – stupid physician," said Amanda. Catherine was delighted as well and agreed with Amanda.

When I retired for the night I remembered the night when I floated up to the Reservation and Tala yapped and howled; she knew that night I'd conceived. The Great Spirit must have heard Tréville's wish. I put my hand on my stomach and the tears started to flow, I was happy but also sad at the same time. I just wanted Tréville here in my arms. I also then realised why my eyes didn't return to their normal colour quickly after healing Porthos. Tala was delighted, she had two cubs to look after. As I was now with children and needed all my strength, it meant I would not be able to heal Tréville, or my brothers, if they were injured, and nor could Tala and I go running. I gave Catherine more responsibility in the bakery, so when my time came she would be able to take over, if the bakery survived. I had already told Amanda and Catherine that I wanted to have our children at the dwelling, war or not. Catherine became well versed in the running of the bakery. I showed her how to pay the workforce and gave her the key to the safe. In return I rewarded her with more wages, and told her when I left she was to take over my rooms permanently.

Weeks later, in the morning, one of the guards from the palace called upon me to say that the King would like an audience with me that afternoon and a carriage would be sent at the appropriate time. Why on earth did the King want to see me? My mind was everywhere but I always came back to the same answer – Tréville. The carriage arrived and by this time I was really worried. Catherine walked to the carriage with me, gave me a hug, said everything would be all right and helped me in. When the carriage pulled up to the palace, another guard helped me out and I was escorted to a room where I was told to wait. I paced up and down the room and then the door opened and Amanda walked in. "Lesley, how lovely to see you, why are you here?"

"Oh, Amanda I have no idea. The King asked for an audience with me, have you heard any news about our husbands?" I said as I held my hands out to her, which she took. She replied she had heard nothing, but was curious as to why the King wanted to see me. "You don't think it's bad news, do you, about Tréville?" I asked, tears welling in my eyes.

"Lesley, try and stay calm, it's not good for your babies, or you. I'm sure it must be about something else." Hopefully it was. At that moment the escort came. Amanda walked with me, as far as she could go, and said she would wait for me – just in case. We went out of the room, down a corridor and then the escort opened another door where the King was.

The King was sitting on a chair looking out of the window. "Ah, Lesley, or should I say Madame Tréville? There you are," he said, smiling.

"Your Majesty," I said as I curtsied to him.

"Come sit by me," he said. As I moved to the chair he indicated to, he saw I was shaking slightly and took my hands.

"Oh Lesley, please calm yourself, this has nothing to do with Tréville... well, I suppose in a roundabout way it does. Amanda told the Queen you were with children and Tréville does not know. I know he is going to be away some time and wondered if you would like to, maybe write him a letter, and I will get a messenger to take it to him, or I could send a rider to bring him back, but only for a very short time," he said, releasing my hands. I was so relieved it was nothing serious.

"Thank you, Your Majesty, but I would rather Tréville did not know. He has enough to worry about, without worrying about our babies, and me, and his men need him. Hopefully he will return and it will be a lovely surprise for him."

The King looked at me and said, "Spoken like a true Minister's wife. Now if there is anything you need, like my physician, a bedchamber nearer your time, anything, you only have to ask. After all, my Minister for War would not be happy with me if anything untoward should happen to you. I must say, I like your necklace." I smiled and told him it was a gift from Tréville. He smiled and replied, "Well, I never knew Tréville had such an eye for beauty. In a necklace, I mean. Your beauty far outweighs it." I smiled and thanked him.

There was a knock at the door and a guard came in, bowed, and whispered something to the King. "Lesley, please forgive me, an urgent matter has come to my attention that I must deal with immediately, and do not worry, it's not Tréville, or his men."

I stood and said, "Thank you Your Majesty, and it was a pleasure to talk with you again," then curtsied as he walked out the door. The escort showed me back to where Amanda was waiting, and I told her all was well. She told the guard we would go back to her quarters and she would let him know when the carriage was required. I stayed with Amanda for about an hour, catching up on our news. Amanda went to advise the guard I was ready to return to the bakery. I kissed her cheek and hugged her and said I would see her soon. We were about halfway back, when the carriage jerked. I was thrown across to the other side of the carriage and then the carriage turned over and I screamed.

"Madame Tréville, Madame Tréville, can you hear me? Are you all right?" I heard a voice say. For a moment I wondered where I was, then I remembered. My hand went to my stomach.

"I'm here," I replied. I felt no pain anywhere, apart from a little bit in my hip, so hopefully my babies and myself were all right. The door of the carriage was wrenched open and Monsieur Verde appeared. "Lesley, are you hurt?" I replied I felt all right apart from my hip. "Can you stand, Lesley?" I moved and then stood up. Luckily it was a small carriage, so with help from Monsieur Verde and two Musketeers I was soon out of the carriage. "Lesley, you're pale, where is the pain?"

"Only in my hip, but Monsieur Verde, my babies?"

"You are with child?" he said. I replied I was with two. He was surprised he hadn't heard. At that moment another carriage arrived. Monsieur Verde helped me up and I sat down in the new carriage and then he examined me – he said everything was fine. I had only jolted my hip, and the pain would soon go. It turned out Monsieur Verde had been on his way back to the palace when he came across the upturned carriage. Everyone, including the horses, was all right and it turned out the wheel snapped. Monsieur Verde kindly accompanied me back to the bakery, his horse tethered to the back of the carriage. He made sure I was comfortable, had a chat with Catherine and then as he went to leave he said, "Oh Lesley, congratulations." I smiled and thanked him, and asked him to tell Amanda I was all right, as she would be worried. Catherine made sure I was all right every day, and Amanda came round when she could, over the following weeks. Luckily nothing untoward happened and life carried on as normal.

CHAPTER 28

The Village and Return

One very cold, windy December morning, I received a note from Amanda letting me know that a messenger had been sent, a couple of days before, to the border to bring Tréville back as the King wanted news of how the war was going. I had a feeling Tréville would be extremely annoyed at having to ride all the way back to see the King, and leaving his men, but then he was his Minister for War. Oh, I couldn't wait to see Tréville, and show him our news, and ask him about Porthos for Amanda. Alas, that was not meant to be. As soon as the King had his report, and he had discussed tactics with Tréville, which took some time, he was given a fresh horse and sent back immediately, with new recruits, who had ridden to the palace from the garrison. Even Amanda didn't see him. I was now six months, and Christmas was near. I was really missing him, as I was sure Amanda was missing Porthos. At least I knew Tréville was alive, my necklace told me every day. I was having problems with my back and hip, walking was painful, and this should have been our first married Christmas together. It was also the first Christmas I would spend without my brothers and Amanda, but I had my lovely workforce. The lead up to Christmas had been extremely busy, but all the orders were now fulfilled, and we could all relax for a couple of weeks.

A couple of days later, I looked out the window and saw it was snowing and for a time as the snow settled everything looked clean and fresh. Oh, how I wished I could go to my safe forest and let Tala run through the snow, we would have had so much fun. I stood by the window daydreaming of what might have been, when all of a sudden something hit the window and I jumped. A couple of children were having a snowball fight and let's just say one of them aimed high! I smiled and went down to the kitchen, but a knock at the door stopped me going in. Laurens and Pierre were at my side in a second. I opened the door and there stood Gaston. "Please, Gaston, come in and warm yourself," I said.

I must have looked a bit worried because Gaston replied, "It's all right, Madame Tréville – sorry, Lesley – it's not bad news." He had in fact come to invite my workforce and myself to a Christmas Day meal at the garrison. He knew we would be on our own and the King would be sending "special rations" for the day. Naturally I accepted on behalf of all of us.

We all left the bakery early afternoon on Christmas Day but now the lovely white snow had turned to slippery slush. Pierre and Laurens walked arm in arm with me, mainly to make sure I did not fall. When we got to the garrison we entered the meeting room and I was amazed. There were chickens that had been roasted, hams, cheeses, other meats, fruits, wine and ale. "Good heavens above, Gaston, where did all this come from?" I asked.

"All I know, Lesley, is that before our Minister Tréville left, he asked the King that we all be well fed on Christmas Day. This letter was also to be given to you today."

I smiled and thought to myself, *Oh my love, I so wish you were here with me.* I took the letter, and recognised Tréville's handwriting, opened it and it read:

My dearest love,

I'm saddened not to be with you this day, I'm sure we will have many more Christmases and New Years to celebrate together. Just to let you know that I am well, as are your brothers, and they send you their love. I was hoping to surprise you, but alas, the King told me I had to return to the border immediately, and instead of me coming to the garrison to get the new recruits, they were sent to the palace.

I hope you are well and I think of you every day and long to be back in your arms. I so wanted to take you in my arms and kiss you, hold you, I miss you so very, very much.

Apologies I can write no more, I have to go. Stay safe my beloved, and as always, I will love you until my very last breath.

Je t'aime de tout mon cœur.

Tréville xxxxxxxxxxxxxxxxxx

I smiled and tears came to my eyes. Catherine came to see if I was all right, I replied I was fine, just missing Tréville. There was a roaring fire going and the room was lovely and warm. There were only about twelve Musketeers that joined us. The rest of the Musketeers were in and out, after duties were done. We all sat around the tables and thoroughly enjoyed the best meal we'd had in a long time. Amanda was at the palace and enjoying the festivities there. I must send thanks to the King and Queen. I saw Gaston and thanked him again, I also asked him to make sure none of the Musketeers, if they were sent to fight, relay my condition to Tréville. Gaston was a father himself and understood, and assured me none of the Musketeers would say anything. We left the garrison very late that night, and all of us were happy, merry and full. There was enough food left over to feed the garrison the following couple of days as well.

A week later, the snow fell again and it was deep, everyone had huge problems getting around and it was also New Year. It was suggested that I did not go out on my own, in case I slipped, but I still helped in the bakery. I tired easily so mid-afternoon I would go to my parlour and rest. I saw the beginning of the New Year in with Catherine and the rest of the workforce. Bread, pastries and a cake had been made, and everything was put on the kitchen table. We all sat round a roaring fire, talking, laughing, drinking (apart from myself) and telling ghost stories. They all got very merry, but at least they didn't have far to go to fall into their beds. When I retired to bed that night, like most nights, I talked to my babies about their papa, thought about Tréville and my brothers, and even though they were at war, I hoped they had time to somehow have a drink to each other.

Suddenly Swallowtail appeared. "Swallowtail, is something wrong?"

"No, Spirit of the Wolf, I came to let you know that Tréville and your brothers are all well. Tonight the pistols, swords, muskets and cannons are quiet, all the men, on both sides, realised it was the start of a New Year, and decided hostilities would cease for a day." I wondered if Swallowtail had been sensing my thoughts. We talked and then I thanked her, we kissed and hugged each other, she left and then my father and mother appeared. We talked for a short time, then after their hugs and kisses they left. I smiled to myself and thought of Tréville and drifted off to sleep, feeling his arms around us.

Musketeers returned now and then so at least Amanda and I knew that Tréville, Porthos and my brothers were all right. They never stayed more than a couple of days, usually to get the new recruits, of which there were plenty, and I never saw them, so none of them could tell Tréville of my condition. Amanda, and/or Monsieur Verde, were always called to look after the wounded, and Gaston would keep me informed as well. At seven months, with Amanda and Catherine's blessings, I left to go to the dwelling. The bakery was in Catherine's capable hands and she moved into my rooms. The bakery was still going, but only just. On Gaston's orders, I had two Musketeers to escort me to the dwelling, Henri and Paoul. Later on another Musketeer was going to drive a cart with my belongings, all put into trunks. The only piece of furniture I took was a long, low cabinet so that all my dresses could be laid flat. As to Katherine's inheritance, most of the funds Tréville had invested where his funds were, before he left. It was too dangerous to leave my funds at the bakery or the dwelling. What was left now, I took with me. No longer would I be staying at the bakery; I actually had a tear in my eyes when we rode away.

It was a cold, chilly day – thank heavens the snow had gone – so I made sure I was well wrapped up and had a thick, warm hooded cloak round me. As we passed the garrison it looked totally deserted, no Tréville to wave to on the balcony or my brothers at the table. I had two pistols and some daggers concealed under my cloak. When we got to the crossroads we took a different route, it was the way I went to my safe forest. "Gentlemen, why are we going this way?" I asked. Henri replied that Gaston did not want us going through the centre of Paris, as it was too dangerous. As we passed the forest, which obviously I hadn't been to for a long time, it was bigger than I remembered, but then Tala and I had never covered the whole of it.

All of a sudden we heard horses galloping, and there was nowhere we could hide. Henri and Paoul had their pistols ready. My hand went to one of my pistols but I did not draw it. "It's horses and a carriage," I said. I had learnt over the years to listen for the different sounds. At that moment four horses drawing a very large carriage appeared.

A voice bellowed, "Stop the carriage."

A gentleman put his head out of the carriage and said, "You, you Musketeers, I need you to escort me to the palace, your wench can make her own way to wherever you were going."

Who did he think he was, calling me a wench? He was no gentleman but a very arrogant, rude man!! Henri and Paoul put their pistols away, and I took my hand off mine. We trotted back to the carriage and Henri replied, "I'm sorry, Monsieur, we have our orders to escort this lady to her dwelling."

The man glared at me and replied to Henri, "I think I'm more important than... than... that," he said pointing to me, "and if trouble lies ahead I will need you, I'm a very important nobleman to the King."

Paoul then said, "Monsieur, please do not be so rude to the lady we are escorting. She is not one of our wenches, as you so delicately put it, she is the wife of our Minister for War, Madame Tréville."

At that, the man alighted from the carriage and came over and bowed. "Madame Tréville, please accept my profound apologies for my rudeness, I have not had the pleasure of meeting you before. Our Minister Tréville is held in high esteem at the palace. I see you are with child, would you not have been better travelling by carriage, especially in this cold weather?"

I replied, "No, Monsieur, believe me it's more comfortable, for me, on horseback than being in a carriage where I would feel every bump, and I am warmly wrapped. May I make a suggestion? Maybe Henri or Paoul could escort you, as I do need someone with me." He agreed and got back in his carriage, again after apologising, and Paoul went with him. As Henri and I carried on, I saw where the man had come from. To the right of us was a small tree-lined lane, with a house at the end. I could not see a lot of the house as trees surrounded it. What I could see, it looked very grand.

As we were riding I realised I wasn't sure where we were. "Henri, where are we going?"

Henri replied, "It's all right, Madame Tréville, Gaston came out and had a look at the area and decided this was safer than riding through the village, just in case." I then saw the medium area of various sized trees, which I recognised. We were at the top end of the village.

"Henri, did you see that?" Henri replied he saw nothing. I reined my horse to a stop and then saw it again. It was a young boy, who looked frightened and was running and hiding from tree to tree. The boy saw me and I beckoned him over. I recognised him as one of the boys from the village. He was about seven years old, covered in dirt, but at least he had a thick jacket round him. "It's all right, we won't hurt you, who are you hiding from?" I asked him gently.

"The soldiers. You're the lady from one of the dwellings, aren't you?" I replied I was. Henri dismounted from his horse and crouched down and asked him what was happening. The boy called Edouard told us that soldiers had arrived the day before and taken all the women and young children to the church, the men and boys taken somewhere else. He had been out collecting berries and saw the soldiers ride past, went to watch at a distance, and then hid in the trees. He had found a tree, which had been uprooted, and had a large hole underneath. He covered it with branches and leaves and stayed there all night, eating the berries he had collected. He had hardly slept, frightened of the noises he could hear, and at sunrise he got up and started running around to keep himself warm. Then he started crying. Henri helped me dismount and I took Edouard in my arms to calm him.

"Madame Tréville I am going to see what I can, I suggest you and the boy stay here. Is the village far from here?" I replied the top of the village was at the end of the treeline, and the church was on the left, halfway down. Henri left us on foot.

I led the horses further into the trees and tied them to a branch, then found a large fallen tree trunk and Edouard and I sat down. "You have baby in there?" said Edouard, pointing to my stomach. I smiled and told him I had two. His eyes went wide and said, "How did you get two in there?"

I didn't really know how to answer that question, so I just said, "The other one was a special gift." We talked for a short time and then I heard a twig break. I put my fingers to my lips to tell Edouard to be quiet, and put my hand on one of my pistols.

In a hushed tone I heard, “Madame Tréville, where are you?” It was Henri.

“We’re here, Henri, did you see anything?”

“Yes, there’s about fifteen soldiers and as Edouard said the women and children are in the church, the men and boys are tied up and gagged in the tavern. I’m going to ride back to the garrison and get more men, but I worry for you. You are in no condition to ride back.”

I replied, “Can I get to my dwelling?”

Henri replied, “No, they seem to be just walking round as though they are waiting for something or someone, and they are not Spanish – they are Red Guards.”

“Red Guards?” I said totally stunned. “Why on earth would Red Guards take our village?”

Edouard tugged my cape and said, “I know a safe place we can go, it’s not far, if you can get back on your horse.” I smiled at him and said I would be all right. We mounted our horses, Henri took Edouard and we went back the way we came. Edouard pointed to another small forest of trees, which we went to, down a gentle slope and came to some large boulders. “There,” said Edouard. I looked to where he was pointing and could see some large boulders and trees, but nothing else. “It’s hidden,” said Edouard. We all dismounted and Edouard took my hand and led us to where some trees were. I then saw an entrance behind the trees into the boulders. It looked ideal and I could also see if anyone approached. There were large flat boulders inside that we could sit on, and it was even big enough to put the horse in. Henri gave me his cape for extra warmth, left and rode back to the garrison and said he would only come and get us when the village was safe.

I was feeling quite weary now and needed to rest. I sat on one of the boulders with Edouard at my side; I wrapped both cloaks around both of us, mainly to keep Edouard warm, and I drifted off. When I woke Edouard was not with me. I started to panic and went to look outside the entrance. How could I have been so stupid to drift off? He was a seven-year-old boy full of curiosity. At that moment I saw him coming back with something in his hand. He had a basket with some berries for us to eat, and a flask. Where had he got the flask? "Sorry Madame, I didn't mean to wake you," he said. I smiled and told him he hadn't, but I worried when I saw him missing, and to call me Lesley.

"Where did you get the flask?" I asked him.

He replied, "This is my secret place, I found it with my papa and have things here I need."

I then looked properly round the area and saw a couple of baskets, flasks and other things. I looked at him curiously.

"I come here to play after school and weekends. My maman has three others who are younger than me, and since Papa died, I come here to feel close to him. I was going to come here last night but was frightened more soldiers would see me. I got us some berries, you hungry?"

I found a rag and wet it and cleaned his face and hands, then brushed the dirt off him. He was a handsome boy with blonde hair and his eyes were the greenest I had ever seen. I could see him breaking many young ladies' hearts when he was older. We sat and ate the berries and drank the water from the flask, apparently there was a stream further in the forest. He found a bucket and said he would go and get some water for the horse and off he went. I smiled and thought if I had a boy or boys, that they would be as kind as Edouard.

Edouard returned with the water, which he gave to the horse. I was starting to get cold, as was Edouard, so we cuddled up together. It was a shame I could not light a fire but the smoke would just have filled the inside. After what seemed a long time I heard horses approaching. I put my fingers to my lips and Edouard nodded that he understood. I got up and stroked my horse to keep him quiet as well. I carefully looked out of the entrance, hand on my pistol, and saw to my relief it was Gaston and Henri.

"It's all right, Edouard, it's Musketeers," I said. I walked out of the entrance as Gaston and Henri dismounted their horses.

"Lesley, are you all right?" asked Gaston, quite concerned. I replied we were both fine, just very cold, and asked what had happened. Gaston replied they were in fact Spanish soldiers wearing Red Guard uniforms. Somehow they knew recruits were being taken to the border, and were going to ambush them later on that day.

They saw the village and took it over so no one would escape and get to the garrison or palace. None of the villagers had been injured. They were all just frightened. Everyone was now reunited but Edouard's maman was frantic with worry, until Henri explained where he was. Helene had gone to my dwelling to get the fires going, and was making hot broth. The cart had arrived with my cabinet and trunks and they had put everything in the parlour.

Gaston looked at Edouard and said, "Time to go home, young man, and see your maman. In a way you saved the village and a lot of our men."

Edouard smiled and said, "I wouldn't have come out, but I saw Madame Lesley and knew her." Gaston helped me onto my horse, and realising how cold I was, gave me his cape as well. Edouard rode with Henri, who wrapped him in his cape, but before we left Edouard turned and looked at his secret place and said, waving, "Bye bye, Papa. See you soon." That brought a lump to my throat and a tear to my eyes. Gaston looked at me and I said I would explain later.

As we rode into the village, I saw several Spanish soldiers in a cart waiting to be taken back to the garrison, and the other cart had the dead. I looked at the soldiers and then said, "Gaston." Gaston reined his horse to the side of mine. I pointed to a soldier and said, "That soldier is a Red Guard, he used to ride with Rochefort." The soldier tried to leave the cart but his shackles held him.

Gaston said, "Now it makes sense, he would have known the movements of the recruits, he would have known of the village, and who better to get Red Guard uniforms? He will go to the King for his punishment, as a traitor of France."

Suddenly a woman was screaming, "Edouard, Edouard!" and came running up the village.

Henri dismounted and helped Edouard down, who then ran into his maman's arms.

"Oh, thank you for saving my son," she said.

I looked and smiled and said, "Actually it was Edouard who saved the village and the recruits, and as my husband would say, 'he is a brave young man.'"

Edouard looked at me and said, "May I come and see you,

Madame Lesley?" I replied he could come and see me whenever, with his maman's permission. He walked off with his maman, turning and waving, I waved back.

I sighed, I felt exhausted. Gaston said, "Lesley you are looking pale. Come, let's get you to your dwelling, you have had quite a day."

We rode to my dwelling where Helene was waiting and I dismounted my horse with Gaston's help. Helene looked and saw my condition and said, "Ah, Lesley, ce sont d'excellentes nouvelles, combien de mois?"

I replied, "Un peu plus de sept mois."

"Come, mon amie, you are so cold and weary. The dwelling is warm and cosy and I have some hot broth for you."

Gaston came in and asked where I would like my trunks and cabinet putting. I replied in the bedchamber. Between Gaston and Henri they kindly moved them from the parlour. I then thanked them both for all they had done and they then mounted their horses and rode out of the village with the prisoners, and the dead. Helene and I had our hot broth, which I was grateful for, and then she said she would leave me to rest. She would come in every day to make sure I was well, and would also introduce me to the midwife, who was called Marianne.

The following day, after Helene had helped me put my dresses, undergarments and other items away, and put the empty trunks in the barn, she told me that times were hard for the villagers. The grain was gone, so no flour, and no sugar, or salt. Oh no, I had totally forgotten about all the supplies in the barn that had been completely covered over. I told her, the villagers must go to the barn, and help themselves. There was plenty for everyone. Luckily the barn was totally dry and secure, no rats had found their way in. The cheeses had mould round them, but once scraped off was edible. The village wasn't big, probably only thirty people in total. The villagers were so happy, they only took what they wanted and within a month the tavern re-opened, people were happy again, and one day I even heard dogs barking and children playing. I just hoped this war wouldn't go on much longer or we could all end up starving, or worse.

About two weeks later, Tala became very agitated. "Hush, Tala, you know I cannot run."

"She doesn't want to run, Spirit of the Wolf, she knows your birth is near, and I need to make Tala sleep deeply." I turned and saw it was Swallowtail.

"What do you mean, Swallowtail?"

She took my hands and said, "Spirit of the Wolf, you know you are a healer wolf, and Tala knows your time is near, and if I don't put her into a deep sleep she will come forth and give birth to her cubs. If you were still on the Reservation it would not be a problem, but here is different." I looked at Swallowtail, shocked, "Do you mean Tala would appear and actually produce two wolf cubs?"

Swallowtail laughed. "No, Spirit of the Wolf. If Tala is awake her spirit will enter both your babies and they will become healer wolves and will change, like you do. This must not happen. I need to put Tala into a deep, deep sleep until after you give birth. It will not hurt her, or your babies, I promise." I asked what I had to do. She replied all I had to do was lay down on the bed, if I could. I did and Swallowtail started chanting.

I slowly drifted off to sleep and started dreaming. I was on the Reservation, and three tipis were in front of me. The first one I went into, a woman was giving birth. I saw the pain she endured, but seeing her baby born was incredible. I smiled but soon my smile turned to tears – the child was stillborn. Then I was in the second tipi, this time the birth was quick and the baby survived. The boy grew quickly and was four years old. I saw the boy running towards the forest, and suddenly stop. Wolves surrounded him. The alpha went to him, sniffing as he went, and then he stretched his front paws out and bowed his head. An injured wolf appeared and the boy held his hand out, and the light came forth and he healed the wolf – this boy was a healer wolf. Then I was in the third tipi, the woman had a horrendous time giving birth, and she had to be cut open, and the baby taken out. There were anxious moments waiting to see if they both lived or passed. The baby lived, but the mother passed. The mother's relatives looked after the child. It was a normal child, and its life was normal.

Slowly I woke and I told Swallowtail what I had seen. She replied she wanted me to see what childbirth was like, and the difference in Tala being awake and asleep; now I understood. Swallowtail told me Tala was now in a deep, deep sleep and when the time was right, she would return to bring Tala back. I thanked her and she left. I put my hand on my stomach and said, "Sleep well, Tala, you will soon be back with me."

Helene came and saw me every day, as I was finding things quite difficult now. It really hurt for me to walk, I felt like a huge waddling beast. I was so big I couldn't even see my feet, so some of the time I was confined either in my bed or sitting on a chair – the bed was more comfortable. I found it difficult to sleep, my thoughts were always with Tréville and now being away from the bakery, I heard no news of him, or my brothers, but my necklace was still beating. It was a delight to feel my babies kick and I hoped they would both survive. Many mothers lost their babies or both died. Marianne was a lovely midwife, who would massage my shoulders and back, which helped. She also made sure I did walk, as it was good for me, even though it was painful. I missed seeing and talking with Amanda, but the weather was not good and she needed to stay safe. I don't know why but I had a feeling something wasn't right with Amanda. Helene said very soon she would move into the spare bedchamber and be there for me, as my time was getting close.

One day there was a knock at the door and Helene opened it to see Edouard standing there. "My maman said I could come and see Madame Lesley," he said. Helene told him to come in.

"Edouard, how lovely to see you. Would you like some hot chocolate?" I asked him.

He looked at me with a frown. "What's hot chocolate?" he asked. Helene made him a mug.

"Oohh, that's lovely," he said. We talked and he told me about school, how one of his sisters had fallen and hurt her ankle badly, but Marianne had bandaged it. Then he said, "When you first arrived my maman and some of the villagers thought you might not talk to them because you were dressed like a lady, then when you went missing they thought you left because of them, until they found out it was all your husband's doing, next thing you're a Madame and wed to him."

Both Helene and I looked surprised at that remark. I replied, "Yes, now I'm married I am a Madame, just like your maman and Helene, but life was very different for me when I lived in England. I used to be a servant and worked very hard, some nights I would go home with my hands bleeding where I had to scrub tables with a wire-like brush. When I came here I was very, very lucky to meet Monsieur Rennard and then my husband, who through his hard work was made a Captain of the Musketeers, then Minister for War. I'm just as down to earth as everyone in the village, and I look upon all the villagers as friends."

Edouard smiled and said, "That's what my maman said after you rescued me. All the villagers like you and your husband now, including me. I had better go, Maman said not to tire you out. Please don't get any bigger or you'll go 'pop.'" I laughed, gave him a hug and kissed his cheek, and in return he gave me such a tight hug.

After he had left Helene said, "I think someone has taken a liking to you." We both smiled.

One night, a couple of weeks later, I was woken by the sound of a key in the door.

"Helene, is that you? Is something wrong? It's late," I said as I struggled out of my bed. I now slept with a couple of lit candles in lanterns and went out to the parlour, and couldn't believe my eyes. "Tréville, am I dreaming? Oh Tréville, my love, you're here," I said as I went to him, tears in my eyes. Tréville wrapped his arms round me.

"My love, are you all right? I heard all about the Spanish," he said. I just kissed and kissed him and tried to wrap my arms around him, but a rather large stomach stopped me from doing that.

"I'm fine, my love. I can't believe you're here, are you all right? Are you wounded, how are...?" His lips on mine stopped me saying anything else.

"Hush, my love, let me get a word in," he said, smiling and taking my face in his hand, wiping my tears away. "Amanda told the King your time was very near, and you'd left the bakery to come here, so he sent a messenger to bring me home and the King told me our brilliant news, and before you say anything I understand why you did not tell me. I'm now to stay here or at the garrison until the war is finished. We have more or less won and I would think another month and the war will be over, and everyone is alive and not too badly wounded. Athos is more than capable to take charge of the men. Now if it's all right with you, I would like to get out of these clothes, have a wash, get into bed, hold and kiss my wife and baby and go to sleep with you in my arms, I have missed you so much," he said.

"Ummm, just one thing, Tréville, I'm not carrying one but two babies." His smile radiated happiness at the news.

As he undressed, I went to him and put my hand on his back. "Tréville, what happened?"

He had a long scar across the back of his shoulder. "Let's talk about it another time, not now," he said. I washed his back, and when he finished he took me in his arms, unplaited my hair and ran his hands through it. It was a long time since I'd seen my husband naked, and I blushed slightly.

He went to remove my night garment and I said, "Oh, Tréville I don't look very nice under my night garment." Tréville smiled and slowly undid the laces at the front and then gently pushed it down from my shoulders, where it then fell to the floor, kissing my neck at the same time. He then went to remove my necklace. "No, Tréville, please, my necklace is part of me now and I never remove it. I know it sounds stupid but I know you are safe if it's round my neck. Please my love, promise me you will never take it off unless I leave this world."

He promised, smiled, and as his eyes took all of my naked form in he said, "So you've gained a bit of weight, you still look so beautiful," and helped me into our bed. Our arms went round each other, our kisses deepening and then he went down and kissed my stomach with such tenderness, it brought tears to my eyes. The passion in our eyes for each other was overwhelming, but that would have to wait until after the births. Our arms entwined around each other, as much as possible, and that night I slept soundly in the safety of my husband's arms.

The following morning Tréville woke early, got the fires going then filled the tub and we bathed together. Whilst we were in the tub, I grabbed Tréville's hand and placed it on my stomach. "Ouch, was that...?" he said.

I smiled and said, "That was one of your sons or daughters kicking." I then took both his hands and put them on my stomach and said, "And that's both of them kicking."

Tréville kissed me so tenderly, helped me out and we dried each other. He took my hand and said, "Back to bed now, I want to hold you in my arms, so I know I'm not dreaming." I smiled and we went back to our bed where he wrapped his arms around me, kissing me, telling me how much he had missed me, and how much he loved me. I told him the same. I so much wanted to love him, hopefully once the twins had been born we would do so. I then fell asleep on his shoulder.

Later on that morning, Helene came round as usual and was stunned to see Tréville making me something to eat. "Oh Tréville, what a lovely surprise to see you. Are you well, and your men?" she asked, giving him a hug. Tréville replied all of them were exhausted but well. I entered the parlour and she said, "Well you have a glow about you now, mon amie, I'm so pleased. I will give you time to yourselves, but any signs of labour, Tréville, you come and get me straight away." He replied he would.

The next five days Tréville stayed with me, and we just relaxed in each other's company. I wanted for nothing, he saw to everything including the cooking. Marianne came round and Tréville wanted to know all about birthing. She told him all scenarios and I think afterwards he rather wished he hadn't asked! I noticed as the days passed he started to relax and didn't look so drawn as he did when he arrived back. I didn't ask him about the war, but sometimes I noticed he seemed far away. Tréville knew I would listen if he wanted to talk, and he would – in time.

Day six when I woke, I noticed the bed was wet.

"Tréville, wake up, I think I need Helene and Marianne."

Tréville woke immediately, jumped out the bed, dressed and went to Helene's. Helene and Marianne entered the bedchamber and closed the door. Tréville was banished to the parlour. Marianne got everything ready and examined me and said all was well. Then my pains started, it was pain like I had never felt before. Sometimes I would scream out, and I could have killed Tréville many times for the pain I was enduring. In the end Tréville could take no more and burst through the door and said he was staying with me. Helene and Marianne tried to soothe me, but once Tréville held my hand I calmed. He took the cloth from Marianne and kept wiping my face, and talking softly to me. Suddenly I felt a massive pain shoot through my body, I grabbed Tréville's hand so hard that it took him by surprise, then I heard Marianne say, "It's coming, bear down Lesley, bear down," and I did, screaming. I heard a baby cry and then the pain hit me again and exhausted as I was, with Tréville's and Helene's encouragement, my second baby was born. Both babies were crying and so was Tréville. I saw Swallowtail was also with us and she was chanting a blessing over the babies. I was absolutely exhausted, but suddenly I felt strange, the room was spinning; another pain hit me and I knew no more.

CHAPTER 29

What Happened to Rochefort?

When I opened my eyes Tréville was sitting at my side, holding my hand, talking to Monsieur Verde.

"Tréville... What happened?" I said drowsily.

"Oh, my love, I have been so worried, you left us for two days."

"Two... two days?" I said, concerned. "Our babies, are they all right?"

"They are fine, my love, you have given me two sons," said Tréville, smiling, and I could see how proud he was, but his eyes betrayed him.

"Tréville, what's wrong?" I said. Tréville's smile left him and he looked at Monsieur Verde.

"Lesley," said Monsieur Verde, who took my other hand in his, "after the births, you had, let's just say, a complication. Tréville sent for me immediately. Marianne looked after you, until I arrived, and she did an excellent job. You are going to be absolutely fine, but I'm so, so sorry to have to tell you, you will not be able to have any more children."

At that moment I felt an absolute failure to my husband. Tears flowed down my cheeks. I took my hand away from Monsieur Verde and held Tréville's hand in both of mine, and said sobbing, "Oh Tréville I'm so sorry, please forgive me."

Tréville's hands went to my face and he wiped my tears away with his thumbs and said, "My dearest love, you have nothing to be sorry for, and no forgiveness is necessary. You have given me two beautiful sons, and as long as all of you are all right, that is all that matters. I'm just so relieved that I am here with you." I looked into his eyes, which were full of love, devotion and sincerity, and it made my heart melt. "Now my love, if you're ready, I think two little people would like to be introduced to their maman."

"Oh, yes please, I can't wait to hold them in my arms." Tréville kissed my lips, and put my necklace inside my night garment. He left and went to the spare bedchamber, whilst Monsieur Verde helped me to sit up. Tréville came back, with Helene, a baby in each of their arms.

Tréville placed the baby in my right arm and Helene put the other one in my left arm. This time tears of joy fell down my face. They were so tiny, but I could feel they were strong. I kissed both their foreheads and whispered, "Welcome, my little ones, I'm your maman."

Monsieur Verde told me he had examined them and both were well, even though they were born less than a minute apart. One had dark brown eyes, who was the first born, and the other blue, which was unusual. Monsieur Verde also told me until I was stronger, three wet nurses would be feeding them. It had all been arranged, they had been wet nurses for one of the Queen's ladies in waiting. Two would stay with us during the day, the other night-time. I would have to stay in bed for about a month and slowly regain my strength. He then kissed my hand and said, "Congratulations to you both."

Helene came and hugged all of us and said she would be back later, and then they both left. Tréville sat on the bed with me and placed some stray hairs behind my ears, then took my face in his hands and kissed me so tenderly, and then kissed the twins' foreheads. His arm went round my shoulders and I lay my head on his shoulder. "My love, what do you think we should name them?"

I looked into Tréville's twinkling blue eyes and said, "Oh that's easy, my beloved, after you." We named them Jean and Armand. (Tréville's proper name was Jean Armand de Peyrer.)

I noticed some wild flowers in a tumbler, on the windowsill.

"What lovely flowers, Tréville."

Tréville replied, "Edouard brought them for you, he thought you had passed until I told him you were just asleep."

Edouard visited us often and got on really well with Tréville. The three wet nurses we had were lovely ladies. They helped me, whenever I needed it, and made sure I was involved with everything for the twins. One night, when Tréville returned, he told me he had come back, when the sun was high, to see me asleep with the twins in my arms. "My love, that was the most angelic sight I have ever seen, I will never forget it," he said, and took me in his arms and kissed me tenderly.

Two months later, after nearly a year, we were all celebrating – the war was over. I had now regained my strength and was feeding our twins. Tréville helped as much as he could, but naturally the King wanted him at either the palace or the garrison, but I always had Helene and the villagers. Everyone in the village had been wonderful and helped out where they could. Unbeknown to me, the day after the twins were born, Amanda turned up with Monsieur Verde, and was deeply concerned. Tréville promised her he would keep her updated with news, good or bad. Swallowtail returned and brought Tala back to me, I had missed her. As I was on my own she gave me some special healing.

One night, as Tréville and I laid together in each other's arms in our bed he said, "My love, your necklace, why will you not remove it? Is it because the heart beats?"

I looked at him totally stunned and had to think quick. "Tréville, have you been on the wine? My necklace doesn't beat, how can it? It's just a piece of jewellery, beautiful jewellery I must say."

He took the necklace in his fingers and said, "When you left me for those two days, I thought I was losing you and thought it might be a bad omen and went to remove it, until I remembered what you told me. I held the necklace in my fingers, like now, and I could have sworn the heart was beating, and you were saying, 'The Reservation,' over and over."

"Is it beating now?" I asked. He replied it wasn't. I noticed a movement and saw Swallowtail, who put a finger to her lips. I understood. She had stopped it beating, but the minute Tréville removed his fingers, it started beating again, and Swallowtail faded away.

"Oh my love, I'm sorry you were so desperately worried, maybe, because you thought you were losing me, if you held my necklace it would keep my heart beating. The Reservation, as you know, is where my people go when they leave this earth. Only honoured people are allowed though."

I took his face in my hands and gently kissed him and he said, "Umm, that's probably what happened. There was something else I wanted to tell you, which is very important." I looked at him and he said softly, "I love you so much."

I replied, "And I love you too, my beloved."

Our arms entwined around each other and after goodnight kisses we slept, for a short while, as I then heard the twins stirring. Tréville got them one at a time so I could feed them. He then rocked each of them until they fell asleep, and put them back into their cots, at the side of our bed.

Things very slowly started getting back to a way of life. Even though the war was over, it wasn't. My Musketeer brothers had not yet returned as skirmishes still broke out. I prayed they would all stay safe. It didn't feel right me having Tréville back and Amanda not having Porthos back. Amanda came and saw the twins and myself when she could, but she was very busy. The fields were starting to grow grain again, people were pulling together and trying to make the best of everything, but there was still a lot of unrest. The twins were now four months old, and Helene offered to look after them whilst I went to the bakery to see the damage. As I didn't know how long I would be gone, I asked one of the wet nurses if she would kindly help out. She was happy to go and feed the twins. Catherine had visited, and fallen in love with the twins, and explained they only had enough supplies left to feed the five of them, so the bakery had been closed these past two months. I told her the workforce must stay there, as I didn't want the place being ransacked by Red Guards. Since Rochefort died, another Red Guard had replaced him, who was just as bad as him. He never inflicted any hostilities towards Amanda or myself, well, not that I knew of. He did believe though, that he ruled Paris and not the King. There were lots of clashes between him and Tréville. My brothers would have plenty to keep them occupied, when they returned.

Six months after I'd left the bakery, I returned. Lazare, the farmer, said he was going into Paris with his cart to deliver goods, and could take me to the bakery. As we travelled through Paris, I noticed large stones were being placed outside the city – strange, I would have to ask Tréville. Outside the bakery the whole area looked so derelict. I thanked Lazare and went inside and everything was spotless. The workforce said they had to do something to say thank you for letting them stay. Laurens and Pierre had even made a new cart as the other one was falling to bits. It was so lovely to see them all again. Catherine and I talked about what to do next. I then went to the garrison to see Tréville, as I had thought of a plan, and hoped it would work. I went up to Tréville's office and he was talking to Gaston. "Lesley, how lovely to see you again. I trust you are well, and belated congratulations."

"Thank you, Gaston, and I am feeling well." I asked Tréville if I could borrow a couple of horses.

He looked at me with a raised eyebrow and said, "What on earth are you up to now, my dear, and who's looking after the twins?" I explained about the twins and told him I wanted to ride out to the farmer and miller, to see how things were for them now. "Why two horses?" he asked. I replied I wanted to take Catherine with me. "Oh no, I'm not having the pair of you riding over there on your own, I will accompany you instead of Catherine."

I raised my eyebrow and looked at him, and said, "Why?"

"Excuse me, I think it's time for me to see to my duties," said Gaston, and left.

I stood there with my hands on my hips, "Well I'm waiting for an answer, my dear husband."

Tréville walked over to me, took me in his arms and placed his lips on mine and I melted, I should have learnt by now, he did it every time! "If I may, my dear wife, I would rather I went with you. You do not know what hostilities may await you and I would rather be at your side, instead of sitting here worrying. In fact we only need take one horse, it's a long time since we rode together, and I have missed that."

I looked at him and replied, "Well, seeing as you would be so worried perhaps it would be an idea for us to ride together," and with that I gave him a kiss on the lips and walked out to go to the stables, with a satisfied smile on my face. My plan worked. It was never my intention to take Catherine!!

I sat astride the horse with Tréville behind me, holding me close, like he always did before. I always felt safe and protected in his arms. Whilst we were riding I mentioned to Tréville what I had seen in Paris. He told me The Royal Court had ordered the placing of thirty-one stones to mark the edge of the city. Building beyond the stones without Royal approval was forbidden. (It took eight months for the work to be completed.) We encountered no trouble, but the miller and farmer had fallen on hard times, like everyone else. The farmer now only had one cow, which could only keep milk going for his family. The miller's fields were barren. Both of their barns were in ruins. Tréville asked both of them what they would need to start producing again. The list was long, but with the help from the Musketeers rebuilding their barns, the finding of a farmer's wife whose husband had been killed and who was happy to sell her cows, within months things started to flourish. That day I was pleased that Tréville had gone with me. I needed to get the bakery up and running again, but I could not leave our twins.

When we rode back into the garrison Remy came to us and said, "Minister Tréville, there is someone to see you and Madame Tréville. I asked him to wait in the meeting room."

"Thank you, Remy. Did he give a name?"

"No, Minister Tréville."

Suddenly we heard a shriek and I looked at Tréville and said, "That sounded like Mertyl."

Tréville helped me down and drew his pistol and I took his other one, then both of us went into the meeting room, pistols aimed. "Don't tell us we survived the war to come back here and get shot," said Athos. I then shrieked, put my pistol on the table, and threw my arms around each one of my brothers, and hugged and kissed them. I noticed they were all thinner, there was such sadness in their eyes and they looked totally worn out. They all hugged Tréville and patted each other's backs. It was so wonderful to see them back again. Porthos had Mertyl in a bear hug.

"I think this calls for a celebration, how about all of us going to the tavern for a meal? Porthos, please, go get Amanda," said Aramis.

I looked at Tréville and said, "You go, my love, and I must get back to the dwelling."

Aramis looked at me and said, "So pray tell us, sister, what is more important at the dwelling than us, your brothers who you haven't seen for over a year, and we have all missed you greatly?"

Tréville stood behind me and wrapped his arms around my waist and said, "Do you think we should tell them?"

I looked at each one of them and said, "I'm not sure, how do you think they will take the news?"

Athos said anxiously, "Minister, Lesley, has something happened?"

I smiled and said, "The answer to your question, Aramis, is... our four-month-old twins."

They all looked stunned. "Well, never knew you had it in you, Minister," said Athos, smiling.

They all congratulated us and decided they would all come over to the dwelling the following day and celebrate then. I left Tréville with his men to catch up and went back to the dwelling, and started baking some rather large pies – well Porthos was coming!

The following day they all arrived, along with Amanda. I had arranged with the tavern to do us a huge picnic, so we got a large table and put all the food on it, and we put lots of blankets out at the back of the dwelling, for us to sit on, after we had finished eating. Luckily there was a clump of four large trees, so some of us could rest our backs against them. Tréville got the tumblers and wine, and put the large pies with the chickens, ham, cheeses, fruit, breads and various other fares. Naturally, Amanda and my brothers wanted to see the twins, so very quietly I took them into our bedchamber but all they could see was two covered little bundles asleep. Back in the garden Athos said, "Lesley, before we enjoy this wonderful meal, I think you should know we brought someone else with us, but he was rather shy and stayed outside." I looked at Tréville and he shrugged his shoulders. We all went out to the front of the dwelling and tears of joy filled my eyes. There in all his glory stood Sunkwa. I ran to him and put my arms around his neck and kissed his nose. Sunkwa nuzzled into my neck. I noticed he had quite a few battle scars, but Aramis assured me he was well. His horse had been shot, and the rider of Sunkwa also died, so Aramis took him and looked after him.

"Thank you, Aramis, how can I ever repay you?" I said.

"Your smile is thanks enough," said Aramis.

I led Sunkwa towards the field, where the other horses were, and watched him join them. I couldn't believe he was back with me.

The sun was high in the sky and we all sat round the table on the benches, eating, drinking, and catching up with everything. Porthos said, "Until now, Lesley, I didn't realise how much I had missed your pies. Thank you, they're delicious." I had made four large ones, of which Porthos ate two!! After we had finished eating, we all went and sat on the blankets and relaxed.

I heard the twins crying so I went in and fed them, and then took them outside. Tréville jumped up and said, "My love, give me one of them." He always took Armand. His men just looked at him, not believing what they were seeing. Their Minister for War, who could be abrupt, stubborn, and sometimes extremely bad-tempered, now drooling over his sons.

I looked at each one of them and laughed, and said, "If only you could all see your faces now." I gave Jean to Amanda and noticed how she and Porthos looked at each other. I knew of Amanda's heartache and my heart had gone out to her, it was so upsetting. Hopefully one day she and Porthos's wishes would be granted. Tréville gave Armand to Aramis, and then D'Artagnan took Jean and Athos took Armand. I went to the parlour to get some more wine and looked out the window. What a wonderful sight it was, as everyone looked happy and relaxed. It had been a wonderful day.

They all left early evening. Tréville brought his horse and Sunkwa back to the barn. I now felt complete, all my family were back together again, including Sunkwa.

After the twins had been fed and eventually went to sleep, I walked back into the parlour. Tréville was sat in the chair with his eyes closed. I looked at him and my heart was overwhelmed with love for him. We had shared our bed together, but we had not lain with each other in such a long time. There was the war, and then I had to heal completely after the twins had been born, and that healing process took over three months. (Instead of going to my physician, I saw Monsieur Verde, as he had attended me, who confirmed I had healed.) I took Tréville's face in my hands and kissed his lips so tenderly. Tréville opened his eyes and I saw the passion in his eyes as he did in mine.

"Tréville, love me this night."

"My love, are you sure?" said Tréville.

I replied, "I'm sure, and I have missed my husband's loving so much," and kissed him deeply.

He took my hand and led me into our bedchamber, where he started kissing my neck and then slowly we undressed each other. He picked me up and laid me on the bed and very slowly we got to know each other's bodies again, and then, our hearts entwined into one and our passions for each other were wonderfully and gently fulfilled. We were a couple again, and it felt so good. Our arms entwined around each other, and we slept until the sound of a baby's cry woke me up.

The following day I asked Helene if she would mind looking after the twins for a short while, as I wanted to ride Sunkwa again. Helene was more than pleased to look after them. I had fed them and they were sleeping. I got onto Sunkwa's back, no saddle, and it was like he had never been away. We trotted out of the village and then we galloped all the way to the crossroads, the long way round, and then back again. It felt so good to ride him again. Once back I rubbed him down with straw and then took him over to the field so he could do what he wanted. I watched him for a short time, and he trotted round, jumped around and then started rolling over on his back. He knew he had his freedom back again.

A couple of weeks later Tréville arrived back at the dwelling with my brothers. I looked at Tréville and said, "Is everything all right? None of you look happy."

Tréville replied, "Nothing for you to worry about, my love, we needed to speak somewhere private to plan a strategy."

I smiled and said, "Go sit at the table in the garden and I will prepare you all a meal."

Tréville took me in his arms, kissed me and whispered in my ear, "I love you," so I whispered back, "I love you too." Luckily I had made some pies the day before, so along with cheese, fruit, bread, chicken and ham. I took it out to them, for which I was thanked.

The twins woke up and I fed them in the bedchamber and was rocking them in my arms in the parlour, when Porthos walked in. "May I?" he asked. I let him take Jean. He looked so small in Porthos's huge arms. Within a very short time they were both asleep and I put them in their cots in our bedchamber, and then Porthos and I walked back into the parlour. "One day, Amanda will make a wonderful maman just like you, my dear sister," and he gave me a hug and kissed my forehead.

I smiled and replied, "I was so upset when Amanda told me of her miscarriage, and you would both have your own child in your arms now." Porthos looked at me in stunned silence, and I saw tears well up in his eyes. Oh no, Amanda must not have told him, what had I done!!

"Oh Porthos, please forgive me, I thought Amanda would have told you by now."

He looked at me and said, "She has said nothing, but I knew something was wrong, maybe she had fallen out of love for me, but I never gave that a thought."

I took his hands and said, "Porthos, Amanda loves you as deeply as I love Tréville, and always will. I didn't know until after the twins were born, and then she didn't really want to tell me. I guessed and then she told me. I'm sure Amanda is waiting for the right moment, as she probably wants you to settle back to married life again. Please, Porthos, don't be too upset with her, it tore her apart and she felt a failure to you. Believe me, Porthos, as I know how that feels. There is something that none of you know. I was very ill after I gave birth and, due to a complication, I can have no more children and I felt a failure to Tréville. Amanda and I know we have wonderful husbands, who will support and care for us no matter what happens."

Porthos looked at me and said, "Oh Lesley, you and Amanda have had your own wars to contend with, I'm so very sorry."

I took Porthos in my arms and kissed his cheek; he hugged me so tightly. "It's a good job I don't get jealous of your brothers." We turned to see Tréville stood in the doorway. "I suppose you forgot to get the wine?" he said.

"No, Minister, I was helping with baby duties," said Porthos.

Tréville smiled and replied, "That's more important than wine."

Tréville got some bottles of wine, and they went back outside. When it was time for them to leave, they all gave me a hug and a kiss and Porthos whispered, "Thank you, sister, I promise to look after her." That night Tréville asked me if Porthos was all right, as he had ridden back to the garrison in silence. I told him about Amanda, and it saddened him greatly.

Over the next couple of months, Tréville and my brothers had lots of encounters with the Red Guards and the very unhappy people of Paris. One night, after we had put the twins down, and as Tréville got into our bed, I ran my hand over the long scar across the back of his shoulder, kissed it and asked him what happened. Tréville moved the pillows behind us so we were sitting up and put his arm around me and I rested my head on his shoulder, and he said, "Six of us set out to see if we could find the supply wagons, as we were desperate. We had no ammunition, pistols, muskets, bombs, rations or medical supplies. Your brothers were elsewhere. Suddenly from nowhere about twenty Spanish soldiers appeared and we were attacked. The next thing I knew I felt something go across my shoulder. Your brothers must have seen where we went because they turned up and eventually the Spanish were killed. We found the supply wagons and took them with us. Aramis looked at my shoulder, and said luckily it wasn't too deep but would still need stitches. When we got back to camp he put alcohol on it, put the stitches in and then applied some ointment. I had to be careful not to move my shoulder too much or the stitches would have given way. Aramis checked the wound as often as he could to make sure there was no infection."

I looked at Tréville and said, "Is it me, or are my brothers different now?"

Tréville replied, "There is a change in them, they have seen things they will never forget, and they have become harder.

"When you're on a battlefield it does things to your mind. Fear takes over, but in the end fear has no power over you. I saw men leave the battlefield, but in the morning they were always back, they never knew I had seen them. One night I overheard two men talking, one of them must have left but returned. 'I came back for my men and friends. However bad it is, you must watch their backs and also you fight for the people of France,' he said. Your brothers have been through some bad times. Athos was thrown from his horse and badly hurt and nearly bayoneted to death. His brothers saved him. Porthos, as you know suffered a bad wound across his stomach. D'Artagnan is not a boy anymore, he is now a man who has grown up too quickly, and as for Aramis, it brought back bad memories of Savoy. His horse was shot out from underneath him, and luckily he fell into a bunker or he would have been blown up by cannon fire. Naturally we thought of how things were here – you, Amanda and Constance. We all had someone to come home to. Sometimes I would watch and listen to your brothers and they all seemed far apart, but deep down they are still brothers, and always will be until death."

I put my hand on his face. Tréville looked at me and I could see the sadness in his eyes and I gently kissed him. "May I ask you something else?"

"Yes my love, what is it?"

"What happened to Rochefort? You knew, didn't you?"

Tréville looked at me and said, "No my love, I knew nothing about the details of his death until the King told me, after I returned from the war. It is rather a gruesome story. He told me that Rochefort had been plotting evil against you and Amanda after we had left, and no, I will not tell you what he was going to do to you. Let's just say neither of you would have been alive when we returned."

I looked at Tréville and said, "Tell me, please."

"I would rather not, my love, it will probably give you nightmares."

"Tréville, he is dead, he cannot harm us anymore. I know my death by his hands would have been slow and brutal."

Tréville sighed and said, "Very well. Both of you were to be hung, drawn and quartered in a secret place only known to Rochefort."

I gasped and said, "I knew it would be brutal, but not that." I felt physically sick at the thought.

"My love, you have gone pale, are you all right? I knew I should not have told you."

I looked at Tréville, sort of smiled and said, "I am fine, my love, please tell me the rest."

Tréville said, "Whilst Amanda, Porthos and both of us were away on our honeymoons, Rochefort assaulted the Queen, and she was badly hurt. The King, obviously, was outraged, and had to tell everyone the Queen was indisposed due to a very bad cold, and decided he could take no more of Rochefort's evil ways – it was time for Rochefort to go, but how? The King spoke to one of his other ministers who told him he knew of at least a dozen men who hated Rochefort with a vengeance, and six of them would do the deed. One of these men had very carefully become one of Rochefort's men, and had relayed all Rochefort's plots to this Minister, who then told the King. So it was decided that a trap would be set for Rochefort once and for all. The King told Rochefort he had a secret mission for him and three of his men, who he named. Again, through information relayed to him, the King had found out who had bitten you and helped Rochefort with your kidnap. The same three men had also helped Rochefort in his persecution of Amanda. They were told under no circumstances to wear their uniforms because if anything untoward should happen, nothing must be traced back to the palace. The King had convinced Rochefort, that a Spaniard he knew was actually a French spy, and he needed to be rescued quickly as his life was in grave danger. He also told him only swords must be taken, no pistols. Rochefort understood. An ambush was set up and Rochefort and two of his men were killed.

"The other one managed to escape, but not until after he had seen Rochefort and his friends killed, and got back to the palace, and advised the King what had happened. They say he died of his injuries later, personally I think he was dealt with. Apparently, Rochefort put up a good fight, but was eventually stabbed through his heart and fell. All of them stood round his body and cheered. They all congratulated each other, and then dug a grave to put the bodies in. (This is when the other one fled.) When they turned, one of them said, 'What... where's Rochefort?' His body had gone. Rochefort had dragged his bloody body behind two large boulders, where they found him. Rochefort said, 'You'll never kill me, you haven't got the stomach for it and you will all be hanged by the King.' They all laughed and told him it was the King who had sent them. Rochefort paled and then said, 'Oh, my revenge on that idiot will be so drawn out.' The men had no pistols with them, as the King didn't want anyone hearing gunfire. One of the men, who was tall and solid built, then said, 'There's only one way to deal with vermin like you,' and went to his horse and came back with a very wide sharp sword. Rochefort sneered and said, 'Oh look, he's got a big sword. My men will find out who you all are and will get revenge.' The men grabbed him and laid him over the boulder. Rochefort tried to fight each of them but he had little strength left. The man with the sword said, 'Need to see how sharp it really is,' and with that slashed Rochefort across his chest; blood spurted everywhere. Rochefort laughed and said, 'Oh, ouch, that really hurt.' The man raised his sword up high and said, 'Goodbye, Rochefort, this will be a pleasure.' Suddenly Rochefort realised what was about to happen and screamed as his eyes watched the sword come swiftly down. It was the last sound he ever made. 'This is for the King, the Queen, Madame Tréville and Madame du Vallon,' said the man. In these four strikes, Rochefort's head left his body.

"The bodies and head were thrown in the grave and covered. They returned to the palace and advised the King of the gruesome outcome. The King sent these men back to retrieve Rochefort's body. A funeral took place, purely for the Red Guards, but Rochefort's body was not in that coffin. The King did not want him being celebrated so his body was buried in one place and his head in another, deep in a forest on the outskirts of Paris. Justice had been done for his Queen, and you and Amanda."

I replied, "I would like to thank the King for what he did, but obviously I cannot."

Tréville looked at me and said, "I know you would, but it was a long time ago now, you must not tell anyone of this and that includes Amanda, as I was told in the strictest confidence. Enough of this now, my love, let's think and talk of nicer things, like the christening of our sons."

I looked at Tréville and said, "Thank you for telling me, and his death was a fitting end, compared to what he was going to do to Amanda and myself."

We talked for a while about the christening and other things, and then I wrapped my arms round his neck and gently kissed him. I saw the passion in his eyes. I ran my right fingers through his hair and kissed him again, but deeply. My other hand slowly trailed down his chest to the top of his undergarment. "Thinking of nicer things, do you... maybe... know a way to show me instead of us talking?" I said with a mischievous smile.

Tréville smiled and took my face in his hands and kissed me deeply and then said, "Umm... I think I know a way," and started trailing kisses down my neck, and unlacing my night garment.

Over the next couple of days Tréville and I made plans for the twins' christening. The event was going to take place in the village church, but the problem was getting everyone there on the same day. We went and saw the priest and arranged a date for two weeks later, on a Saturday. A list was made of everyone we wanted to invite, including all the villagers. The small church was going to be overflowing. Tréville had to ask the King if time off would be allowed for him and my brothers. The King agreed and said both himself and the Queen would like to see the twins. Luckily the tavern offered to do us some food, wine and ale afterwards. One week later, Helene and Marianne showed me how to make a sling around my shoulder and arm so I could carry one of my babies on horseback, so Tréville and I had one each and rode to the palace. A guard helped Tréville dismount and then helped me down. The King and Queen were delighted to see the twins. The Queen was fascinated by the colour of their eyes, whereas the King held both of them whilst walking round the room talking to them. I noticed the Queen had such a longing in her eyes for a child, hopefully one day. I could see a child would be most welcomed. When we left I got onto Sunkwa, Tréville handed me Jean and then Armand. He mounted his horse and then took Armand from me and we rode back to the dwelling. The twins were so good, they were awake the whole time but not once did they cry.

The day of the christenings arrived and it was pouring with rain! "Oh, Tréville, we can't take the twins out in this, we will all get soaked," I said, rather upset.

"We have a couple of hours yet, maybe the weather will be kind to us," he replied.

True enough the rain went away and the sun came out. When Tréville and I got to the church all the villagers, Catherine and the workforce, and other friends were already seated. "Tréville, where's my brothers and Amanda? We can't start without them."

"One day they just might get somewhere at the right time," he said with a sigh.

All of a sudden three horses came galloping into sight. It wasn't the ones we were expecting. One of the riders dismounted and came over to us. They were from the palace. "Minister Tréville, Madame Tréville," he said, bowing, "we are on a mission for the King, but he asked us to come to you first to give you this present from him and the Queen." Catherine had come out to see if anything was wrong, so I gave her Jean, Tréville had Armand. I took the present and opened it, and inside there were two small gold crosses on beaded chains. They were beautiful. I showed them to Tréville, who then thanked the rider and asked that our thanks be conveyed to the King and Queen. Naturally Tréville would also give thanks to them both, when he was next at the palace.

As they rode off, so five other riders arrived, full of apologies. They said they had got lost, how many times had they been to the dwelling!

At last the christenings took place. My brothers and Amanda made a promise to look after the twins should anything happen to both of us. I noticed Amanda was a bit hesitant; I knew only too well that she was still in turmoil after losing her own child. Behind the priest I saw Swallowtail and my father and mother. Swallowtail was doing a christening chant, but as soon as the ceremony finished they faded away. All my brothers and Amanda took turns holding the twins, but when they got to Athos they started crying, so Tréville and I took them. "Something I did?" said Athos.

I smiled and said, "Of course not, Athos, I think they are hungry and tired."

Everyone went back to the tavern, except Tréville, and myself. We took the twins back to the dwelling where I fed them. We both decided to put the crosses around their necks when they were a bit older. With a bit of rocking in our arms Jean and Armand went to sleep, so we put them in their cots.

I went to re-lace my bodice, but Tréville stopped me and took me in his arms and said, "I have my beautiful wife and now I have two beautiful sons, what more could I ask for?" and with that kissed me deeply and passions flared in both of us.

"I think, my love, we should perhaps continue this later, we have a celebration to attend," I said. He replied by kissing my neck and unlacing the rest of my bodice. Moments later our clothes were on the floor, and our love for each was fulfilled. Helene had already offered to look after the twins and arrived with her friend about an hour later.

As we left Helene took my arm and said, smiling, "I hope we didn't interrupt anything?" I smiled and blushed slightly. Tréville and I went to the tavern and celebrated with all our friends and had a lovely time. My brothers and Amanda stayed the night at the tavern, and then along with Tréville in the morning, they all rode back to the garrison.

About a week later Helene came to see me. She had become a very dear friend to me, well more like an older sister, especially before and after the twins were born. I don't know what I would have done without all of her help. She had heard that a daughter of a friend of hers had lost her job because the master of the house had passed and his widow was going back to England with her children. "What has this to do with me, Helene?" I asked curiously.

"I wondered if you required someone to help you with the twins. One child is hard enough, but two? I also know you need to get back to your bakery. She has been given a reference," said Helene.

I replied, "I would like to meet her, but first I would like to talk to Tréville."

When Tréville came home a couple of days later, we talked about it and both agreed it would be a good idea, but Tréville would leave the decision to me. I arranged with Helene to meet this person and would take it from there. The day she arrived the twins were screaming at the top of their lungs, which was unusual for them. She went straight to both, picked them up one by one, and sang to both, and within a very short time they were both gurgling away quite happy. I was impressed. "What is your name?" I asked.

"My name is Chloe Surcouf and I am twenty years old, Madame Tréville."

"And how long have you looked after children?" I asked.

She replied she was brought up in a home of ten siblings, she was the eldest, and it was her job to look after them all. When she was sixteen she was sent to her employer as a chambermaid, but after a couple of years was asked to look after his children and had stayed until he passed. I took an immense liking to Chloe and that's how Tréville and I got someone to look after the twins.

Chloe turned out to be very good with the twins and after a couple of months we suggested that she move in with us and she could have the spare bedchamber where the twins would now sleep. We rearranged the room and put in a small desk and a couple of chairs. There was already a fireplace in there, so if Chloe wanted to spend time on her own, she would be warm and private. She was paid a very good wage and we let her have most weekends off to visit her family. I would, obviously, not work at the bakery on a Saturday and Sunday, it was closed, so I would spend every weekend with the twins. I also taught Chloe how to bake. I found it very strange that Chloe called us Madame Lesley and Minister Tréville, as we were always called by our first names, but as my husband pointed out it was the correct way.

I was glad to get back to the bakery, and saw Tréville when I could. Tréville came to the dwelling as much as he could, but when he couldn't he stayed at the garrison. I loved seeing Tréville with the twins, as he would have one on each of his legs and would bounce them up and down, until the pair of them were giggling. He would crawl round on the large blankets I put out in the back garden, pretending to chase them.

One Saturday, Athos turned up and quietly I led him to the back garden and he watched Tréville and then laughing, said, "Forgive me, Minister, and are these new duties your men need to learn?"

"Perhaps you should come and try, Captain," said Tréville.

I was stunned as Athos put his sword, pistols, daggers, hat and jacket on the table and joined in!! Helene turned up and the pair of us stood there laughing, watching a Minister for War and his Captain chase giggling babies. A short while later Tréville asked Athos why he had come. Athos replied he just needed to talk to him about something, so Helene and I left them and went inside. Eventually Tréville and Athos came in with our sons who were firm asleep. The love Tréville had for them shone in his eyes, as they did for me. Athos and Helene stayed for a meal and left quite late.

At the bakery, things slowly got back to normal. The miller and farmer started sending us supplies and it was so good to get the bakery ovens going again. The lane also started looking better, people started returning to the taverns, the market came back and soon it was like the war had never happened. The chocolate room flourished again, and we started getting orders from customers for celebrations. Soon Christmas would be upon us. At last the bakery was getting busy again, thank heavens. There was also good news from the palace – the Queen was with child.

CHAPTER 30

The Summer Ball

Christmas week arrived, or as the French called it, Noël. This Noël would certainly be better than the last one. Tréville and my brothers were home, and we had the twins, who were now nine months old. I would have loved to cook a Noël meal for my brothers and Amanda, but alas, the table in the parlour was not big enough for all of us, so we agreed we would meet them the following day for a meal at the tavern. Tréville also said it would be nice for me not to cook and relax for once. I had an idea what to buy Tréville as a special present, but he also needed new shirts and undergarments. I went to the seamstress in Paris and she made him four new undergarments and four new shirts. Once I got them, I wrapped them in plain paper and asked Helene if I could leave them with her, along with his special present, until Christmas Eve.

On Christmas Eve, before children went to bed, they would leave their shoes by the fireplaces for gifts from Père Noël. Sweets, nuts, fruit and small wooden toys were placed in the shoes. A Yule Log Cake called Bûche de Noël was made and served at a grand feast called Le Reveillon. After nearly everyone had attended midnight mass, they would either go back to someone's dwelling, or the tavern to celebrate. Le Reveillon was made up of poultry, ham, cake, fruit and wine. On the farms a wooden Yule Log was made and burned from Christmas Eve until New Year's Eve. Once New Year arrived a part of the log was made into a wedge shape for the plough. It was a good luck omen for plenty of harvest in the coming year. We had one small farm in the village and this ritual was done every year. In the church a small area was closed off where a table was placed and had figures on a straw bed. These figures were made from moulded clay and were then dressed in different colours and occupations of what the people did. They were called Santons. Sometimes you would see figures of high officials and village characters. (I'm sure one year I saw a Musketeer!)

Christmas morning arrived. Tréville had got a chicken, which had to be cooked, and he had ordered a piece of ham for the New Year. I had every intention of getting up early to start cooking, but Tréville had other ideas. As I was about to creep out of our bed, a pair of arms went round me and pulled me back in. "And where do you think you're going?" he asked.

"My love, I have a chicken to cook, along with other things. The twins will soon need feeding, don't forget we let Chloe go home for the festive time, and we have to go to church," I replied.

"I can't hear the twins crying yet, and yes, we have the dwelling all to ourselves. Church is a lot later, so come here and give your lonely husband a kiss."

I looked at him, he was smiling and his eyes twinkling. "And since when have you been lonely, my poor husband?" I said, trailing my fingers down his chest.

"Since you tried to leave my arms without my good morning embrace," he replied.

I laughed and said, "Has anyone ever told you what a load of...?" I never finished my sentence. His arms entwined with mine, our lips meeting and our kisses deepening with each kiss. Our passions for each other were overwhelming and were lovingly fulfilled. Tréville looked at me and said, "Happy Noël, my love." I was so lovely and warm entwined in his arms, and was just about to drift off when the twins woke up.

I fed the twins and then later on Tréville took over. He bathed, dressed, and then played with them. I cooked the chicken and vegetables, made a cake for later on, and after we had partaken of our meal I went and got one of his presents. We were sat in the parlour in front of a roaring fire, and the twins had fallen asleep and were in their cots. He opened it and said, "Oh, undergarments and shirts, just what I needed. Thank you, my love. Let me go and get yours." I could see he was a little disappointed. "I got these for you, my love," and he handed me two boxes. In the first box was a pair of earrings that matched my necklace perfectly, and in the other was a lovely fleur-de-lis bracelet with earrings.

"Oh Tréville, they are beautiful, thank you my love."

He smiled and kissed me and said, "Only the best for my true love."

I got up again and quietly went back into the twins' bedchamber and picked up a large box I had hidden in a cabinet. "My love, you honestly didn't think I would only give you undergarments and shirts for our first Christmas together. I saw this and thought you would like it."

He carefully unwrapped it and his eyes lit up. "How on earth did you know I was looking for a new one? It is a wonderful present, my love." He took me in his arms and kissed me so deeply. I had bought him a rosewood writing box, with three gold-like latches on the lid. The writing box was attached on top of a large drawer and could be locked for private papers. In front of the box were two inkwells, and a groove where quills could be laid. Inside the drawer were various quills and sheets of parchment.

Late afternoon, we dressed the twins up warmly, as we did ourselves, as it was a cold day. Tréville had Armand, and I had Jean, and we went to the church for the Christmas blessing. Both the twins were awake, eyes looking everywhere. They were good and didn't cry, but both of them would point at something and start giggling and kicking their little legs!! Outside the church, Helene came over as did the other villagers and we all wished each other a happy Noël. Helene had a friend staying with her for the festive period called Ana, and we asked both of them if they would like to join us later for a light meal. They were delighted and arrived just as I was putting the twins down for the night. Helene loved the twins like they were her own, so I let her lull them to sleep. Tréville poured them a drink of wine, and I put cheese, chicken, bread, fruit and cake on the table. We had a thoroughly enjoyable evening. Helene and Ana were more than delighted to look after the twins the following day so Tréville and I could join Amanda and my brothers at the tavern. We were meeting around noon and said we would only be away three maybe four hours.

The following day, I made sure everything that the twins would need was done, and had fed them, and after Helene and Ana arrived, Tréville and I set off for the tavern. I was glad we went on one horse, as it was really cold, so even though I had my thick cape on, Tréville put his cape round me also, so we kept each other warm. We left the horse at the garrison, and went to the bakery, but Catherine must have gone to her aunt's as it was all locked up. The tavern was packed.

"Minister, Lesley, over here!" shouted Athos. We made our way over to them, and I kissed each one of them on their cheeks, and gave them a hug. Tréville patted their backs and shook hands. He kissed Amanda's cheek and gave her a hug. Amanda gave me a package for the twins. Inside were two beautiful hand-stitched nightgowns, I was delighted and gave her a hug and kissed her cheek. I carefully re-wrapped them and put them in my cape pocket so they wouldn't be damaged or lost. The atmosphere in the tavern was full of merriment and happy drunks. A huge log fire was burning. Mertyl came over and placed chickens, ham, bread, fruits, cheeses and plenty of wine on the table for us. We all talked and laughed and had an excellent meal. Neither of us noticed how time had gone by until I realised it was just starting to get dark.

"Oh Tréville, it is getting dark. Alas, we must go, our twins will be screaming to be fed."

He looked at me, smiled, and said, "Not sure I can get on the horse, never mind feed the twins." I raised my eyebrow. He was merry. Oh, this was going to be fun getting him home!

All of them were merry, except me, I couldn't drink, but I was very happy. "My love, you stay and enjoy yourself, and I will go back to the dwelling. I'm sure you will be able to stay at the garrison," I said, giving him a kiss on his cheek.

"Like hell you will, Lesley, I'm coming with you. Once I'm on the horse I will be fine," he said sharply, in a raised voice.

I looked at the rest of them, who had lowered their eyes, so I bent down and whispered in his ear, "Don't speak to me in that tone or you will walk back from the crossroads. Do you understand?"

Tréville looked at me and then said, "Apologies, my love, I should not have spoken to you in that way," and gave me a quick kiss. He then stood and said, "Amanda, men, it is time for us to depart, thank you for a wonderful day."

Athos looked at us and said, "I think it's time we all returned to the garrison, we can continue our evening there." We all walked back to the garrison, after thanking Mertyl and everyone else for a wonderful meal. The cold air chilled my bones and I was so pleased I had my thick cape on. When we got to the garrison Remy got Tréville's horse. I smiled, kissed and hugged my brothers and Amanda goodbye, and asked Porthos if he would help me get Tréville on his horse. Porthos helped Tréville up, I was going to sit behind him, but Porthos said not to. Should Tréville fall he would take me with him, so I sat in front as usual. Tréville put his arms round my waist, under my cape and then Porthos put Tréville's cape round both of us, and I took the reins.

On the way back Tréville started kissing my neck. "Have I ever told you, my love, you have a beautiful neck, I just want to kiss it all the time."

I slowed the horse to a walk and turned, and put one of my hands on his face and we kissed deeply, and I said, "Thank you, my love."

As we rode on I felt Tréville's hands creeping up my body, until they rested on my breasts. "Can I kiss these now?" he asked, as he tried to unlace my bodice.

"Tréville I think we should wait until we get back to the dwelling, it's not far now," and pushed his hands back down to my waist – twice. The next minute one of his hands was taking the pins out of my hair.

"I like your hair down, so I can run my fingers through it," he said. Before he had chance to unplait my hair, I stopped the horse.

"My love, we are back at the dwelling, now dismount and then help me down, take your horse to the barn, rub him down, feed and water him, put his blanket on and shut him in his stall. Can you do that for me?"

Tréville replied he was quite capable of seeing to his horse, but instead of dismounting, he slid off him backwards, and fell into a bush. I had to stop myself from laughing. He stood up, looked at me and said, "Don't think that was right," and then put his arms up to me and I put my hands on his shoulders and his hands went to my waist. I really hoped he wouldn't drop me – he didn't. He then took the reins and led the horse to the barn, or did the horse lead him?

I went straight into the dwelling and apologised to Helene and Ana, but Helene said the twins had been fine, and they grizzled but didn't cry out. I went and fed them immediately. I talked with Helene and Ana for a time and then said my goodbyes to them. I put Amanda's present for the twins on the table so I could show them the following morning. I wondered where Tréville was. I went to the barn, and what I saw I could not believe. Helene had kindly lit the two candles in the lanterns for us. First of all I saw his boots, then his jacket, shirt and breeches on the floor. The poor horse was stood in his stall, still with the saddle on, snorting and pawing the ground!! Sunkwa was nodding his head up and down and looked like he was laughing. Where was Tréville? The straw bales were stacked three high, and there he was sprawled face up on the top of one of them with a leg and arm dangling down the side with just his undergarment on!!

"Tréville, wake up!" I said sharply.

"Ah my love, you've come to bed at last. Come lay with me."

"Tréville you are in the barn, not the bedchamber, now dress yourself, or go to our bedchamber, and don't wake the twins." I heard him moving so I went and sorted his horse out. I rubbed him down with straw after I took the saddle off, put fresh hay in his trough, filled the bucket with water, put a blanket over him and finally scattered fresh straw on the floor. I locked him in his stall for the night, and then patted Sunkwa. Tréville had not dressed but was back on the straw bale gently snoring. I went back into the dwelling, checked on the twins who were now firm asleep, got four large spare blankets, went back to the barn and put them over Tréville. He was going to ache in the morning!

In the early hours of the morning I felt the bed dip. I turned and looked at Tréville, who still had his undergarment on and was laid on top of the bed. "Tréville, get under the blankets or you will catch a chill," I said.

"Sorry, didn't mean to wake you and I'm sorry for my behaviour, can I kiss you goodnight?"

"If you get under the blankets I will let you." I smiled, as he was under the blankets in seconds. He took my face in his hands and gently kissed me. "Tréville, you are so cold," I said.

"Perhaps I need warming up my love," he said.

"Perhaps, my love, that will teach you not to undress in the barn."

"I didn't undress in the barn," he said.

"Then where are your clothes?"

"Ummm... I don't know," he said.

I smiled and took him in my arms. I couldn't be mad at him, as it was very rare for him to get merry, unlike my brothers. I kissed him gently and our arms wrapped round each other, our kisses deepening, and soon my night garment was off, as was his undergarment. Slowly our passions for each other were reached and afterwards Tréville whispered in my ear, "Mmmmm, I must get merry more often if this is what happens, and I'm lovely and warm now." I playfully slapped his arm and then our arms entwined around each other and we slept until two little people woke us up. In the morning Tréville found his clothes in the barn. I never said a word.

The day of New Year, all of us celebrated it at the tavern in the village. Amanda and my brothers stayed at the tavern and returned to the garrison the following day. All of them got very merry and as Patric had some of the locals playing their musical instruments we all had a dance with each other. I helped Tréville stagger back to the dwelling, thanked Helene, helped Tréville undress and as soon as he lay down he was asleep. After I had checked the twins were sleeping soundly, I then undressed, washed, put my night garment on and got into our bed. Tréville's arms went round me, as mine did him. He kissed me deeply and said, "I love you, my beautiful Lesley," but before I could reply he was gently snoring.

Nine months later, a couple of weeks before the King's birthday in September, it was announced that the Queen had given birth to a son and heir, Louis XIV, who would be known as The Dauphin, until he was older. The bakery was asked to help out for the christening meal at the palace, which again was an honour. Amanda and myself had been invited by the King and Queen to attend the christening at the cathedral. Tréville and his men were all in full military uniform, all looking very splendid. The King and Queen looked magnificent and both of them radiated their happiness. After the ceremony everyone returned to the palace and celebrated.

Six months after the birth of the Dauphin, the King surprised everyone by saying a masked ball was to be held, three months later, on the day of the summer solstice in June, which fell on a Friday. This day was called the Fire of Saint Jean and was a celebration day. The King would light a large bonfire. Later in the evening fireworks would be lit and brighten up the night sky. The fireworks would be in white or pale gold colours. The ball would start early evening and then everyone would go into the gardens to see the fireworks, as a finale to the ball. My main problem was what to wear. When Tréville told me, I sighed. "My love, what's wrong? I'm sure Helene would only be too delighted to help Chloe look after the twins."

I looked at him and replied, "It's not that, Tréville, look at the state of me – I feel big now, how on earth am I going to look good in a ball gown? I am your wife and I mustn't let you down."

Tréville laughed and took me in his arms and replied, "My love, you are not big, you have regained your figure since the twins were born. Maybe your breasts are bigger, but I like them bigger." I just looked at him – trust my husband to come out with that statement!! "Seriously my love, you will find something and you will look beautiful like you did at the first ball I took you to," and gently kissed my lips. I smiled as a memory of that ball came back to me – the day I had surprised Amanda, and the start of my love for Tréville. "I understand from the King, that myself and your brothers are to have new uniforms, and they will be ready for the ball."

"Oh, what will they look like?"

"I have no idea, my love." Umm, that gave me an idea.

The following day I went to a seamstress in Paris and explained what I would need. She took my measurements and assured me I was far from big, told me to go back in two months for a final fitting, which I did. I had talked to Tréville about the ball, mainly to see if we would be allowed to dance with each other and with my brothers. He replied they would all be on duty at the palace, and would have to wait until the night. When I next visited the garrison, I asked Porthos if he could kindly ask Amanda to come and see me at the bakery. Amanda came round a couple of days later and I told her about a plan I was thinking of. I thought it would be a good idea to mask ourselves so well that our husbands would not recognise us. Amanda agreed, it could be fun. I went and had my final fitting and the dress was beautiful, the mask she had made was better than I thought, and she had also got me a lovely fan. At last the day of the ball arrived.

The King and Queen decided not to have a formal meal, but to have about a dozen long tables filled with various sorts of fare. I had been asked, again, to help out. Various cakes, pastries, breads and biscuits were made at the bakery, and the Queen had specifically asked for two Croquembouches to be made, and these would be made in the palace kitchen. I spent the morning at the dwelling with our twins and made sure Chloe would be all right, and had everything she would need for them. Helene had said she would stay with Chloe for as long as she needed her. I did mention that depending on how late it was, we might not be back until the following morning. Chloe told me not to worry, as the twins would be safe with her and Helene, and to enjoy myself. I rode Sunkwa into Paris, picked up my dress, mask and fan, and then rode to the palace, where a stable boy took Sunkwa to the palace stables. The Queen had kindly offered me a spare bedchamber I could use, and, if needed, she was happy for Tréville and me to stay the night. I laid my dress out on the bed, which was in a cover, then laid out my other garments and unpacked the small bag I had brought with me.

I then headed down to the kitchens, but not before I spotted Tréville stood at the entrance to the palace ballroom watching what was happening. I quietly crept upon him and put my hands over his eyes. His hands took mine and kissed them both, before turning to me and kissing me quickly. "Now, now, you two love birds, you will have to leave that until later."

We both turned to see the King walking towards us.

"Sire," said Tréville, and bowed.

"Your Majesty," I said, and curtsied.

"Lesley, lovely to see you. How are your twins?" asked the King.

I replied, "Growing too fast, Your Majesty, they are now two years old." I asked him how the Queen and the Dauphin were and I had never seen such a huge smile from him.

"They are both quite well, thank you. Doesn't everything look splendid? Do you have everything you require for the Queen's request?" I replied I was on my way to the kitchen. We both left Tréville and the King walked a little way with me, and then I curtsied and left him.

As I had helped in the palace kitchen before, all the ingredients I needed were ready. Between myself and three other kitchen staff, the two Croquembouches were made and ready to be taken up to the room adjoining the palace ballroom. I was so pleased I didn't have to carry them! Catherine had also arrived with everything from the bakery, so we started setting everything out on the tables. The kitchen staff had brought up various poultry, hams, cheeses, fruits, and other fare. We had just finished when a voice said, "Oh Lesley, it looks wonderful." We both turned and curtsied to the Queen.

"I'm glad it's to Your Majesty's liking," I replied, smiling. "I trust you and the Dauphin are well?" She replied she was, and was so looking forward to the evening. With that she left and we both curtsied.

Suddenly an arm went round my waist and a couple of small kisses were placed on my neck. "I think it's time you went to get changed, my love. You and Amanda are supposed to arrive before the King and Queen, not after." For that remark he got a slap on his backside. Catherine laughed and I escorted her to the door and said I would see her after the weekend, and then I made my way quickly to the spare bedchamber.

I undressed, washed and then unpinned my hair and started brushing. I had seen in La Gazette de France (published years ago), how to braid my hair and had been practising every day to do it correctly. It looked extremely complicated, but in fact it was quite easy, but needed lots of pins. Starting from the front I gathered my hair up from the sides and pinned it. Then I did an eight-plait section, nearly to the end. I then brought the plaited section back up and pinned the sides together. The unplaited hair I separated into two sections and wrapped each section around a hair rat (a soft pad), and pinned them to the plait, then carefully removed the hair rats, so that it looked like a large bow. Once I was happy with my hair, I then put on a clean thin-strapped petticoat, and then my dress. I had Tréville's necklace round my neck, as usual, and wore the matching earrings and the bracelet that he had bought me. Finally, on went my mask, which I tied underneath the top of my braided hair. I looked in the mirror and was delighted, even though I was showing more chest than I would have liked, but I could always use my fan. The seamstress was the one making Tréville and my brothers' uniforms, but she did not have enough material left over from Tréville's, to do my dress. The way the dress had been made showed me I wasn't as big as I thought I was. Tréville was right, I had regained my figure. The bodice and overskirt were in dark blue, nearly the colour of Tréville's uniform; the underskirt and sleeves were in gold and blue damask. My mask was also made from the damask cloth with gold ribbons.

Now I was ready. I went to Amanda's quarters and knocked on her door. She replied, "Come in." I entered and she looked at me and said, "Are your lost, Madame?"

I burst out laughing, and said, "It's me."

"Oh Lesley, you look wonderful. I really didn't recognise you, but I should have done by your necklace."

Amanda looked beautiful. Her dress was in dark lavender, with the bodice and underskirt in lighter lavender, and once she put her lavender and gold mask on I didn't recognise her either. As I went to open the door I said, "Oh, Amanda, our wedding rings, we need to hide them. I'll keep mine hidden holding my dress. Now let the fun begin." We left her quarters, and as we walked down the corridor we saw Porthos, Athos, Aramis and D'Artagnan walking towards us. I quickly, with my right hand, put my fan up to hide my necklace.

"Ladies," said Aramis, doffing his hat. We both nodded and as they walked past us, I turned to see Aramis looking at us, and he winked. Amanda and I giggled. We quickly went into the room where the food was, so I could check everything was all right. One of the other Queen's attendants was talking to Amanda, so I sat on a chair and waited. Amanda and I then entered the palace ballroom, which was full of people, looking wonderful, with all the different colours of the ball gowns.

Straight away I spotted Tréville and my brothers. "Oh, Amanda, look at them now in their new uniforms, I have never seen them look so handsome." As Minister for War, Tréville's uniform consisted mainly of different colours of blue. He had a white shirt on with beige ruffs on the collar and at the end of the sleeves, dark blue waistcoat and trousers, a navy-blue sash that went round his waist, tied at the side. On top of his sash was a brown belt, onto which he had linked another leather belt, which held his sword in a silver sheath. He could also attach his pistols and whatever else. His jacket was navy blue and came down to just below his knees, with dark blue motifs at the top on either side. His boots were brown and the tops turned down. Around his neck was the official gold Minister of the Crown medallion, with two crossed swords in the middle, which stood for Minister for War. This was secured with a dark blue ribbon. He wore a ring on his small right finger, which was the Minister for War seal. Naturally he was wearing his wedding ring, on his other hand. Athos, Aramis, Porthos and D'Artagnan had now changed, and all had different uniforms and looked very impressive, and still wore their new pauldrons at the top of their right arms.

Amanda agreed and couldn't take her eyes off Porthos. I nudged her and reminded her we didn't know them. We looked at each other and smiled. We wandered round the room arm in arm, getting quite a few admiring glances from the men, and actually walked past Tréville and our brothers. I put my fan against my chest so he would not recognise my necklace. As we passed our men we both nodded. Porthos looked and said, "Evening ladies." I could see Tréville was looking all round the room. We managed to stand at the side of them and heard Tréville say to Porthos, "Where the hell are they? I knew they'd be late, and now here come the King and Queen."

Glad he had faith in both of us!!

"Ladies and gentlemen, the King and Queen," said one of the King's guards.

Everyone moved into lines from the door to Their Majesties' thrones and as they walked past all the men bowed, and all the ladies curtsied. As they passed Amanda and myself I saw the King glance at us and smile. Once they reached their thrones, the King said something to the Queen, who looked in our direction and smiled. The Queen looked stunning and the King magnificent. The King then made a short speech, and afterwards the music started. The King and Queen took to the floor and then other guests joined in. When they returned to their thrones, Tréville and my brothers took up their places behind and at the side of them.

CHAPTER 31

The Twins

Two gentlemen came to Amanda and myself, and we danced with them for a short time. All the time I kept glancing over to Tréville. Suddenly his eyes met mine, so I lowered my eyes for a couple of minutes and then glanced back. He was no longer looking at me, but had gone back to looking round the room. I noticed Athos, Aramis and D'Artagnan were walking round, taking everyone and everything in. The Red Guards were standing at various entrances. I could see Tréville was getting anxious, as was Porthos, because neither of them could leave Their Majesties, and try to find us. In between the dances I suggested to Amanda that we just walk past and wink at them both. We did it twice. Aramis nudged Porthos and nodded at us both times. Amanda and I giggled. Eventually I suggested we go and ask them for a dance. We walked up to them, curtsied to the King and Queen, and I said to the King, in a broken accent, "Your Majesty, we wondered if we might have your permission to have the pleasure of a dance with your Minister for War and Musketeer Porthos?" Again, I had my fan against my chest.

The King looked at both of them and then Tréville looked at us and said, "Apologies, ladies, but we are on duty."

"Tréville," said the King, "Athos, Aramis and D'Artagnan are here with myself and my Queen, you and Porthos have my blessing to dance with these two beautiful ladies – after all, they are your wives."

All five of them looked at us, stunned, and once I dropped my fan and they saw Tréville's necklace, we all smiled at each other. Aramis chuckled and said, "Good luck, gentlemen, you should have recognised them."

To which I quickly replied, "As I recollect, Aramis, none of you recognised us in the corridor earlier," and then I winked at him.

"Aaahhh," he said.

"Thank you, Your Majesty," I said, and we curtsied. Tréville and Porthos bowed, unbuckled their swords, and we led them onto the dance floor. Amanda and Porthos danced away from us.

Tréville took me in his arms, and I looked at him and said, "We heard you say you thought we were late, when we weren't. We even walked past you, Porthos nodded and said, 'Evening, ladies.' I thought you might have recognised me from my dress, earrings or bracelet, do they not look familiar?"

Tréville looked at my dress and suddenly it registered. "My love, you said you were wearing peach, not the colour of my uniform, and yes, I should have recognised your earrings, they were your Christmas present, as was your bracelet. I'm stunned I did not recognise either of you. I must say one thing, though, you look absolutely beautiful and your hair is so different. I can't wait to get you back to the dwelling."

I smiled and said innocently, "Why Minister, what are you suggesting?"

"How did the King know it was you?"

I replied I had let him in on our secret. "I must say, my love, you and your men look very handsome in your new uniforms. Perhaps I can't wait to get you back to the dwelling."

Tréville smiled and said, "Now who's suggesting?" We both looked into each other's eyes, and could see the passion in them. A slow dance started to play and Tréville held me so tight, giving me gentle kisses on my neck. My chest was rising and falling with every kiss, so I danced us to the nearest opened double windowed door, which led out to the gardens.

Once outside our arms went round each other and our kisses deepened with every one. "I love you so much, my dearest love, and I always will until my very last breath," said Tréville.

"I love you too, Tréville, and I always will until my very last breath, hopefully for a long time to come yet. When our time comes I hope we are like this, entwined in each other's arms, kissing each other to show how much our love means to us." Tears came to my eyes.

"My love, why the tears?" I took his face in my hands and said, "Because the thought of losing you would break my heart. You are my lover, my friend, my protector and the most wonderful husband and father, and my life without you would have been nothing."

He put his arms around me and held me so close. "I'm not going anywhere without you, my love," and then his lips met mine and we kissed each other with such a tenderness that both of us could feel the passions rising in us.

"Tréville, I think maybe we should take a walk round the garden to cool our passions, you in particular, I can feel you through my dress, and hopefully we will continue this later."

Tréville smiled, and we walked arm in arm in the cool night air, then Tréville kissed me again, and said, "I had better go back, I will find you when the fireworks start."

We went back in, and I looked to see where Porthos and Amanda were. The connecting door had been opened so the people could eat. I should have known – he was eating. I made my way over to them and Porthos kissed Amanda and went back to the King and Queen. Nobody was allowed to touch the Croquembouches until the Queen said so. Amanda and I had a dance with each of our brothers and other gentlemen. The King and Queen also had many dances together. The Queen loved to dance. The King then stood, clapped his hands, and said, "Ladies and gentlemen, everyone out into the gardens for the bonfire and fireworks. Afterwards, once the Queen and I have partaken of our share, the remainder of the Croquembouches can be eaten."

We all went outside and Tréville and Porthos found Amanda and myself. Tréville's arms went round my waist, my hands rested on top of his. Now and then I had a gentle kiss on my neck, and we watched the King light the bonfire and then later on the fireworks lit up the night sky to "aahs and oohs." There were a lot of superstitions, with regards to the bonfires lit all over the towns and villages, on this night. In some villages at the end of the evening lots of dancing and singing went on throughout the night, and chairs were put round the fire so that the deceased could join in as well. The most common superstitions were:

For the brave and not very intelligent, jumping over the dying fire guaranteed you a marriage by year-end.

For the more reasonable, parading around the fire several times made you look like an idiot but promised you true love for the rest of the year.

For those more interested in money than love, throwing a coin into the fire and retrieving it later from the ashes insured you riches all year long.

If you just wanted a good harvest, throwing in a rock that you retrieved later and buried in your fields assured you the best crop ever (the bigger the rock, the bigger the harvest).

You could also throw some garlic heads into the fire and then feed the roasted cloves to your children to keep them from getting sick all year long.

In Paris a huge bonfire was always built, in front of the Hotel de Ville, as it was this year, burning up to twenty metres high, which the King always lit. This year, however, the King decided to clear an area in the palace so he could have his own bonfire and fireworks. After the fireworks, the bonfire would be doused with water.

Once everyone returned to the ballroom, and the Croquembouches were eaten, the King and Queen decided to retire and left. Again, everyone bowed or curtsied. After that everyone started to leave. Soon there was only Amanda, Tréville, my brothers and myself left. Tréville said he would check all was well and then we would be on our way. We both said our goodnights to Amanda and my brothers and I watched them ride away, back to the garrison. When Tréville returned I said, "The Queen kindly let me have one of the spare bedchambers and said, if needed, we could stay the night. What do you think, my love?"

Tréville took me in his arms, kissed me and then said, "What a splendid idea," and with that, hand in hand, we both walked down the corridor to the spare bedchamber.

Once in the bedchamber I saw how plush the bed really was. I looked at Tréville and could already see the passion in his eyes. "Come here, my dearest love," he said, and took me in his arms and kissed me deeply. He removed my mask, dress and petticoat. I helped him out of his uniform and undergarment and he picked me up and laid me on the bed. It was so comfortable. "Now how do I let your hair down?"

"Why don't we leave that until later?" I replied and kissed him deeply, our arms going round each other, and then our passions were fulfilled. The bed was so big four of us could have slept in it. I wondered if Chloe was all right with the twins. Tréville said she was more than capable, and did have Helene, but it was the first time I had left them all night. Slowly Tréville was removing the pins holding my hair in place and my hair fell down into the long plait I had done. Tréville unplaited it and combed his fingers through, and then gently pulled me on top of him, kissing me deeply. I looked into his eyes and they were ablaze again with his love for me, as mine were for him. Our passions for each other were overwhelming and both of us were left breathless. We entwined our arms around each other and fell into a deep slumber.

We woke early, washed and dressed. I put my dress back in its cover and everything else into my bag, and after I tidied up, we left for the dwelling on our horses. The only person we saw was the maid and Tréville advised her that the room could be cleaned. As we passed the ballroom I noticed it was spotless. The staff must have worked well into the early morning. When we got to the dwelling two little boys came tottering into our arms, and we kissed and cuddled them. Chloe said they had been no trouble at all. Tréville stayed with them for a couple of hours and then left for the garrison, and Chloe made her way home.

During their first couple of years, Tréville had long times away from the twins, due to outbreaks of skirmishes on the borders, and various other duties. He hated being away from them, which I could understand. The twins were now walking and into everything. They had also found their voices, but only saying a couple of words. I remembered when they both said "Ma man" and "Pa pa." Luckily Tréville had been home and was washing them when Armand pointed at him and said, "Pa pa." Tréville was so proud and called to me to tell me. I went to them and then both of them started saying

"Ma man" and "Pa pa" – it was wonderful.

One weekend Tréville and my brothers rode up with a cartload of wood. Apparently some of the trees at the palace had been chopped down and Tréville asked the King if he could have some, so that he could enclose our back garden and make it safe for our twins. All of them worked hard over the weekend and did a great job. Now the twins could run free, when allowed, and not fall in the stream, or wander out of the garden.

When Tréville returned after being away for some time, for a couple of days their maman didn't exist. I noticed, quite quickly, that when Tréville was away, Armand would be slightly quieter than Jean. On one such occasion Tréville had been away for nearly a month. On this Saturday morning the sky was very dark – a huge storm was looming. The twins were playing happily, in an area that Tréville had made for them in the parlour, when I noticed the winds had picked up greatly. I quickly went to the stables and made sure everything was lashed down, and Sunkwa was safe. I also made sure nothing was loose on the ground that could be blown away and cause damage. I had just got back in when the first thunder hit, followed by lightning. Then came the very heavy rain, beating so hard on the windows, I thought they would break. Both the twins screamed, "Maman, Maman!" I picked both of them up and took them into our bedchamber, and put them on the bed.

"It's all right, my little ones, don't be scared. It's only the naughty spirits in the sky having an argument." A huge flash of lightning crossed the window, and both of them clung to me, frightened and crying. I lit the candles and closed the shutters, at least they couldn't see the lightning then. The storm raged on for hours, bringing down one of our small trees in the back garden. Luckily it fell towards the stream and not the dwelling or the stables. A couple of times I could hear Sunkwa neighing, but I couldn't get to him. Then I heard a loud banging at the door. I had locked it as it rattled so much I was worried it might blow in. "Who is it?" I asked. A familiar voice replied and I opened the door.

"Oh my love, you are soaked through. Come, get out of those wet clothes immediately." I had been playing a game with the twins, where they hid under the blankets and I pretended to find them. They had both come into the parlour, took one look at Tréville, screamed and went running back into our bedchamber.

I saw the hurt in Tréville's eyes. "My love, don't be upset, look at you. You have your large hat on, with your cloak, you must look like a giant to them and they haven't seen you for nearly a month. Now take these two cauldrons of hot water and go to the tub room and get undressed before you catch a chill. I will put two more cauldrons of water on and bring them to you." I asked him if Sunkwa was all right and he replied he was a bit on edge but settled down now his horse was there. Whilst the water was warming up, I went into our bedchamber and found the twins, cuddled up to each other, under the blankets. "Jean, Armand, there is no need to be scared, it's your papa come home. Will you come with me and welcome him back? He's very upset he scared you," I said gently. They both looked at each other and then me and nodded. "Let Maman take this water to Papa first and then I'll take you in."

Tréville was already in the tub, so carefully I poured the water in for him. "Thank you, my love. Are the twins all right?" I took his handsome face in my hands and kissed him gently, and said I was bringing them in to see him. I held the twins' hands and took them into the tub room. Tréville looked at the twins and smiled and held his hands out to them.

"Hello Jean and Armand, I have missed you both so much. Will you not come and say hello to your papa, and let me give each of you a cuddle and a kiss?"

I knelt down and put my arms round their waists. "Go on, Papa will not hurt you and if he does, hit him," I said, smiling at Tréville. Tréville raised his eyebrow at me.

As usual Armand was the first to take a step. He looked at his papa with curiosity, then looked at Jean and said, "Is Papa, is Papa." Jean went to Tréville and he held both their hands. Armand looked at me and said, "In Maman."

"Looks like you have company, my love," and I undressed both of the twins and put them in the tub with Tréville. As I prepared a meal I could hear all three of them giggling, and I smiled to myself.

After we had partaken of our meal, Tréville settled the twins down for the night, reading them a story, until they were both asleep. When he came into the parlour, he looked so tired. "Are you all right, my love? You look exhausted."

"All I want to do now is go to bed with my lovely wife, hold you, kiss you and then sleep."

I led him into our bedchamber and we did exactly that. A lot later a hand gently tapping my arm slowly awakened me. I opened my eyes to see Jean and Armand stood at the side of the bed. "In Maman," said Jean. Since Tréville had been away the twins, who now slept in a small bed, on the odd occasion would come and sleep in our bed.

"Hush, don't wake Papa, he is still asleep."

Quietly, and without disturbing Tréville, I moved out of his arms and got out of bed and lifted Armand in, and he cuddled into Tréville's chest. Then I put Jean in, and I got in and he cuddled into my chest. I must have gone back to sleep when I was awoken by a hand stroking my cheek. I opened my eyes and looked straight into Tréville's gorgeous blue eyes, which were twinkling. "This was not the way I was going to wake you up, and I see we have company." The twins were still asleep. Tréville took my hand and kissed it and said, "I love you and our boys so much."

I replied, "As I do you, and you are all my life. Now sleep a little longer while we can, because once they're awake..." Tréville closed his eyes and as I closed mine I felt a heat radiating and opened them to see a rainbow swirling round all four of us, and in that moment my heart was filled with so much love from the people who I loved the most, my husband and our twins.

A couple of hours later, the twins were awake, and pretending to fight with Tréville, who was tickling them. I got up, washed and dressed and started making them all something to eat. The twins could now eat what we did, but smaller portions. Chicken, ham, and fruit was cut up very small so they could chew it; bread, they only had the soft middle. Most of their vegetables I mashed up and put in their broth. Armand liked water, Jean did not, so I would make a small herb tea, and then let it cool. Most of this day was spent washing, cleaning and baking.

Tréville went out into the back garden and looked at the damage the fallen tree had done, but didn't get much done as he had two little helpers!! Unfortunately it had crashed through the fencing. The twins were running round squealing and giggling and saying, "Papa, Papa."

One of the branches from the tree they found they could climb. Tréville got one down to turn around and see the other one climbing up. Armand nearly fell in the stream, but Tréville caught him just in time. Jean then hid in a bush so his papa couldn't find him (I had to point to where he was). Both of them splashed in the puddles, laughing, and were soon covered in mud. Tréville now knew what chaos was. I watched most of this out of the parlour window and just laughed.

Helene came over to see if we were all fine and told us the village was blocked both ends by fallen trees, and the river had flooded. The men from the village were trying to clear everything. She watched Tréville and the twins and laughed as I did. Eventually Tréville gave up and brought in two very tired, dirty boys. I had warmed some water up so Tréville put them both in the tub. After a couple of hours' rest, the twins were up and causing chaos again. I got the impression they loved having their papa home; they didn't want to play with Maman. That night both of us fell into an exhausted sleep, but it had been a lovely day for all of us.

Soon it was time for the twins to attend little school. They also now both wore the crosses that the King and Queen had sent them for their christenings. Tréville had taken them to the garrison blacksmith to have the beaded chain made longer. (When they were older, again, the beaded chain was added to, and neither of them took them off.) The priest did lessons every day, for about an hour, except the weekends, and taught the children very basic reading and writing. Armand loved playing with the other children; Jean held back, but eventually joined in. Even though the twins were identical in every way, same build, same dark hair, it was their eyes that separated them. Armand had Tréville's blue eyes and Jean had my dark brown eyes. We had been blessed with lovely twins. They never argued or fought with each other. They shared everything. If Jean was playing with a toy, later he would give it to Armand to play with and vice versa. Chloe would meet them after their lesson, take them back to the dwelling and give them a meal and drink. In the afternoon they would have a rest, then back out to play for a time. Chloe would also help them with their reading and writing. Early evening they would be washed and ready for sleep when I returned. (They stayed at little school until they were five years old.)

A couple of months later, I started noticing things about the twins. The first time it happened I thought it was my imagination. Tréville was away and Chloe had gone to her family. We were sitting at the table when I noticed Jean look at Armand and then the bread. Armand passed the bread to Jean. Again, Jean looked at Armand and then a piece of apple – Armand gave him the apple. The following weekend some of the younger village boys came to play in the back garden. Jean was playing with a boy showing him his toys. Armand was pretending to fight and fell over. I went to Armand who pointed to his elbow and said, "Hurt, Maman." I rubbed and kissed it better and thought no more of it until the following morning. As I was washing them I saw that both of them had a small bruise on their elbow. I had to think, as surely it was only Armand that fell!! Other small incidents like this happened; if either of them was hurt, they both had the marks. I would have to watch them more closely, but as soon as it started it stopped so I thought no more about it.

CHAPTER 32

The Cave

One bright sunny day I was sitting outside watching the twins playing quite happily, when I felt a huge sorrow in my heart. I had put it to the back of my mind for all these years, but now the thought I could have no more babies came back to me and tears welled in my eyes. I would so love to have given Tréville more children, maybe a couple of daughters. I felt a hand on my shoulder and looked up to see Swallowtail stood at my side. "You are hurting, Spirit of the Wolf. Let your grief out, for too long you have not grieved deep in your heart."

Before I could reply Jean said, "Maman sad?"

Both of the twins were stood in front of me. Armand then said, "Lady," and pointed at Swallowtail. Both of us looked at each other, stunned.

I chose my next words carefully, and said gently, "Can you see Maman's friend?"

They both nodded. The next minute the twins held each other's hands and walked to Swallowtail and held her hands with theirs. Swallowtail knelt down and cuddled both of them and kissed their cheeks. She looked at me and said, "Worry not, Spirit of the Wolf, they will think it was a dream later on. You know the twins have a gift?" I told her about what I had seen and happened. "The twins are developing a gift that Tala must have passed onto them. If one of them is hurt, they both hurt. Jean could be ill, but both would have the illness. This bond will grow very strong as they get older, and can cause huge problems, but now while they are so young it can be stopped, if you wish."

I looked at the twins, and both of them came to me and said, "Kiss, Maman." I bent and kissed both their cheeks, as they kissed mine, and then they went back to playing with their toys.

"What would happen to them, Swallowtail, if I don't break this bond?"

Swallowtail said, "It is difficult to explain but I will try to make you understand. The twins will always have a special loving bond between them, which cannot be broken and will never hurt them. It is what happens, if the other side of the bond is left. As they grow older, events in their lives could break them. The main one would be jealousy. One of them could fall in love, and slowly the other one is not thought about as much, and does not like it. His relationship with his twin is being taken away. I have seen this happen and both the twins ended up passing away, the grief was too much for them to take."

That thought worried me greatly. "What would you have to do, Swallowtail?'

"Nothing more than a potion and a chant, which is best done when they go to sleep. Apologies, Spirit of the Wolf, I must go. I am sorry to leave you but your father is calling me. I will return to you tonight and put the dream into the twins," and with that she faded away. The rest of the day this "bond" played on my mind; I did not want our twins to come to any harm. When Swallowtail returned I told her my decision. Swallowtail went back to the Reservation and returned with the potion. The twins, already drowsy, drank the potion, whilst Swallowtail did a chant. In the morning I watched them closely as they were playing and could see the loving bond was still there. I asked them if they remembered the lady who had called on me the day before. They both asked, "What lady?"

One weekend, many months later, I asked Helene if she would

like to accompany the boys and myself for a picnic. She replied she would be delighted to come, and would take us to a place where her and her husband used to go. We rode for about twenty minutes. I had Jean, Armand and myself on Sunkwa. Helene had blankets and the picnic box attached to her horse. Helene led us down a gentle slope, through a forest I'd never been to before. At the bottom of the slope the land turned into a small field of green with red, yellow and blue flowers. A bit further on there were large and small boulders, which surrounded a lake with a small waterfall. It was beautiful. We dismounted and tied the horses up under the trees to keep them cool. The boys were off running round, exploring. Helene and I laid out the blankets and put the picnic basket on the rug for later. The boys came back and Armand said, "Please Maman, can we go in the water?" I replied I would make sure it was safe first, so I found a small slope to the lake and saw the water was not deep, so I told the boys they could go in. Seconds later both of them had thrown their clothes and shoes off and were playing at the edge. I told them not to venture too far in the water. They might be five years old, but accidents happened.

I went back to Helene and we talked for a while, and then laid out the picnic, but I was still keeping my eyes on the boys. They had left the water and were exploring the boulders. "Maman, come look, we find something." Helene and I walked over to see the boys had found a cave. It was dry inside, and quite big. As the sun was shining, we could see inside.

"Secret cave, Maman," said Jean. It reminded me of Edouard's secret cave.

"Come, boys, I don't want you catching cold, so let's go back. You can dress and then we will eat," and that's what we all did. After a rest the boys were running around again pretending to be a Musketeer and a Red Guard. I watched them pretending to fight, but all they did was fall over laughing, as did Helene and myself. Soon it was time for us to pack up and leave, after what had been a lovely time.

Helene went to get the horses but on the way back she slipped. "Ouch," said Helene. All three of us ran to her. She had twisted her ankle, and hit her head. I tore off some of my petticoat and wrapped it round her ankle, and the other bit I got Armand to soak in the water, then held it to her head. There was no way Helene could ride and I could see the sun was slowly going down. I needed to get help, but how? I couldn't leave Helene on her own and take the boys back, neither could I go, nor leave the boys with Helene.

"Jean, Armand, can you help Maman put everything in the cave?" They carried the blankets and picnic box into the cave. I took the horses and tied them behind the side of the cave. I got the boys to collect twigs, so if I had to, I could make a fire. Slowly I helped Helene into the cave and then helped her to sit down. I wrapped a blanket round her to keep warm.

Suddenly the boys came running in and said, "Maman, riders coming." This reminded me of when Tréville and I had been at another waterfall and Rochefort had turned up. Well I knew it wouldn't be Rochefort, but it could still be Red Guards.

"Boys, stay here, don't move and keep very, very quiet, and look after Helene." I saw about six men coming down the slope, but they weren't Red Guards. I noticed their horses looked different to the French horses, and were laden with blankets, rolled up things and pistols. Two of the riders moved away and came nearer to the boulders. Unless they actually explored the boulders, they wouldn't find the cave and we would be safe.

"This looks all right, Captain, got water to drink and wash in, probably could stay here for the night, then carry on to Paris tomorrow." I was shocked – they were English!

"Make camp, men, build a small fire so nobody can see it," said one of them with authority.

I felt something tug my dress. "Maman," said Jean, "Helene wants you."

I put my finger to his lips and said quietly, "Hush." I quietly went back to Helene.

"What is happening, Lesley? The boys said something about riders. Can they help us?" I told her what I'd seen and heard. "English? What on earth are they doing here?" I replied I had no idea. I went back to the entrance and listened.

One of them said, "What's the drill, Captain?"

The one that seemed to be the Captain said, "Paris isn't far now, men, if we've followed this map correctly. We will set off early morning and get to the palace, hopefully before many people are around. We need to find this King Louis and his Queen and kill them, but quietly – daggers, not pistols, and then get out of there. We must be on guard though for this Minister Tréville and his Musketeers. I'm not sure if they stay at the palace or the garrison, which is about a ten-minute ride away, but if needs be we will kill them too." My hand went to my mouth. I must get to Tréville and warn him. The sun was nearly down and the moon would soon be rising, so that meant all of us had to stay in the cave until they left, but that could be too late. I went back to Helene and told her what I heard.

"Lesley, you must go and warn Tréville. I can't ride and my head still hurts slightly. Leave the boys with me, I promise they will be safe." I looked at Jean and Armand, who were cuddled up to each other on the other blanket. Hopefully they would sleep through the night. I had no idea where we were though.

I asked Helene for directions, which she gave me, but we were about forty minutes away from the palace – on horseback. I would have to walk. Then an idea came. Sunkwa knew his way to the garrison. I would have to let him go free and hope he would go there, and hopefully Helene's horse would follow. I told Helene what I was going to do, kissed the boys and told them they must look after Helene, but more important they must be very quiet – no noise whatsoever.

Jean said, "Maman, pipi." Armand wanted to go also, so I took them as far back in the cave as I could so they could relieve themselves. They then went and sat either side of Helene, with both blankets wrapped round them.

Helene said, "Lesley, why don't you ride out?"

I replied, "if I do those men will see me and probably capture me and then find you all, and I'd rather not think of the consequences. I'm so worried about leaving you and the boys." Tears started to well in my eyes.

Helene put her hand on my face and said, "It's all my fault, but if I hadn't slipped we would never have seen and heard their plans. You must go, as the King and Queen's lives are at stake. Look, the boys are asleep, go now and take care." I told Helene there was food left in the picnic box, and a flask of water. I kissed Helene's cheek and the boys' cheeks and then quietly went to the entrance.

I saw the men had made a small fire and were all around it looking like they were asleep, except one. I slipped round the back of the boulders, hoping I wouldn't spook the horses. Sunkwa just nodded his head up and down. As Helene had put the saddle back on her horse, I now quietly took it off. The only way for the horses to go was the way we came in. This was going to be tricky, and I prayed it would work. "Sunkwa, you must go to the garrison, find Tréville, understand, find Tréville." I looked into his eyes, as he did mine and I knew he understood. I picked up a small stone and threw it as far as I could, hoping it would make a noise. It actually hit a tree then bounced into the lake. The guard looked around and then walked over to the lake. Quickly I slapped both horses on their rumps and both of them took off, but quietly, as though they knew danger was ahead.

The guard said, "Who's there?"

Another voice said, "No one, probably just those deer we saw earlier, now shut up and let us sleep." Relief flooded through me. I made my way to the back of the boulders, and very slowly started to climb, in the dark, up the side. The spray from the waterfall had made the boulders slippery and I kept losing my footing on them. Some of the small stones fell down and I froze. I heard nothing so carried on, desperately trying not to make any more noise. Eventually I cleared the boulders and was now in the forest.

Quite a few times I tripped over roots of the trees that were exposed. My skirt kept getting snagged on twigs and thorns. Eventually I took it off and put it round my shoulders. As I knew I would be riding, I had put my long undergarment on, which came to just below my knees, so I tucked my petticoat into it. Heavens, what a sight I would look if I did meet anyone. The forest was far from quiet and I could hear different noises in all directions. I could see eyes watching me. I could hear a snorting ahead of me, it just turned out to be a couple of deer, which then ran off. The forest was dense, so hardly any light came through. I just hoped I was going in the right direction. I knew there was a full moon, but clouds obscured it, just when I needed it. Then I walked straight into a large thorn bush. I used my hands and arms to protect my face. I could feel the branches pulling my hair, which had fallen down into my long plait.

It felt like the tree was trying to rip the hair from my head. The more I struggled to get out, the more the thorn bush seemed to wrap its branches round me Then a gap in the clouds let the moon shine down on me. I eventually untangled myself and got to the top where the road was.

My arms and legs hurt from where I received cuts and scratches, my hair was a tangled mess, but I didn't have time to worry about that, all I knew was I had a long walk ahead of me. I pulled my petticoat out of my undergarment and put my skirt back on. All the time I was walking all I could think of was Helene and the boys. Had I done the right thing? I don't know how long I'd been walking, but my feet and hip were hurting badly, and I looked for somewhere to sit down. I found a fallen tree log and rested on that. I must have fallen asleep as when I opened my eyes I could see the moon was down, and the sun just rising. Oh no, I had wasted so much time. I started walking again, albeit in great pain, then I heard horses' hooves. I quickly made my way off the road and hid behind a bush. I looked out and saw Sunkwa. "Sunkwa," I called. Sunkwa stopped and trotted back to me. Obviously he didn't go to the garrison and I didn't have the strength to get on him. What a stupid mistake I'd made, what would become of Helene and the boys?

Suddenly I heard a voice cry out, "Lesley."

I turned and looked and saw Tréville, my brothers, and other Musketeers riding towards me. Sunkwa had gone to the garrison after all. I kissed his nose and said, "Thank you."

Tréville was off his horse and took me in his arms and said, "My love, what's happened, who's done this to you? Sunkwa came galloping into the garrison, with another horse, neighing and prancing round, we couldn't calm him. I thought he had escaped from the barn, so we put them both in the stables. Remy said Sunkwa was restless all night. A short time ago he started crashing his stall and Remy let him out. We all went to see what the commotion was. Then D'Artagnan said it looked like Sunkwa wanted us to follow him, and that's what we did."

I quickly explained what had happened. Athos, Porthos and D'Artagnan immediately rode off to the palace with most of the other Musketeers. Aramis asked me if I was all right. I replied I would be fine. I just wanted to go back to the boys and Helene. I didn't say how much pain I was in with my hip and feet. "Tréville, please, we must get to Helene and the boys, never mind about me." Tréville raised his eyebrow, got back on his horse and Aramis helped me onto Tréville's horse, and we all set off to find Helene and the boys. Sunkwa just trotted at the side of us.

Eventually I saw the slope down. Tréville said for me to stay at the top, with the horses, until they had seen what was happening. I gave him a look that said, "No chance," but I knew he had a job to do. Tréville helped me dismount and found a log for me to sit on, whilst the rest of them dismounted and off they went. Sunkwa came and nuzzled my neck, and I patted him. Tréville and his men returned and said there was no sign of the men, or Helene and the boys. I gasped. "Did you find the cave?" I asked, concerned. Tréville looked at me, blank. "Tréville, I told you they were in a cave, but it looks like boulders. Come, I will show you." Tréville helped me onto his horse, and then got on behind me, holding me tight. All of us went down the slope and I guided them to the cave.

"Lesley, stay here," said Aramis.

All of a sudden two little boys came running out. "Maman, Papa!" they cried.

Aramis came out with Helene in his arms. Tréville helped me dismount and the boys ran into my arms. My heart was overjoyed, as they were all safe.

"My love, I'm sorry, I must get to the palace. Will you be all right riding back with the boys and Helene? Two of my other Musketeers will accompany you back to the dwelling and I will send Monsieur Verde to attend to you and Helene." I replied for him to take care and I would see him at the dwelling. Tréville kissed the boys and myself, made sure Helene was all right and then, with Aramis and the others, they galloped off.

One of the Musketeers helped me onto Sunkwa, and then the boys. They then helped Helene onto one of their horses, with a Musketeer holding her, and the other Musketeer had the picnic box and blankets, and slowly we all set off for the dwelling. Once we got back to the village, I asked one of the Musketeers if he would kindly go and get Marianne for Helene. Marianne came immediately. "Oh, Madame Lesley, Madame Helene, what has happened? You both look awful." I explained about Helene and told Marianne to see to her first, I was fine. I went and lay on our bed and the boys joined me.

Jean looked at me and said, "You're hurt, Maman?"

I looked at my arms that were covered in cuts, bruises and blood. I must have hurt myself more than I thought, but it was the pain in my hip that was in agony. I heard a banging at the door, and then heard the voice of Monsieur Verde. There was a knock on the bedchamber door and I said to come in.

"I hear you've had a bit of a night, Lesley," said Monsieur Verde.

"Look, Maman hurt," said Jean.

"Armand, Jean, could you go and play in your bedchamber, just whilst Monsieur Verde has a look at Maman?"

They were both a bit hesitant and Armand said, "You won't hurt Maman will you?"

Monsieur Verde smiled and assured them he would not. "Lesley, can you remove your shirt for me so I can take a look at those cuts? I don't want any infection getting in."

"Never mind me, Monsieur Verde, how is Helene?" He replied that she was fine. Marianne had checked her ankle and put a new dressing on, and the cut on her head was very small. She was waiting to see how I was before going back to her own dwelling.

Monsieur Verde cleaned my arms and put ointment on them. I told him I had also hurt my feet, so he took a look. I had lots of cuts on my lower legs, but the bottoms of my feet were badly cut. Not thinking I would be walking for hours, I had only worn thin flat shoes. Again, he cleaned them in alcohol, put ointment on and bandaged them. I went to get up and a pain seared through my hip and I screamed a bit louder than I thought. The door burst open and the boys came running to me. "You hurt, Maman," said Armand. "I wish Papa was here."

A voice behind them replied, "Papa is here."

The boys turned and ran into Tréville's arms. "He hurt Maman," said Jean.

Tréville looked at me, and I pointed to my hip. "No boys, Monsieur Verde would never hurt any of us. Let's go see Helene," and with that he took them out. Monsieur Verde examined my hip, but I knew it was all the climbing, and slipping and walking that had caused the pain. Monsieur Verde agreed all I needed was rest.

With Monsieur Verde's help, I hobbled out to the parlour to see Helene. She looked a lot better, and I knew she was feeling better when she said, "Now I know why you always ride with Tréville, rather nice to cosy up to someone holding his arms round you." I laughed and kissed her cheek. Tréville came in from the back garden, leaving the boys to play out there. Helene said, "What happened, Tréville? Are our King and Queen safe?"

Tréville said, "Athos, Porthos and D'Artagnan arrived ahead of the English soldiers – they knew a short cut. The King, who was rather upset at being woken early, and his Queen, were moved to a secret chamber within the palace. The English soldiers made their way to the King and Queen's bedchamber. Two of them acted as lookouts at the end of the corridor, two others stood guard outside the bedchamber and the other two went in. With daggers ready, they went to the bed, and threw the blankets back to find only pillows. When they turned they were stunned to see Athos, Porthos and D'Artagnan stood behind them with pistols aimed. Meanwhile Aramis, the other Musketeers and myself had arrived, and quietly captured the other four. They were all immediately taken for questioning. All they would say was that one of their English Ministers had given them orders to come to Paris, with the intention of killing the King and Queen. For what reason they didn't know, they were just carrying out their orders. Once the King and Queen heard about both of you, I was sent home to see to you all."

"Oh, what a relief," said Helene.

Tréville looked at me and said, "The King and Queen would like to see you, my love, when you are well."

"Me, what for?"

"It's all right, my love, they want to thank you for what you did, you probably saved all their lives."

Helene said it was time for her to go to her dwelling. Marianne was going to stay with her. The next thing she knew Tréville had picked her up in his arms. "Tréville, what on earth are you doing? I'm quite capable of walking," she said.

Tréville just looked at her and replied, "Makes a change to have another woman in my arms," but turned and winked at me. I smiled.

The boys came running in and said goodbye to Helene. "Maman, we're hungry," they said.

I bent and kissed both of their cheeks, told them to go and wash and I would prepare something.

When Tréville came back he said, "Oh no, my love, you have to rest. Leave that, I will see to the boys." With that, he made a plate of food for both of them, put two cauldrons of water on, whilst I went and lay down. A bit later Tréville came into the bedchamber and said, "I've got a surprise for you," and picked me up in his arms. He took me into the tub room and I saw he had filled the tub with water for me. "Thought this might help with your aches and pains. Monsieur Verde has given me plenty of ointment so I can re-apply it and re-bandage your feet."

I looked into his eyes and said, "I love you, Tréville," and kissed him deeply. "Where are the boys?"

Tréville replied, "In their bed, curled up to each other, firm asleep, under the blankets."

Tréville quietly closed the door and helped me undress, but when he removed my petticoat, he gasped. "Oh my love, your back is covered in cuts, and you have a nasty cut above your left breast." I looked and saw it was a cut of about four inches and was very deep, but luckily there was no infection. To my surprise Tréville undressed. I looked at him and he said, smiling, "I need to help you in the tub and sit down and I can't do that dressed, can I?" He got in the tub and then helped me in. He helped me to sit down and then he sat behind me. I had pinned my hair up so it would not get wet. Tréville gently washed me, and then I laid back and put my head on his shoulder. The water was lovely and warm and I could feel my body relaxing, so I closed my eyes and drifted off.

"My love, wake up," said Tréville gently. I opened my eyes. "Time for me to dry you," he said.

He got out and wrapped a cloth round his body, then helped me out. He wrapped a cloth round me and dried me off, then gently applied the ointment to my chest, back, legs, arms and feet. He had brought my night garment in and helped me into it. He then got dressed. Again, he picked me up in his arms, opened the door and carried me back to our bedchamber, pulled the blankets back and put me in the bed. I wrapped my arms round him and kissed him deeply. "Thank you, my love, I feel so much better now."

I moved a bit too quick and my hip felt like a knife had gone through it. Tréville felt me tense and said, "Now you rest. I will look after the boys for the rest of the day. I will bring you some food in a moment." He kissed my forehead and went out.

A short while later he came back with a large tray of bread, ham, cheese, chicken and fruit. We sat and ate together and then two heads appeared around the door. "May we come in, Maman, Papa?" Tréville moved the tray and the boys got on the bed slowly. One came either side of me and wrapped their arms round me. "Papa, we stay with Maman now." I looked at Tréville and smiled. A lot later Tréville made the boys a meal, then washed them and got them ready for bed. They came into our bedchamber to say goodnight to me, but Jean said, "Papa we sleep with Maman, Maman hurt."

I looked at Tréville and nodded so he said, "Of course you can, but you must be very gentle with Maman, especially her left hip, it's very painful."

They both replied, "Thank you Papa," and got under the blankets.

Tréville helped me to lie down and Jean came to my right side and Armand to my left. The next thing I knew Tréville was in bed kissing my lips. I slowly opened my eyes and he said, "Sleep my love, sleep." The boys were between us. I must have rolled over onto my right side, because as soon as Tréville got under the blankets Armand cuddled into his chest, Jean into mine. I dreamt that night of the night before, but in my dream it had a very different ending.

"Maman, Maman, wake up." I slowly came round and saw Jean was crying.

"Hush my little one, what's wrong?" I said quietly so as not to wake Tréville and Armand.

"You upset and crying."

"Oh, I'm sorry Jean, Maman was having a bad dream, but it's gone now. Go back to my sleep, little one." I kissed his forehead and wiped his tears away.

I looked over at Tréville, who was watching me. He put his hand on my face and said, "Are you all right, my love?"

I nodded, kissed his hand and said, "I am now, my love. I am now."

CHAPTER 33

Paradise

The following morning Chloe was back and could not believe her eyes when she saw me. Tréville had to go back to the palace. "Don't worry, Minister Tréville, I will make sure Madame Lesley rests as much as possible." Tréville thanked her, kissed me and left.

Two weeks later I could walk properly again and the pain in my hip had eased, and most of the cuts had healed. Tréville and I rode to the palace on his horse, Tréville holding me close as usual. Once at the palace, we both sat in a spare room waiting to see the King and Queen. I was feeling quite nervous, and Tréville held my hand. The guard came and escorted us to the throne room. Tréville bowed and I curtsied. "Ah, Lesley, so good to see you. I hope you have now recovered from the event that took place?" said the King.

I replied, "I am quite well now thank you, Your Majesty."

The King stood up and walked towards me and took my hands in his. "Thank you is not enough for what you did for me and my Queen. Your courage and determination saved our lives, along with the Dauphin's. I wanted to give you something from all of us and I hope you will like it." He nodded to the guard who gave the King a small box, which in turn he gave me. I opened it and inside was a beautiful brooch.

It was a frame of acanthus leaves, with a fleur-de-lis in the middle. Either side of the fleur-de-lis was three very small cut diamonds, and the top of the brooch had the Royal Crown, also set with small diamonds. "Oh, Your Majesties, it is absolutely beautiful, I will treasure it always."

Tears welled in my eyes and the King said, "Now, now, no need for tears."

I looked at Tréville and he smiled.

"Tréville, I believe we have some business to discuss. Please forgive us, ladies." With that, the King and Tréville left.

The Queen came to me and said, "May I?" She took the brooch and pinned it on my dress.

"I really don't deserve this, Your Majesty."

The Queen looked at me and replied gently, "Nonsense, of course you do. Now, come sit with me and tell me all about Jean and Armand."

One of her ladies in waiting brought in refreshments and both of us talked about our sons, until Tréville returned. I curtsied and Tréville bowed and we left. Tréville got his horse, but as he went to help me up he took me in his arms and said, "And this is from me," and kissed me deeply.

The following weekend, on the Friday night, Tréville told me the following morning we were going away for the weekend. It had all been arranged. Chloe was staying, and with Helene, was going to look after the boys. The following morning, after we said our goodbyes, we mounted our horses, with a small bag each, and rode out towards Chartres.

"Tréville, where are we going?" I asked.

Tréville smiled and said, "It is a secret."

I saw a signpost that said Village Paradisiaque. As we passed through the village, which had about a dozen dwellings, it was as the signpost said – paradise. About a five-minute ride away we came upon a single dwelling. "Here we are," said Tréville.

"Oh Tréville, it's beautiful," I said. The dwelling had a small garden at the front, but the entrance was an arch of gold/yellow roses. A path went down the middle. Either side was grass and the borders had different coloured flowers growing against the fences.

We dismounted from our horses and Tréville picked me up in his arms, kissed me deeply and carried me into the dwelling, and then put me down. Inside the dwelling it was split into three: a parlour, a bedchamber with a tub room leading off it. I saw a door that led out to the back garden. On the parlour table was a vase of beautiful red roses, chocolate, a cake and a bottle of expensive-looking wine.

I looked at Tréville and said, "Are these for us?"

Tréville smiled, his blue eyes twinkling, and said, "It's a bit late, but Happy Fifth Wedding Anniversary, my beloved." I wound my arms around him and our lips met. Our kisses were full of tenderness and passion. "I think, maybe, I should get the horses in the barn first, bring our bags in and then we can decide where to eat and drink those."

Whilst Tréville saw to the horses, I looked round the dwelling. The parlour cabinet was full of bread, cheeses, fruits, cakes, vegetables and more wine. The parlour had a medium-sized oven and fire. There was a small table and two chairs. The bedchamber had a large bed in it, with drapes tied round the posts. There were a couple of cabinets. A door led into the tub room. I raised my eyebrow at the size of the tub – large. There were different sized cloths, soaps I had never seen before. Again, there was a large fire that would take three cauldrons. Windows with shutters were back and front in each room. I opened the door and went out into the back garden. It took my breath away. Rose trees were either side, with large and smaller trees. At the bottom was a very wide stream, and on the other side were fields filled with various coloured flowers. I walked down and saw the stream seem to meander down past the back of the village, and to my surprise it had swans and ducks on it. I felt a pair of arms go round me. I turned and kissed Tréville deeply. "My love, it's beyond words, who owns it?"

"Let's just say it belongs to royalty, my love. Now where were we before horses had to be seen to?" I kissed him deeply and I could feel and see Tréville's passion.

"My love, why don't we fill the cauldrons, relax in the tub, then eat and drink in the bed?"

I agreed that was a good idea. Tréville filled the tub, and I found a tray and put the cake, chocolate, wine and glasses on it and put it on the table at the side of the bed. I took my boots and dress off, unpinned my hair and was brushing it when Tréville came in. "May I? It's been a long time since I brushed your hair." I smiled and gave him the brush. When he finished I plaited it and loosely put it on top of my head and pinned it. Tréville took me in his arms and kissed me deeply and slowly; I undressed him and he removed my petticoat and undergarment. He picked me up in his arms and carried me to the tub and put me in, and then he got in facing me. I got a cloth and soaped it and slowly we washed each other. He took my face in his hands and said, "I love you so much, Lesley."

I replied, "Not as much as I love you."

Our arms entwined around each other, our kisses deepening with each kiss, and our passions were fulfilled. Tréville got out of the tub and then helped me, and we dried each other off. We went into the bedchamber and got into the bed, and I laid the tray between us and we fed each other and drank the wine. There was no need for words, as our eyes did all the talking. I put the tray back on the table, blew the candle out and Tréville took me in his arms, and started trailing kisses down my neck. Our passions for each other were overwhelming and then we slept entwined in each other's arms.

The following morning neither of us was in a hurry to arise, so we let our passions take over instead. It did seem strange that the twins did not come running in, but this was mine and Tréville's time alone, and I was enjoying every moment. I made us a late breakfast of bread, cheese, fruit and tea. Later on, as it was such a glorious, hot sunny day, we went out the back and watched the swans and ducks on the stream.

"Fancy a swim in the stream?" said Tréville.

"Someone might see us," I said.

Tréville kissed me and said we would keep our undergarments on, just in case. We got in the stream slowly, so as not to frighten the swans and ducks and swam away from the village, then turned and swam back. The stream was lovely and cooling. The lovely part of it was the swans and ducks swam with us. I so wanted to put my hands out and stroke them but thought better of it. When we got back to the dwelling Tréville got out first and then helped me. I had left large cloths just inside the door and got them. We undressed and wrapped them round us. I wrapped another one round my hair. Unbeknown to me Tréville had laid a large blanket out, so we lay down on it, side by side holding hands. I looked up at the sky and looked at the clouds. "Look, Tréville, there's a rabbit, there's a lake and mountains."

Tréville rolled over and kissed me, as he pushed my cloth away. "Have I told and shown you lately how much I love you?" he said. I didn't get the chance to answer. Afterwards he said, "Come, sit up and I will dry your hair." I did and he unwrapped the cloth and rubbed it through my hair and got most of the wetness out. "Stay there, my love, and dry your hair and I will go and get us something to eat." He came back with the tray, which had on it the rest of the chocolate, cake and wine, which we ate and drank. My long hair was now more or less dry and as the sun was going down we went in. "Come, let me brush your hair," said Tréville, which he did. I didn't bother to plait it, as Tréville liked it loose so he could run his fingers through it. We got into bed and our arms went round each other, our lips meeting and then our bodies and hearts entwined into one.

The following morning I tidied the dwelling, remade the bed with clean blankets and put the ones we used in the basket. Tréville saddled the horses, but before we left, I took Tréville in my arms, under the rose archway and said, "Thank you, my beloved. I have had such a wonderful weekend, and I will always remember it. Never forget I love you with all of my heart and I always will for many, many years to come." We kissed each other with such a passion that both of us knew only one thing would ever separate us, and that would be death. We mounted our horses and arrived back to our dwelling later on to be greeted by the boys running into our arms, and I knew both of us had missed them.

About a month later Tréville came home to the dwelling, sat at the parlour table and burst into tears. "Tréville, my love, what's wrong? Has something happened to one of my brothers or Amanda?" He took my hand and I sat on his lap.

"What I am about to tell you, you cannot repeat my love. It is to do with Louis, he has just told me he is dying." I looked at Tréville, absolutely stunned.

"Oh my love, I am so sorry, I know how close you both are. How is the Queen?"

"He won't tell her."

"Oh Tréville, he must, think how distraught she will be if she is not told. Can you not, somehow, tell her?"

Tréville replied, "The King said if I told the Queen or anyone else, he would hang me."

"He said what!! It must be his illness talking. Does he know how long he has?"

Tréville replied he had no idea, but it was probably less than a year. I held Tréville tightly in my arms and he broke down, sobbing uncontrollably. I had never seen my husband so emotionally upset before, but then he and Louis had been lifelong friends. Eventually the Queen was told, but not by Tréville. The King and Queen now had a lot to sort out, with regards to Regency and other important matters.

The following month the King decided to have a huge celebration for the Dauphin's fifth birthday. People couldn't understand why this birthday was so special. Only a handful of us knew the real reason. Eight months later, in May, the whole of France was in mourning – our King had passed away. The last three days of the King's life, Tréville never left his side. The Dauphin was now King Louis XIV, but was far too young to reign, so the Queen became the Regent Queen. The King's funeral took place forty days after his death and was a state funeral; thousands of people attended. Amanda and myself stood beside each other in the cathedral and watched as Tréville and our brothers carried the King's coffin. In the King's memory, I wore the brooch he gave me. I looked at the Queen and my heart went out to her. She looked so lonely following the coffin, holding the Dauphin's hand. The King was buried in his family tomb, which was a private affair. Two things Louis did before he passed away were set up a Royal Printing House, and the first permanent theatre in Paris opened. The King and Queen loved the theatre.

Amanda and I sat on a bench outside the cathedral waiting for our husbands and brothers to return, catching up on each other's news. Amanda and Porthos were now the proud parents of a boy. I was so delighted for them, and hopefully more would bless them. When they did, apart from Tréville and myself they returned back to the garrison. The Queen had summoned Tréville to the palace. When his audience had finished, he found me in the gardens and we walked round arm in arm. "The Queen has bestowed a great honour on me," said Tréville, "she has made me Commander of the Musketeers, until the Dauphin, as King, is old enough to take his command back."

"Oh my love, that is wonderful news, congratulations," and I took him in my arms and kissed him. I glanced up to one of the windows and saw the Queen looking out and she had a smile on her face.

"There is a downside, my love. It means I will now be staying at the palace and not the garrison and might not be able to come home to you and the boys as much as I do now."

I looked into Tréville's blue eyes and replied, "As much as I need you, my love, at the moment our Queen needs you more. She has few friends now in the palace, and I'm sure the Queen will not mind me visiting you, and the boys will understand."

Tréville took my face in his hands and said, "And that's why I love you so much," and kissed me deeply.

The following day both of us went to the garrison and told my brothers the news. D'Artagnan said, "Are you still our Minister for War?" Tréville replied he was.

Aramis said, "Another uniform, Commander?" Tréville just smiled.

We went up to his office and he packed away everything that had to be taken to his new office, including his new writing box. So much had happened in this office, memories that would never be forgotten. Silently I was quite upset that he was leaving. I would still see my brothers when I delivered their pies, but Tréville would be missing. A memory returned. It had been a hot sunny day and I brought the pies to the garrison as normal. Tréville and my brothers just had their shirts and breeches on, no jackets. I heard Tréville say, "Ah, gentlemen, here comes my beautiful wench with her lovely pies."

I raised my eyebrow at Tréville. Did he just call me a wench? My brothers looked at each other. "What did you just call me, Tréville?" I said as I put the pies on the table, except one.

Tréville looked at me and smiling said, "It's an endearment, my love."

I looked at him and said, "Really? Well perhaps this 'wench' should give you your pie personally," and with that I slapped it in his face. The crust broke and the warm meat and juices ran down his face. I looked at my brothers who were laughing, behind their hands, and winked.

I went to get a cloth and as I passed Tréville I slapped him so hard on his backside he said, "Ouch!"

I looked at all of them and said, "If any of you call me a wench you will get the same treatment, understand?" They just nodded. I helped Tréville clean his face, and then whispered in his ear, "This wench will see you later, and if you're very lucky..." and I winked at him. I gave him a kiss on his lips and as I went to leave I turned and said cheekily, "My love, I think you need to change your shirt, not a good impression for your men," and then I walked back to the bakery giggling.

Athos came up and Tréville told him he must now move into what was rightfully his office as Captain. Tréville knew he would see less of his men being at the palace, but told them he would always be there for them, whenever they needed him. His office at the palace was very large. As you entered, his desk was at the far end, in front of a large cabinet. There were tall, wide windows either side of the cabinet, that looked out over the palace gardens, with shutters. There were cabinets on both sides of the walls full of various parchments, ledgers and books. At the end of the left wall was a very large curtain. Behind this curtain was a door, which led into Tréville's bedchamber. The bed was bigger than the one at the garrison. There was a washstand with jug and a bowl, a cabinet for his uniforms, various coloured shirts and waistcoats, and other garments. He had one tall wide window overlooking the gardens, with shutters. There was also a door that led into the corridor. In both of the rooms there were tall candelabra's, and various sized chairs.

After Louis's death, the people of Paris became unsure of their Regent Queen. A lot still looked upon her as Spanish, rather than French and wanted her gone, and she was accused of giving military secrets to her brother in Spain. A lot of unrest broke out, some of it was quite ugly, which Tréville and my brothers had to keep under control. She raised taxes and created new ones. A period of civil war broke out and she had many enemies. Her leading noblemen demanded the restoration of privileges that had been set by Cardinal Richelieu, but she refused, and this also caused a lot of ill will. Two of the Queen's Counsel were murdered, and I worried for my husband.

One day, about a year later, I had just finished baking pies and cakes at the dwelling, when there was a loud banging on the door. I opened the door to see Athos stood there, covered in blood.

CHAPTER 34

Last Breath

"Athos, you did not have to... Athos, what's wrong? Are you injured?" I asked, concerned, looking at his blood-covered uniform.

Athos replied, "Lesley, I'm sorry, there's no easy way for me to say this. I need to get you to the palace immediately, it's Tréville, he's been shot."

I just looked at Athos and in that moment I felt my whole world crumble and felt faint. Athos caught me as I grabbed the door. "Is he...?"

Athos replied, "Not yet."

Luckily Chloe was there to look after the twins. Athos had brought a spare horse so I got on it and we were on our way. Why was it taking so long to get there? We were galloping but if felt like everything was in slow motion; my mind was wandering.

"**Lesley look out!**" shouted Athos. I looked up just in time to see a low branch coming at me and quickly lowered my head. After that, Athos took my reins.

At last we were at the palace, I was off the horse and rushing inside.

"Athos, where is he? Where is he?"

We ran down a corridor; had the corridors always been this long? And then I saw my brothers sitting outside a door.

"Lesley, wait," said Aramis.

I totally ignored him and burst through the door. All I could see was Tréville laid on the bed, which was covered in his blood. I then saw Monsieur Verde was there and about half a dozen other people. It was then I noticed the Queen. "Your Majesty, my sincere apologies, please forgive me for my entrance," and I curtsied.

"Lesley, please come to your husband, and I will let Monsieur Verde explain about his condition. Please, everyone else leave the bedchamber."

Tréville had taken a musket ball just above his heart, and he was deathly pale, cold and clammy. Monsieur Verde explained the ball had got lodged, but had been removed, and now it was a waiting game, but the outlook did not bode well and he would probably pass that night. He had lost a lot of blood before and after they moved him.

I went to Tréville, kissed him on his lips, then sat at the side of him and took his hand in mine and the tears started to flow and they came like a river and I couldn't stop. "Tréville, please come back to me. My world is nothing without you, I need you, our boys need you, I love you so much. Please don't die, please don't die my love." He just lay there, his breathing very slow. Quite a few times I thought he had gone and cried, "No, no!" but then I could see his chest rising, albeit very slowly. I was losing him and my heart was breaking.

I have no idea how long I had been sat there when I heard a knock at the door and Aramis came in. He drew another chair up and took me in his arms, and the tears came again, "Oh Aramis, what happened?"

Aramis said, "There had been a skirmish just outside the palace grounds as the Queen and the Dauphin returned from a prior engagement, and then they were under attack. Tréville had already sent a message to Athos for us to attend the palace on another matter and when we arrived we went to help. Tréville and other Musketeers had fought off most of the attackers and managed to get the carriage to safety when a shot rang out. We all watched in shock as Tréville went down and rushed to him, somebody else went for Monsieur Verde. Between us we gently managed to get his jacket off and I looked at the damage. The ball was lodged above his heart and it had to be removed immediately. By this time Monsieur Verde and others had arrived. I got the ball out and left the rest to him. They worked on him for quite some time and only when they had stemmed his blood, did we manage to carry him here, but his blood started flowing again, hence the state of our uniforms."

I looked at Aramis, tears rolling down my cheeks, and said, "How are the Queen and the Dauphin?"

"The Queen is in despair, you know how much Tréville means to her as her Commander, and the Dauphin was frightened, but he is well. Tréville had saved both of them." I looked back at my husband who looked to have passed already. "Lesley, you have been here twelve hours, you need to rest. We are all here to stay with him."

I looked at Aramis and said, "Thank you but until he passes or whatever, I will not leave his side."

"May the rest of us come in, Lesley?"

"Of course, Aramis, you all love him like I do."

Athos, Porthos and D'Artagnan came in, hugged and kissed me and made sure I was all right. I noticed all the blood on them. "Come on, Commander, we need you to keep us in order," said Porthos. I smiled and looked at them – each one of them had tears in their eyes.

Athos said, "We are staying outside the door, if you need us, Lesley." I smiled and thanked them and they left.

The door opened again and Monsieur Verde came in. He came to me and hugged me and then I broke down in his arms. My sobs were so loud that Aramis came in and held me. Monsieur Verde was saying something but I could not take it in. Then I noticed some other people come in and looked. "It's all right Lesley, Monsieur Verde needs to get rid of the blood-covered sheets on the bed, but he needs help," said Aramis. I just nodded but I never took my eyes off them.

They were all so gentle with Tréville and soon the bed was clean. Aramis released me and I went back to Tréville. "Would you like me to stay with you for a while?" said Monsieur Verde. I thanked him and said I would be all right. It was only when I looked around, that I realised we were in the spare bedchamber we had stayed in the night of the masked ball. This night I tried chanting for my healer wolf to help me, but nothing came. Tala just whimpered. Every time I tried – nothing.

Days passed, Tréville's condition stayed the same. His men came in and sat with me; Amanda, Monsieur Verde and the Queen also came. I had not eaten or drunk anything the whole time. I just sat there holding his hand, talking to him, mopping his brow with a cool cloth, and hardly sleeping. Everyone was getting increasingly concerned for me, but none of them could persuade me to move from his side. Tréville always said, "I will love you until my very last breath." I would be there for his very last breath. On the fourth night, suddenly my necklace stopped beating. I looked at Tréville and his chest was still. I was about to scream out when a voice said to me, "Spirit of the Wolf, listen to me, my daughter." My father appeared in front of me, and I went to him sobbing and he held me tight.

"Oh, Father, he's gone. What will I do? I tried but my healing light would not come. I have let the love of my life pass."

"Calm, my daughter, calm. Tréville is still with you. He is at the Reservation, and his heart has been stopped for a reason. We are all doing what we can for him but his wound is very deep. Luckily he is strong, though. You must help him, you must build your strength. He feels you slipping away from him, and that is breaking his heart. You know your hearts are entwined by love. Please, my daughter, we need your help."

"Oh Father, I never realised, of course I will help, but will he live?"

"I cannot answer you, my daughter. We have six chiefs and three medicine women, along with Swallowtail and myself working on him. His love for you is very, very strong, I can say no more. Is your necklace now beating again?" I felt it beating and replied it was, very slowly. "It's now up to you, my daughter." My father hugged me, kissed me on my forehead and then faded away.

I went back to Tréville and held his hand. "I'm here my love, I'm here. Please stay with me, and I love you with all of my heart." Again, the tears fell.

The following morning the Queen and the Dauphin came to me. In the Dauphin's hand was an apple, which he held out to me and I thanked him and took it. He looked at the Queen and said, "What long hair she has." I suddenly saw myself in the mirror – oh heavens, what a sight I looked. I had on what I called my baking dress and apron, my hair was down in a plait, but a lot had come loose and was just hanging down. I was so embarrassed.

The Queen took my hands and said, "Please Lesley, I can see you are embarrassed. There is no need, we all worry for you. Would you like me to send a messenger to your dwelling for some of your belongings to be brought for you?"

I replied, "Please forgive me, Your Majesty, I had not given my appearance a thought, all I have on my mind is Tréville. Thank you, I will make a list for Chloe."

The Queen smiled and then said, "You have nothing to be forgiven for, Lesley, I will arrange it for you. Now, will you not try and eat and drink something? Tréville would not want you to be ill as well, and you have your boys to care for." I thanked the Queen and replied that it would be a good idea, and she smiled. She went to the door and a couple of maids brought a small meal in for me, with fruit and water. As she went to leave I stood and curtsied and thanked her.

When the Dauphin got to the door, he turned and said, "Please eat the apple, Madame Commander." I smiled, curtsied and replied I would, and I did. I made sure I ate every meal that was brought after that, even if I had let it go cold. I wrote a small list for Chloe and later that day a maid brought everything to me, along with fresh water. I immediately undressed, washed, dressed into clean clothes, brushed my hair, replaited it and pinned it up. Now I looked respectable.

My brothers had been keeping Chloe and Catherine informed as to what was happening and also all the villagers. They were all praying for Tréville; everyone in the village thought the world of him, especially Edouard. He had sort of become our third son.

A couple of days later when I was holding Tréville's hand I felt him move his and it took me by surprise. I went to the door and shouted, "Please, someone come quickly." It sounded like everyone in the palace came running down the corridor, it was only Monsieur Verde, and my brothers.

"What's happened, Lesley?" asked Athos.

I looked at Monsieur Verde and said, "His hand, it moved in mine."

Monsieur Verde went to Tréville and examined him. "I am sorry, Lesley, there is no change, you must have imagined it."

I went back to Tréville's side and took his hand in mine. Nothing. "Lesley, you are tired, why not let us stay with him and you get some rest... please?" said D'Artagnan.

"You all think I imagined it, then why can't I move my hand out of his?" I said, looking at Tréville. Monsieur Verde came to my side and could see what I meant. Tréville had a firm grip.

Porthos said, "Look, he is not as pale as he was." Then I felt my necklace beating in a better rhythm.

I put my other hand to his cheek and whispered in his ear, "Tréville, come back, I love you so much. Please come back to me, my love."

Suddenly Tréville took a small breath. We all stood waiting and then very slowly he opened his eyes. He tried to speak but I put my finger to his lips and said, "Hush, you need rest."

He managed two quiet words. "Queen, Dauphin."

At that moment the Queen came into the bedchamber, the men bowed and I curtsied. "I heard something had happened," she said, looking at each of us with concern. I smiled and looked at Tréville. The Queen came to my side and saw he had his eyes open; he tried to say something but she stopped him. "I am so pleased you are back with us, Tréville. I will never forget what you did for me and my son. Please rest and I'm sure Lesley and Monsieur Verde will give you all the tender care you need to regain your health," she said, smiling. "Lesley, as you know you are more than welcome to stay with Tréville as long as you need, and bring the twins whenever you wish. Maybe our sons could play together like Tréville and my husband did."

"Thank you, Your Majesty, and I am sure the twins would love it." They then all left and I leant over and gently kissed Tréville; the relief was enormous.

That night my father appeared. "Spirit of the Wolf, as you can see we have helped him, but he still have a long road to climb. You must make sure Tréville not overdo it. It will take many months for him to regain strength, but with your care, he will get better."

I hugged my father and said, "How can I ever thank everyone? You, Swallowtail, the chiefs and medicine women who worked so tirelessly on him. Thank you is not enough."

My father kissed my cheek and said, "My daughter, they have heard you. Now I must go, I hear your mother calling me. Take care, Daughter, I am always with you," and with that he faded away.

A couple of days later Tréville tried to get up!!

"What do you think you are doing, my love? Please, you must rest, your wound is not yet healed."

Tréville looked at me, smiling, and said, "When did you become my physician?"

"The day I wed you," I replied.

"Oh, well maybe a couple of kisses would make me behave myself." I just looked at him and smiled; he was coming back to me. I took his face in my hands and gently kissed his lips; one of his hands went round my waist and he tried to pull me to him.

"Oh no," I said, wagging my finger at him, "the more you behave, the more kisses you will get, but nothing else, you must heal."

A week later Tréville had gained a bit of his strength back. I washed him every day, the Musketeers came every day to keep him updated with current affairs, which actually annoyed me, but I never said a word, and our twins came at the weekends. They were so pleased to see their papa. They wanted all the gory details, but I had to stop them bouncing on the bed! My time was then divided between the palace, the bakery and the dwelling. I was so lucky to have Chloe looking after the boys, and Catherine looking after the bakery. I really don't know what I would have done without them.

On one of the weekends I stood by the window watching the boys playing with the Dauphin. The Dauphin was now six and the boys were seven and half years old. They were pretending to be Musketeers and Red Guards, and took turns in being killed with toy swords. Quietly Tréville had got out of bed and came and stood at the side of me, and put his arms round my waist. "Tréville, what are you doing out of bed?"

"Like you, my love, I'm watching our boys play with the Dauphin. Reminds me of when I played with Louis, I still expect him to walk through the door and tell me to get back to my duties."

I looked into his eyes and could see the sadness. I took his face in my hands and gently kissed his lips. At that moment there was a knock at the door and a guard entered, followed by the Queen. I curtsied and Tréville tried to bow. "Commander, why are you out of bed? I thought you were told to rest," said the Queen with concern in her voice.

Tréville replied, "I wanted to see our sons all playing together, Your Majesty."

The Queen walked to the window, looked out, and smiled. As though they knew they were being watched, the boys turned and looked towards the window, and then dropped their toy swords and ran towards the door. Seconds later all three of them came charging into the bedchamber, and started talking all at once. I saw Tréville's face and before he could say anything I said abruptly, "Jean, Armand, have you forgotten your manners? You are in the presence of Her Majesty." They both bowed immediately and apologised to all of us. Even the Dauphin bowed, which made me smile.

The Queen took my hand and said, "It's all right, Lesley, please do not scold them."

I replied, "Thank you, Your Majesty, but they must remember their manners, as we all must."

Suddenly Jean grabbed my hand and said, "Maman, Maman, what's wrong with Papa?"

I turned to Tréville who was holding his chest and had paled. "Guard, fetch Monsieur Verde immediately," said the Queen. Between the two of us we got Tréville back into bed. Monsieur Verde came straight away and everyone left, apart from myself. Monsieur Verde examined him and said annoyed, "Did I or did I not tell you to rest, Commander? What part of **rest** did you **not** understand?" I had never heard anyone tell Tréville off before, except me. I had to smile. "Your heart is racing, you have done too much. Now no more visitors today, you will stay in bed and rest. **Do I make myself clear, Commander?**" Tréville replied he was sorry and would do as he was told. I raised my eyebrow and thought, *That would be a first.*

I went to find the boys, who were in the palace ballroom with the Queen and the Dauphin. I curtsied. They both came running towards me saying, "We're sorry, Maman, we're sorry."

I cuddled both of them and said, "It wasn't your fault, and your papa will not do as he's told so now he must rest. When we go back in you must be very quiet and let Papa sleep." They both nodded. The Queen came to me and told me if I needed anything to ask a guard; I thanked her.

The Dauphin looked at me and said, "I'm sorry, Madame Commander, I did not mean to make our Commander poorly."

I smiled and replied, "It was not your fault, sire, the Commander is naughty and will not do as he is told."

The Dauphin looked at the Queen, then me and said, "I will tell him to not be naughty." Both the Queen and I smiled.

I took the boys' hands and was halfway back to the bedchamber when I heard footsteps behind me. I turned to see my brothers. "How is he, Lesley?" asked Aramis. I raised my eyebrow.

Athos said, "Not doing as he's told then, now why doesn't that surprise me? Would it help if we took the boys for a ride and then maybe something to eat?"

"Please Maman, can we?" I agreed and off they went. I went back to Tréville who was resting.

"I'm sorry my love, please come and sit with me," he said. I sat on the bed looking at him; he put his hands on my face and pulled me forward and kissed me so tenderly. I wrapped my arms round him and kissed him back.

"I love you so much, Tréville."

"I love you too, my dearest love, and as I always say, I will until my very last breath."

Tears welled in my eyes, as it had nearly been his last breath. Tréville just held me.

"Where are the boys?"

"My brothers are looking after them."

Tréville looked at me and said, "Good, then we can just enjoy each other's company until they return," and kissed me again. Tréville actually fell asleep in my arms.

A couple of hours later, there was a knock at the door. I opened it and Athos and Porthos stood there with the boys firm asleep in their arms. Tréville said, "Put them one either side of me," which they did, after I'd removed their shoes. Tréville put his arms round both of them, and they cuddled into him.

I went outside the bedchamber and had a quick talk with my brothers; they hugged and kissed my cheek and then left. When I went back in, all three of them were firm asleep. I carefully removed the boys' clothing and put their night garments on and then pulled the blanket up around them. Tréville had to sleep sitting up, and had a couple of very thick blankets draped around him so he would not get cold. I kissed his lips gently, blew out the candles by the bed, quietly closed the window shutters and went to the desk. I read for a while, then undressed, washed, put my night garment on and got into my bed, after I had blown the rest of the candles out. A spare bed had also been set up for the boys. The following morning the boys were in my bed, cuddled into me. When I asked why they had left their papa they said, "He snores too loudly." I laughed, cuddled and kissed them. Later on, Chloe came and collected them.

Six weeks after Tréville had been shot he came back to the dwelling. Monsieur Verde said he needed complete rest and being at the palace was not helping his recovery, and I totally agreed. I think the first couple of days every villager must have come to see him. His first visitor was Edouard. Helene came every day. We had not shared a bed since the incident. That night it felt so good to be back in his arms. I always slept with my head on his left shoulder so I could hear his heart beating, but now I rested my head on his other shoulder. The boys were delighted to have their papa home, and helped him as much as they could. Tréville would help them with their reading and writing and other things. The boys, since the age of six, now attended Boys' School.

Neither Tréville nor myself wanted them to go to a school where they never came home, so we had looked around and were lucky enough to find a fee-paying school for day teaching only. The school was split into two. Age six to ten they had to attend from mid-morning until just after mid-afternoon (about four hours). Ten and upwards they had to be there for seven in the morning, lessons started at eight, and would last a couple of hours, then a break. An hour later was study time, followed by another break for a meal, and then lessons would finish at four in the afternoon. Chloe would them meet them, take them back to the dwelling, feed them and then get them ready for bed. Whilst they were there, they were taught on an individual basis, more in-depth reading and writing, where each pupil would take turns to read or recite at the master's desk. Every day began and ended with prayers. Other subjects taught were geography, history, music, arithmetic, literature, French and Latin. For recreational lessons they could build model forts, wage mock battles and play games to strengthen body and mind. Both of the boys hated school and got up to no end of mischief, I really did feel sorry for Chloe.

After three months Tréville was back to his normal self and work. The Queen and the Dauphin were delighted to have him back. My brothers had visited him often to keep him updated on affairs, but I made sure they did not tire him too much. One night after the boys and Chloe had retired for the night, Tréville took me in arms and kissed me so deeply; we had both missed each other so much. We went to our bedchamber, Tréville unplaited my hair and then we kissed each other, deepening our kisses each time. We undressed each other slowly and then Tréville picked me up and laid me down on the bed, our eyes both reflecting each other's passion. I kissed the large scar above his heart. Our arms entwined around each other as did our hearts and as our passions reached its realm, I knew I had my love back, and my head went back to his left shoulder, and again, listened to the beating of his heart.

The relationship between the Queen and her people eased and life was better. Skirmishes still broke out but nothing as bad as when Tréville was shot. The Musketeers did find the culprit responsible and he was sent to the Bastille. The boys played with the young king when we visited Tréville at the palace, mainly weekends, but when he was crowned King, naturally, things changed. They always remained friends and had a mutual respect for each other.

CHAPTER 35

Edouard and An Apology

One afternoon as I was riding through the village I heard someone calling me. "Madame Lesley, Madame Lesley." I turned to see Serena, Edouard's maman.

"Serena, is everything all right?"

She replied, "I wondered if I may have a word with you about Edouard?"

"Of course, let me take Sunkwa back to the dwelling and see to him and then I will walk down to you," I replied. I saw to Sunkwa and went back to Serena's dwelling. We sat at the parlour table and Serena told me that Edouard had gained employment on a farm in another village, as he was now fifteen. The farmer had taken Edouard to a blacksmith for one of the horses to be shod. Edouard was fascinated. He now wanted to become a blacksmith; he knew the work would be hard but rewarding, and there was so many other things that could be done. Serena wanted to know how she could try and do this for her son. I replied I would ask Tréville for her, he would have more of an idea than me.

When I saw Tréville I mentioned Edouard. Tréville replied, "Leave it with me, I have a feeling the garrison is looking for an apprentice, if not I know a few blacksmiths and I will ask them."

About a month later I went to see Serena and asked her if Edouard could come and see me and I would take him to the palace to see Tréville. That weekend Edouard turned up; what a handsome young man he was now. We rode to the palace and as we walked through the corridors to Tréville's office, quite a lot of the maids and ladies in waiting smiled at Edouard. All he could do was blush. I knocked on Tréville's door. "Enter," he said. I went and gave Tréville a hug and kiss, and then he shook hands with Edouard. I think over time Edouard had come to look upon Tréville as a replacement father. Our boys had a good rapport with him as well.

"Edouard, my boy, nice to see you again," said Tréville. "I understand from Lesley, via your maman, that you want to become a blacksmith. May I ask why?"

Edouard replied, "It is good to see you again, Minister Tréville. As you know I have employment on a farm and was lucky enough to be taken to a blacksmith where he put a new shoe on the horse. I love horses and watching this being done, without hurting him, had me in awe. I know it will be hard backbreaking work, but I am ready to take on a new path, if I can. The blacksmith also showed me other things that were made as well. Maybe one day I could have my own blacksmith's."

Tréville looked at him and replied, "It will be very hard labour, Edouard, but you seem prepared for that. There is a blacksmith on the outskirts of Paris, who is looking for an apprentice. He is a friend of mine, and I know you will both get along nicely. It will mean leaving your family, but we came to an arrangement that you could have one Sunday a month off to go home. He will provide you with board and lodging at the blacksmith's, your wages will be low, until you advance. Would you like to meet him?"

Edouard replied he would, and thanked Tréville from the bottom of his heart for helping him, and would never let him down. I looked at Tréville and smiled, but I had a tear in my eyes. Tréville said they could go at that moment, so I said my goodbyes to them both and went back to the dwelling. Tréville told me later that Edouard had accepted his apprenticeship and would start in two weeks. I was so pleased. Edouard came to see me before he left and I wished him well. He gave me such a hug and said Tréville and myself would always have a special place in his heart. Serena, his maman, came and thanked both of us, but I knew deep down that she and his sisters were going to miss him dreadfully.

One evening, as I was going to read to the boys, I heard them talking. "Why is it smaller than Papa's?" asked Armand. I raised my eyebrow.

"Maybe it gets bigger as we grow up," said Jean.

"It can't, Papa is so tall, it would be longer," said Armand.

"Maman is bigger here than Papa, but Maman doesn't have one. Papa also has hair above it." Oh no, I realised what they were talking about.

Jean said, "Perhaps we only pipi with it, what else would we do with it? And look when we jump up and down it does it as well."

Armand replied, "Perhaps if we pull them they'll grow."

Jean replied, "I'll pull yours if you pull mine."

Armand replied, "I wonder what Papa does with his? It's so much longer than ours. Does it just hang down?"

I was quietly laughing and tears were filling my eyes. I heard the door open and turned to see Tréville. "My love, what's wrong? You're crying."

I spluttered quietly, "I'm not crying my love, I'm laughing. I will tell you later."

The boys had heard their papa's voice and came running out shouting, "Papa, Papa!"

Tréville scooped them up in his arms and kissed them both. "Why aren't you two in bed asleep?" he asked.

"We were waiting for Maman to read us a story, now you can," said Armand. With that Tréville went and read them a story, whilst I made him a meal.

After they were asleep and Tréville and I had gone to our bedchamber, as we were undressing each other I told him what I heard the boys saying. The pair of us laughed so much. "I think they're too young to be told yet, think I'll leave it for a couple of years," said Tréville. We got into our bed and Tréville's hands went to my breasts and said, "So these are bigger than mine then?"

I looked into his eyes and said, "Umm, I think so, my love." He pulled me on top of him and kissed me deeply. "Now I wonder what

I do with my long one?" he said, laughing.

"I haven't got a clue my love, but I'm sure you'll think of something..." and he did.

A couple of weeks later, Tréville and the boys were in the tub, and as I carried some more water in for them Armand said, "Papa, can I ask you a question?"

"Of course, Armand, what is it?"

The boys looked at each other and Armand said, "Why is yours bigger and longer than ours?" I stopped dead in my tracks and nearly dropped the cauldron of water. I looked at Tréville and put my hand over my mouth to stop myself from bursting out with laughter.

Tréville looked at the boys and said, "Umm... err... well... umm. I think you are a bit young for Papa to explain now, but when you are older I will." I looked at Tréville, raised my eyebrow, poured the water in the tub, then went to out bedchamber and burst into laughter.

On the odd occasion Chloe would bring the boys to the bakery, after school, but I suddenly noticed Chloe brought them more often, and then she told me she had met a Musketeer and they had become sweethearts. Chloe stayed with us until the boys were about fourteen, and then she married her sweetheart, and moved away. As the boys got older we had put drapes round the beds so both Chloe and the boys could have privacy whilst undressing and dressing. When I looked back, the boys seem to grow up so quickly, but one thing I made sure of was that I was with them every night before they went to bed, every morning before they went to school and we always spent the weekends together. When Tréville was free we would take them down to the river and have a picnic, or take them into Paris and have a meal somewhere, or go out into the countryside. When they visited the palace, the young King had a pony, and they all loved having rides. Tréville asked the Queen if it would be all right for him to teach all of them how to ride a horse, to which she agreed. The boys used to love going to the garrison and talking with my brothers; they called them their "uncles" and Amanda was their "aunt", and they also loved being at the bakery.

One weekend as the boys and myself were walking down the corridor to Tréville's office, I could hear Tréville shouting at someone. The boys stopped immediately and Jean said, "Papa sounds very angry, Maman, perhaps we should go home."

I replied, "Papa is expecting us, we will just sit quietly and wait for him."

Suddenly, Tréville came storming out of his office with the Captain of the Red Guards, looking absolutely furious. I smiled. Tréville stopped, looked at me and said brusquely, "What are you doing here, I don't have time for frivolities."

I looked at him absolutely stunned, but at the same time felt my right hand go into a fist. "Come, boys, obviously your Papa doesn't want us here," and with that I took their hands and walked straight out of the palace. As we left, the Queen and the Dauphin arrived.

"Lesley, are you all right? You look quite distressed." I curtsied and the boys bowed.

"My husband has just advised me he doesn't want us here, so we are returning to the dwelling," I replied.

"Jean, Armand, would you like to play with Louis, if your maman agrees?"

I looked at the boys; it wasn't their fault their papa was in such a foul mood, and so I smiled and agreed. Off all three of them went to heavens knows where.

"Come, Lesley, we will go to my chambers."

It was a long time since I had been to her chambers. Once there she asked one of her Ladies in Waiting to bring refreshments. We sat and talked, mainly about our boys. She told me since the King had passed, both herself and the Dauphin were very close and she spent most of her time with him. She even attended his classes at the palace, to make sure he was taught correctly.

Suddenly we heard lots of laughing and both of us moved to the window. The boys were pretending to be horses and were jumping the small borders in the garden, and then falling over, and just lying on the grass areas laughing. "Oh no," I said as I saw Tréville walking towards them.

The Queen put her hand on my arm to stop me going. She opened the window. I heard and saw Tréville bow to the Dauphin and say, "Sire, do you mind if I quickly talk to Jean and Armand?"

The boys stood frozen where they were. The Dauphin went and sat on a bench watching. Tréville knelt down and held his arms out. The boys looked at each other and then ran to him and he cuddled and kissed their cheeks. "I have an apology to make. I am so sorry for my temper, I hope you will both forgive me? Where is your maman?" They both shook their heads, they didn't know. The Dauphin went to Tréville and whispered something in his ear. Tréville smiled and gave him a hug.

I looked at the Queen, who had a tear in her eye, as did I, and said, "I think it's time I went and had a word with my husband."

She replied, "Come, we will go down together, you can go to Tréville's office and I will send him to you," then she laughed. "Oh, forgive me Lesley, I was thinking how Louis laughed when you gave Tréville a fist in the face."

I replied, "He just might be getting another one," and we both laughed.

The Queen went into the gardens and I went to Tréville's office. Tréville came rushing in and said, "My love, there you are."

I just looked at him and replied, annoyed, "Don't you 'my love' me. How dare you speak to me like that, and in front of our boys! More embarrassing was that you 'reprimanded' me in front of the Captain of the Red Guards. I would imagine now all the Red Guards know what you said to me. I have never felt so humiliated, Tréville." Tréville held his arms out to me, and I said, "You don't seriously think I'm going to fall into your arms. If you do, you're greatly mistaken. I'm now taking the boys home, what you do is entirely up to you," and with that I turned and walked out of his office, slamming the door. I said my goodbyes to the Queen and the Dauphin, the boys waved goodbye, and we mounted our horses and rode back to the dwelling.

Hours later I heard a horse. Tréville had decided to come home. The boys had eaten, washed and were asleep in their bedchamber. I had already changed into my night garment and went to our bedchamber, took my hair down and started brushing it. I heard Tréville come in, and as he did the nights he came home, he went and said his goodnights to the boys. A hand appeared around the bedchamber door holding a huge bunch of flowers. "My love, may I come in?"

"If you wish, Tréville, after all it is our bedchamber," I replied. I glanced at him and then said, "I see you bought yourself some flowers."

"Actually, my love, they are for you as a way of an apology. I am so sorry for what happened, I feel dreadful." I got up, took the flowers, walked past him and put the flowers in a bucket of water in the parlour. I would arrange them in the morning. When I entered the bedchamber Tréville had started undressing.

"What do you think you're doing?" I asked.

"I thought..."

"You thought wrong, you can sleep with the boys, Tréville. You will not share my bed this night." Tréville looked absolutely downhearted, and walked out into the parlour. I closed the door, plaited my hair, went to bed and read for a short time, blew the candles out and then slept.

When I rose the following morning, Tréville had already left. As I went to call the boys, I heard Armand say, "Maman must be very annoyed with Papa, he slept in the parlour last night. I have never known them be apart before."

Jean said, "I didn't hear Papa come home." Armand told him it was late and he had woken from a dream, and Papa was kissing them goodnight.

"I'm never getting married, I don't want to kiss girls," said Jean. I had to smile. I then called to them both. Tréville came home early evening, and the boys sat at each side of him, with his arms round their shoulders, and told him what they had been learning at school, and then he read to them when they had gone to bed. Later on I retired, said goodnight to Tréville, went to our bedchamber and closed the door. I wondered if he would come to me but he didn't. I heard a noise in the parlour and slowly opened the door. Tréville was sitting by the fire with his head in his hands. My heart went out to him, so I quietly walked up behind him and put my arms around him and whispered, "Our bed is cold without you in it."

He turned, stood up and took me in his arms and kissed me deeply. "My love I am so..." I put my finger to his lips. "Tréville, hush and just be with me." We went back to our bedchamber where I helped him undress, he took my night garment off, our arms went round each other and he started kissing my neck. After our love for each other had been fulfilled I asked him what had happened.

Tréville replied, "The Musketeer Cadets were in a field being taught how to fight with their fists, with your brothers, but not causing any actual bodily harm. Unbeknown to them some of the Red Guards had hidden in the trees, and were watching and then grabbed one of the young cadets, took him to a barn, about five minutes from the palace, and started fighting him. The poor cadet was badly beaten up. Another cadet had seen the incident and had run to tell his Captain. Athos told D'Artagnan to come and get me. When your brothers arrived at the barn, the Captain of the Red Guards was there, just watching. Athos tried to reason with him, but he was having none of it. They got the cadet out of the barn, but as they were leaving the Captain of the Red Guards grabbed Athos and hit him. You can imagine what happened next. I arrived and shouted, **'Stop this now.'** I have to be honest, the Red Guards lost that battle. I told the Captain of the Red Guard to attend my office immediately. I made sure your brothers were all right, and they were, and told them to take the cadets back to the garrison. The badly hurt cadet was being helped by Aramis. I then rode back to the palace. As you know I was absolutely furious and laid into the Captain of the Red Guards and was on my way to confront the Red Guards who had taken the cadet when I saw you walking towards me. I had totally forgotten you were coming, and then..." I put my finger to his lips, and then kissed him deeply; our eyes showed our passions, and afterwards we slept in each other's arms.

Once Chloe had left us, the antics the boys got up to in their bedchamber sometimes left me speechless. I walked in one morning to see Armand in the tub room, stood on a chair, relieving his bladder down the pipe that went outside. "Armand, what on earth do you think you are doing?" I said crossly.

He went crimson and said, "Maman, avert your eyes, this is embarrassing you seeing my private part. Papa does it, instead of using the chamber pot, and then we pour the tub water down it."

I couldn't believe what I was hearing. "Oh, does he? Well I will be having words with your Papa, and as to your private part, I think I have seen it since the day you were born."

When I left them I heard Jean saying, "Ha ha, I knew Maman would catch you, wonder what she's going to say to Papa?"

Armand replied, "We'll have to listen outside the door." I smiled and raised my eyebrow – oh will they!

The next time Tréville came home, just before the boys went to bed I said, "Tréville I wish to talk to you about a certain matter after you have said your goodnight to the boys." Both Jean and Armand looked at each other. When he came back out, I took his hand and led him into our bedchamber, and pushed the door so it was nearly closed. "I have something I want to ask you, Tréville. Did you or did you not tell the boys they could relieve their bladders down the pipe in the tub room?" Tréville looked at me in amazement. He went to say something but I put my fingers to his lips. Quickly I pulled the door open to see Armand and Jean stood there. "Did you two want something?" I said angrily. "Do you think your Maman is so stupid she doesn't know when you are lying?" I said, looking at Armand.

"I'm really sorry Maman, Papa," said Armand.

Tréville looked at both of them and said angrily, "Go to your bedchamber, I will deal with you both in the morning."

They returned to their bedchamber, and I made sure they were in their bed. When I returned to our bedchamber Tréville asked me what had happened. I closed our door and as we undressed each other I told him and he smiled and said, "He actually had it down the pipe?" We got into bed, looked at each other and burst out laughing. Their penance was mucking out the garrison stables for two weeks.

We had to decide how the boy's futures would go. Even though they both hated school, they both did well, but we now had to guide them down the right path. One night we sat them down and asked them what they would like to do. Jean replied he wanted to learn all about the bakery, and Armand wanted to follow in his Papa's footsteps and become a Musketeer. Neither of their decisions surprised us, it was what they had both been brought up with. Tréville said he would have a word with Captain Athos and see what could be arranged. Athos was pleased that Armand wanted to be a Musketeer, but he would be treated like everyone else, no special advantages because he was the Commander's son. He would have to start at the bottom, keeping the stables clean, grooming the horses, and Remy would teach him. There would be time for other training as well. As he was only fourteen he would be able to come home every night.

Now the boys were going to accompany me, I suggested to Tréville we buy another couple of horses; we couldn't keep borrowing the garrison horses. Tréville said there was plenty at the garrison and brought two to the dwelling. My horse Sunkwa had passed and I missed him greatly. The barn had three stalls so it was not a problem. As I was at the bakery for six in the mornings, the boys rode on one horse and I rode the other. They always took turns who sat in front. They were good like that, as they shared everything. I left Jean with Catherine and then took Armand to the garrison. All my brothers were there, and I noticed Armand was looking a bit hesitant. I asked him if he was all right and he replied, "I will be, Maman, I mustn't let Papa down." I took him to one side and told him being a Musketeer was a very hard career. As long as he did what Captain Athos or my brothers told him, he would be well looked after. He smiled and went to Athos. I smiled and went back to the bakery.

Catherine was explaining about baking of the bread to Jean, and so I left him in her capable care. Once the pies were done I took them to the garrison. As I entered I saw Armand being doused in water. I raised my eyebrow and looked at D'Artagnan. "It's all right, Lesley, he had a bit of an accident – he slipped in the stables and fell in some horse..."

I put my hand up to stop him and said, "Is that what the smell is? Well I'm sure you'll sort him out, I'll leave the pies with Pascal." Poor Armand, he looked like a drowned rat. I mustn't let him see me laughing.

About six months later, Tréville told me he was going to make a surprise visit to the garrison to see how things were progressing. In other words, he wanted to see Armand, who was now learning to use a sword. (Athos told me how much more they had been seeing the Commander at the garrison with some excuse or other. I had to smile.) I agreed to meet him and we slipped in and went to Athos's office. Athos and my brothers knew we were there. It seemed strange being back in Tréville's old office, and Tréville sat in his old chair.

Athos came in and said, "It's yours if you want it back,

Commander." Tréville smiled. Athos said he was going to give Armand his lesson. Tréville and I watched and both of us agreed he was doing well. As we turned to leave we heard a scream. Tréville looked out the window and paled and said, "Armand." I have never seen him run down the steps so quickly. When I got there Armand was lying flat on his back with blood coming out of a wound on his arm.

"I'm so sorry, Commander, I told him to go left and he went right, and I caught his arm with my blade," said Athos.

"Tréville, may I look please?" I said before he lost his temper with Athos.

It looked a lot worse than what it was, and he had a two-inch scratch. Aramis cleaned it up for him and put a small bandage on it.

Armand looked at Tréville and said, "Look Papa, my first injury, and I survived. That's because I'm a brave Musketeer, I hope you're proud?" Tréville said nothing and just hugged him. I on the other hand, turned away so Tréville could not see me smiling. Even his men were smiling.

I went to Athos and hugged him and whispered, "I think he'll live," and kissed his cheek. Athos smiled back.

Jean was doing really well at the bakery and Catherine was impressed, as was I. He now knew how to make the dough, cut it up into the right sizes, weigh it and put it into the tins. He was too young, in my eyes, to load them into the ovens. Jean was always full of ideas and Catherine and I would sit at the kitchen table discussing them with him. He always went with me if I had to visit the farmer or miller, and like myself, he was shown how the produce was done. He was given the hard jobs to do as well. The tables had to be scrubbed clean every night, the fires doused, cleaned and new logs laid, the utensils cleaned and put back in their correct places, ready for the following day. His hands suffered badly when scrubbing, but, like myself, he soon learnt. Tréville was concerned, but as I pointed out to him, we learnt on our own, they were lucky. They had us to look after them.

CHAPTER 36

New Beginnings

Two years later Armand asked to speak to his papa in private. I had a strange feeling I knew what it was about. I rode with him to the palace and whilst he spoke to Tréville I walked round the gardens and then sat down on one of the benches and waited. Eventually Tréville and Armand appeared; I could see Tréville looked slightly sad, so my feelings must have been right. They joined me on the bench and Tréville said, "Have you told your maman what you have decided?"

Armand said, "I wanted to tell you first, Father, and then I was going to ask Maman."

I looked at him and said, "Ask me what, Armand?"

"I have just told Father that I do not want to be a Musketeer anymore, and again Father, I apologise if I have disappointed you. I would like to join Jean in the bakery, if you will allow me."

I looked at Tréville, who smiled at me. "Well Armand, I must say I am completely surprised by your decision, but at the end of the day, you need to be happy in what you do. I'm sure you have not disappointed your papa, and I know whatever both of you do, we will always be proud of you."

Armand hugged me and kissed my cheek. "Thank you, Maman."

At that moment the young King appeared. We all stood, I curtsied and Tréville and Armand bowed, and we said, "Your Majesty." He asked if Armand could go riding with him, we agreed and with that they left us.

I looked at Tréville and said, "Are you deeply disappointed, my love?"

Tréville replied, "I would have liked one of them to follow in my footsteps, but Athos told me Armand had seen a lot of injured men coming into the garrison, from various skirmishes, and he didn't like what he had seen. Looks like you're going to have your hands full with both of them. They might be coming up seventeen, but they still get up to mischief."

I took his face in my hands and kissed him tenderly and said, "I wouldn't have it any other way, as long as they're happy."

Tréville kissed me deeply and we walked back to his office, with our arms around each other's waists. Once we were there, Tréville locked his door, grabbed my hand, and led me into his bedchamber. "Tréville, we can't, you might be needed," I said.

Tréville closed the window shutters and said, "Our boys can be mischievous, so can we. The Queen is away from the palace, and those two have gone riding." I laughed and he took me in his arms, we quickly got undressed, and then fulfilled our passions for each other. Afterwards Tréville said, "Have you noticed our boys now call me 'Father'? It makes me feel old."

I laughed and said, "My love, in their eyes we are old."

Tréville smiled and said, "I would still rather be called Papa."

Armand knocked on the door a couple of hours later; we said goodbye to Tréville, rode back to the bakery, and got Jean. As we rode back to the dwelling, Armand told Jean his news and Jean was delighted – he had missed his brother. Heaven help me, now I had both of them!!

"Jean, Armand, may I ask you why you now call Papa 'Father'? You still call me Maman."

They both looked at each other and Armand replied, "You will always be our maman, but we called Papa 'Father' now because of respect. I was told that at the garrison."

I smiled and replied, "Ah, I understand now. Well it makes him feel very old, so do you think you could go back to calling him Papa, or else you will have to call me 'Mother'."

"Papa sounds fine to me," said Jean.

When Tréville next came home I heard the boys call him Papa, and I saw the smile on his face – he was happy. The boys got on extremely well at the bakery and the entire workforce loved them, especially Catherine. Jean was more than happy to show Armand how things worked, and surprisingly, there was never a cross word between them. Both of them were extremely hard workers.

About three months later, on a Sunday, the sun was shining, the birds were singing and I decided to do a picnic for the boys and myself. We rode out into the country and found a lovely spot by a river. Once we had eaten, the boys went for a walk and I started to read my book, but fell asleep. I slowly awoke as I heard the boys talking, but did not open my eyes.

"I'm sure Papa understood why you asked to leave the garrison," said Jean.

"I felt like I had deeply upset him, I am sure he wanted one of us to follow in his footsteps, but I couldn't take the horrendous injuries the men came back in. I hate to think what Maman and Papa must have endured during the War," said Armand.

"Tell me, Armand, what happened?"

I heard Armand take a deep breath and say, "The first day I went I had to muck the stables out with Remy. Alas, I slipped in horse muck and D'Artagnan had to douse me with water. Maman turned up and looked quite concerned, but I'm sure after D'Artagnan told her what had happened, I saw her laughing. I laugh myself now. My duties every day, to start with, were muck the stables out, help clean the dishes in the kitchen, brush the yard, stack the straw, clean the chamber pots – that was disgusting, put buckets of fresh water from the well in our uncle's rooms, fresh straw for the horses and feed. Slowly Remy showed me how to groom the horses. Our uncles always looked out for me, though, when they were there. I thought being Papa's son I would eat with them, but no, I ate in the stables with Remy. There were other lads there older than me, and they always picked on me. I soon learnt how to use my fists and on more than one occasion one of our uncles had to rescue me.

"As time went on, I learnt to stay out of trouble. I didn't want Maman or Papa annoyed with me. Athos seemed to take me under his charge and slowly showed me how to use a sword. Porthos showed me how to fight a little, D'Artagnan showed me how to fire a pistol and Aramis showed me how to clean everything in the armoury. One day I heard horses and a cart come into the yard, with men groaning and covered in blood. I saw some of them had limbs missing. They were taken to the infirmary. I never went in there, as didn't want to see them. A couple of weeks later, that changed. I had a bucket of fresh water with me when Monsieur Verde came out. 'Ah, just what I need, Armand, can you bring it in here for me please?' I said, 'What, in there?' Monsieur Verde replied, 'It's all right, Armand, a Musketeer just has a cut on his leg, nothing bad.' I followed him down the corridors until we came to the Musketeer. I looked around and there were seven others, nothing too bad. As I walked back out I heard loud groaning and ran. A couple of weeks later another lot of Musketeers arrived. Again, Monsieur Verde asked me to take him some water, but when I went in I went down the wrong corridor. Jean, it was awful. Musketeers lay on beds with horrible injuries. One man I saw had both legs gone and was screaming, another had half his face missing, another had his stomach ripped open, and the smell. Those screams and smells haunted me for months. Monsieur Verde eventually found me cowered in a corner, and took me out. Remy saw I was unhappy about something and eventually I told him, and he told me to speak to Athos, which I did. That was the day Maman and Papa turned up at the garrison to watch me. I wasn't listening to Athos and turned the wrong way. I think if Maman hadn't been there, Papa would have hit him. A couple of weeks later I decided I didn't want to be a Musketeer anymore and was frightened how Papa would react, but he understood."

Jean said, "Is that why some nights I would hear you cry out in your sleep and you would toss and turn? I would hold your hand until you calmed, but you never knew."

There was a silence between the boys, and then Armand asked Jean how it had been at the bakery. Jean replied, "I was always watching Maman bake, I just knew I wanted her to teach me. My first day, I spent with Catherine. She was so lovely, as were the rest of the workforce. After a couple of weeks, I knew how to cut the dough, weigh it, put it in the tins, or roll it into balls. Maman said I must never touch the ovens, as they were so hot, so I didn't. Maman took me to the miller and farmer, and what nice people they were. They showed me how the grain was grounded, the way cheese and butter was made. The more I learnt the more different ideas I got, where from I don't know. I would talk with Maman and Catherine round the kitchen table and they listened. We would try things out, and sometimes they worked, sometimes not. Same as you I had a certain routine; start off making the dough, weighing, cutting ready for the ovens. Maman and Catherine made various pastries and cakes that I helped decorate with fruits. Later on I was allowed to serve in the shop. As you know Maman would make the pies for the garrison. Once everything that was to be baked was finished, I had to clean all the pots and pans, the tables had to be scrubbed down with a wire-like brush. That was how I got all those cuts on my hands, but as time went on I understood how to do it properly. The floor had to be washed, scrubbed and dried. The shop had to be cleaned and made ready for the next day. Just before Maman came to get you, the fire had to be doused, cleaned out and the logs put ready for the following morning. It was hard work, but I always enjoyed it. I always missed you though, and now we're working together it's even better."

It went quiet for a moment and then Jean said, "Do you think we should wake Maman?" It was then I slowly opened my eyes and looked at our two sons. I obviously knew what Jean had been through, but my tears fell for what Armand had gone through – if only we had known.

"Maman, what's wrong?"

I replied, "I was dreaming how much I love you both and your papa, and how lucky I am."

They both came over to me and gave me a hug and a kiss on the cheek. "We love you too, Maman, and Papa of course. We couldn't have asked for such loving and caring parents," said Armand.

I noticed the sun was starting to go down, so we packed everything up and then rode back to the dwelling. That night I couldn't sleep, all I could see was Armand and injured Musketeers. I wished that Tréville was with me. He arrived back the following night and when we retired to our bedchamber, I hugged him so tight. "My love, what's wrong?" I told him what I had heard. Tréville entwined his arms round me and said, "I never knew the full reasons, but now I understand. He will be fine, my love, they both will be. After all, they are working for you now." I looked at Tréville and saw a cheeky grin, his eyes twinkling and the next thing his lips were on mine.

Some nights later, Tréville said we really needed to look for somewhere bigger to live. The boys were now seventeen years old, young men, and still sharing a bed. Not only that, whenever Tréville and I wanted to bathe together, it meant we had to go through their bedchamber – not ideal. About a week later, I went to the palace to see Tréville, after seeing our sons at the bakery, and he told me he had received a note from our solicitor with regards to a house that had just become available. We went to see him the following day and his apprentice took us in the carriage to the house. I recognised the road we travelled; surely after all these years it couldn't be. It was. It was the house that the nobleman had come from when Henri, Paoul and I were going to the dwelling, when I was seven months with the twins. The lane up to the house, which was longer than I remembered, was very overgrown and the trees had branches overhanging. As we approached the house, the lane finished and went into a field, with trees and shrubs. The house did look very neglected. When we alighted from the carriage I looked at Tréville, who had a glint in his eyes; he liked what he saw. We walked up about a dozen steps to the front door and the apprentice asked us to wait while he went inside and opened the wooden shutters on the windows, so we could see.

He led us into the hall, which had stairs at the left to the next level. A door on the left led us into an office. The door in front of us went into the parlour, which was a good size. To the right through another door, from the hall, was a dining room, which again was a good size. By the front door, again on the right, was another door that led down and up some steps. The steps down took us to a rather large kitchen, storage room, parlour, and what were the servants' quarters with three separate small bedchambers. Apart from the kitchen all the other servant rooms were empty of furniture. I asked the apprentice how many servants there used to be and he replied six. We returned to the hall and ascended the main staircase to the next level. There was one large master bedchamber, with a smaller one leading off from it, and three separate smaller bedchambers. The last room we entered made me gasp. "Good heavens, what a large tub," I said.

The apprentice replied, "Yes, there is quite a story to it. Not the present owner or his father, but the owner before them was, as you can see, a very tall, rotund man. He was over a toise (six feet, four inches) in height. The tubs here were so small for him and uncomfortable. He used to travel a lot and once on his travels he came across a tub just like this one.

"He made enquiries and found the blacksmith who had made it. It was impossible for the blacksmith to make another one there and transport it, so it was agreed that he would come here and make it. As you can see, it looks like two tubs made into one. Naturally, it was very expensive."

I agreed and then had a thought and blushed. Tréville looked at me and I whispered, "Just think of the fun we can have in that," and he burst out laughing and gave me a quick kiss.

There were also a couple of tall cabinets and a square box thing. All the rooms had fireplaces. A door at the end of the corridor turned out to be a continuation of the steps from the kitchen (so the servants didn't go up the main staircase), and carried on up to the next level that was the roof. (The steps were in one of the two towers either side of the house. The other tower had the stairs up to the bedchambers only.) Windows had been put in just for light; no one could live up there, and the roof was too low. There was furniture in the house but it was all covered over, dust, cobwebs and dirt everywhere, the fireplaces were absolutely filthy. There were candlesticks on the walls. I think a lot of new candles would be needed. The apprentice told us it had been empty for over two years. A lot of work would be needed to bring it back to its former glory.

The apprentice then took us outside. The stables, which had six stalls and room for a couple of carriages, were in serious need of repairing, mainly the holes in the roof. As we walked round to the back of the house we saw there were steps from the parlour that led down to four medium-sized gardens. All of them were neglected and again, a lot of work would have to be done. A low wall surrounded the gardens and had a gate at the bottom. I left Tréville to talk with the apprentice and walked to the end of the gardens, and out of the gate. There was a field that led down to a river and beyond that in all its glory was my safe forest. I noticed further down there was a bridge. I walked over the bridge, which I'm glad to say was safe, and just stood and looked at the forest and thought of the happy times when Tala and I had run there – maybe we would again. Tala and I still went for our runs, but not as much as we used to, life was too hectic. Two arms encircled my waist followed by kisses on my neck and I turned to look at Tréville, who had a huge smile on his face. His lips met mine and our arms entwined around each other. Passions were starting to flare until both of us remembered where we were.

Tréville looked at me and asked, "What do you think, my love, is it to your liking?"

I replied, "I think it's lovely, but you and I have been used to living at the garrison, the bakery or the dwelling. Do you not think it a bit too big and grand for us?"

Tréville smiled and replied, "It looks big, but the rooms are not that big, I expected them to be bigger. It would be nice for Jean and Armand to have their own bedchambers. I want to provide a house for my beautiful, loving wife and our sons. The house will be how we want it. It might look grand but that won't stop us asking our friends from wherever."

I looked at Tréville and smiled and said, "My love, as usual, you are right, all we need to know now is do we have the funds to buy it?"

Tréville took my face in hands and looked into my eyes and said, "That's for me to worry about, my love," then gently kissed my lips and arm in arm we walked back to the apprentice, who was locking everything up. As we walked back I noticed the house and land had large and small trees all the way around, so anyone passing would have no idea it was there.

When we got to the front of the house I asked the apprentice if we could quickly have another look round. He replied he would wait in the carriage. I grabbed Tréville's hand and pulled him up the staircase back to where the tub was. "What on earth is going, on my love?"

"I want to see you in the tub."

"Woman, have you lost your senses?" he said.

"Take your boots off and get in."

Eventually he did as I asked and true enough he could lay flat. He was only 0.925 of a toise (five feet, eleven inches). I then took my shoes off and lay at the side of him. I was only 0.86 of a toise (five feet, six inches). "My love, what is the point of this?"

I looked at him, smiled and said, "Well, if you misbehave or come home very merry, you can sleep in the tub."

Tréville just looked at me and then burst out laughing, pulled me on top of him and started kissing me. "My love, this is not very comfortable and I'm sure the apprentice must be wondering what we are doing," he said. We both got out, put our footwear on and went back to the carriage. We then went back to the solicitor's. Tréville made an arrangement to see the solicitor in a couple of days to discuss matters.

When we returned to the dwelling that night, Tréville and I discussed the house with our sons and decided on Sunday, we would ride back there and they could have a look. Tréville sent a messenger to the solicitors to see if we could borrow the key; the apprentice kindly delivered it to Tréville at the palace. Jean and Armand absolutely loved it. Armand loved the gardens and he and Tréville had all sorts of ideas. Jean and I were more interested in the kitchen. They had even decided which bedchamber they wanted. Tréville returned to the solicitor's and they discussed what would happen next. When Tréville returned he told me the story. The owner had passed over four years ago and willed the house and lands to his son. The son, who was already married, had moved in with his father as his mother had passed a couple of years before. Two years after his father passed he found his wife was with child. Alas, happiness was not meant to be. The child was stillborn and the wife went mad and one day ran into the woods and hanged herself. When the husband found her, he buried her by the tree. (I shuddered, thinking that more than likely Tala and I had run over her grave.) It was then he decided the house was a bad omen, so he sacked the servants and closed the house and went to England. He was now very ill and could not travel and, as he hated the house, he wrote to our solicitors to tell him to sell it, for whatever he could get for it. The furniture was brand new as when his wife died he cleared the house and totally replaced it all. The new owners could buy what they wanted.

Our solicitor wrote back and explained that we would like to buy the house and suggested a figure. The son replied and said it was too much. He only needed enough funds to live on, as he himself did not have long to live, but he would take half. The solicitor sent him the legal documents, which he signed, and returned. After six months the house and lands were ours. Tréville told me what funds he had paid and I was stunned, we had got it for a lot less than I thought, but there was a lot of money to be spent on the house, gardens, barn and servants' quarters. As Captain of the Musketeers, Minister for War and now Commander, I knew Tréville was very well paid and he had, through a friend, some sound investments. Tréville had also invested most of Katherine's inheritance along with his own. I had the bakery and the dwelling, so in our own rights both of us were very well off, some might even say rich.

The first thing we did at the house was to remove all the covers to see what furniture was there. We opened the windows so the dust could go out. We had to leave the covers on the pieces we wanted, the rest would be taken away to a huge seller in Paris. We ended up keeping about half of it, as to me, it fitted in with the house. The rest was taken away by wagons including the beds. News had got round our village but we assured them we would not be selling the dwelling. Helene asked if we would need help; we replied we would and that weekend about ten villagers arrived to help us. The first room to get cleaned was the kitchen; it was hard, backbreaking work, and it took all of us all weekend. Jean or Armand brought food from the bakery for us. Tréville had his duties at the palace and sometimes was away for weeks, I was helping the boys at the bakery as lots of private orders were required, and after three months hardly anything else had been done to the house.

One night Tréville came home with some good news. The Regent Queen and Louis had been invited to go a huge ball about thirty miles south of Paris for the weekend. The Queen told Tréville as long as Captain Athos and his men escorted them, she would be happy for Tréville to take some of the other Musketeers from the garrison to help out at the house. On the Saturday, Tréville left the dwelling early and when I got to the house, after getting supplies, I couldn't believe my eyes. There must have been at least thirty Musketeers cutting the tree branches away, cutting the overgrown weeds; others were sorting out the barn roof. On the Sunday there seemed to be more and by the time the weekend was over, the lane was cleared, all overhanging branches cut and chopped up ready for the fires, and stacked in the barn that had been repaired. I spent most of my time cooking.

Over the next six months we got our bedchamber sorted, we had great fun picking a new four-poster bed, which had drapes hanging on each bed pole; got the parlour more or less sorted which had a couple of long fabric-covered benches, chairs, and a couple of small tables and pictures on the wall; cleaned the dining room which had a large table with eight chairs around it, a large cabinet where the plates, glasses and other things would go, and all the fireplaces had been scrubbed, and had logs in them ready for being lit.

The bedchambers all had cabinets, jugs and basins in them, along with fabric drapes that we had bought from the dye mills down on the River Seine to cover the windows during the night. The tub was thoroughly scrubbed until it shined, but what I thought was a box turned out to be something totally different. I pulled up the lid of the box to find a hole cut out in the middle. "Tréville, what is this? It doesn't look or smell very nice," I asked. Tréville told me it was used like a chamber pot and, whatever, went down a long pipe with a curve at the bottom and probably went under the gardens and departed somewhere deep into the river. Also, the water from the tub could be poured down it as well. Thank heavens the Marseilles soap we now used had a lavender smell to it that would hopefully keep it smelling nicer. Tréville said they had two of them at the palace. The first time I used it was strange indeed.

All the cobwebs were gone, new candles in the holders. All was nearly done inside, but nothing had been done on the gardens or the servants' quarters. Tréville and I could now move into the house and that's what we did. We also had a lot of help from Amanda and my brothers. They loved the place. Our sons had sorted their bedchambers out, and divided their time between the bakery, the dwelling and the house. Little did they know that I knew they both had special ladies in their lives. I mentioned to Tréville that it might be time to have a "man to man" talk with our sons, and he did, much to his embarrassment. I cheekily listened at the door and had to go out in the garden because I was giggling so much. Tréville bought four horses – two blacks, a chestnut, and a grey, as we always borrowed horses from the garrison, but now we had a field they could graze in and the barn for night-time.

CHAPTER 37

Resignation

One year later Tréville came to a tremendous decision – he was going to relinquish his commission as Commander of the Musketeers. He wanted to spend more time with our sons and me, and he so wanted to sort the house and gardens. As much as he had loved being with the Musketeers he said it was time to move on. I wasn't sure how I felt about this, but in the end, he did make the right decision. I loved being with him all day and all night. He had enjoyed a great life at the garrison, as Captain of the Musketeers, then Minister for War, then Commander of the Musketeers. It was a sad day for my brothers and his men when he left. The Queen did all she could to try and persuade him to stay, but he advised her that now King Louis XIV had had his Coronation it was time for the King to decide who he would like to appoint Commander of the Musketeers, until the day came that he took his title back.

One day, Catherine asked me if she might have a word with me. She was going to get married. I was so pleased for her, and her husband-to-be was our banker. Catherine's first love had been a Musketeer, who decided he wanted to go the Americas; he did ask Catherine to go with him, but she did not want to leave France. A couple of years later she met Francois, an apprentice at the bank, but also the banker's son. Over the following years Francois's father passed and he took over. Love came to both of them and now they were to be wed. I would miss Catherine so much; her devotion to me, and the running of the bakery, I would never forget. She had become my younger sister. I remembered when I returned from England to find Monsieur Rennard had employed her. She was one of the beggars in the street that I fed when I could. A saying came to my mind: "from rags to riches." Catherine deserved her happiness. I promised her I would do her wedding cake and celebrations. When her wedding day arrived, and she saw her cake, she hugged me and cried.

Over the next couple of years Pierre, Laurens and the other three girls all left. With Jean and Armand's help a new workforce was found and I made sure our sons gave them the same good rapport as I had with my workforce.

Now our boys were nearly nineteen, they asked about the rooms over the bakery. I knew what was coming. They asked me if I would give permission for them to move in. They wanted to put the two rooms together again, but each have their own bedchambers. Tréville and I agreed, and helped with funds to help them change it round. They took turns in who stayed. At least someone was on the premises, and should I need to stay over, there was a spare bedchamber.

After Tréville retired, a new Cardinal was appointed. Within weeks he was the most hated man in Paris, and my Musketeer brothers did not get on with him at all. In his first year, anyone who had built a home close to the city walls was heavily taxed. Two years later taxes were imposed on fruit and vegetables brought into the city, and that affected us quite a lot in the bakery. The following year anyone who had built their home on property that officially belonged to the King would have to re-buy the rights of the land. Then came the riots, and both Tréville and myself were glad Armand was not a Musketeer. My brothers had a dreadful time trying to control these riots, and quite a lot of Musketeers were killed. The reason was another war broke out with Spain, and again, victory went to France. My brothers did not go, as they were needed in Paris. After this victory, the Cardinal arranged a special mass at the cathedral, which the young King attended. Red Guards lined the streets. As soon as the event was over, the Cardinal had three prominent members of the Parlement arrested – why? – because he had tried to stop payments of salary to three of the city councils for four years. They were furious and the Cardinal had to change his mind. This was his retribution. News spread of the arrests, hence the riots. Hundreds of barricades were erected to make sure various buildings were safe. Violent scenes broke out between the people of Paris and the Red Guards; hundreds were killed. In the end the Regent Queen attended an audience with the leaders of the Parlement, and the prisoners were released.

Tréville asked for a private audience with the Regent Queen, who agreed and was delighted to see him. Tréville suggested that if she and the young King needed to escape Paris, they would be more than welcome to come and stay with us. She was delighted but advised him that the following night, under the cover of darkness, they were leaving Paris and going to Chateau de Saint-Germain-en-Laye. The riots had frightened her greatly and she feared for her son's life. Over the following years the Regent Queen and her son fled twice to the chateau. Later on in his life, the King distrusted the Parisians so much, that he moved, with his mother, to Versailles. After that the King very rarely came to Paris.

When our sons reached the age of twenty-four they asked if they might discuss a certain matter with us. They both wanted our blessing to get married, and they wanted to get married at the same time. Naturally we gave them our blessing and were delighted for them both. Armand and Jean had both met Anne and Marie, who were sisters, at a ball held by our solicitor to celebrate forty years of marriage. Jean and Marie lived at the bakery, and had only been married over a year when tragedy struck and she passed after a short illness. Jean stayed at the bakery for a couple of months and then asked if he might move back to the dwelling. Naturally, we both agreed. Armand and Anne had moved into the dwelling after their marriage, but within nine months Anne was with child, so they found another dwelling, about half an hour's ride from ours. I went back to the dwelling about once a month just to check everything was all right. If Jean was at the house then the villagers would keep an eye on it for us.

Armand and Jean had made a great success of the bakery and Tréville suggested it would be a good idea for me "to let go" and then we could spend even more time together. I agreed it was time for me to enjoy my life with Tréville now. We saw our solicitor and made more or less identical wills. The bakery and dwelling, which was in my name, I left to Tréville, and when he passed it went equally to the boys. With regards to the house, that was going directly to the boys.

One day when I was walking through the village, about two years after we had moved into the house, I met Celeste, the wife of Patric who ran the tavern. During our conversation she asked me if we were looking for any servants. It seemed strange someone asking me if I wanted servants, when I used to be one myself. I asked her why. She told me she knew of a husband and wife who were looking for work. The husband was used to working in a garden and with horses; the wife was a maid, and also worked in the kitchen. I told her I would be interested but I would talk to Tréville and let her know. Tréville wanted to meet them, especially the husband. I gave Celeste the details and we arranged for them to come to the house. They turned out to be a lovely couple. Solange and Maurice were both twenty-five, and had borrowed a horse and cart to get to us. We showed them the servants' quarters, which we had not done anything to. Maurice said it wasn't a problem, they would see to it, if they got the positions. Tréville, to put it politely, put Maurice through his paces, especially about horses. Maurice took it all in and answered his questions. I showed Solange around the house.

I made everyone a drink in the kitchen and we made our excuses to Maurice and Solange and went to the parlour where we discussed the idea of taking them on. Tréville was highly impressed with Maurice; he knew a lot about trees, plants and horses, and I liked Solange. They had brought references with them, which were very good. Two weeks later they moved into the servants' quarters. They told us they were staying with friends and had no furniture so I went to a market in Paris and got a big and small bed and straw pallets, pillows, a small table and two chairs and some cooking utensils, and various other things. Tréville sorted out tools for the garden and whatever for the horses. Tréville and I cleaned the fireplaces and shutters so all was clean if nothing else. They were stunned at what we had done and thanked us so much. Within a month the servants' quarters took on a cosy look, and both of them were extremely hard workers.

The garden work was still too much for Tréville and Maurice, so Tréville took on two other men from our village. A couple of months later, Solange asked us if we needed more staff as her sister and husband, Esther and Claude, had lost their positions to a huge fire which had totally destroyed the château where they were employed. We met them and took them on and they moved into the servants' quarters. Luckily they didn't live at the burnt-out château so they had all their own furniture, which they brought with them. Solange and Esther did the household duties, but I still did a lot of the cooking, and Tréville and I would partake of our meals with them sometimes. Claude and Maurice helped Tréville with the garden and horses.

Within a year things were looking so different. It took another two years before the house and gardens and surrounding areas were back to their former glory. The lane up to where the field used to be was now wider and had a gate, which was rarely closed. The field was now divided in two with the path going through the middle, and was now grass. The path then branched out to go left and right, around the side of the house and into the gardens. The path on the right continued on down to the field at the back of the house, and passed the stables. At the back of the stables a plot of land had been dug and vegetables and herbs had been planted. When the trees were full of leaves, looking from the house down to where the lane started, it looked like an arch.

At the back, the four separate gardens had all been replanted with various types of small trees and flowers, none of which I knew the names of! Outside the gate the field now had a hedge running round it so the horses would not escape, had plenty of trees for shade and two large troughs for food and water. The hedge finished just before the bridge, so I could still go walking in the forest, which Tréville knew I loved. During the summer months Tréville and I would sit in the garden, and entertain our friends. The gardens would be in full bloom, flowers of various colours and smells, different sorts of birds singing in the trees. In the winter months, he would worry about his gardens. If there was snow, like children, we would go out and throw snowballs at each other, and then one day I lay down in the snow.

"What on earth are you doing, my love?" said Tréville, looking perplexed.

I replied, "Do you remember one of your nieces told us how to make snow angels? Well that's what I'm doing." I started moving my arms and legs and then asked Tréville to help me up. "See, my love? There is a snow angel, now it's your turn."

"Oh, I don't think so my love, I'll leave that to you," he said, laughing. Thanks to a certain move Porthos had taught me, Tréville was soon on his backside in the snow. He sort of did a snow angel but as he went to get up he grabbed me and we both ended up in the snow, rolling, laughing and kissing each other. We then decided because we were so wet a hot bath would be in order and then go and cosy up in the parlour by a lovely log fire, with a hot chocolate for me and wine for him.

We must have been at the house for five years when a really bad winter set in, it was so bad that Jean and Armand and families could not get to us for Noël. I had woken and everything seemed so very still. I quietly left the bed so as not to wake Tréville, and opened one of the drapes and gasped. Tréville immediately woke and asked what was wrong. I told him to come and look. "My gardens, my gardens," he said. I had never seen him wash and dress so fast. The reason – the snow was so deep it totally covered the top of his gardens! I quickly washed and dressed and went down to the kitchen where Tréville was talking to Maurice and Claude, asking them what they were doing in the kitchen and not outside.

Maurice said, "Sire, the shrubs you've planted will withstand the snow, what plants are there will not. Not only that, sire, we cannot get out of the door, the snow is halfway up it."

Tréville started to get into one of his rare tempers so I put my hand on his arm and said, "Tréville, look, the sun is rising and soon we can probably go out the parlour way and then move the snow away from the door."

He looked at me and then at Claude and Maurice and said, "My apologies."

We had our breakfast in the dining room as usual. Solange and Esther had both turned out to be good cooks, and Esther was also an excellent seamstress. If we were entertaining I would sit in the kitchen with them and decide what food was required and they would then sort out what had to be bought. It felt strange not doing it myself.

A couple of hours later the sun had melted enough snow so Tréville could get out of the parlour doors. There was a very cold wind blowing so I made sure he was warmly wrapped up, to quite a few coughs and tuts. He went to the barn and got a shovel and moved all the snow away from the back door. The first thing they did was tend to the horses, and then started moving the snow off some of the paths. There was nothing he could do with his gardens but wait. The one thing I asked was for the path to be cleared to the forest. A couple of days later I wrapped up warm, and put boots on and went over the bridge, carefully, to the edge of the forest. The sun had melted the snow a bit so it wasn't too deep. There was snow all over the branches of the trees, icicles hanging from some of them and twinkling in the little bit of sun. I didn't venture deep into the forest, as the snow there was even deeper. As I turned to return to the house an icicle fell from a high branch and hit the back of my hand. I flinched and look down and saw it was bleeding quite badly. I touched another icicle on a branch and it too was sharp at the bottom. I had a handkerchief with me and wrapped it round the wound.

I looked at the house and was so stunned. It took my breath away. It looked enchanting and magical. It had started snowing lightly again and it looked like white petals were falling from the sky around the house. I saw Tréville walking towards me and smiled. "Tréville, look at the house," I said when he reached me.

He turned, wrapped me in his arms and said, "What a beautiful sight, our own magical castle." He then gently kissed my lips and went to take my hand in his when he saw the handkerchief. "What happened, my love?" and I told him. He took my hands in his and was surprised at how cold they were. "Please be careful walking in the forest with all this snow, I couldn't bear it if something happened to you." With a twinkle in his eyes and his arms around me he said, "I think we need to get back and maybe have a hot bath or I can warm you up in other ways." I smiled and kissed him. We then walked back to the house, had our hot bath together and then our arms entwined around each in our bed and we let our passions take over. The snow lasted two months. Thank heavens we had stocked up with supplies. Needless to say, his gardens survived.

Solange, Maurice, Claude and Esther settled in well and neither of us saw them as servants. I asked Solange one day why they always called us Sire and Madame. Solange replied that it was the correct thing to do; if we were entertaining and they called us by our first names, people would be shocked. I understood what she meant. Helene and quite a few of the villagers would come and visit, along with our friends from different walks of life. Naturally my brothers and Amanda were always welcomed with open arms, when time allowed them. Our sons and families came down at least twice a month. Tréville and I would go into Paris, walk by the river and have a meal, go to the theatre, watch puppet shows, and be invited to friends quite often, and then we would return the favour. All in all, Tréville and I had a very happy contented marriage, rarely had crossed words; we celebrated every year of our marriage and for our 25th anniversary Tréville bought me a gorgeous fleur-de-lis ring, which I treasured, and we loved each other with such a passion that never went away. We always went everywhere together, we always slept entwined in each other's arms, and we also had great fun in the tub!!

Over the year's Tala and I had some great runs in our safe forest. Sometimes I went during the day and would, through Tala's eyes, sit by a couple of huge trees, which gave plenty of cover, and watch Tréville working in the garden, and knew he was my alpha male. Alas, the years caught up with Tala and I, and the runs became less and less. It would take longer for Tala and I to return, and I would be so drained, but we always remained content with each other – after all, she was my spirit wolf, and she would always be with me.

Then all our lives changed...

CHAPTER 38

Memories

I woke, totally drained. I looked at Tréville's side of the bed – he wasn't there. I rose, washed and dressed. I looked out of the window at the view, but it was blurred – I felt like I wasn't there. There was a knock at our bedchamber door, and it was Solange. "Morning Madame, I thought you might like some breakfast."

"Thank you, Solange, please put it on the table. The house seems quiet considering our two sons are here with their wives and children," I said. Solange replied that they had already had breakfast and were in one of the gardens. I really didn't feel like eating but a long day awaited me, and so I ate my breakfast. I looked out of the window and saw carriages arriving, so I made sure I looked presentable and went out. I walked down the stairs to the hall where Armand and Jean were greeting Athos, Porthos, Aramis, D'Artagnan (now no longer Musketeers, but they were all in full Musketeer uniform) and Amanda. Each one of them greeted me with a kiss on the cheek and a hug.

Jean advised me that everybody else was outside. "Gentlemen, it is time, if you would care to follow me," said Armand.

Amanda came and stood at my side, and put her arm around me and said, "Oh Lesley, I am so sorry." I tried to fight back the tears but to no avail.

I heard Athos say, "Turn, lift." The men emerged from the small office bearing the coffin of my beloved on their shoulders. They then walked out of the main door towards the back of the house where the funeral and burial was to take place, in the beautiful garden at the side of the house which Tréville and Maurice had redesigned and tended. The priest and quite a crowd of mourners were waiting, including Edouard who now had his own blacksmith's, and tears were flowing down his cheeks. Tréville always visited Edouard when he could to make sure he was all right – they were very close. Thank heavens it wasn't raining! I had wanted Tréville to be buried at the small church where we married, but alas it was too far away. The grave was already dug and ready to accept him. The priest conducted the service; I don't remember much of what was said, I just looked at the coffin and thought, *It can't be true,* and, *I'm never going to see him again,* tears flowing down my cheeks. I felt a hand take each of mine and glanced up to see Armand on one side and Jean on the other; they too were weeping for their father. As the coffin was being lowered I bent over and placed a red rose on the coffin. I went to step forward, I so desperately wanted to be with him, but hands held me back.

My sons then led me back to the house where food, wine and ale had been laid out for the mourners. I felt a hand on my shoulder and turned to see Tréville's niece, Aurore. I was so pleased to see her. Tréville had told me of her bravery for France, especially in the war. We sat and talked for about an hour and then, alas, she had to go. She told me Michelle sent her apologies, but she was in England. We hugged and kissed each other – Tréville thought the world of them both, but I think Aurore more so. I had met Aurore and Michelle on various occasions over the years, and we were the best of friends. The first time I met Aurore was, let's say, not quite the way I would have liked it.

One day, after Tréville had told us we were at war with Spain, and we had returned from our honeymoon, he sent a note to me at the bakery "summoning" me to go to his office immediately. He knew I was really busy and being summoned made my blood boil. I stormed out of the bakery, covered in flour and heaven knows what else. As I crossed the garrison Aramis spotted me and said, "Morning Lesley, looking lovely as ever." I just glared at him. "I think maybe the Minister is in trouble," I heard him say. I hitched up my dress and stomped up the garrison steps, went to his office and banged on the door.

Tréville replied, "Enter."

I entered and he was stood by his desk. I looked straight at him, slammed his note down on the desk and with my hands on my hips said, "Well, I'm here, Minister, you summoned me. Who do you think you are? You may be my husband but..."

A female laughed behind me and said, "You've met your match at last, uncle, I like her already."

I turned to see a lovely woman, who looked a little bit like Michelle, stood in the door of the armoury. "I'm Aurore, Tréville's other niece. I believe you've met Michelle, sorry about that," she said. I wished the ground had opened and swallowed me up. Tréville smiled at me, came and put his arms around my waist and kissed my lips, and my temper passed as he knew it would, and said, "After the last time I thought I'd better introduce you properly, perhaps 'summons' was the wrong word, and... I love the new look." For that, he got a slap on his arm.

I looked at Aurore and said, "Please forgive me, if I'd known exactly why Tréville had summoned me I would have made the effort to turn up clean and tidy."

Aurore laughed and said it wasn't a problem, but seeing as "Uncle Tréville" was busy, how about the pair of us go back to the bakery? She would love to see it.

We went back to the bakery and Aurore saw how busy we were and actually helped out. She was so easy going, but I knew deep down her allegiance to France was to her credit. After we had finished I took Aurore up to my parlour and excused myself so I could freshen up. I changed my dress and brushed my hair, replaited it, but left it down. Aurore and I then walked back arm in arm to the garrison. As we entered the garrison my brothers were sitting at the table. "Aurore, lovely to see you again," said Athos, who kissed her cheek and hugged her. Porthos and Aramis did the same.

"Well Captain Athos, how do you like your new title?"

Athos just scowled. Aurore laughed. I saw D'Artagnan nudge Aramis. "Aurore, may I introduce you to our new Musketeer D'Artagnan," said Aramis.

D'Artagnan bowed, took Aurore's hand and kissed it, saying, "The pleasure is all mine."

"Knock it off, you're married," said Porthos. We all laughed whilst D'Artagnan blushed.

Tréville came down the steps and called for our horses. I looked at him and he said, "Athos, we are going to the dwelling, should anything important happen." Athos nodded. Remy brought the horses round, and put Sunkwa by the steps. I walked up a couple of steps and got onto Sunkwa's back.

"Lesley do you not ride with a saddle?" asked Aurore.

I told her I didn't. She looked worriedly at Tréville, who smiled and said, "Lesley always rides without a saddle, unless it's necessary. She will be absolutely fine." Athos helped Aurore up. All three of us then rode out of the garrison and went back to the dwelling.

When we got there Tréville asked Aurore if she would like to stay with us. Aurore replied she would love to. We decided we would go and eat at the tavern, and had a lovely meal with wine. When we returned to the dwelling I got the spare bedchamber ready and decided to retire to bed and left them to talk about the war.

Aurore stayed with us for two days. One of the days Aurore and I went into Paris and had a meal at the tavern by the river. She wanted to know how I had met Tréville, our wedding, and how I got on with Tréville's men. I told her my story and how his men were now my brothers. I also told her about Amanda and everything both of us had gone through with Phillip and Rochefort. She was shocked. Aurore told me about Michelle's story. Michelle was her sister, but not a blood sister. Her parents had been killed when she was about three months old, and Aurore's parents took her in, and brought her up as their own. She made me promise not to say anything; nobody knew, not even Tréville. I promised.

The day she left, Tréville, my brothers and myself all went to the tavern for something to eat, and then back to the garrison for her departure. We hugged and kissed each other on the cheek. I had made her a picnic to take on her journey, which Tréville attached to her saddle. I was worried about her going off to war, but she told me she had a "very special friend" who would protect her. She also told me of a time when she and her friend had a snowball fight and making something called "snow angels". Tréville and I watched her ride out of the garrison, our arms around each other's waists, waving, and agreed we must try the snow angels. It was two years later before we met up with Aurore again.

We didn't see Michelle until after the war. This time a message was sent to Tréville so I was prepared. She was, to start with, the opposite to Aurore – very critical of everything, looked down her nose at my staff and rather aloof, but after a couple of weeks she mellowed and we became friends. She apologised for the last time we met, she even apologised to Catherine, and as with Aurore we went into Paris and had a fabulous day. She absolutely loved the twins. Michelle was quite happy to stay at the tavern so she could be close to them, and she was a great help to me. She stayed a month, told me how she had met her husband and then, alas, the time came for her to depart. I was actually sorry to see her go. Strange how events turn. Tréville's nieces became more of my extended family.

I mingled with everyone, caught up with the news from Athos, Aramis, D'Artagnan and Porthos and Amanda. It was so good to talk to them. After Tréville had left the garrison we still met up with Amanda and my brothers, but not as much as I would have liked, but they all had their own lives to live. People started to leave until there was only myself, my brothers, Amanda, and my two sons and their families. Amanda came to me and said, "What are your intentions now, Lesley, are you staying here?"

I looked at her and replied, "No, as much as I love the house, in a couple of weeks I am returning to the dwelling. The house is now in the hands of my sons as Tréville requested, and I have so many memories of him at the dwelling. I will come down as much as I can, but it is quite a journey, and I'm not young anymore, and now his spirit is with the others, and I know my sons will take care of the grave. They both now have huge decisions to make with regards to the house and the bakery, and they both know if they need my advice I will always be there for them." I said my goodbyes to them, wondering if I would ever see them again. Tréville's most loyal and courageous men – The Musketeers.

Again it brought back a memory, which I smiled at. After the house and gardens were finished, one day because it was such a beautiful sunny day, I suggested to Tréville that we took our meal and went and sat by the big tree at the front, which was to the left of the house. I laid the rug out in the shade. We had chicken, ham, cheese, bread and wine. We partook of our meal and then I sat against the tree with Tréville's head in my lap. Tréville looked up at said, "I love you so much, my love, and I don't know what I would do without you." I smiled and bent my head and kissed him so gently. The next minute our arms entwined and when we looked at each other, we saw the passion in both of our eyes.

I knew where this was leading and said, "Tréville we cannot, what would happen if someone came?"

"And who is likely to come all the way out here, my love? Maurice, Solange, Esther and Claude have gone to visit their family," he replied. He took me in his arms and kissed me deeply.

Just then we heard horses' hooves. We both looked up to see Athos, Aramis and Porthos riding up. Tréville sighed and said, "They never did have good timing, and we will continue later."

We both stood and greeted them, Athos looked at us both and said, "Sorry, did we interrupt something?" Tréville just raised his eyebrow and gave him a look!!

We all hugged and kissed and then I said, "Captain Athos," for which I got a scowl, "Porthos, Aramis, please join us, there is some food and wine left. What brings you all the way out here? Is everything all right?" Athos then told us that they wanted Tréville to be the first to know, apart from D'Artagnan, they were going to resign as Musketeers. They no longer felt they could go on under the new regime. I was shocked but could understand.

Tréville said, "And what will you do now, my friends?" Athos was going back to where he used to live, Porthos and Amanda were undecided, and Aramis was going back to Noisy-le-Sec to the Abbey. D'Artagnan had been promoted to Lieutenant of the Musketeers and was staying.

A couple of hours later, after news, laughs and then hugs and kisses, they left. Tréville had felt honoured that they had come to tell him first. He put his arm round my waist and said, "Now where were we?" and started kissing my neck.

After our passions had been satisfied we heard hooves and a cart approaching. We quickly dressed, and gathered up the remnants of our picnic, and as we walked back to the house Solange, Esther and their husbands arrived. I looked at Tréville and said, "Um... I feel rather hot, maybe a bath would cool me down."

He looked at me with a twinkle in his eyes, smiled and said, "Now that sounds like a lovely idea," and it was.

That night after I had retired, I stood by the window unpinning and unplaiting my hair, and then brushing it whilst I looked at his grave. Tears rolled down my cheeks. Suddenly I saw a figure walking towards his grave and lay something on it. The figure turned and looked up at me – it was Anne, who had been our Queen, and had passed six years before. I nodded to her in understanding. She stayed at Tréville's grave for about five minutes and then as she walked away she faded. Tréville and I had attended her funeral at the Basilica of Saint-Denis in Paris, and afterwards she was laid to rest with her husband, Louis XIII. Anne had been quite ill for some time and passed away at Val-de-Grace convent, also in Paris. The church of Val-de-Grace was built by Anne, and was on lands that used to have a Benedictine convent on it. The Dauphin, as he was then, laid the cornerstone when he was of the age of seven. It took twenty-two years to be totally constructed. After the ceremony Tréville and I were honoured as the King came over and spoke to us. He thanked us for attending and asked if we were both well. We talked for about ten minutes and then he departed. Neither Tréville nor myself ever saw the King again.

I changed into my night garment and went to draw the drapes on the window when I noticed another figure at Tréville's grave. They stayed for about five minutes and as they turned to look up at me, I saw it was Liz from England, who had also passed. She waved to me and I waved back, but in the moonlight I could see tears glistening down her face. Both Tréville and I attended Liz's funeral in England, over ten years ago.

Tréville and I had been taking breakfast when Solange came in and said a letter had arrived for me. I could see it was from England, but it was not Liz's writing. Liz and I corresponded at much as we could, since Katherine had passed. I opened the letter and it read:

Dear Mrs Tréville,

I would like to introduce myself. I am Mr Elijah Brown of Brown and Jones

Solicitors in London, England. I am the solicitor to Miss Liz Bramwell, whom I understand is a very great friend of yours. I am sorry to advise you that Miss Bramwell has suffered a serious illness and only has, maybe, about two/three months before her life expires.

On many occasion she has been asking for you, and I wondered if there was any way, at all, that you might be able to travel to England to see her. I know it would be her greatest wish to see you.

Should you be able to make the journey, please reply to me with dates and I will ensure that a carriage will await you at Dover.

I remain

Elijah Brown

Solicitor

A tear rolled down my cheek. "My love, is it bad news?" asked Tréville. I handed him the letter to read. "Oh my dear, I am so sorry, we must go immediately. I will make all the arrangements for us."

I looked at Tréville and said, "We?"

Tréville took my hands in his and said, "You honestly don't think I'm going to let you go on your own. I will be at your side, as always, to protect you."

I smiled and replied, "How on earth did I ever find such a loving, caring husband? I would love for you to come with me, but are you sure there are not more important things here to be done?"

Tréville replied, "Nothing in this world is as important to me as you are. Now I will go and see Athos to see if there is a quicker route to get to Calais and arrange for horses along the way. All you have to do is pack for both of us. Not a lot though, we will have to travel light," and with that gave me a kiss and went off to get his horse.

Later that day, when Tréville returned from the garrison, he had a route that was a lot quicker and would only take three days instead of four. Athos had sent a rider ahead to the two tavern stops to make sure a room awaited us, and fresh horses for the next day. Athos also told Tréville a boat would be leaving Calais for Dover in four days' time. Again, the rider would go to Calais and book passage. I must thank Athos when I next saw him. Tréville had also gone to the bakery and told Jean and Armand that we would probably be away for a month, if not more. He gave them Liz's address and said if anything important happened to contact Athos and he would get a rider to us. Jean and Armand were concerned and said, as we were not young anymore, perhaps they should come with us. Tréville never did tell me what he said to that comment, but I could think of a couple of replies!

That night Tréville packed what he needed, as I did. I had two cases, and he had one. "My love, what on earth are you taking?"

I looked at him and said, "Tréville I cannot wear the same dress and underwear for a month. All I have packed is three dresses, one black in case it is needed, undergarments, night garment, my brush and other small items I will require."

He looked in my cases and said, "Do you really need to take all those undergarments? And you have four petticoats, four long undergarments – just take two of each. I'm sure when we reach England we will be able to wash them." As much as I loved my husband there were times when I wished him elsewhere.

"Tréville, I need my four long undergarments for riding, I can roll them up small."

Tréville took me in his arms and said, smiling, "Have I ever told you how stubborn you are?"

I replied, "No, but then I had a good teacher, didn't I my love?" and kissed him.

Early the following morning, after Tréville had talked to our servants, who I preferred to call friends, we loaded our horses, with one case each. Tréville looked and just smiled. I had taken a dress and two each of the undergarments out, and managed to tightly put everything all in one case. The morning was cold and misty, so I put a thick dress on, and wore my warm hooded cape. Both of us had pistols and daggers on us. We rode until the sun was high in the sky, the mist and cold now gone, and stopped at a tavern, where we had refreshments and gave the horses a rest. After a couple of hours we continued on to the tavern for our overnight stop. We did the same for the next two days and arrived in Calais on a very wet and windy day. I looked at the sea, it was angry and I worried for Tréville; he had never been on a boat before. Luckily we had a cabin all to ourselves, so if Tréville got the seasickness it would be in private. As it turned out, once we had left the port of Calais and got out into deeper water, the sea calmed and we had a good crossing, which took two days.

As we went to leave the boat, the Captain came to us. "Mr and Mrs Tréville, I hope your journey was comfortable?" We replied it was and thanked him. "Two horses are waiting for you at the dock side, all arranged by a gentleman called Athos. Go to the end of the dock, be careful where you put your feet, and you will see a small shack. Enter and ask for Thomas, he will then take you to where your horses are. I wish you a pleasant onward journey and hopefully see you again on your return journey." Again, we thanked him, went to the shack and got our horses. Four hours later, we entered the outskirts of London.

Tréville looked at me and said, "I thought Paris was bad for the air, but this is whole lot worse." I smiled and told him we were not going into London itself, and when we got to the first crossroads we turned left and went back out into countryside. "Aahh, this is better," he said.

Soon we came to the village where Liz lived. My, how it had grown. There was now a large tavern with stables attached, and lots more dwellings. I couldn't even remember where Liz's dwelling was because I could not find Katherine's house. We stopped at the tavern and asked if they had a room for maybe a couple of weeks. The owner replied he had a room, so we took our cases up, refreshed ourselves and then went back down. I asked the owner if he knew where Liz's dwelling was. He looked at me and said, "You must be Mrs Tréville from Paris?" I looked at him, stunned, and he said, "Liz talks of no one else but her great friend who left these shores and went to Paris. My name is Peter, and I assume you must be Mr Tréville?" and he shook hands with Tréville, who replied he was. "Come, I will show you the way," he said. Liz's dwelling was about a five-minute walk from the tavern. We thanked him and I knocked on the door.

A woman opened the door and said, "May I help you?" I told her who we were and the next minute she was hugging Tréville and me. "My apologies, I am so pleased you have come. She asks for you all the time, but be prepared, she is now very weak and sleeps a lot, as she has reached a good age of seventy. Come, please sit in the parlour and I will make you a drink. Tea, coffee?" We both declined politely. She left us and went into another room that I knew was Liz's bedchamber. "Please come, both of you."

As I entered the room Liz was sitting up in bed, but her eyes were closed, and she looked like a skeleton. I was quite overcome. Tréville put his hand on my arm. I went to Liz, sat at the side of her on a chair and said, "Liz, it's Lesley. I'm here, my friend."

Liz opened her eyes and tears fell. "Oh Lesley, you came, I thought I would never see you again." Her eyes then looked at Tréville and she said, "No wonder Lesley wanted to go back to Paris, now I see why. Handsome, aren't you?"

Tréville smiled, took her hand and kissed it, and said, "It is an honour to meet you."

Liz looked at me and said, "Any chance he can stay the night with me?"

I laughed and Tréville blushed. I never told him what a wicked sense of humour Liz had. Tréville said he would leave us to talk in private, and he would have a wander round the village.

"Be careful, Tréville, a lot of the villagers don't take kindly to strangers," said Liz. He assured her he would be fine.

Liz and I talked for about an hour and then I could see she was getting weary. I wondered where Tréville was. I asked the woman, who was called Martha, if she knew which way Tréville had gone. She replied she didn't. I told Martha I would be back in the morning, but if Liz took a turn for the worst, no matter what time, to come and get me. She said she would. As I left Liz's dwelling I looked to see if I could see Tréville – nothing. What used to be Katherine's house was just down the lane so I walked that way, but as I passed the cemetery I saw Tréville sitting on a bench. "Tréville, are you all right?" I said with concern in my voice, walking towards him.

"Yes my love, I have walked round the village and started to feel weary, so I thought I would rest a while."

"What, in the cemetery?" I asked.

He looked at me and smiled and said, "Why not? It's peaceful here, and I was looking at the graves. I found Katherine's whilst I was looking." Tears came to my eyes as I remembered the last time I had visited here. "My love, I did not mean to upset you," said Tréville.

I took his hand and kissed it and said, "Memories." I went and paid my respects to Katherine and then hand in hand, Tréville and I walked to where I used to live.

I was surprised to see the house was looking run down. It didn't look like anyone had lived in it for some time. I would have liked to have gone and looked in the windows, but it was not my place to. I pointed out which room I had, and the layout inside to Tréville, then we made our way back to the tavern. We had a quick wash, went down and had a lovely meal and then retired. It had been a long six days. Tréville and I talked about Liz, then he blew the candle out, our arms went round each other and after goodnight kisses, we slept deeply.

The following morning, both of us woke early, but did not get up. The bed was really comfortable so we laid there for another hour. When we went down for our early morning meal, Peter said, "Good morning Mr and Mrs Tréville, I trust you both slept well?' Tréville replied we had. He asked me if Liz had been happy to see me. I replied she was, but how poorly she looked to when I last saw here. "You been here before then, Mrs Tréville?" he asked. I told him I used to live there with my aunt Katherine, until I went to France. Peter told us he had only taken over the tavern three years before, after he lost his wife, and the first person he met was Liz. Apparently she took Peter under her wing. She introduced him to all the villagers, gave him advice with regards to who he should purchase wines, ales and food from. They had become very good friends and he was very upset now that she was so ill. He asked Tréville if he would like to accompany him into London. He had to go to the markets and purchase some goods and would like the company. I advised him that Tréville had never been to England before and he replied, "Sites to be seen then." I watched them depart and then went to Liz's.

Martha told me Liz had had a good night, and was looking forward to seeing me again. I knocked on her door and entered. She smiled and looked past me. "Where is he then, that handsome husband of yours?" she asked.

"Tréville has gone into London with Peter. I hope he will be all right, he hasn't been to England before."

Liz looked at me and laughed. "Gone with Peter, has he? Well, he won't be sober when he gets back."

Oh no!! Liz and I talked of the old days. I told her all about Jean and Armand and the bakery. She told me all that had been happening in her village and London. The hours went by so quickly, before I realised it, it was late afternoon. I hugged and kissed Liz's cheek and said I would see her in the morning, said my goodbye to Martha and went back to the tavern. No sign of Tréville or Peter. I had my evening meal and retired. I was now starting to get anxious as to where they were. Suddenly I heard such a row. I opened the window to see the horse and cart coming down the lane with Peter and Tréville sort of singing at the tops of their voices. As they neared the tavern I saw a window open and a voice said, "Shut up, Peter, some of us are trying to sleep." The next thing a huge bucket of water was thrown over them. They both stopped immediately. I couldn't help it, I just laughed and laughed. Talk about two drowned rats.

I grabbed a large cloth and went back down to see the pair of them walking in the door. "Slorry, Mrs Trev... him and me... we had some ale," said Peter, who could just about stand.

I looked at Tréville and he said, "Oh dear, I think I'm in trouble, have I ever told you what a wonderful wife you are?"

"Upstairs now so I can get you out of those wet clothes before you catch your death," I said. trying to sound annoyed.

Tréville looked at me and said, "Now there's a reason I can't say no to, night Peter."

Peter didn't answer, as he was on the floor firm asleep.

Another man appeared and said, "Please don't worry, Mrs, I'll see to Peter. You sort your husband out." I helped Tréville up the steps and got him into our bedchamber.

"Why am I all wet?" said Tréville as I helped him out of his wet clothes and hung them on a chair to dry. I eventually got him dried and into bed. Within seconds he was asleep. I undressed, got into bed, and blew the candles out. Tréville turned and took me in his arms and said sleepily, "Goodnight my love, sorry." I smiled.

CHAPTER 39

Ritual and Return

In the morning, as I opened the shutters the sun shone through the window. I heard a moan and turned to look at Tréville. "Why on earth does my head hurt so much?"

"Do you not remember, my love? You went to London with Peter and came back rather merry."

"Oh yes, and I don't like London. The air is dreadful, no way could l live there. Peter showed me lots of different places, then on the way back he seemed to stop at every tavern and everyone knew him. I hope I didn't disgrace you in any way, my love?" I told him he had been fine, but he had no recollection of getting wet. He laughed when I told him. We washed and dressed and went downstairs to see Peter as good as new.

"Ah, Mrs Tréville, I think I have an apology to make to you." I smiled and said he had nothing to apologise for, and to call me Lesley.

Both Tréville and I went to see Liz, but when we got there the physician and her solicitor were with her. I asked Martha what had happened. Martha told us Liz took a turn for the worse in the early hours, and asked for her physician and solicitor, so one of the village men rode to London to get her solicitor, who had arrived about an hour ago. The physician who lived in the next village had come straight away. I told Martha we would come back later on, but as we went to go, the door of her bedchamber opened and two men walked out. "Good morning, you must be Mr and Mrs Tréville. Allow me to introduce myself. I am Elijah Brown, who wrote to you. I assume you received my letter?" I replied I had. He then introduced us to Liz's physician, Dr Walter Moorhouse. Both men shook hands with us.

"How is Liz?" I asked.

Dr Moorhouse replied, "I fear Liz will depart us by the end of the day. I am so sorry to give you such bad news." Tears fell from my eyes and Tréville held me.

I calmed, wiped my tears and asked if I may sit with her; the physician said she had been asking for me. I knocked on the door and entered. Liz was sitting up, and smiled as I went to her.

"Lesley, my friend, don't look so sad. I have had a good life and I am ready to meet my maker. Hopefully I will see Katherine again. Now tell me, how did Tréville get on with Peter?"

I told her the story and she laughed so much she started coughing, so I got her a glass of water, which helped. She asked me if I was on my own and I said Tréville was in the other room. "Get him in here. Let me see your handsome man before I depart, I want to talk to him."

I went and got Tréville, again he kissed her hand, but Liz wanted a kiss on the cheek, so he obliged, and gave her a hug as well. "Cor, I bet he's lovely to cuddle up to in bed." she said. I replied he was. She looked at Tréville and said, "I'm not going to be around much longer, and I want you to promise me you will look after this lovely lady, because if you don't I will come back and haunt you."

Tréville replied, "You have my promise, I love Lesley with all of my heart and will always protect her." Liz smiled and asked if we would mind if she spoke to her solicitor again.

That was the last conservation I had with Liz; she passed an hour later. Tréville held me in his arms whilst the tears fell down my face. Eventually we went back to the tavern and told Peter – he was inconsolable. That night it felt like every villager came to the tavern and they all paid tribute to Liz. A week later Liz was laid to rest in the village cemetery and as the coffin was lowered I saw Liz and Katherine together. We all smiled, and I blew a kiss.

The following day Tréville and I decided it was time for us to return home and we would ride back to Dover to see if a boat was there, going back to Calais, but before we left Elijah Brown came to see me. "Mrs Tréville, as you know Miss Bramwell was unattached. Such a shame, she was such a lovely lady, I'm sure she would have made someone a wonderful wife. Apologies, I digress. Miss Bramwell has named you in her will and has left you everything, including the dwelling. As you know, Liz had a good occupation of being a seamstress. Her work was well known and nobility would come to her. This made Liz a very respectable lady. Through my father, the late Elijah Brown, Miss Bramwell invested her funds wisely, there will be a substantial amount."

I was absolutely stunned. "Excuse me, Mr Brown, I'm rather overcome at this news, do you mind if I take some air?" I walked down to the cemetery and sat on the bench.

Five minutes later Tréville joined me. "My love, are you all right, can I help at all?"

I sighed and said, "I can't believe Liz left me everything, it's not like I've been here all this time, and Liz knew I would never leave France."

Tréville put his arm round my shoulder and I put my head on his shoulder. Tréville then said, "My love, I have a suggestion, see what you think. What is the one thing that's missing from the village?" I looked at him and shook my head. "A school," he replied.

I looked at Tréville and thought what an excellent idea. I would never have thought of it. As we left the cemetery I wanted to take one last look at Katherine's house. Peter had told me that the owner has passed over a year ago, and had no family left. I went through the gate, and up to one of the windows and looked in. To me it looked the same, as nothing had changed. Then I saw the future and smiled. I took Tréville's face in my hands and kissed him. "Thank you, my love," I said.

Tréville looked at me and said, "For what?"

"For being here," I replied.

We went back to the tavern and I spoke to Mr Brown on my own and told him of my idea. His reaction was one of delight – he thought it was a wonderful idea, mainly because everyone in the village had loved Liz.

Tréville and I said our goodbyes to everyone and five hours later we were in Dover. We took the horses back to where we got them and Thomas told us a boat was going to Calais the following day. We found a tavern, of which there were plenty, and stayed the night. After we had retired Tréville asked me what I had decided. I told him that I had asked Mr Brown to sell Liz's dwelling and once he had a buyer to put those funds with Liz's investments. He was to also look into how to buy Katherine's house. The funds from the dwelling and investments were to be put towards Katherine's house and then turned into a school. So it was agreed that the papers, when ready, would be sent to our solicitors, for me to sign and send any shortfall required. Mr Brown, along with Peter, would oversee the school. One thing I did insist on, it was to be called KatLiz School. Tréville agreed that had been an excellent decision. The following day we got passage on the boat and as we set sail, I gave a wave to England, knowing I would never return. Six days later we were back home, and it felt so good. Tréville had been there for me, as I knew he would be. That night after we retired to our bed our arms entwined, our kisses deepened and our love for each other was overwhelming.

About three months later I received the papers from Elijah Brown. Someone from London had bought Liz's dwelling. Mr Brown had to go to the courts to buy Katherine's house, and once everything was settled, no extra funds were needed. Katherine's house was now the new school. I was pleased. I received a yearly report from Mr Brown for another six years, and then I received a letter with very sad news. The village, along with three others that were nearby had suffered an epidemic of the plague. All the villagers had perished and soldiers were sent to burn and raze every building to the ground. The village where I grew up with Katherine and Liz was now lost forever.

I looked at the now empty bed. How could I get used to life without Tréville? He was my life, my friend and my greatest love and he was gone. Again, the tears fell from my eyes. The bed was cold, but soon I closed my eyes and slept.

The following day, as I sat having breakfast with our sons and families, Solange came to me. "This letter has just been sent by a messenger for you, Madame." I thanked her and saw the seal of The

King. The letter read;

Dear Madame Tréville,

I wish to convey my heartfelt sympathies to you and your family after hearing of your sad loss of one of my most loyal, courageous and faithful Ministers, who I will always remember affectionately as Commander Tréville. I will never forget the day he was shot, and both my mother and I were delighted when he recovered. I have so many fond memories of him, as I do Jean and Armand. Please convey my regards to them.

You are all in my prayers and thoughts.

Louis XIV

I felt so honoured to have received his letter and showed it to our sons.

A week after the funeral a message came from Helene asking if I could visit her. She was too old to travel these days, and was upset she couldn't make the funeral. I went to see her a couple of days later. "Oh Lesley, I'm so upset about your loss as a lot of the villagers are. Would you like a drink?" I replied I would and I made us both a drink with mint leaves and hot water. "May I ask, if it's not too painful, what happened, mon amie?"

I replied, "Two weekends ago Armand and Anne came down with the grandchildren. The house always came to life when they were there, especially Christmas. The grandchildren had gone out to play when all of a sudden one of them came running back in, saying, 'Grandpère on floor in garden.' We all rushed out to see Tréville face down on the grass. I asked Tréville what was wrong. Armand rolled his father over carefully, and I cradled Tréville's head in my lap. 'Had pain in chest, felt funny, fell,' said Tréville. I told Armand to go quickly and get our physician, and to take the chestnut horse, as she was the fastest. Armand called to Maurice and Claude to help me, they came running and slowly we got Tréville back into the house and into the parlour. Tréville looked deathly pale and the sparkle in his eyes had gone. About half an hour later two riders came galloping in, it was Armand and our physician Dr L'Enfant. He examined Tréville and then between Maurice and Armand they slowly took

Tréville upstairs to our bedchamber.

"After what seemed like ages, Dr L'Enfant came back down to the parlour and said, "I'm sorry Lesley, I don't have good news, it is his heart and I have told him he must have absolute rest. I have left medicine, which he must have four times a day. I will come back in a couple of days to see how he is doing." I thanked him and went straight upstairs to see Tréville. As soon as I saw him I knew something was wrong. I called for Armand to get Dr L'Enfant back. I walked over to Tréville, the colour had gone out of him, but he looked peaceful. I took his face in my hands and kissed his lips. Tréville slowly opened his eyes and put his hand on my face, and said slowly, 'My dearest love, I will love you until my very last breath.' His hand fell from my face, Tréville had left me. (My necklace stopped beating.) Dr L'Enfant confirmed Tréville had passed, and even he was shocked." Tears started to flow down my face. Helene took my hands in hers and I continued, "I sat on the bed next to him, took his hand in mine bent over and kissed his now cold lips, lips I would never kiss again. I then laid my head on his chest, no heart beating anymore and my arm went round his waist, and I felt like my heart had been wrenched out off my chest. Armand put his hand on my shoulder and said, 'Come, Maman, Dr L'Enfant needs to see to Papa.' I composed myself slightly and looked at Armand and said, 'I would like your papa to be laid out in his Captain's Musketeer's uniform, which is in his cabinet, his hat to be in his hands.'

"Armand and Anne escorted me from the bedchamber. Armand informed the staff and then rode out to tell his brother of his papa's passing."

What I didn't tell her was I didn't know if Tréville's spirit had risen but as I left the bedchamber I saw Swallowtail stood there and she said, "Tréville has risen, he is safe and with us." I smiled and she vanished. It was also an Indian custom to put bundles of personal belongings with the deceased to help their journey to the spirit world, so before the lid was closed I put his sword, pistol and other items in. I plaited a piece of my hair, cut it off and placed it in one of Tréville's hands, under his Musketeer's hat, and placed red powder on his hands which stood for the colour of life. The last thing was my necklace, which I placed in his other hand. I looked at Tréville's wedding ring; it would not go with him, it would be left in his coffin, and I couldn't bear that, so I took his ring off, found a long piece of ribbon and tied it round my neck.

Helene said, "All the villagers, and myself, held Tréville in great esteem. He was a great, loved man and we will all miss him terribly. Will you come back to the dwelling?" I replied I would be returning soon, after things with our sons had been sorted out, like the house and the bakery. I gave Helene a hug, said my goodbye and returned to the house.

The following day I went for my walk in the forest, sat against my normal huge tree and thought about the last time I had been here. The day after Tréville passed I quietly made my way out of the house to the forest. I didn't want to be seen, and I didn't want anyone following me. I had to perform an Indian ritual in honour of Tréville. I cleared a small area and got stones and put them in a circle, collected small sticks and tinder and made a small fire by rubbing two sticks together. I sat cross-legged on the ground, closed my eyes, and again, very quietly, started chanting and Tala howled with my grief. When I opened my eyes, my father, mother and Swallowtail were with me, also chanting. My father then did a grief blessing.

"May the sun bring you new energy every day,

bringing light into the darkness of your soul.

May the moon softly restore you by night, bathing

you in the glow of restful sleep and peaceful dreams

May the rain wash away your worries, and cleanse

the hurt that sits in your heart

May the breeze blow new strength into your being,

and may you believe in the courage of yourself.

May you walk gently through the world, keeping

your loved one with you always, knowing that you

are never parted in the beating of your heart."

Swallowtail then came to me, and I knew what she needed. I plaited a piece of my hair, and then cut if off with the knife I had brought, and then made two deep cuts on my arm. I put my bleeding arm over the fire and at the same time put the plait in the fire. Swallowtail chanted and brought forth a vision of my love. Tréville looked at me and said:

"I give you this one thought to keep

I am still with you – I do not sleep.

I am a thousand winds that blow

I am the diamond glints on snow

I am the sunlight on ripened grain

I am the gentle autumn rain.

When you awaken in the morning's hush

I am the swift, uplifting rush

Of quiet birds in circled flight

I am the soft stars that shine at night.

Do not think of me as gone

I am with you still – in each new dawn."

Tears welled in my eyes and the vision of Tréville slowly faded. Swallowtail took me in her arms and said, "As you know we do not let just anyone enter the Reservation, but Katherine, Liz, Monsieur Rennard and especially Tréville have been here in your heart and have been allowed by the tribe to join us. We will look after them until your time comes to join us, which will not be yet, as your earth time is far from over. I know your grief consumes you and you want to be with Tréville, but you have sons who need you, grandchildren who need you. Tréville will always be at your side, and as he said, he is everywhere you look – the forest, the dwelling, the rising sun and the moon. Tala will grieve the same as you, but again, Tala is always with you and will guide you too." I looked round me and saw what she meant – Tréville was everywhere. My mother and father blessed me, and held me so tight and I felt their love so much, and then along with Swallowtail they faded away. The fire had died but I made sure nothing was still smouldering as I moved stones over the remains. As I left the forest the rain started, my tribe were mourning with me. When I entered the house Solange appeared and said she would help me out of my wet clothes. Suddenly I remembered the two deep cuts on my arm. How would I explain them? I told her I would be all right, but maybe a lovely hot chocolate would be nice. I needn't have worried, when I took my dress off, the cuts were already gone.

A couple of days later I was sitting on the terrace when my sons and their wives came and sat with me. Jean asked me if I minded recalling my love story to Charlotte, as they had only been married about four months. Jean had met Charlotte about two years ago, when he was asked by a friend to do her a birthday celebration. Jean made the birthday cake, breads and other pastries. Charlotte was a widow of five years, and according to Jean they both had an immediate attraction to each other, and things took their course from there. I looked at Charlotte and said, "Of course I will." I started from the first time I met Tréville up to the present day. I told her all about Amanda and my brothers and some of the fun I'd had with them all. "Tréville and I would have been married forty-four years next month, and now I'm on my own, and my heart is totally broken."

The tears started to flow, and both my sons put their arms around me and hugged me. "You have us, Maman, you have all of us," they said.

A month after we had laid Tréville to rest, whilst the grandchildren had been taken off for a picnic, Jean, Charlotte, Armand, Anne and myself talked about the house and the bakery. Jean really didn't want to give up the bakery, so by mutual consent, Armand and Anne decided to become the new owners of the house, with their three children, and they would also keep Solange, Maurice, Esther and Claude on. I was, quietly, delighted. I told Armand and Jean that I would not be upset if they wanted to change the furniture, after all it was what Tréville and I had bought. Armand replied they would keep it, as it was part of the house and also a part of his Papa and myself. Armand and Anne wanted me to stay with them but I could not. I told them that since Tréville had passed, the house, to me, felt different. There was a silence in the rooms, the house felt cold and unloved. I looked for him in the gardens and he wasn't there; waking up in our bed was hard, it felt like a horrible dream and then I knew it wasn't, Tréville had gone. Tears started to fall down my cheeks and Anne comforted me. I looked at Jean and Charlotte and asked if I could move back into the dwelling with them.

Naturally they agreed but then Armand came up with an idea. He offered their dwelling to Jean and Charlotte who were surprised, but delighted, and agreed it would be a shame to sell it. They didn't have a lot to pack up so they decided it could all be done when I returned to the dwelling the following day. Jean already had someone staying in the rooms at the bakery.

The next day my bags and trunks were packed and put onto the cart along with Jean and Charlotte's. The horse and cart were going to be driven by Maurice, but we were to travel back in the carriage driven by Armand. Jean and Charlotte would pack their items and put them in the carriage, which would then be driven by Maurice, as the horse and cart were to stay at the dwelling. Armand would then guide Maurice to their dwelling, pack his and Anne's items up, Jean and Charlotte would move in and then Maurice would drive Armand back to the house. I told them there was no rush. Maybe they knew that deep down I wanted to be in the dwelling on my own. I said my goodbyes to Anne and my grandchildren. I asked my grandchildren if they were happy to stay at the house, their response was to run and hold hands and dance in circles on the grass. I got the impression they were pleased. I would hate to think they would be unhappy. I then said a very emotional goodbye to Solange, Esther and Claude. I thanked them for everything they had done for both of us. It seemed strange Armand driving the carriage, and once we arrived back at the dwelling Jean and Charlotte packed their items and I said my goodbyes to them and promised I would visit them both soon. Again, it was another emotional goodbye to Maurice. I knew I would see them when I visited, but it was now different not living at the house anymore.

I then went to see Helene to let her know I had returned. It was a Sunday and most of the villagers were in church. Helene asked me to help her over to the church, as her walking now was quite bad. She said she had something to show me. "All the villagers wanted to do something to remember Tréville and we knew he liked his gardens, so we hope you don't mind and you like it." She took me to the side of the church, and my eyes welled up. A small garden had been designed, with a bench, and a small headstone with the inscription: "A notre ami Tréville – il reposer en paix." (To our friend Tréville, may he rest in peace). I hugged Helene and as I turned I saw all the villagers had come out from the church. "Vous mes amis remercier ses absolument magnifique." (Thank you, my friends, it's absolutely beautiful). All the villagers took turns to hug me, and I was overwhelmed. I walked Helene back to her dwelling, said my goodbye and went back to my dwelling. The dwelling felt the same as the house, cold and unloved. I went into our bedchamber that hadn't been used for a long time, as my sons always used the other bedchamber. "My love, light the fires, don't forget the guards."

"Tréville?" I said, but he wasn't there; but he was right. I lit the parlour and bedchamber fires and soon the dwelling was cosy. Years before, the blacksmith at the garrison had made something called a "guard" which was to be put round the fire so if any of the wood crackled out it would not cause any damage. I put one round the parlour and bedchamber fires. This would be the first time I slept in the dwelling without him, knowing he would never join me again.

I looked at my trunks and bags and decided they could all be unpacked another day. As I looked round the bedchamber I saw Tréville's cabinet and went over and opened it. I'd forgotten he had left some of his clothes here. I had brought the rest from the house with me. One of his old Captain's jackets was there and I held it against me, and then put it round me. It felt like he was holding me again. Tears started to flow. I felt something in his inside pocket and put my hand in. I drew out two letters and an eagle feather. This was the jacket he wore when he was at war. One of the letters was from me, and the other was from Aurore, but signed "The Red Rose." Tréville told me Aurore used to send messages in code, and this obviously was one he kept. It read,

Captain Tréville
My loving uncle

Forgive my tardiness between letters life in the county is so invigorating to ones health. the wound from the fall from my horse troubles me so infrequently now that I am immersed in the duties you so rightly prescribed.

Many new friendship's have been forged in the time spent away from Paris. I request my dear uncle, may I extend my stay at the estates in Gascony and return with the blooms of summer when once more the roses will flourish in the gardens of France.

The Red Rose

Captain Tréville

My loving uncle

Forgive my tardiness between letters. Life in the country is so invigorating to one's health, the wound from the fall from my horse troubles me so infrequently now that I am immersed in the duties you so rightly prescribed.

Many new friendships have been forged in the time spent away from Paris, I request my dear uncle, may I extend my stay at the estates in Gascony and return with the blooms of summer when once more the roses will flourish in the gardens of France.

The Red Rose

Your loving servant

After I had read it, I put them back in his pocket, where they had always been. I made myself a hot chocolate and retired for the night, and as I slowly drifted off I felt Tréville take me in his arms and kiss my forehead and say, "I'm here my love, I'm with you." To anyone else it would have sounded ridiculous, but I knew Tréville was with me and he always would be. Even Tala sighed with contentment.

CHAPTER 40

My Purrfect Friend

About six weeks after I arrived back at the dwelling, I heard a carriage pull up outside. I went to the door and was surprised to see my daughter-in-law, Charlotte. "What a lovely surprise, Charlotte, is everything all right?" I asked.

She came over and hugged me and kissed me on both cheeks. "Oh Maman, I was just on my way back home and thought I'd drop by and see if you were all right, everything is fine with us."

"Oh, my dear, how kind. I'm well. It's a lovely day, shall we partake of some mint tea in the back garden?"

"That would be lovely, Maman." (Neither of my daughters-in-law felt comfortable calling me Lesley, so they decided on Maman, which I thought was lovely.) I went back inside, made the tea and put out some homemade biscuits. We talked about the bakery, her and Jean settling into their new dwelling, and other things. She told me both of them loved their dwelling, and had enjoyed going to the market in Paris and buying furniture. The villagers welcomed them and Charlotte had made some lovely friends. Naturally Jean was at the bakery all day, and on the odd occasion Charlotte would help. As we were drinking our tea, Charlotte looked at me and said, "Maman, may I ask you something?"

"Of course my dear, what is it?"

She hesitated and then said, "I've noticed a small grave at the side of the dwelling, I wondered who it was." I looked at the small grave and tears welled up inside me. "Oh Maman, I did not intend to upset you."

"It's all right Charlotte, even after all these years I still miss my most loyal, faithful companion – my cat Snooka who passed at the age of seventeen. Would you like to hear her story?" Charlotte smiled and nodded.

"Just after I'd inherited the bakery, there was a loud banging on the back bakery door. I asked who it was before I opened the door and a childlike voice said, 'Please, Madame, take her or she will be killed. Please, Madame.' I opened the door and saw a child of about six holding a bundle in his hands. 'Who's going to kill what?' I asked. With that, he pushed the bundle into my hands and ran off. I took whatever it was inside and put it carefully on the table. Slowly I removed the cloth and was surprised at what I saw. A small brown/black kitten with large eyes looked up at me. I then understood what the child meant. Every now and then the horrific practice of rounding up cats and kittens took place, and I'm glad to say I never saw it. Men would catch them and then throw them alive onto a bonfire. I looked at this kitten and said, 'Well, what on earth am I going to do with you?" The kitten miaowed, slowly stood up and looked around, then sat down and started purring. I found an old saucer, and filled it with water and gave it to the kitten, which lapped most of it up.

"All of a sudden it jumped off the table and ran into a corner. Had I frightened it? I heard a scuffle and the kitten came to me and dropped a dead mouse at my feet. I looked at the dead mouse and shrieked louder than I thought. The kitten ran under the table, and then someone banged on the door. 'Lesley, it's Aramis, are you all right?' I opened the door and pulled him in and pointed to the mouse. 'Lesley, it's a dead mouse, nothing to be frightened of,' he said, laughing. 'Oh Aramis, sorry I shrieked louder than I thought, I have seen dead mice before,' and with that picked the mouse up by the tail and threw it out the back door. I then told Aramis the story. 'Where is it?' he asked. I replied it was under the table. Aramis found the kitten, picked it up and it snuggled into his jacket. He examined it and said, 'You have a lady mouser and she's gorgeous, and I would say she is about six months old. She doesn't have any injuries or unwanted guests, in fact she's in fine health. She will make a good companion and keep the bakery mouse free.' Aramis handed me the kitten that immediately cuddled into me, purring.

"That night I took the kitten upstairs to my parlour, and as soon as I was in bed she was there cuddled up to me and fell asleep." I wasn't sure how Tala would react to this but she took to the kitten straight away, of course I couldn't tell this to Charlotte. "The following morning I showed her to the workers, and they all fell in love with her. I wasn't sure what to feed her. Laurens went out the door and five minutes later came back with fish, which he gutted and cooked for her, and he did that most days. He also made a couple of boxes and filled them with dirt. One he put in my parlour, the other by the back bakery door. She knew what they were for. I had to think of a name for her. She had a habit of sneaking up behind the workforce and one day Laurens had bent down to put some fish in her dish when she jumped up onto his back. Catherine laughed and said, 'She snuck up on you, Laurens.' I looked at the kitten and she ran over to me and I picked her up. 'Umm, snuck, snucks, snucki, snoki, Snooka. That's it, I'm going to call you Snooka."

"Snooka soon settled in and she was a good mouser, and soon no mice were to be seen. She made 'friends' with Hercules the carthorse, and sometimes would jump from the beams onto his back! She never made any attempts to escape, she never extended her claws; she'd found a loving owner and friends, but there were times when Snooka snuck out. One day I'd gone to the garrison to ask Tréville's advice on a matter and after I'd been there for about ten minutes we heard a noise at the door. Tréville opened the door, and yes, cautiously in ran Snooka. I was stunned, how on earth...? Tréville picked her up, smiled and said, 'Well where did you come from?' I told him what had happened. He couldn't believe she got up the steps, never mind followed me. She snuggled up against his neck and slowly licked his ear, and he fell in love with her. When I went to leave he carried her down the steps to where my brothers were sitting at the table. 'Aahh, our newest recruit,' said Aramis. The others looked at him as he took her from Tréville. 'Gentlemen, meet Snooka, who now lives with our sister.' She was cuddled by all of them; I was worried Porthos might crush her, but he was a gentle giant, and like everyone else, they all fell in love with her. I'm sure the Musketeers visited the bakery only to see her. One of the strange things she did was to curl around your neck and go to sleep.

"When I had got back to the garrison, after Rochefort had kidnapped me, Catherine told me Snooka was miaowing all the time, it was like she knew I was hurting. Eventually Catherine brought her to me, with Tréville's permission. I had moved up to his office, and Tréville carefully put her on the bed. Straight away she was purring and curled up at my side. Snooka was happy to go up the steps, but going down was difficult for her, so she thought of a way. If Tréville was in the office she would go to the door and miaow, Tréville would then carry her down the steps. If Tréville was not there she would go and sit at the top step and again miaow. My brothers or any of the other Musketeers would then walk up, pick her up, and put her down at the bottom of the steps. She would spend hours playing in the stables or around the training areas. Tréville always made sure she was fed and had water, and always went out to do what she had to do before we all slept for the night. Usually she would curl up by my side, but sometimes she would be under Tréville's blanket curled up with him. One day she must have been a bit bored; Tréville was working at his desk, she jumped up and laid across all of his paperwork. Tréville smiled and said, 'Now what do you want? How can I do my work with you laying there?' Snooka replied by rolling onto her back – she wanted her tummy rubbed, so Tréville obliged. Then she got up, went to the edge of his desk and sat there. Tréville picked up his quill to carry on doing his writing, but Snooka had other ideas. Every time he moved the quill she put her paw out to play with it. I had awoken and was watching her and giggling. Tréville looked at me with his eyebrow raised, and said, 'Look, Snooka. Lesley is awake." That worked, she was off his desk and on the bed with me in seconds. I'm sure Tréville never thought one of his duties, as Captain, would be cat sitter.

"She had her 'days', with each of Tréville's men. When D'Artagnan was on stable duty, which was often, Snooka would sit and watch him from one of the stalls, then suddenly she would jump on his back – how many times did he fall over? She would then walk round the stables, like she was inspecting them, and would then start scratching the hay all over the place. D'Artagnan would then chase her with the broom – it was hilarious to watch.

"Aramis had the job of cleaning all the swords, muskets and

pistols. He would lay them out on the table, and every time he moved the rag up and down, Snooka would paw at it. I think it took Aramis twice as long! One day he put his bag of shots on the table. Snooka's curiosity got the better of her and she pawed the pouch around until it fell on the floor. All the shots rolled out of the pouch all over the yard. Naturally, Aramis was not amused, and as he bent to pick them all up, Snooka decided to pounce on them and scatter them even further. In the end Porthos picked her up whilst everyone else picked up the shots.

She was always wary of Porthos and I think that was because he was such a big man – a giant to her. One day all of us were sitting eating at the table in the yard when I noticed Snooka jump on the end of the bench by Porthos. As he had his back to her, he didn't see her 'steal' his piece of chicken, and jump down. I nudged Tréville and pointed to her with my eyes. Tréville put his hand over his mouth to hide his smile. Porthos went to get his piece of chicken and couldn't believe it gone, but shrugged it off and thought he'd eaten it, so he got another two pieces and put them on his plate. Again, Snooka jumped up, but apart from Porthos we all saw her take one piece, and we all burst out laughing. Porthos looked and looked again and then saw Snooka. He scooped her up and was about to scold her when she licked his nose. All he did was cuddle her.

"Athos, funnily enough, she looked after. Whenever he had a hangover, most mornings, she was up and out of the bakery early. She would jump up to Athos's windowsill and push the half-drained wine bottles under his bed. When one of the normal Musketeers put the water on his sill, she would jump up on his bed and start purring in his ear. This would wake Athos up. Sometimes he went to push her off, but she was too quick for him. If he put the blanket back over himself, she would pull it off. If that didn't work she would lick the bottom of his feet, and that did wake him up. He always cuddled her – in fact they all did – she was a part of their family.

"I remember our wedding day. I left the bakery a week before the wedding and took Snooka with me. I took a carriage as I had a couple of bags with me, and I was worried Snooka might try and jump out of my arms, whilst on the horse. Snooka curled up on the seat and slept most of the way. When we arrived she was very wary, and stayed on the bed, and never ventured out. Tréville made her a large tray with dirt, where she could do what she had to. Helene met her and when she came round Snooka would curl up on her lap. The day of the wedding, I made sure she had something to eat and drink, and left her curled up asleep on my bed. I wasn't sure how she would take to sharing it with Tréville as well. Everybody was in the church and I was at Tréville's side and just about to say my vows. All of a sudden people started giggling. Tréville and I turned to see what was going on, and giggled as well. There was Snooka walking down the aisle, looking at every pew as she walked past. She walked past both of us and round the back of the priest, and then came and sat down and shuffled back so she was right between us. She looked up at the priest, who was also smiling, and miaowed, as though to say, 'Carry on,' which we did. When we both walked back down the aisle together, Snooka had fallen asleep on what little bit of a train I had. Catherine picked her up and carried her back to the dwelling.

Later on after Tréville and I had moved to the dwelling and Catherine had taken over my rooms, I thought Snooka would stay with her, after all she was only used to the bakery and the garrison. Oh no, not Snooka. After I left to have our sons, Snooka went missing. Everyone, even some of the garrison Musketeers, were out looking for her – alas, nothing. I was heartbroken, if only I'd taken her with me to the dwelling, as I thought she would be content at the bakery. The day I gave birth, as you know, I had a complication and was sleeping for two days. On the fifth day, in the evening, after Tréville, Helene and the wet nurse had settled the twins down, he came in with something in his arms. 'Look who I found in the barn the day you gave birth,' he said. My eyes lit up and tears welled up in my eyes, it was Snooka. 'Oh Tréville, is she all right? She looks so thin?' He replied, 'Hush my love, I have had her checked by the Head Stableman, who looks after the horses at the palace. He said she has a few bites and scratches, which will heal, and apart from those she is fine. I have made her a small straw pallet and she has been sleeping contentedly in the barn, in a closed pen, until you are well enough and then she can move back in with us. Now, sleep, you need your rest, my love.' Oh, what a relief, but we would never know how on earth she left the bakery, crossed through war-torn Paris to get to us, and stayed alive.

"After I was well, Snooka came back into the dwelling and Tréville put her bed in the parlour. Slowly she gained the weight she had lost. When I returned to the bakery, I worried she would try and follow me, so I arranged with Chloe to look after her. As time went on we realised Snooka was going nowhere. She never made any attempt to leave the dwelling or the back garden. Maybe something had happened on her adventure and that's why now she stayed close to us. She also loved to lie in the sun. She adored the twins until they started screaming – off she went to the barn. The day my brothers came round, after they had returned from the war, she ran straight to Aramis. She never forgot them. A huge fuss was made over her and eventually she curled up on Aramis's lap and slept, until I came out with the twins. Then she just went and laid by another of the trees, as if to say, 'I've had my time, now it's theirs.' I did have to laugh at her antics.

"Once Sunkwa returned, they were inseparable. When Sunkwa was in the field, both of them would run around. I worried Sunkwa would accidentally kick her, but it never happened. If she wasn't asleep on her pallet, in the parlour when we retired for the night, we knew where she was as Tréville had seen her with his own eyes one night. 'My love, come and look,' he said. He took my hand and we quietly entered the barn. Sunkwa was laid down sleeping and Snooka was curled up under his chin. She raised her head and gave us a look that said, 'Do you mind? Animals trying to sleep here.' Both Tréville and I smiled and left the barn. Most of the time though, even though Tréville and I slept entwined in each other's arms, when we woke she would be between the pair of us. How on earth she never suffocated was beyond me. She eventually ventured out into the village. Everyone knew her and looked out for her, no wonder she gained a little weight!!! When Sunkwa passed, Snooka must have gone into mourning. She would miaow every night in the barn, until Tréville or myself went and brought her into the dwelling. Snooka lived a long, happy and contented life until she was seventeen. One night I noticed she was having problems moving. Tréville got Aramis to look at her and he told us her time was coming to an end. Two days later Snooka passed away in my arms, and I saw her spirit rise. I was absolutely heartbroken; for months nothing would console me but eventually I coped with my grief. I will always remember something Porthos said – 'Grief fades, you'll still have your memories. Treasure them, it's a gift.'"

Tears were rolling down my cheeks and when I looked at Charlotte she too was in tears. "Oh Maman, what a lovely story," she said.

About an hour later Charlotte left and I promised I would visit her at her new dwelling the following week, and then my thoughts went back to Snooka. What I couldn't tell Charlotte was about Snooka and Tala. The first time, after the twins had been born, I decided I was fit enough to let Tala run, and so I went over to the forest. As Tala was trotting round, all of a sudden something jumped on her back – it was Snooka. She shook her off and Snooka fell to the ground. Tala went up and nudged her, took her in her mouth and ran gently through the forest, then put her back on the ground when the run was over. After that Snooka always came with me; sometimes she would run with us, or she was on Tala's back, or if she was tired Tala would carry her in her mouth. They became great friends.

One night we were so busy playing in the forest I didn't hear the hooves of horses. All of a sudden my father appeared, and put his fingers to his lips and made the sign for us to lay flat. Snooka had never seen my father's spirit and his wolves before, so she backed up and hissed and all her fur stood on end. Tala quickly calmed her by licking her fur and nudging her towards her side. Luckily we were near a very large shrub where all of us could hide. I looked through Tala's eyes and saw about twenty riders coming towards us. As they drew near I signed in relief – they were Musketeers, who seemed to be lost. They couldn't see my father, so he went up to the lead horse and guided them all out of the forest. When he came back I knew he would be angry with me, I had nearly made a fatal mistake. "Tala return, Spirit of the Wolf appear," he said angrily. Luckily my dress was nearby and I hurriedly got dressed. "My daughter, what do you think you were doing, and what is that?" he said, pointing to Snooka, who had jumped into my arms.

"Oh Father, I am so sorry," I said with my head down, "I have been here many, many times and never has anyone come, and this is Snooka, my cat."

He came towards me and put his finger under my chin and I looked up at him. I could feel Snooka shaking, she was afraid of him. "Daughter, even though they were Musketeers, you would have been shot on sight. Don't ever let your guard down again. I cannot be at your side all the time, in fact it was my wolf who picked up on the danger." He then looked at Snooka, who had her ears back. "Come, little one, do not be afraid, I will not hurt you," he said, and then stroked Snooka's head. She immediately calmed and started purring at him. "I am being called, Daughter, I must go. Please listen when you are Tala, next time I might not appear." I learnt a lesson that night.

When Snooka passed Tala whimpered and grieved for a long time at the loss of her friend. We had lovely and happy memories.

R.I.P. SNOOKA

CHAPTER 41

Back Together

Ten years have passed since the love of my life went away. My heart is still broken in two and will never mend.

I visited Armand and Anne as often as I could, and I always had a warm welcome. Sometimes I would stay for a couple of days at the house, but it never felt the same. I always stayed for the Christmas time. It was also lovely to see my grandchildren growing up, and Jean and Charlotte always joined us. Jean and Armand had decided, in memory of Tréville, to have a statue done of him, and now it was at the head of his grave. Both of our sons and their families were happy and contented with their lives.

Amanda and I still wrote to each as often as we could. She told me the sad news, in various letters that Athos, Aramis, D'Artagnan and Constance had all passed. I though how nice it would be if they were all with Tréville. Amanda's letters stopped coming and via a friend I found out she and Porthos had both passed as well. Lots of our friends in the village had now passed, including Helene. That was another very sad day for me, but at the reading of her will I was in for a shock. As she had no family she had left her dwelling to me. All I could do was sell it, which seemed wrong. Then Jean said to me one day, "Mother, I have had an idea about Helene's dwelling. Why don't I buy it for myself and Charlotte and then we would be close to you? Your health worries us."

I replied, "Helene would have liked that."

Jean sold his dwelling, but I would take no funds from him. I told him to make use of it, maybe in the bakery. So after three months Jean and Charlotte moved into the dwelling and I saw them nearly every day.

I went and visited the solicitors to change my will, so when I passed, the bakery would go only to Jean. The dwelling would go to both of my sons, which I wanted them to keep. I knew one of my grandchildren, Amilee, was in love with the dwelling, and she always said she would live there, so maybe one day her wish would come true. I decided to go and have a look at the bakery. It looked so different now, as did the lane. The bakery now had a double window with a new door in the middle and various pastries, bread, pies and new things that Jean had produced on the shelves. The chocolate room was now part of the shop. The wall that divided them was gone, making a huge area. They still did chocolate and something new called tea and coffee. Jean had decided to promote one of the men so he and his wife now occupied what used to be my rooms.

Jean had lots of private orders, which kept him very busy. The day I visited he was away doing a wedding so I did not venture inside. The lane was longer than I remembered and had various outlets of different suppliers. Where there only used to be one tavern there was now three. The market had really grown in size. You could now buy livestock (mainly chickens), rugs, flowers, utensils, lots of stalls with vegetables and fruits – one stall sold a drink called cider, which was made by crushing up apples. Cider became the second-best drink, after wine of course. I then slowly walked to the garrison, which hadn't changed much at all. I stood by the gate and looked up to the balcony and could have sworn I saw Tréville stood there waving to me. Tears welled in my eyes and I returned to my carriage, which I'd left at the bakery, and drove back to the dwelling.

When I got back to the dwelling I was very tired and closed my eyes to rest. All of a sudden I was walking through the forest listening to the birds singing, taking in the clean air with all its different smells. Oh, how I wished Tala and I could run, but Tala was now too old to run, as was I. We had had many brilliant runs over the years. I was then walking round the village, past the tavern, over the bridge and then sat on the bench, where Tréville first told me he loved me, and then I was at his memorial that the villagers had done. I opened my eyes and I was back in my parlour. I knew some of the new people in the village and I believe I was called the "nice old lady"! They were right, I was an old lady now, on sticks to help me walk. I partook of a small meal and later on retired for the night. I had always shed tears for my beloved Tréville since the day he passed and this night was no exception, but then his arms would encircle me and I would know he was with me.

As I started to drift off, I started dreaming. I was standing in a large field with a river flowing by. My father, mother, the four wolves (Motomo, Father's wolf, and the two spirit wolves), and Swallowtail appeared to me. As soon as I saw them I ran to them, feeling like a young woman again. I hugged and kissed my parents. It felt so good to be back in their arms. I hugged Swallowtail. "Welcome, Spirit of the Wolf. Come, we have surprises for you," she said. I looked behind her and saw three tipis. From the first tipi Katherine, Liz, Monsieur Rennard and Helene emerged. They all walked towards me as I did to them and we all hugged and kissed each other on the cheek. The flap of the second tipi opened, and much to my surprise out walked Athos, Aramis, D'Artagnan, Porthos and Amanda. I went to them and they all hugged and kissed me as well. I looked around and smiled at my family and friends, but could not speak due to the emotions inside of me. "Come," said Swallowtail, "there is someone who has missed you very much."

I walked into the last tipi and there stood Tréville, wearing his Indian wedding shirt and breeches. I looked down and saw I was also wearing my Indian wedding dress and my hair was in plaits with the sacred feathers. "Oh my love, my love, how I have missed you." I ran into his arms, tears rolling down my face and we kissed and kissed, making up for what we had missed for years.

He said, "My beautiful Indian wife."

I felt something go round my neck and looked down to see Tréville had put my heart necklace on, and I felt the heart beating. I then felt something brush my legs and I looked down to see my beloved Snooka. I picked her up and she cuddled into me, purring in my arms. Tréville and I talked about everything and anything. About an hour later, Swallowtail called us out, and we walked out of the tipi hand in hand.

"Spirit of the Wolf, I have someone who very much wants to

meet you," said Swallowtail, and as she moved aside I saw the most beautiful wolf I had ever seen.

"Spirit of the Wolf, meet Tala." I looked at Swallowtail in shock.

"Tala? But Tala is with me."

"Not anymore, Tala is a free spirit now."

Tala padded over to me and I put my arms around her neck and hugged her. Snooka jumped from my arms onto Tala's back, and was head rubbing her.

"Thank you, Tala, for being with me all these years. What am I going to do without you?"

Suddenly I looked at Tréville and he smiled and said, "It's all right my love, Swallowtail has told me everything. I always knew you were very special. Swallowtail has also honoured me by telling me your story and the healing you did on me when I was stabbed, and why you could not tell me," he said.

I went to him and kissed him gently on the lips and said, "You have to thank my father, as it was him who helped me to heal you. I loved you even then and have never stopped." Tears filled my eyes and Tréville took me in his arms and kissed my forehead.

Swallowtail then said, "Tréville, as you know Spirit of the Wolf is Indian. You did not know this when you wed her, and now you are one of us, the Tribe has asked me to honour you with an Indian name. You will be known as Takoda, and it means 'a friend to everyone'.

I looked at my husband and smiled. "That name suits you and is true," I said.

Swallowtail then said, "It is time for us to depart now, the Reservation awaits."

I looked at Tréville, and he held his hand out to me. "Come, my loving wife." I walked over to Tréville and put my hand in his. I watched as Katherine, Liz, Helene and Monsieur Rennard walked one way and then my mother, father, the Musketeers along with Amanda, and the wolves walked another way, and one by one vanished. Tala came to my side and Snooka jumped back into my arms.

I looked at Swallowtail and said, "Thank you, Swallowtail, for letting me be a part of this, I will now have more memories to hold on to. I will miss you all so much, until it is my time."

I looked at Tréville and said, "Tréville, you'll need to take Snooka." Snooka would not leave my arms. Swallowtail took Snooka and gave her to Tréville, and she immediately curled round his neck, purring so loudly.

Swallowtail then smiled, took my hand and put it into Tréville's, and said, "Come, Spirit of the Wolf, you are with us now forever," and led myself, Tréville, Snooka and Tala towards the Reservation. That was when I then realised my earth world was over.

"Swallowtail I must go back, our sons will be so upset to think I have passed without them being with me."

Swallowtail looked at me and said, "Do not worry, they were with you. White Wolf made sure Jean and Armand were with you, he guided them to you just before you passed. Take my hand, close your eyes and I will show you."

I took her hand and closed my eyes. I was back in my bedchamber floating above my bed looking down at myself. I heard voices and saw Jean and Armand walk in.

"Did you feel something was wrong?" said Jean to his brother.

"Yes, I just knew I had to get here immediately," he replied.

I was mumbling something and both of them sat either side of me on the bed and took a hand each. "Mother, if you can hear us, we are both here," said Jean. My eyes flickered open quickly, I looked at both of them and then closed my eyes again and I smiled. Suddenly I sat up in the bed and held my arms out in front of me and said, "Tréville, oh Tréville, you're here. I can see you stood there with your arms open, waiting for me. I'm coming, my beloved, I'm coming." As suddenly as I sat up I laid down again.

Armand looked at Jean and said, "Mother is with Father again." They both kissed my cheek and I saw the tears fall.

I opened my eyes and I was back with Swallowtail. I looked at Tréville and he looked at me, then he gently kissed my lips. From now on I would always be with the love of my life, my loyal Snooka, my family, my friends, Amanda and the Musketeers and Tala and the wolves forever.

CHAPTER 42

The Epilogue – Part 1

Slowly I opened my eyes and looked around. I seemed to be in some sort of tent, and I felt so weak. The flap of the tent opened and a woman walked in dressed in what looked like strange clothes. "Welcome, Tréville, please do not be afraid, I am here to help you."

"Where am I, and why do I feel so weak?" I asked.

"All will be told to you, Tréville, but now you just need to rest, eat, drink and regain your strength. I have made you a remedy that will help, please drink." I took the drink, sipped it at first; it tasted fine, so I drank the rest. I felt warmth go through my body, and I also felt a calming effect. I closed my eyes and drifted back off to slumber.

When I woke later, a younger woman was sitting on the floor, and she looked like she was doing something with some clothes. My eyes seem clearer now and I looked around the tent. I saw a uniform hung up, along with a sword, pistol, hat, boots and a necklace. The necklace seemed familiar, but I could not think. I put my hand up and touched my chest, to find I was naked. Slowly I moved my hand down lower – thank heavens, I had something on.

"Welcome, Tréville, I am pleased to meet you at last." I turned and the woman was stood at my side. She looked like somebody, but who? "My name is Chipara. The other lady from earlier is Swallowtail and you are on the Reservation." I looked at her. What on earth was she talking about? "Tréville, what is the last thing you remember? And I ask for a reason."

"I can remember nothing, my mind is confused," I replied.

"Please do not worry, you are in a safe place, but time is needed, all will slowly become clear. I will leave you to rest, but first, drink, it will help you." I thanked her and took the drink.

As I slept, dreams came to me, but they were all muddled up. In one I was wearing the uniform I had seen hung up, in another a beautiful woman was in my arms, then I was a child running with other people, then I was on a battlefield. I woke up, sweat pouring down my brow.

"Calm, Tréville, calm," said a voice. I looked to see the other woman with me. She smiled and said, "My name is Swallowtail, and I hope, with time, I can help you through this time."

"Maybe it would help if you told me where I am, what's going on, why can't I remember?"

She took my hands in hers and said, "I cannot help you with regards to your memories, and it is against our laws. As you gain your strength so your memories will return and then everything will become clear. I can, however, help you regain your strength and I think it's time you left the tipi and went outside for some air, it will do you good. You have been in here for a month. Let me help you up."

"Did you say I've been here a month?" I said, stunned.

"Don't worry about it, time here is endless. Here are clothes for you to wear, when you are ready, come outside," and she walked out the tent. I put the strange clothes on. They fitted well and I went out of the flap. I put my hand to my eyes; the light was bright but I soon adjusted.

The air felt good as I breathed it in. I looked around and saw I was in a large field, and there was a river to my left and another couple of tents to my right. On the horizon were a lot of trees. There was a sense of calm here. It was peaceful. I heard a noise behind me and turned to see two white animals approaching me. "Fear not, Tréville, they will not hurt you, wolves are our protectors," said Swallowtail. "Come walk with me down to the river," she said. I went to walk but as my feet touched the ground it felt strange and I thought I was going to fall. "Let me help you," said Swallowtail, and took my arm. With her help we walked down to the river, to a spot where a blanket was laid on the ground and what looked like food.

Suddenly I said, "Picnic, men, wife, children."

"Tréville, are you all right?"

I replied, "What?"

Swallowtail looked at me and said, "You just said, 'Picnic, men, wife, children.' Did you remember something?" I looked at her and I had no idea what she was talking about, I just smiled and sat down on the blanket. "Please, Tréville, help yourself, you need nourishment and I hope the wine is acceptable."

I took a piece of meat, which Swallowtail told me was chicken, it tasted lovely. There were other things to eat also. I then realised how hungry I actually was and ate rather a lot, but Swallowtail didn't seem to mind. The drink was very acceptable but I only had a small glass, not sure what wine was. I was looking at the river; it looked so inviting, but at the same time, it meant something else to me, but what? I cried out, "Why can't I remember?" and put my head in my hands.

"Tréville, please stay calm, it is going to take time. I know you want answers straight away and everything is strange, but soon all will be well," said Swallowtail gently.

I looked at her with tears in my eyes and said, "I feel so lost, please help me."

Swallowtail took my hands and said, "I will help you as much as I can. Let's start at the beginning. I can see some things you know. Tell me what you see."

I looked at her and said, "We are in a field, that is a river, this is a blanket, these are clothes, that is food, this is a glass, those are plates, over there are trees. The sky is blue, and the sun is yellow. There are three tents."

Swallowtail smiled and said, "We call them tipis, not tents. Come, let's go to your tipi, see what you can tell me is there." My walking was better now.

As I entered the tipi, I said, "Bed, blanket, pillow, uniform, sword, pistol, hat, boots, necklace, chair and table."

"What is your uniform made up of?" asked Swallowtail. I looked at her. I was feeling like a child!!

"Breeches, shirt, doublet, belt, boots and hat."

"See now how you are remembering things? Your strength is returning and soon your memories will start appearing. I will get you a quill and ink, and something to write on. It will help you when you start remembering your dreams to write them down. Do you remember if you can swim?"

I replied, "I think so, I do this with my arms," and moved them out in front of me and then to each side.

"I will have large cloths brought to you, and then, when you wish, you can swim in the river, but do not go too far to start with, build slowly. I can see by the look on your face you think I am treating you like a child. I do not mean to insult you, Tréville, that is not my intention. You are doing well and as I have said before I will help you all I can, but everything will be done in stages until you are whole again."

At that moment I felt embarrassed and said, "I apologise, Swallowtail, and I thank you for helping me. Can I ask, where am I?"

Swallowtail smiled and said, "You are in a place called the Reservation. This will mean nothing to you at the moment, but you are free to walk wherever you want, by no means are you a prisoner. If I am not here and you need anything, Chipara is in the other tipi. You will always have company to start with, as the two white wolves will stay with you, just in case you have a problem. This will seem stupid to you, but they communicate with me by their howls, so if you fell down and hurt yourself I would know immediately. I can see the confusion in your face, don't worry, and the wolves will not hurt you. They are your friends. Whenever you want to eat or drink, food and drink will always be available either in your tipi, outside your tipi or down by the river. The clothes you are wearing are Indian clothes and more shirts and what you call breeches and undergarments will appear in your tipi soon. You will also have moccasins to wear on your feet; you will find them comfortable, but if you wish to wear your boots that is fine. I'm sorry, I have to go now, I am needed elsewhere. I suggest you now rest, your day has been exhausting."

She was right, I was feeling quite weary. I undressed, washed and got into my bed and closed my eyes. As usual I dreamed but in the morning, I couldn't believe it – I remembered. I saw the quill, ink and paper and wrote it down. I also noticed on my chair a pile of Indian clothes for me.

I decided to go down to the river and see if I could swim. I took a couple of large cloths with me and another undergarment and walked down. Strange, I didn't remember seeing that clump of trees there before. I went into them and undressed, but leaving my undergarment on, and seeing a gentle slope down to the river I walked down and slowly eased myself into the water. Well, time to find out. I put my arms out in front of me and pushed off into the water. I went straight under the water, but it didn't frighten me. After a couple of times, I was swimming. I didn't go far, I remembered what Swallowtail told me. I went back to the clump of trees, took my wet undergarment off, and then I remembered I had a long scar on my leg, but now it was gone. Strange. I dried myself, dressed and returned to my tipi.

Swallowtail was stood outside my tipi. "Tréville, I see you can swim, I am so pleased."

I smiled and said, "That's not all, and I have something to show you."

We went into the tipi and I gave her the paper. She read and smiled. "Tréville, this is great news. Please don't lose heart if tonight you do not remember. You are on the way. Come, let's eat and I will ask Chipara to join us," and with that she went to the other tipi. I watched as Swallowtail and Chipara walked towards me. My eyes never left Chipara, I didn't realise I was staring so intently at her until Swallowtail said, "Tréville, I think you make Chipara feel not welcome."

I said, "Please forgive me, Chipara, but you remind me so much of someone, but at the moment I can't remember who."

Chipara replied, "Do not worry, it will come, now eat and drink, please."

After we had finished our meal Chipara asked me about my dream. I said, "I started in a village with quite a few dwellings. The village was empty, as were the dwellings. I was then in a yard, with buildings all round it. I walked through the yard and went under an arch. One way was a large area of ground, and the other way also had ground with trees and something you get water from. My last part was a large house, so many rooms, again all empty. There was a garden out the front and back and a river. It was strange, there was only me, no other people."

Chipara and Swallowtail both glanced at each other, and then Chipara said, "A well is where you get water from. You lower a bucket down on a rope, until it reaches the water, and when it's full you bring it up again."

"Thank you, Chipara, I can see that now."

That night I dreamed of the same places as the night before, but this time a few people were there, but I could not make out their faces. The next day, and every day, first thing, I went down to the river to swim, longer and longer each time. I could feel my body adjusting to this daily task, and it also gave me something to look forward to. I also started walking further afield – this Reservation went on forever. No matter how far I went though, when I decided to return I would turn around and the three tipis would be quite near to me. The two white animals I now knew were wolves, went everywhere with me. Hopefully soon all this would make sense to me. Every night I dreamed the same dream; more and more people appeared but I could still not see their faces. Then one night I was dreaming of being in the yard when a man passed me in a uniform, sitting on a horse. Then I was a child running through a field. I could see the faces of the other people, and I knew them.

In the morning Swallowtail was standing outside my tipi. "You remembered something, Tréville?" she said. I looked at her, stunned. How did she know these things? "Go swim, Tréville, we will talk on your return." So I did. When I returned, food and drink were on the table and after we had eaten she asked me what I remembered.

"I was running through a field towards two other people. It was my mother and father. Two other children were running with me, they were my brother and sister. I can't remember their names though. When I dreamed of the yard, a man in a uniform passed me on a horse, something tells me he was a soldier."

Swallowtail said, "I am so pleased, now things will come, hopefully, to you quickly, and then everything can be revealed to you. Don't forget to write it all down, and then as you remember names you can put them at the side. Now this is going to sound not right, but do you know your name?"

I looked at her and said, "It's Tréville."

"No, Tréville, your full name. Your last name is Tréville, but that is what everyone called you."

"Called me," I said, and then something dawned. "I'm dead, aren't I?" I could see by the look on Swallowtail's face I was right. "It's all right, Swallowtail, you can tell me because now all this makes sense to me."

Swallowtail took my hands and said, "Are you sure?"

I replied, "Yes."

"Very well then, yes, you are right, you passed six months ago. As you know I am Swallowtail and I am a medicine woman for an Indian tribe. Chipara is actually English, and she married White Wolf from my tribe, you have yet to meet her husband. Everything you see is called the Reservation, but the Reservation will change due to events in your life. There are three of them. When people of my tribe pass, this is where they come. For reasons I cannot tell you yet, there is a special reason why you are here, as are a couple of other people. Your strength is gaining every day. Time here is quicker, but endless. Does this make any sense to you, Tréville?"

I listened to everything she said. "Yes, it does, it's like a puzzle in my mind slowly being put together, and I know I will get there, I'm determined to. I need to go to my tipi and get something." I went in and picked up the necklace and took it back outside. "This is something significant in my life, isn't it? Now I hold it a vision of the heart beating comes to me."

"I'm sorry, Tréville, as I've said before, I cannot help you with your memories."

I smiled and said, "Thank you Swallowtail, for telling me. I feel better now I understand. There is one thing I don't understand. I remembered I had a long scar on my left leg, now it's not there, how can that be?"

Swallowtail replied, "As you regain your strength, the nourishment we give helps mend all injuries." I looked at my chest and saw I had a huge scar there. How did I get it?

As time went on more and more of my memories returned. I remembered my parents were called Jean and Marie, my brother and sister Pierre and Louise. I also had half brothers and sisters – Pierre, Arnaud, Marie and Jeanne. My full name was Jean Armand de Peyrer and when my father died I became Comte de Troisville, but my father had already changed the name to Tréville. One night I dreamed of a palace, and I was stood in front of the King with four other soldiers, but I had the uniform on from my tipi. I now saw more people in the village and the yard, and the faces of four people in the house.

One day as I returned from my swim, I saw a tall Indian man standing outside Chipara's tipi. He came to me and said, "You Tréville, me White Wolf, Chipara wife." We shook hands. "Come, sit, eat," he said.

Suddenly Swallowtail appeared. "White Wolf, you have returned, it is good to see you again. I see you have met Tréville."

He nodded, then said to me, "Memory, how does it go?"

I replied my memories were coming quickly, but there was still lots to remember and names were not good.

"Will come, you must not think much too. Drink new remedy Swallowtail make, and draw faces." He looked at her and she nodded. "I go now, see wife. You good to see," and with that he left.

Swallowtail smiled and said, "His English is not good." I smiled as well. That afternoon I got more paper and started drawing the faces from my memories. Soon, as I had lots of them, White Wolf made a large board, and with his dagger made tiny sticks so I could stick them in the paper and put them on thc board.

The more I looked at the drawings, the more frustrated I got that I couldn't remember, so when I got to that stage I either went for a swim or a walk. Then a really weird thing happened. As Chipara and I were talking she sneezed. *Aattchoo.* Suddenly I said, "Athos."

She looked at me and said, "Who?" I went and got my drawings.

"This, this one is Athos," I said. "This is Porthos, this is Aramis, this is D'Artagnan, they were my men – they were my Musketeers. Oh, Chipara, I remember. I was Captain Tréville of the King's Musketeers; the King was Louis XIII and his Queen was Anne of

Austria. The yard in my dream is the garrison. The uniform in my tipi is my Captain's uniform."

Chipara was delighted and laughed and said, "All that from a sneeze. Oh, Tréville, I am so happy for you," and kissed my hand.

I looked at her and said, "I kissed a lady's hand and I know she is the key of my memories. Why can't I see her or remember, Chipara?"

A voice behind me said, "Now more of your memories have returned it will come, soon you will know, but do not dwell on it, let it come naturally." It was Swallowtail. "Come, I think you deserve a hug," she said, and all three of us hugged each other. I felt good, really good.

That night I dreamed as usual, but this time it was a nightmare. There was a woman, no face; she got shot, and I saw myself running to her. My men were there and another woman, whose face I could see. Then the same woman was at the garrison with an injury to the side of her head and other injuries – her hip gave her problems. Then she was in another room and her body was mutilated, blood flowing from lots of wounds. She had been cut down her chest and arms. I could not look at her, so much anger; she died, she came back. My last bit of the dream was her riding away on a horse. I followed but she went further and further away. I woke crying out, "Come back, please come back." Sweat was pouring from me.

A hand touched my shoulder and I looked to see White Wolf. "Calm, Tréville, you in tipi. Here, drink, will calm you." As I drank I could feel the warm liquid going through me and I drifted back to sleep. In the morning I drew the picture of the woman. Again, she was familiar, but it was the faceless woman who troubled me the most.

Chipara was outside and gave me a hug. "You all right, Tréville? White Wolf told me what happened. Do you think you can tell me your dream?" I said I would but first I needed to swim and refresh myself.

Later on I told both Chipara and Swallowtail my nightmare. I looked at the drawing of the woman and said, "I don't know why but she is connected to one of my men." Both of them could see I was struggling about the faceless woman and told me to calm, think about something else. Chipara gave me some books to read, which helped.

It was whilst I was reading that another memory came back. I was reading about a wedding and then realised the woman I had drawn was with Porthos, but as of yet her name did not come to me. She was also linked to my faceless woman. That night as I slept I returned to the village, to one dwelling in particular. It now had furniture in it and in one of the cabinets was my uniform. I then returned to the house, again full of furniture. The house had lots of rooms and the four people I had dreamed of before lived in the basement. Then I was at the garrison and started walking down a lane. I stopped outside a bakery shop. I went in, people were there working. I woke up. As usual, I drew what I had seen. I talked to Swallowtail about it but she would give me no answers. I now had more faces. I went for a walk. The wolves didn't follow me anymore now, as they had gone back to White Wolf.

Days later I decided I would try and walk to the forest in the distance. Eventually I got to the edge of it. The forest looked very dense and for some reason I didn't want to venture into it. I saw a clearing with some large rocks and sat down. Suddenly I heard something growling behind me. I turned to see one very large wolf, a smaller one, and four even smaller ones. I knew not to move or look them in the eyes. "Motomo, he is friend, not enemy," said a voice. I looked around – nobody was there. The lead wolf came to me, sniffed and then sat down at my side. He nudged my hand and I stroked him. His fur was so soft. The other wolves also sat with me but at a distance. I stayed there, feeling completely content, until Motomo decided it was time to go, and they all went back into the forest. I could see the tipis in the distance, and was feeling hungry, so started to walk back.

As I passed Chipara's tipi she came out. "Did you enjoy your walk, Tréville?" I replied I did and told her about the wolves. "So you have met Motomo. The other wolf was his mate and their four cubs. I hope he behaved, he can be very naughty," she said, laughing. I told her about the voice and she said it was White Wolf, and he was probably in the forest and I didn't see him. Strange, why didn't he come and speak with me?

After that day I would walk to the forest more often; sometimes Motomo would be there, and we would start playing. He would roll over and let me rub his belly, but the next minute he would be trying to knock me over. I enjoyed it, as it was fun. It was whilst I was running with Motomo that I tripped over a small rock. Motomo came to me immediately, nudging me to get up and whimpering. I told him I was all right and unhurt. At that moment another name came to me – Rock, Rockford, Rochefort. This name put a dread through me and I knew it was linked to my faceless woman. This worried me. I tried to put a face to the name but I couldn't. As I had been told, I didn't dwell on it, my memory would remember when it was ready.

When I returned to my tipi, I looked at the unnamed faces. I looked at the woman. She was linked to Rochefort, but how?

Swallowtail came to me. "Are you all right, Tréville? I believe you had a fall. You are not hurt?" I replied that I was all right and thanked her. How on earth did she know these things, she wasn't there!!

My days were now filled with swimming, walking, reading, eating, talking and sleeping. My dreams came and went and, what seemed like a long time later, another different dream came to me. I was walking round the palace when I saw the woman I'd drawn being held by another man; she looked frightened. Then the Queen called for her, he released her, and she walked towards the Queen. She curtsied and then they walked towards the Queen's chambers. In the morning I looked at the picture. Her name was Amanda, and she was Porthos's wife. The man was Rochefort. I went and sat down by the river and closed my eyes. All sorts of visions came to me. When I opened my eyes I knew exactly who Rochefort was and what he had done, especially to my faceless woman.

When I next saw Swallowtail I told her everything. "You have done so well, Tréville, now you just need a few more to complete all of your memories. They will come, as I always say, give it time. The last one will be your biggest memory."

Nothing happened for some time. I still dreamed but always the woman remained faceless. In one dream though, I was back in the bakery. A man was helping his workforce sort out different items to be baked. I knew this man. Then the man and my faceless woman were on a cart going to the palace, then my dream changed to a huge castle where a wedding was taking place, and I was visiting there and then somewhere else. Then I saw the man in the dwelling in the village, and then he passed away. The faceless woman took his place. When I woke I went for my swim and then walked to the forest. Motomo appeared, but on his own. He came and sat with me. "I wish you could help me remember, Motomo. It's hurting me that I can't remember her, she is obviously someone special to me," and at that tears fell from my eyes. Motomo put his head on my lap and for the first time ever, gently howled. I seem to sit there for a long time, with Motomo, then he took his head off my lap and left, and I walked back to the tipis.

Chipara was waiting for me. Why did she look so familiar to me? "You look sad, Tréville. Can I help in any way?"

"Tell me what I don't know," I replied, and then said, "Sorry, I know you can't but it's getting hard now."

Chipara took my hands and said, "You are trying too hard, Tréville, you need to relax, let your mind think of other things. The last memories are always the hardest. Sometimes people do not want to know the ending, it frightens them, but once they do they are pleased. You have not eaten or drunk today. Come, you need your nourishment."

We sat and ate our meal and I drank some water. Later that night dreams came to me again, but all was muddled and I sat up suddenly. I put my head in my hands and tears came again. "Tréville, drink this to calm you," said Swallowtail. I did and I drifted back off to sleep. The following morning, for the first time ever, it was raining. Swallowtail brought me a board that had food on it, which I ate.

"I've never known it rain before," I said.

"It is raining because another of our tribe has passed and the rain is our people mourning them," she said.

"You must have had some great chiefs pass away then, by the downpours I can remember," I said cheekily.

Swallowtail laughed. "It will clear soon and then you can go where you would like," and with that she left my tipi.

I sat and looked at all my writings and drawings, but nothing came. I got a book but couldn't concentrate. I was restless, and I needed to walk. Soon the rain stopped and I walked to the forest. Motomo didn't appear, so I sat on my rock and closed my eyes. The air smelled good and fresh. Then another smell came to me – pies and bread. I thought of the bakery and could make out the name on the door. "Rennard's Bakery." The man was Monsieur Rennard, my great friend, and then I remembered my other friend, Henri L'Enfant from Chartres. I opened my eyes to see Motomo, his mate and cubs all asleep at my feet. I slowly put my hand out and stroked Motomo who woke immediately. He sat up and held his paw out to me, which I took. His paw was huge, but then he was a large wolf.

"You make friend forever, he guards you, great honour." I looked and saw White Wolf, along with his three white wolves, stood at my side.

"White Wolf, it is good to see you again," I said.

"You are well, Tréville, I think you now have one memory left? I tell you, once this memory comes, you will awake in other part of Reservation. It will be better for you. I say no more now, I go, I needed elsewhere." With that, White Wolf left, with his wolves, as did Motomo and his wolves. I walked back to my tipi.

That night, as I retired to my bed, I took the necklace in my hand and closed my eyes. I thought I felt the heart beating, but it couldn't, it was just a piece of jewellery. I slowly drifted off.

In my dream I was saying to someone, "I will love you until my very last breath." My faceless woman had a face but I only caught glimpses of it. We were at a ball, and she was at the garrison, the dwelling, and the house. Then I saw a dwelling with a rose tree arch. Out the back was a wide stream with swans and ducks on it. I knew I'd taken her there, but why? I could see us swimming in the stream, the swans and ducks following us. I was drying her long hair. I was loving her. Why, oh why couldn't I see her properly?

When I woke I knew my last memory was coming, I couldn't wait to tell Swallowtail and Chipara. When I went outside they were waiting for me. I looked at Chipara and suddenly I felt faint. "Tréville, sit down, are you all right?" said Swallowtail.

I looked at Chipara and said, "It's you, isn't it? In my dreams, you are my faceless woman?"

Chipara paled and looked at me and said, "No, Tréville it is not me, you see, I promise you."

I looked at Swallowtail and she nodded, confirming what Chipara had said. I was confused, and then something dawned on me. "Is the woman I see in my dreams a relative of yours, maybe your sister, cousin? Please help me." She shook her head. I knew she could not tell me.

"Tréville, you are nearly there, try and remain calm," said Swallowtail.

"I want to know and I want to know now. This is driving me mad, why won't you tell me? You all know, but why is it such a big secret? I wish I'd never come here, I can't take it anymore," I snapped and walked off towards the river.

I sat and stared at the river and then felt incredibly guilty for the way I had spoken to them both. I had to apologise, and now. I walked back to my tipi but neither of them were there. I went to both tipis, but they weren't there. What had I done? All of them had done nothing but help me on this journey and look how I had repaid them. I saw there was food and drink on the table so I ate and drank.

"Tréville, my love, what have I told you about that temper of yours?" said a voice.

I whirled round but nobody was there. Where did I know that voice? I waited a long time but neither Swallowtail nor Chipara came. Sadly, I retired for the night, slept and started dreaming. My dreams were muddled but then they calmed. I was stood in a church and a bride was walking towards me, but again her face I could not make out clearly. Then the same person was giving birth to twins, and I realised this woman was my wife and these were my children. I felt proud – I was a husband and father. Then I was riding back into the garrison and after I had dismounted my horse I saw a beautiful lady on the balcony looking down at me, smiling. Her face was clearing. I climbed the steps and she came to me, hugged me and kissed me. When we parted I looked into her gorgeous dark brown eyes. Suddenly I sat up in bed and shouted, "Lesley, my beloved Lesley, I remember you!" The tears rolled down my face, and I sobbed. I felt arms go round me and opened my eyes, to see Swallowtail, Chipara and White Wolf were with me.

"I am so sorry for what I said, I didn't mean..."

Swallowtail took my hands and said, "Hush, Tréville. We know, and now you have remembered all your memories, especially Spirit of the Wolf, we now welcome you properly to the Reservation."

Chipara then took my hands and said, "Lesley's Native American name is 'Spirit of the Wolf', and she is daughter to White Wolf and myself."

I looked totally stunned and said, "I can't take this in."

White Wolf then said, "Welcome, my son, you are now one of us. My daughter, as you know, was born on Reservation in the Americas. As she was of my tribe, she was given her name 'Spirit of the Wolf'. Swallowtail, Chipara and myself have visited Spirit of the Wolf on many occasions as she alone can see us. We can touch her as you could and will again when her earth time is over, but that will not be yet. There are many things you need to know but now you need rest. Sleep, my son, and more explanations will come later." I closed my eyes and drifted off to sleep, but this time my dreams were of my beloved Lesley.

The following morning when I woke I felt like a huge burden had been lifted from my shoulders. I went outside my tipi and could not believe what I saw. There were lots and lots of tipis and Indian men and women walking round.

"Tréville, come." I looked and saw White Wolf and went to him. He was sitting at a table with Swallowtail and Chipara. "You feel today good?" he asked. I nodded. "Eat, drink, I tell you more. Now memories have all returned, as you see, you now on second part of the Reservation. These are our people, with the exception of a very few special people, who are allowed to visit. You will meet them later on. You go where you like, speak to who you like, this now where you stay. You still have river and forest. They just bit further away. I need to tell you more about my daughter. When Spirit of the Wolf was born, we knew she had gift, but not know what. When she was four she go forest and was surrounded by wolves. The alpha bowed to her, I then knew, and you will find this hard to understand, she have wolf inside her – a Spirit Wolf. Her Spirit Wolf is called Tala and she protects her as best as she can. Spirit of the Wolf needs to run and as she runs she becomes Tala."

I looked at him, stunned. "Do you mean my wife is a wolf?"

CHAPTER 43

The Epilogue – Part 2

Swallowtail said, "It is difficult to explain, let me see if I can put it better. A lot of our tribe have special gifts. I am a medicine woman along with many others, but we do not change. The Great Spirit gives our powers to us. Even though Spirit of the Wolf has a Spirit Wolf inside her, her wolf is also a healer, which we did not know until you were stabbed. Every now and then a wolf needs to run to keep its strength up. It does not hurt either of them to change. Some of our tribe are bears, coyotes, eagles, bison and deer. These powers are all put to different uses. Going back to when you were stabbed, you were at death's door. Spirit of the Wolf was already deeply in love with you and was desperate. White Wolf felt his daughter's distress and appeared to her. He looked at what the physician had done to you, and it was not good. He asked his daughter to put her hands out over your injury. As she did White Wolf chanted for the healing light. The light came out of her hands and she healed you inside and you survived. She also healed Porthos, and yes, Amanda knows her secret, but she is the only one.

"Once Spirit of the Wolf knew she was a healer wolf, White Wolf taught her the chanting words, how to call to Tala, and then return to her normal self. Before, Tala would decide when to return. Once she had had a long run she was content. Spirit of the Wolf and Tala have a great respect and harmony for each other. Two spirits sharing the same body, both minds operating as one. Tala is a primal creature, whereas Spirit of the Wolf relies on logic and reason. They also feel each other's distress. When you were shot, unbeknown to you, you came here. We had Chiefs and other medicine women working on you to make sure you survived, but I will let Spirit of the Wolf tell you that story."

I replied, "I must thank these Chiefs and medicine women for what they did. Where can I find them?"

Swallowtail replied, "All over, but they have heard your thanks."

A lot of it made sense, but I couldn't believe I never knew. "Who's Motomo?" I asked.

"Motomo was the alpha wolf who Spirit of the Wolf met when she was four years old. He knew straight away what she was and watched over her, until Chipara decided to leave the tribe. Motomo passed many moons ago, but was honoured and was allowed onto the Reservation. His mate and four cubs came with him; they mate for life," said Swallowtail.

My mind was trying to take it all in when Chipara said, "I think Tréville needs a rest or a walk or swim. You have been told a lot and I'm sure you want to think it through. Our tipi is there, and Swallowtail's is there. If you need us, you come to us." I thanked them and decided to go to the forest.

As I walked through the tipis everyone smiled and greeted me. I noticed none of them seemed to be old. I looked at my hands and the skin was smooth again. I undid my shirt and looked at my chest. The scar over my heart was gone. When I got to the forest Motomo was there with his family. He came bounding up to me and knocked me over. The next minute he was licking my face and I laughed. Eventually he let me get up. "What on earth was that all about, Motomo?"

"He is pleased you have all your memories back and you are here." I turned to see Swallowtail. "I wanted to make sure you were all right, you have been told a lot today that you didn't know about Spirit of the Wolf. I hope you are not too upset?"

I looked and smiled and said, "From the first moment I met Lesley I knew she was very special, to me anyway. Now to hear who she really is and what she has done, I can never repay her. In no way am I upset, I admire her even more. Will Lesley come here too?"

"Oh yes, Spirit of the Wolf is one of us, but she will not have to go through what you did, she will come to us whole. When Philip shot Spirit of the Wolf, she came here and we worked on her and she recovered as much as we allowed. That is why you are here; you never knew Spirit of the Wolf's story, before or after you married her. The Great Spirit entwined your hearts for a reason. When her time comes to leave earth, you will be together forever. Now I will leave you with Motomo and see you tomorrow."

"Swallowtail, can I ask you a question before you go?"

"Of course."

"Why are there no old people on the Reservation?"

"When we pass all things return to a younger time, like yourself. You were seventy-four when you passed, now you are forty, and you will always be that age. That's why time is endless. The other thing you need to know, is our Reservation is for our tribe only. Other tribes have their own Reservations many, many miles away. You will never see them." I smiled and Swallowtail left me. So much to think about!

That night as I was just drifting off to sleep, I felt something jump on the bed. I opened my eyes and looked into two eyes and jumped. When I looked again I smiled. "Snooka, my little friend, you're here as well." Snooka was purring so loudly and cuddled into my neck. "I am so pleased to see you, little one. Come, we will cuddle up and sleep like we used to."

Swallowtail had given me a different remedy to drink that night. Once I had drifted off to sleep my dreams were, let's say, unusual.

I open my eyes and see I am on a different Reservation. A baby is being born, and I hear the cries. White Wolf comes out of the tipi with a baby in his arms. I watch as she grows up. I see her meet Motomo, her heartbreak at losing her father and then leaving on a long journey to England. I realise I'm watching Lesley's life through my eyes. Her life was hard in London, then another heartbreak when Chipara passes. Katherine bringing her up and Lesley turns into the beautiful woman I know. I see her trip to Paris, our meeting, the ball and her reunion with Amanda. I see Philip shoot her again, but then I see her on the Reservation and Swallowtail healing her. I see her heartbreak again when Monsieur Rennard passes. I watch in fascination as she heals me after I was stabbed, with help from White Wolf. Then I see the horrendous ordeal she went through at the hands of Rochefort when he kidnapped her, and what he did to her. I felt the bile coming up in my throat; what an animal. My anger when she was laying so badly injured. I should have comforted her instead of turning my back on her. Next, she leaves me because of the Condesa. I see her time at Chartres and the fun she had, but missing me. Then we arrive and she hides in the secret panel; only Porthos realised she was there. Our reunion back at the garrison, and then our wedding, her healing Porthos, our sons being born, moving, her distress when I was shot and our lives up to when I passed. She had been through so much in her life, and now I knew it all. No one would ever know how much I deeply loved my beloved Lesley, and how much I missed her as well.

When I woke in the morning, I was on my side. Snooka was under the blanket and cuddled into my chest. I had my arm around her, and as soon as I stroked her she started purring; I had tears in my eyes. I never forgot how much Lesley grieved for her, as it was months. As I left the tipi Snooka came with me. "There you are, Snooka, I did wonder if you'd found Tréville," said Chipara. "She's been with us, until one of you arrived. She will not leave you, Tréville, and she gets on with everyone."

I smiled and said, "As Lesley used to say, 'Snooka snuck off,'" and we both laughed.

Chipara and I talked for hours about Lesley and our lives together, and I told her about my dream. She told me that Swallowtail and White Wolf wanted me to know all about Lesley's life so I could understand why things had happened that Lesley could not tell me. She also told me how Swallowtail and White Wolf could transport wherever they were needed on earth, but she could not. She had to hold one of their hands to go with them. It wasn't something she liked to do, but it was the only way she could see Lesley. She told me all about the times they had appeared, even the wedding. I was surprised. She also told me that when Spirit of the Wolf arrived, later on I would be able to go with her and see my sons, daughters-in-law and grandchildren. I then realised how much I was missing them too.

What seemed like a couple of months later, after I had been for my swim, with Snooka watching from the bank, White Wolf came to me. "Tréville, I have some sad news for you, it's not Spirit of the Wolf. One of your Musketeers has passed; he was called Athos and he is where you were, going through the same thing. When he is ready I will let you know."

"Can I see him and maybe help?"

"No, Tréville, you know we could not do it for you. He will be fine."

"Is it all right for him to be here?"

White Wolf smiled and said, "The people who are closest to my daughter come. You, Motomo and Snooka are here. Athos has come, and we will wait for her other brothers and Amanda, but my daughter might be here before them. There are four other friends here, but can only visit. They have own Reservation. You know three – Liz Bramwell, Helene Dubois and Mr Rennard, the other one is Katherine, Chipara's sister."

I was surprised and said, "Can I meet them?"

"Yes of course, I make possible. I go now, as I am needed. I see you soon," and with that he left. One thing I had noticed, when White Wolf and Swallowtail walked away they just seemed to vanish into thin air.

A couple of days later Chipara came to my tipi and said, "I have a surprise for you, please come."

As I went out there were only four tipis, and I said, "Where has everyone gone?"

Chipara answered that when guests were invited they were not allowed on the Reservation. We entered a large tipi and four people stood there. "Oh, Tréville, it's so good to see you and now I can cuddle you as much as I like." I smiled, as it was Liz. I assumed the other lady was Chipara's sister Katherine. The other lady and gentleman were Helene and Monsieur Rennard. I was so pleased to see them again. After Liz eventually let me go, I was introduced to Katherine and then hugged Helene and shook hands with Monsieur Rennard.

"Tréville, I will leave you now, enjoy your friends. There is food and drink on the table outside. Sister, we will speak later," and Chipara left.

Liz said, "Why are you not with us? Why are on you on the Reservation?"

I explained what I had learnt about Lesley, and how I had been honoured to stay at the Reservation. Katherine already knew because Chipara had told her. I could see how Lesley and Katherine got on so well, she was a lovely lady.

Katherine and Liz had great delight in telling me of Lesley's story before I met her. How she had met Amanda at school and their friendship. They were all stunned at the brutality they received from Rochefort. Thank heavens he wasn't here!! I told Katherine and Liz about the school and what happened; they were saddened, not so much about the school, but about all the villagers. Liz hoped that Peter had moved away and was still enjoying his life. Monsieur Rennard told me he had been reunited with his wife and child who had both died at childbirth. He was so happy and was delighted to see me again. We spoke about everything that had happened since he had passed. He so wished he had been at our wedding and met our sons. I replied I would love him to meet our sons, but hopefully not for a long time; they had their lives to live first. He told me he had been allowed to appear to Lesley, and had told her I would make a good husband. I smiled at that and replied how right he had been. He asked if we still had the bakery and dwelling. I replied, "Of course, Lesley would never sell either of them. Our sons now run the bakery and Jean thoroughly enjoys it. Lesley and I moved to the dwelling when our sons were born. We bought a larger house, but never gave the dwelling up."

Helene then brought me up to date with everything since my passing. She told me about the memorial at the village church and how it had brought tears to Lesley's eyes. She told me Lesley had left the house and was now living at the dwelling, Armand and Anne had been delighted to take over the house and Jean and Charlotte had moved into Armand and Anne's dwelling. Lesley was well, but having great problems walking with her hip. She missed me terribly and had told Helene her heart was broken, never to be mended. I was so upset to hear this, but I knew Lesley would be all right. After all, she had married me!!

"Anyone hungry?" asked Katherine. "They would think us ungrateful if we did not partake."

We all went and sat at the table and most of the food and drink soon went. We all got on so well, none of us realised how much time had gone until Chipara came back and said, "I am so sorry, but the time has come for you to depart, my friends. I am sure many more meetings can be arranged. Sister, may I have a quick word?" And with that Katherine and Chipara stood to one side. Chipara then said, "Please, apart from you, Tréville, come back into the tipi." We all hugged and kissed each other, it had been a really good day. I went back to my tipi and found Snooka curled up on my bed. As soon as I sat down, she woke and started purring. I undressed, washed and got into bed, and Snooka came under the blanket and curled up on my chest and I fell into a deep sleep.

When I woke the following morning, I could see Lesley's necklace shining. I went and got it and sat back down on the bed. Snooka came to me and put her paw on the necklace. She looked up at me and then rubbed her head on my hand. I'd never seen her do that before. I tickled her under her chin, then washed and dressed. I went out the tipi and saw everyone was back as before, and then saw Swallowtail. "Can I ask you something please, Swallowtail?"

"Of course, Tréville, what is it?"

I placed Lesley's necklace on the table, "Tell me," I asked gently.

"Tréville, it's nothing to worry about. Do you remember going to the jewellers to get it made?" I nodded. "Well you were sort of guided as to how it was to be made. When you left Spirit of the Wolf and went to war, after she had opened your present, I appeared to her and asked her for it. I put a chant on it. When I gave it back to her she could feel the heart beating. I told her as long as she could feel the heart beating, she knew you were alive."

"So that's why Lesley would never take it off," I said. "After our sons were born and she was taken ill, I told her..."

"I know, Tréville, I was there, but only for a second. I stopped the heart beating, but as soon as you took your hand away, I started it again and left."

"How did it get here then?" I asked.

"Spirit of the Wolf put it in your coffin, along with other things. You probably guessed you were dressed in your Captain's uniform. Spirit of the Wolf did an Indian ritual for you, and it is our custom, when a loved one passes, items are placed with that person to help them travel to the Reservation. Her necklace was the last thing she left with you, so when she arrives here, you can return it to her, if you wish."

I held the necklace in my hand, "The heart does not beat because I have passed. Will it ever beat again?"

Swallowtail smiled and said, "The minute Spirit of the Wolf wears it again, it will beat. Did you have an enjoyable time with your friends?" I replied that I did, and then thanked her and after I had some nourishment I decided to walk to the forest. This time Snooka came with me. I could see Motomo and his family were waiting for me. Suddenly I worried about Snooka, would Motomo frighten her? I need not have worried, Snooka ran to Motomo and jumped on his back and rubbed her head on his. I watched them as they chased each other and then both stopped and fell asleep together. I closed my eyes and also drifted off thinking about Lesley. I missed her so very much, but knew one day we would be reunited.

As I neared my tipi I saw someone walking towards me. He looked familiar and then I realised who it was. "Athos, my friend, it is good to see you again," I said.

Athos smiled and said, "Commander."

We hugged and patted each other's back's, and laughing, I said, "It's just Tréville now. Come, let's eat and you can tell me how you are now."

As we were eating Chipara came to us and said, "Athos, glad to see you have found Tréville, your tipi is next to his. Please, if you need us at any time, come to us." She pointed out her and Swallowtail's tipis. Athos thanked her. We talked about times before, but Athos started looking tired, so I suggested he retired for the night. I had totally forgotten about Snooka, I looked for her but could not see her. As I entered my tipi, I saw where she was – asleep under the blanket. I wondered if she would remember Athos, tomorrow was another day.

First thing the following morning I went for my daily swim, Snooka watching as usual. As I was getting changed I saw Athos walking towards me. Suddenly Snooka was up and running towards him. I should have known, she forgot no one. Athos picked her up and cuddled her. "I might have known this little bundle of joy would be here," he said, stroking her, Snooka purring loudly.

"Did you sleep well, my friend?" I asked. He replied he did. We walked back and then sat at the table and had something to eat and drink. Later on we walked to the forest and on the way there I told him about Motomo and his family and not to be frightened if he was there. Athos told me, same as me, he had got used to them at the other Reservation. Motomo didn't turn up that day, so I asked Athos how had his life been since I last saw him.

Athos replied, "As you know I went back to the area where I used to live and found a small chateau to buy. I became known as the Comte de la Fere again. Athos was buried. One morning I found a baby, about six months old, on my doorstep with a note saying he was mine. There was no sign of anyone else around. I admit I had had a few acquaintances, so who knows? I took the child in, who was a boy, and brought him up. I called him Raymone. All my friends just assumed he was my son and he went everywhere with me. I never married, so Raymone became my life. He grew into a handsome young man and all the ladies fell in love with him. He had a sweetheart, but her parents didn't think him fit to marry their daughter, and she was sent away to England to stay with an aunt. Raymone was beside himself and then made the decision he wanted to be a soldier and joined one of the French Regiments. I worried for him, but as time passed he actually became a good soldier. Before he went off to war, I took him to the Catholic Church and took him down to the crypts, where my family were buried. It was there I gave him my grandfather's sword. Raymone was killed when he was twenty-eight, and had been a soldier for seven years. I was beside myself with grief. I locked myself away from everything and everyone, I didn't eat, just drank, and eventually I passed. What I don't understand is why I am here, do you know?"

I replied I did and told him everything. "I can understand why you're here, but me, I'm not worthy."

I looked at Athos and said, "You were one of Lesley's brothers and she loved you, do you not remember all we went through together, with regards to Rochefort?"

"Oh, please tell me he's not here." I replied he wasn't. Athos sighed with relief. "Does this mean the rest of my brothers will arrive as well, including our sister Amanda?"

"We are all Lesley's family, so yes. That reminds me, they don't call her Lesley, she goes by her Native American name, 'Spirit of the Wolf'."

Athos looked at me and said, "In that case then, I am honoured to be here, and to think that someday we will all be reunited again will warm my heart. All for one, one for all." Athos and I walked back, with Snooka running in front of us.

"There you are, Athos, please come with me, you have someone who wants to see you," said Chipara. Athos looked surprised and I told him to come to my tipi when he returned, and he did. He came in smiling and said, "I don't know how they did it, but I've just met Raymone, it was so good to see him again." I told him about seeing Katherine, Liz, Helene and Monsieur Rennard, and how it worked. He was stunned, but happy.

The next one to join us was Aramis. Both Athos and myself greeted him, but not before a certain young lady had run as fast as she could to him. "Aha, little one, what a welcome and it's so good to see you again, as it is you my two friends." We hugged and patted each other on the back.

Over the next couple of days we explained all to him about the Reservation. He told us after he left he went back to being a monk at the Abbey, but couldn't settle. Athos laughed and said, "When you were a Musketeer you wanted to be at the Abbey, and when you were at the Abbey you wanted to be a Musketeer. I'm glad you never changed, brother." We all laughed.

Aramis told us he stayed a monk for about five years, and looked after orphaned children. One day he was visiting a friend who was ill and met his friend's daughter, and fell in love (how many times had Aramis fallen in love?), but this time he married. They had a happy marriage until their daughter was born, but afterwards the marriage became loveless and he wanted to leave, but wouldn't because of his daughter. He came home one day and they'd left him. His wife's brothers went round, about a week after they had gone, telling him his sister had told him he used to beat them, and not feed them. Aramis was stunned. The brother took a fist to him, hit him and then he fell, hit his head on the stone fireplace, the next thing he knew he was in the tipi.

Next came D'Artagnan; again, Snooka went to meet him. We explained everything to him and asked him how his life had been. D'Artagnan told us that Constance had passed before him, and he never married again. He was still a Lieutenant in the Musketeers and had led many men into battle. He was a great friend of King Louis XIV and was honoured to serve him. At last, what he had always wanted arrived. He received his letter confirming his promotion to Captain-Lieutenant. He was delighted. That day, alas, when he was in battle a musket ball tore through his throat, and he bled to death, and then woke up in the tipi.

There was only two left now. All of us had settled on the Reservation; Athos saw his son now and then, D'Artagnan saw Constance, but it tore him apart, so, after a great talk within the tribe, Constance was allowed to stay on the Reservation as well. We all got on well with the Tribe and there was romance for Athos and Aramis. Athos met Two Feathers whilst he was out walking. He kept his feelings close to his chest, but eventually he realised what Two Feathers meant to him, and they wed the Indian way. Aramis met Humming Bird, so called because she went round humming, but he liked it. They too, wed.

Lastly Amanda and Porthos joined us. Both of them had had a wonderful life with their family. They passed within a week of each other, just through old age. When they arrived we all went and met them. What a reunion it was, all of us back together again, but alas, one of us was still missing.

I woke to the sound of heavy rain. I knew another of the tribe had passed. Swallowtail came to me. I said, "I'm sorry, another of your tribe has passed."

Swallowtail looked at me and said, "Yes, but this is a very special person that now comes to us. There will a huge feast and celebrations tonight and naturally you are all welcome."

Suddenly the flap of the tipi opened and in walked Lesley's brothers with Amanda and Constance, all carrying food and drink. I cleared the table and we all sat down to partake of our meal. "Wonder who it is?" said Constance, "there's a lot going on out there." After a couple of hours the rain stopped and we all went outside. The tipis had been split into two sections with huge fires being blessed by Swallowtail. Many tables were laid out all covered with different food and drink.

Chipara came to me and said, "I'm sorry everyone but we need you to go to your tipis until we call you." Everyone left. Suddenly, for some unknown reason, I felt tired so I went and lay down on my bed, curled up with Snooka, and slept.

Later on I woke to the sound of voices outside my tipi. I got up and noticed I had on the shirt I wore to our wedding, and Lesley's necklace was on the table; all my other clothes had vanished. I could hear Swallowtail talking to someone, the other voice – could it be? I sat on the bed stroking Snooka, who was purring. The flap of the tipi opened and I could not believe my eyes. There in her Indian wedding dress, with her long hair in plaits with the sacred feathers, stood my beloved Lesley. It had been ten years since I last saw her. She ran to me saying, "Oh, my love, my love, how I have missed you." Tears were flowing down her beautiful face.

I took her in my arms and kissed and kissed her so deeply, and then said, "My beautiful Indian wife." I held her so tight. Oh, how I had missed her, now tears were even in my eyes. I looked into her eyes, and could see the love for me in them. "I have something for you," I said, and picked up the necklace. I undid the ribbon round her neck, which Lesley took and put into a small pocket, and placed it round her neck, but this time I felt the heart beating.

Snooka jumped off the bed and came to us, purring. Lesley looked down, saw her and picked her up. "Snooka, my loyal friend, I have missed you so much." Snooka cuddled into her arms purring so loudly. I looked at her; she was young again, like me, and more beautiful than I remembered.

"I have so much to tell you, my love," she said.

"As I have also, my beloved," I said.

She told me everything from the second I passed up to the present, and I told her my story on the Reservation. Suddenly I heard Swallowtail call to us and so hand in hand we walked out of the tipi. Snooka was in Lesley's other arm. I looked around and saw only three tipis: mine, one with Lesley's brothers and Amanda stood outside and the last one had Katherine, Liz, Helene and Monsieur

Rennard stood outside. Motomo was there with his mate and four cubs, as were White Wolf, Chipara and the three white wolves. They had all been here to welcome her. There was a mist all round us. I saw a movement to my right and was stunned, as it was a beautiful wolf. "Spirit of the Wolf, I have someone who very much wants to meet you," said Swallowtail. Lesley looked and was looking as stunned as I was. "Spirit of the Wolf, meet Tala."

Lesley looked shocked and said, "Tala, but Tala is with me."

Swallowtail replied, "Not anymore, she is a free spirit now."

Snooka jumped out of Lesley's arm and then jumped onto Tala's back, rubbing her head on hers. Lesley bent down and put her arms round Tala's neck and spoke to her. It brought a tear to my eyes, this respect and love between them both.

Suddenly Lesley looked at me and I told her Swallowtail had told me her story and I knew all about Tala, what she had done for me after I'd been stabbed, and how the Chiefs and Medicine Women had saved me after I'd been shot. Lesley came and stood by me and took my hand in hers.

Swallowtail then said to me, "Tréville, as you now know Spirit of the Wolf is Indian. You did not know this when you wed her, and now you are one of us, the Tribe have asked me to honour you with an Indian name. You will be known as Takoda and it means 'a friend to everyone'." I smiled and thanked her.

Lesley looked at me, smiling and said, "That name suits you and is true."

Swallowtail then looked at everyone and said, "It is time for us to depart now, the Reservation awaits."

I held my hand out and said, "Come, my loving wife."

I watched as White Wolf, Chipara, Amanda and Lesley's brothers, the three white wolves and Motomo and his family went off, vanishing in the mist, in one direction, and Katherine, Liz, Helene and Monsieur Rennard went off in another direction. Tala came to our side and Snooka jumped into Lesley's arms. Lesley looked at Swallowtail and said, "Thank you, Swallowtail, for letting me be a part of this, I will now have more memories to hold onto. I will miss you all so much, until it is my time to join you." She then looked at me and said, "Tréville you need to take Snooka."

I looked at Swallowtail, trying not to show Lesley my worry. Lesley thought she was dreaming, she didn't realise she was here to stay. Swallowtail looked at me and smiled; she took Snooka and gave her to me. Snooka curled round my neck. Swallowtail then put Lesley's hand in mine and said, "Come, Spirit of the Wolf, you are now with us forever."

I could see by Lesley's face she realised her earth world was over, but she stopped and said, "Swallowtail I must go back, our sons will be so upset to think I have passed without them being with me."

Swallowtail looked at Lesley and said, "Do not worry, they were with you. White Wolf made sure Jean and Armand were with you, he guided them to you just before you passed. Hold my hand and close your eyes." When Lesley opened her eyes she looked at me and I looked at her, I smiled and kissed her lips gently and we walked towards the Reservation, hand in hand.

When we arrived through the mist, which now cleared, all the drums started beating, people were singing and dancing. White Wolf and Chipara came to us. "Welcome, my daughter, we have missed you," said White Wolf. Lesley hugged and kissed her parents, tears flowing down her cheeks. Not only was Lesley a healer wolf, she was also the daughter of an Indian Chief and her tribe were delighted she had arrived. We went and spoke to Amanda, Constance and her brothers. Athos and Aramis introduced her to their Indian wives, and Lesley was delighted. The celebrations carried on well into the early hours. We then said our goodnights and retired to our tipi.

Snooka and Tala were curled asleep together on a large straw pallet, which I hadn't seen before. I took Lesley in my arms and kissed her so deeply. "Oh, how I have missed you, my beloved, and now we will be together forever."

Lesley smiled and said, "Yes my love we will be, but first I must do something." She put her hand in her pocket and pulled out the ribbon she had worn; there was something on it and she slipped it off. She then took my left hand and placed my wedding ring on my finger. "As you know, I put my necklace in your coffin. Your ring I kept and have worn it every day, it made me feel close to you," she said. It felt good to have it back. My arms went round her and our kisses became more passionate.

We could see the love for each other in our eyes. I unplaited her hair, this time the feathers fell to the ground, and then I ran my fingers through her hair. Oh, how I had missed doing this, I loved her hair down. I went to remove her dress and she said, smiling, "Tréville, I have no petticoat on under my dress." I smiled, remembering our wedding night, and removed my moccasins, shirt and breeches, and blew out the candles. I undid the beads on the back of her dress, and then slowly pushed it off her shoulders, where it fell to the ground. At the same time she undid the laces of my undergarment, which also fell to the ground. I picked her up and laid her on the bed. "I think, my beautiful wife, I need to show you how much I have really missed you," and started kissing her neck. It was like we had never been apart; our passions for each other were reached and for the first time I actually felt and saw our hearts entwine into one. "I love you so much, my beloved, and I always will for eternity."

Lesley looked into my eyes and kissed me so tenderly and said, "My love for you has never died, my love, and yes, I will love you for eternity as well." Our arms entwined round each other and Lesley laid her head on my chest, as she used to say, "listening to the beating of my heart."

In the morning, after our passions had been reached, we both washed and dressed. I noticed a lot of Indian dresses were now on another chair, and all my clothes had returned also. I must ask Lesley how things like this happened. I opened the flap of our tipi and met a totally different view. There were a few more tipis but all were in separate circles; some had five or six tipis, with a fire in the middle. There were seven in our circle. Long tables were laid out where people were eating. Children were now running around with wolves, dogs or other small animals. We were in a deep valley with high hills rolling up above us, all covered in green grass. More trees and forests now surrounded the Reservation. The river was still in the same place, but at the side was a field with horses, and then I noticed one of them was Sunkwa. The Reservation looked wonderful, words could not really describe it; the sun was shining brilliantly, and the sky so blue.

I felt a pair of arms go round my waist. I turned and took Lesley in my arms, and kissed her tenderly on her lips. My heart was full of love for her again, not that it had ever gone away. "This is beautiful," I said.

Lesley looked at me and smiled and said, "We are both now, along with our friends and family, truly on the Reservation. This is now where we stay for eternity."

I saw Swallowtail beckon us over to the table, where everyone was seated. I said, "We are all couples now, apart from Swallowtail. I so wish she had someone with her."

Lesley looked at me and smiled. "Swallowtail does have someone, Tréville, but none of us see him. He is a medicine man and only Swallowtail can see him. She is not alone, my love." I was pleased. "Tréville, before we join the others, we must say goodbye to Tréville and Lesley now; we are Takoda and Spirit of the Wolf."

She gently kissed my lips and said, "Welcome, Takoda."

I replied, "Welcome, Spirit of the Wolf."

All of a sudden a huge double rainbow appeared right across the Reservation. I took Spirit of the Wolf's hand in mine and along with Tala and Snooka we walked towards our friends and family.

THE END

24878503R00263

Printed in Great Britain
by Amazon